Advance Praise for *The Wa*

❧

"Shining light upon the work of the original war librarians, Addison Armstrong not only offers a tribute to the power of books and libraries but also manifests the unconventional lives of two women separated by fifty years, both determined to defy society's limitations and forge futures that break the mold. Emmaline and Kathleen stand as worthy testimony to all the women who have blazed trails where none existed before."

—Lisa Wingate, author of
Before We Were Yours and *The Book of Lost Friends*

"*The War Librarian* is a compelling and inspiring tribute to the courageous, groundbreaking women who risked their lives to pursue their heart's desire even when—especially when—their ambitions led them into places where women were at best unexpected, and at worst fiercely opposed."

—Jennifer Chiaverini, author of
The Women's March and *Mrs. Lincoln's Dressmaker*

"If one can measure a novel's success by the emotions it draws from readers, the sophomore work by Armstrong is very effective indeed. Romance and long-held secrets provide additional intrigue in this increasingly powerful story. The values of intellectual freedom, antiracist activism, and female friendship are illustrated within their historical contexts, yet these themes couldn't be timelier."

—*Booklist*

"Armstrong's dark and disturbing tale of prejudice, discrimination, determination, and bravery will resonate with readers caught up in the same issues today." —*Library Journal*

"*The War Librarian* is a touching story of courage and female friendship, with two heroines who will win you over with their honesty, integrity, and resilience—I found myself cheering for them until the very last page!" —Ann Mah, author of *The Lost Vintage*

"*The War Librarian* shines a light on the courage and tenacity of women who blazed trails through male-dominated territory for future generations to follow. A vividly told story of female empowerment with humanity and heart."
—Christine Wells, author of *Sisters of the Resistance*

"*The War Librarian* is an empowering tale of sisterhood and sacrifice, reminding us of the importance of standing up for what is right in the world—even in the face of war and great peril. Timely and enlightening!"   —Sara Ackerman, author of *Radar Girls*

"Two lesser-known areas of fascinating history, two compelling female leads, a little mystery, and a lot of heart make for one captivating novel! Addison Armstrong celebrates the unyielding courage of two women separated by time, circumstance, and experience, and yet united—both forging paths as yet unexplored, overcoming trials and adversity, forming unbreakable bonds of love and friendship, and ultimately discovering strengths found only in themselves and in sisterhood. Meticulously researched, intricately woven, and deeply heartfelt, *The War Librarian* is a testament to the life-giving, life-affirming, and life-changing power of the written word—and of women. Highly recommend!"
—Gabriella Saab, author of *The Last Checkmate*

"*The War Librarian* is a compelling story that reminds us how powerful one person's voice, and actions, can be. Another powerful tribute to our military's female 'firsts.'"
—Kaia Alderson, author of *Sisters in Arms*

"In *The War Librarian*, Addison Armstrong has created both a compelling look at World War I war librarians and a love letter to books and the power of words. Readers will be kept turning pages as both Emmaline and Kathleen fight against prejudice and censorship in their eras. Secrets abound in both timelines, but it's the strong friendships and courageous women that form the heart of this engaging look at forgotten history."
—Amy Lynn Green, author of *The Blackout Book Club*

ALSO BY ADDISON ARMSTRONG

The Light of Luna Park

The
War Librarian

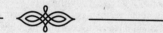

Addison Armstrong

G. P. PUTNAM'S SONS · NEW YORK

PUTNAM
— EST. 1838 —

G. P. PUTNAM'S SONS
Publishers Since 1838
An imprint of Penguin Random House LLC
penguinrandomhouse.com

Library of Congress Cataloging-in-Publication Data

Names: Armstrong, Addison, author.
Title: The war librarian / Addison Armstrong.
Description: New York: G. P. Putnam's Sons, 2022.
Identifiers: LCCN 2022019018 (print) | LCCN 2022019019 (ebook) |
ISBN 9780593328064 (trade paperback) | ISBN 9780593328071 (ebook)
Subjects: LCSH: World War, 1914–1918—Libraries—Fiction. | United States.
Navy—Women—Fiction. | LCGFT: Historical fiction. | Novels.
Classification: LCC PS3601.R5744 W37 2022 (print) | LCC PS3601.R5744
(ebook) | DDC 813/.6—dc23/eng/20220422
LC record available at https://lccn.loc.gov/2022019018
LC ebook record available at https://lccn.loc.gov/2022019019

Printed in the United States of America
1st Printing

Book design by Elke Sigal

I owe my world to the brave women like Emmaline and Kathleen who have come before me. But women today face their own challenges—especially women like my sister Ryan, who studies aviation and is training to be a pilot in a world that can be hostile to anyone who isn't a man. Rye inspires me every day with her resilience, her confidence, her bravery, and the joy she radiates through all the challenges. This book is for her.

Prologue

Emmaline Balakin

November 1918

The familiar light-headedness overtook me. If even Nellie was abandoning me, who did I have left? My pulse throbbed in my wrist as Colonel Hodgson released my arm, and then my vision went blurry. I stood still, too shocked to move, until Nellie dragged me to the motorcar and shoved me inside, then slammed the door and went around to the driver's side. When she spoke, I thought I'd misheard her over the furious beating of my own heart and the desperate waves of my own breath.

"Where should we go, Emmaline?" Her characteristic laugh was absent, her voice trembling with fear. "Where will you be safe?"

Chapter I

$—◈—$

Emmaline Balakin

September 1918

I stood stiffly at the ship's railing and watched New Jersey recede into the distance: the smokestacks puffing, the ships docked at the Hoboken wharf, the industrial warehouses stacked high as the USS *Aeolus*'s mast. I could no longer make out the shapes of the people on land, but I knew they were there. Only a half hour ago, I'd looked down from this very spot and watched soldiers and sailors scurrying around the dockyards. Only half an hour before that, I'd sat in a motorcar and looked out at a silent town of women and children.

I'd grown used to the sight of wives without husbands and children without fathers. And I'd grown used to being alone. The anonymous gray shoreline now seemed a reflection of my own flat and gloomy half-life—I didn't know whether leaving would be the beginning of my story or the end of it.

I fingered Nicholas's letter in my pocket like a talisman and prayed this journey would be not just a blip in my life but the beginning of a new one. After twenty-three years of living in black and white, I deserved something different.

Or did I? Perhaps I had no one to blame but myself. No one had forced me into the shadows; no one had told me I'd be safer in a stack of books than in the real world. But I'd learned it nonetheless. When my mother was killed in a streetcar accident in my fourteenth year, my father retreated into books and I followed. Though he sent me off to boarding school when I was fifteen in the hopes that I would benefit from being around other women, he joined my mother in heaven after a heart attack just a year later, and I became the only student to stay at school through the holidays and the summer. Alone for long stretches of time, I turned back to my old comfort, books my most constant friends and solace.

After I finished boarding school, I got a job at the Dead Letter Office, where I could continue to use words as a shield against real life. But now, five years later, I was sailing away from the only place I'd ever known. Just like Mama and Papa had twenty-three years earlier.

My parents left Russia for the noblest of reasons. As professionals in St. Petersburg, they'd waged a quiet battle against Czar Alexander III's censorship, lending out their own copies of forbidden books and ignoring the government threats—until they learned I was on the way. They'd been willing to risk their own lives, but not mine, and so they packed up and left their homeland so that their child could be raised in a world of intellectual freedom. They used the money they'd been able to take from Russia to purchase a townhouse in Washington, D.C., and my mother had quickly become the center of the city's Russian community. But it all fell apart when she died.

My mother had lived a colorful life, and that was what I wanted to do now. I was tired of being forgettable, invisible Emmaline: the girl who handled dead letters about more interesting lives than her own.

I pulled myself away from the ship's railing. If I was going to embark on a new life, I had to stop gazing backward into the past; I didn't have to watch the shoreline until it receded.

My feet slid on the deck as the ship roiled, but I didn't fall. I took one ginger step at a time, finding my footing, as I explored the place that would be my home for the next two weeks. I couldn't pretend I liked it. The USS *Aeolus* had been seized from Germany's luxury cruise line months ago, but the Germans had ransacked her beforehand. The ship was a metal beast, hulking in size, and the floral wallpaper that peeked through in spots as a reminder of its past life only made it eerier. The razzle-dazzle war paint on deck, zigzagging black and white lines that crashed and intercepted at seemingly random intervals, dizzied me. I supposed that was the point. The camouflage didn't aid the ship in blending in; it simply disoriented the enemy so they couldn't grasp the size, speed, or direction of the ship.

The enemy. I'd read about them in the newspapers and prayed for the men abroad, but I'd never expected to enter a world in which I'd be their target. A world in which I was on a Navy transport ship so vulnerable to German U-boats that we were surrounded by a convoy of ships meant to protect us.

I continued past the mess hall, its polished wood floor

suggesting a past as a ballroom or first-class dining room, and into the belly of the ship. Here, finally, was something familiar: the ship library. There wasn't much to it beyond a few crates of books and a plank of wood that had been fashioned into a sign: TRANSPORT FROM AMERICAN LIBRARY ASSOCIATION FOR ALL MEN ON BOARD. The room had low metal ceilings, and my pumps echoed ominously on metal floors crisscrossed with hatches and handles and levers. But I knew already that I would be more comfortable here than anywhere else on the ship. I set to work immediately sorting the books by genre and author, my hands moving almost of their own accord as I went through everything from textbooks on engineering and mechanical handbooks to collections of poetry and authors like Twain and McCutcheon. In this comfortable, familiar space, it was easier to remember why I'd chosen to join the war effort overseas. The decision went back further than the conversation at Camp Meade when they'd asked if I'd be interested in serving in France; further even than the day a month ago when I'd donated a pile of books to the Library War Service and mentioned to the girl at the desk that I wanted to be a war librarian. It went back to the day Nicholas's letter had landed on my desk at the Dead Letter Office.

The letter meant for another woman.

The letter I'd opened, read, and responded to.

The letter I'd stolen.

Chapter 2

— ❖ —

Kathleen Carre

April 1976

I tried to put the letter out of my mind and tell myself it was a normal day. There was no use focusing on maybes or what-ifs; they wouldn't get me anywhere. So I started the day the same way I'd started every day for the past two years. My alarm went off at five o'clock in the morning, and I was in shorts, my jogbra, and an old tee by 5:10 a.m. I devoured a Space Food Stick, brushed my teeth, slicked my straight hair back into a ponytail, laced up my tennis shoes, and checked in on my nana Nellie sleeping peacefully before jogging downstairs.

I took deep breaths in through my nose and out through my mouth as I ran, imagining that each breath was clearing my head of all its thoughts and worries. Running was the only time I didn't go endlessly through my to-do list—though, strictly speaking, running was part of that list, too.

I knew my route well. Past the strip malls, past the apartment buildings and fire escapes. I kept my Mace tucked into the palm of my hand, though I'd never had to use it before. Better to be too prepared than caught defenseless.

When I returned to the apartment building where I'd lived with Nana for the past fourteen years, I did a series of sit-ups and push-ups, the same sequence I'd been required to do for my Naval Academy admissions test. Then I showered, trying and failing to keep my mind off the letter I was expecting that afternoon. If I got the news I wanted, I wouldn't be able to take long, thoughtful showers for much longer.

I toweled off, brushed out my hair, and dressed for work. The whole process was another thing I hoped would change soon. If all went according to plan, these would be my last few months dressing for work in sheath dresses and pleated skirts with pantyhose.

Nana was in the kitchen with a bowl of oatmeal by the time I passed through on my way out, and I blew her a kiss. "See you this afternoon, Nana."

She looked up from her bowl and raised her eyebrows. "Slow down, you. What makes any granddaughter of mine think she can leave without a goodbye?"

I hid a smile as I backed away from the door and gave Nana a quick hug. "Sorry."

"Have a good day, Kathleen. I love you." She never let me leave without telling me that first.

"I love you, too."

I retraced my steps downstairs and stretched my long legs as I walked to the Metro. I stood in the crowded car to make room for pregnant women and families to sit, and then strode quickly to work, reveling in the feel of my hips opening and my hamstrings aching from my run.

When I arrived at the dentistry ten minutes before opening, the door was still locked. My eyes rolled back at me in the window's reflection. My boss, the dentist himself, was never on time. I spent most of my mornings making excuses for him, patients' vitriol directed at me rather than at the man at fault. I couldn't wait until I was at a place where rank was earned, a place where we worked together for a common goal.

A place like the Naval Academy.

Patience, Kathleen. I squeezed my fingers around the key to the office, and its jagged edges stung my skin. I'd done everything I could have to get an appointment to the Naval Academy: the application, the congressional recommendations, the physical fitness test. Now all I could do was focus on the work I had to do in this moment whether I got in or not.

I unlocked the office door and let myself in, busying myself with tasks long since familiar. I was supposed to be a bookkeeper, not a secretary, but that didn't mean half my working hours weren't spent fixing the thermostat, straightening chairs, and answering phone calls. I didn't mind the routine; it was the meaninglessness of it that I hated. That Soviet lunar robot Lunokhod could have done my job for me. It was rote. But it was a job that paid, so I settled myself behind the desk and opened the appointment book.

Dr. Lloyd rushed in only minutes after I sat down, and I plastered a smile on my face. "Good morning, Dr. Lloyd."

"Good morning, Kathleen."

It rankled me that I didn't deserve the moniker of *Miss*

Kathleen in his eyes, much less *Miss Carre*. But hopefully I'd be *Midshipman Carre* soon, and if not, I'd try again next year in my last year of age eligibility. If that didn't work, I'd enlist. One way or another, I was going to do my duty in a way that mattered.

The day passed tediously, as it always did, so when the dentistry closed its doors two painful minutes after five o'clock, I shot off like a rocket. Surely the mail had come by now.

I fidgeted on the Metro and raced through the streets, ignoring the strain in my ankles as I ran across the uneven concrete sidewalks in my pumps. Inside the apartment building, I skidded to a stop in front of the row of metal mailboxes and unlocked the one that read *Carre, Nellie R.* with trembling hands. There it was, the heavy envelope from Annapolis, Maryland.

This was the letter.

I wanted to open it then and there, but too many other residents were bustling in and out of the mailroom. I sprinted up the stairs with the letter instead, throwing my purse onto the side table and halting in front of Nana in her armchair.

"Is that it?"

I nodded wordlessly at my grandmother as I slid the letter out, the blue inked eagle revealing the tips of his wings. The words on the letterhead, DEPARTMENT OF THE NAVY, unfurled down my spine.

Miss Kathleen Carre
4 Martins Lane
Apt. 321
Washington, D.C.

I am pleased to offer you an appointment to the United States Naval Academy as a member of the Class of 1980.

The Class of 1980: the first class that would graduate from the Naval Academy with women alongside the men. The National Organization for Women had been campaigning for the service academies to admit women since I graduated from high school in 1972, and President Gerald Ford had signed the act into law in October of last year. I already knew the Naval Academy history backward and forward, and it had been all-male since its founding in 1845.

But now, only three more months. Three more months until we charged through the Naval Academy doors with the men. Just three more months of skirts and coifs, of cleaning up my boss's messes and staring endlessly at the swinging door of his office.

Nana was smiling softly up at me. "I take it they accepted you?"

"Yes!" I thrust the letter into her hands, and she squinted down at it. When she looked up, her smile was even wider. But her eyes were hooded and dark.

I fidgeted on my feet, waiting for Nana's congratulations. She was always my most vocal supporter. I held myself to high standards; when I accomplished a goal, I simply viewed it as having met an expectation. But Nana always made me celebrate. She took me out for ice cream when I was elected fifth-grade class president, bought a display case for my track trophy in ninth grade despite the expense, and wrote in all her Christmas cards that I'd graduated from high school summa cum laude. For *this* goal, which had been my dream forever, I expected her to outdo herself.

But instead, hooded eyes. Hooded eyes and silence.

I took back the letter and looked at it again. *I am pleased to offer you . . .*

The tightness that Nana's expression pulled in my chest couldn't stop me from smiling at those words. I'd done so much to get into the academy. I'd written Congressman Walter Fauntroy and Vice President Nelson Rockefeller for a nomination, both of them limited to ten nominations per vacancy and five attending nominees. I'd taken the SAT, two years after my wealthier classmates—though several of the poorer ones had never taken it at all. Then had come the candidate fitness assessment: the one-mile run, the shuttle run, kneeling basketball throws, crunches, push-ups, and flexed-arm hangs. For a girl who'd run track all through high school, the mile run was the easiest. Only the twenty push-ups and sixteen-second flexed-arm hangs had taken much practice on my part, which I blamed on the fact that girls weren't permitted to do anything strength-based in high school gym class. I'd had to start from scratch, working early mornings and late nights to be ready for the fitness test, and I hadn't stopped since. I knew I'd need to far exceed those requirements at the academy itself. If the rumors I'd heard were true, each new recruit did three *thousand* push-ups over the course of plebe summer.

Finally, after all the application paperwork and the physical test, I'd had the interview with a Blue and Gold Officer. Mine was the father of a current midshipman who hadn't seemed all too keen on women entering the academy, but apparently he'd reported my answers and my passion faithfully nonetheless. I took it now as a sign that the academy would be as focused on integrity and merit as I'd always imagined.

What I hadn't imagined was Nana's apathy. "Nana?"

"Sorry, Kathleen." She shook her head and stretched her lips even further into a smile that looked almost garish on my reserved grandmother. "I just want to be sure that this is what you want."

I let out a startled laugh. Nana knew this was what I wanted. She'd been by my side throughout the entire process. Before it had begun, she'd watched the congressional hearings with me as the

NOW president and vice president argued for women's inclusion in the service academies; before *that*, she'd listened to a young Kathleen talk about duty and honor and pride.

"Nana, of course this is what I want." I felt my eyebrows pull together and tried to soften my gaze for this woman who'd done everything for me. "You know that."

"I do." Nana shook her head. "I'm sorry." But she still didn't look convinced, and so I tried to remind her exactly *why* this had always been my dream. There were too many reasons to count. I craved the discipline and the purpose. I wanted to be selfless and honorable.

I wanted to live the life my mother wasn't living.

I'd been eight years old when my mother Jane had decided the "traditional" life wasn't for her. My father had toured Asia and Europe during the Second World War in an Army band, rather than inside a tank like most of the men of his generation, and he'd come home with stories of rich food and rushing waterfalls and great stone fortresses. His descriptions inspired in my mother a passionate jealousy and an urge to travel herself, but it wasn't a desire my father had indulged. The war was over, he was home, and it was time to start a family.

But years passed, and a baby didn't come. At least not before my father was shipped off again in 1951, this time to Korea. He made it through the Battle of Heartbreak Ridge and the Battle of Bloody Ridge, came home on a three-week furlough in 1953, and then shipped off again. He'd survived World War II and two of the bloodiest battles of the Korean War, but it was his last month overseas that killed him. He died in the war's final battle.

My mom was devastated, Nana told me, but she also had the opportunity to do what she hadn't before. She applied to write for

Venture and planned to travel the world—until, one month later, she discovered she was pregnant with me. And so D.C. had remained our home.

At least until 1962, when John Glenn orbited the Earth and reignited my mother's itch to go—if not as far as Glenn—as far as she could. She finally became a travel writer, going where she wanted and using her writing to fund it. My mother left; I stayed. Nana became my mother for all intents and purposes, I became a Carre like my grandparents, and my mother became Jane. I refused to talk to her when she visited one week after my ninth birthday. Eventually I understood her desire for a life beyond marriage and children and meaningless jobs that did nothing but pay the bills. But I also knew that if I ever had a baby, no matter the sort of life I wanted, I would never leave her. I believed in duty over desire.

So it was my nana, Nellie Carre, who'd served as one of the few women in the Motor Corps in World War I, who was my hero. Not my mother, who hopped from city to city without a permanent address or a phone number. Even before she left, she'd constantly changed her jobs and her hairstyles and her schedule. What she'd considered exciting had just seemed unreliable to me, and I'd sworn long ago that I would be the opposite. That I would find a purpose beyond myself. That I would live with precision. And that I would do for others, not just for me.

I remembered sitting at six years old with my pigtails and listening to JFK's inaugural speech: "Ask not what your country can do for you—ask what you can do for your country." He'd been the first Catholic president, the youngest president, the first president born in the twentieth century. At seven, eating a TV dinner in a house with no TV, I wanted to be three things: JFK, my nana, and *not* my mother.

Many of the other girls at school weren't allowed to come over to play with me, apparently fearing that my mother's wayward ways were catching. In high school, I joined the track and field team and learned what it was to have a community. I understood the allure of bonding over a common goal and a shared challenge. I understood celebrating with the girls who passed the baton to you before the final leg of the race. At the Naval Academy, I would find that again.

My whole life has brought me to this point, I wanted to say, but I couldn't find the words. So I just shook my head. "There are so many reasons this is what I want, Nana. It's my calling. I want the duty and the responsibility. I want the organization and the discipline. I want the community. I want the purpose."

Nana smiled softly. "Purpose, community . . . those are things I understand. But it's not that simple."

I sat across from Nana and leaned in. I wanted to know what she knew of discipline and duty, of organization and purpose. She didn't often talk about her time in the Red Cross, though I'd asked her to a hundred times growing up.

Nana took a deep breath. "When I came back . . ."

I tried not to rush my grandmother, who'd always been more of a listener than a talker.

"It was difficult," she finally said. "The things I'd seen. The guilt."

"The guilt? What are you talking about? You were a hero." She'd been a driver for the American Red Cross, not a soldier. She'd never fired a machine gun or launched a grenade.

But she closed her eyes and ignored me now. "You've seen how I can get." She didn't elaborate, but I knew what she meant. There were times, few and far between, when Nana couldn't get out of bed. Days when she wouldn't eat and hardly drank. Days when she flinched each time she heard the honk of a horn outside the apartment building or when I stepped on that creaky spot on the kitchen floor.

"It's gotten better over the years, because I've created a good life for myself. I had my husband, God rest his soul. I had your mother. And I have you." She smiled, though a tear leaked from one of her eyes. "But it happened all the time when your mother was a child. I sometimes wonder if she'd have been more . . . rooted, otherwise."

"No. You can't blame yourself for any of Jane's choices."

"Jane is your mother," Nana said softly. She hated that I called Jane by her name.

I forced down my resentment for Nana's sake. "My *mother* made her own choices. You couldn't control them."

"Still." Nana lifted a frail shoulder. "I know you always loved the idea of having a grandmother in the service. But it wasn't all glory. And things never go back to the way they were before."

That I knew. I'd paraded around in Nana's too-big Motor Corps uniform, peppered her with questions. But they were questions she'd never wanted to answer. Always, there had been shadows on her face when I brought up the war.

"Things are better now. There's more of an understanding after Vietnam."

Nana nodded slowly. "I suppose. It's just that I didn't do right by Jane, and she gave me a second chance when she left you to me. I did it right this time around. And I don't want to lose you, now, too."

"Oh, Nana." I covered her hand with mine. "You could never lose me."

"Then just let me warn you, Kathleen. Though I know you never listen to what others say." She smiled slightly, and I appreciated the effort.

"Seldom," I corrected her with a grin. "I wouldn't say *never*."

Nana nodded and continued. "You need to understand that war isn't a game. It isn't a test. It isn't a book or a film. It's bloody and ungovernable, and I wonder . . . I wonder sometimes if it even has a purpose."

I shook my head. She sounded like a hippie Vietnam protester, not like someone who would have been considered a veteran if she'd only been a man.

She held up a finger. "Let me finish. It's hard to be a woman in a world designed for men."

I laughed at this. "Nana, we both do that every day."

She didn't smile back. "And there are ways to protect this country—improve this country, right this country's wrongs— without taking up arms for it."

I knew that, of course I did. Nana had spent years campaigning for women's rights and civil rights, standing up for blacklisted Hollywood socialists and Vietnamese refugees. But that wasn't what I wanted. And I knew that, in the end, Nana just wanted me to be happy.

"I understand. But this is what I want to do."

She let out a long, weak sigh and collapsed farther back into her armchair. "That's your decision, then, Kathleen. And I'll support you. My one piece of advice is that you find another girl there, another woman. Someone to be your friend. Someone you can always rely on, no matter what." She closed her eyes for a few seconds like she was remembering something too private or painful to share, and then opened them again and forced a smile. "So tell me about it, now. My granddaughter, who has been accepted into the Naval Academy."

Just the name of the school sent a shiver of excitement through me despite every warning my nana had given me. "Well, my first day is in July. And I know it won't be easy, but it's going to be everything I ever wanted."

Chapter 3

—❦—

Emmaline Balakin

September 1918

The first night on the ship, I tossed and turned in my bunk for hours. Ava, the sociable girl in the bunk below me who would be a telephone operator in France, kicked the underside of my mattress. "Stop it," she hissed. "I'm trying to sleep down here."

I tried to still my body, but I couldn't still my mind. I'd left the library that afternoon feeling confident about my decision to serve overseas, but supper in the mess hall had changed things. I'd worked at the Dead Letter Office for five years with a handful of other women and a passel of clergymen, and I was unaccustomed to the chaos and the volume that six hundred young men could produce. I didn't know how to respond to men's attempts at flirting when Nicholas was on my mind, and I had no idea how to insert myself into the group of female telephone operators that had already bonded during training. They'd tried to be friendly and ask me about my work, but I'd clammed up at the mere mention of the Dead Letter Office. It was breaking the Dead Letter Office rules that had gotten me here, after all, and I was afraid of letting the truth slip out. So I'd stammered something about working with a priest and rewriting smudged addresses, and the girls had lost interest quickly.

And rightfully so. The job sounded boring by design. The government employed women and clergymen because they thought we were more moral than the general population; they had no suspicions that we'd read mail not meant for our eyes. I resented the assumption, wishing I were brave enough to do something thrilling—play at Jane Austen's *Emma* and be a matchmaker through the mail, or run a spy ring to bring down the Central Powers—but the government hadn't been wrong about me. Until that fateful day a month ago, I'd never so much as considered opening a letter without authorization.

On the ship now, I pulled out the very letter that had changed it all. I couldn't sleep, and my attempts were bothering Ava as much as myself. Nicholas's letter, despite the way I'd gotten hold of it, always soothed me. Its words were as familiar to me now as the words of *Jane Eyre*, but still I liked to hold it in my hands. Running my fingers along the crease in the center always took me back to the day I'd found it.

The letter was from Vivian Winthrop Callahan, D.C.'s equivalent of the British Princess Mary. In those hot months after Vivian's lavish wedding, everyone had known her name and address. They'd craned their necks outside her white-pillared mansion and planned casual walks down her block the morning of the main event. I wondered how a letter to her, of all people, had been misplaced. How could it have ended up in *my* ringless, ink-stained hands?

I'd flipped the letter over and seen the red *Return to Sender* stamp, explaining it all. The letter was suddenly just as mundane as all the others I'd handled that morning. While the newspapers hailed us as detectives and codebreakers, my job with letters like Vivian's was simple: to see if the sender's address could be ascertained from the envelope or the letter inside if necessary, so it could be sent back. Cutting the envelope open just meant I'd have to resist temptation. The procedures were clear, and I knew them well: I read the greeting and the closing for clues, and nothing in between.

So I had sliced the envelope open and looked first to the salutation:

My Dearest Vivian,

Then forced my eyes to skip to the bottom of the page:

> *Devotedly yours,*
> *Nicholas*

Underneath the signature was an APO address for Private Nicholas Agrapov of the United States Army. I'd held my breath as my eyes traveled over the letters of his name a second time and then a third.

Nicholas Agrapov. Could it be *that* Nicholas Agrapov? *My* Nicholas Agrapov?

I saw a flash of dark hair and gray eyes. A wink from across the table as our feet accidentally brushed underneath it, Nicholas's hand clasped protectively on his mother's shoulder and my own fervent wish that it could be rested on mine. I heard Nicholas's low laugh and my own voice speaking without fear.

And I'd known then that I would break the rules for the first time in my life. That I would read this letter from Nicholas to Vivian. How could I not?

I'd massaged my forehead, looking at the pile of letters I'd already sorted that day. Most of them had been simple cases: one to Boss Town instead of Boston, and one to Ralee, Insee, instead of Raleigh, N.C. One that had been sent to 704 Main Street without a city or state listed had been meant for Philadelphia, which I'd known because no other city's Main Street remained residential past 500.

Strictly speaking, this letter from Nicholas had been equally straightforward. Protocol required that I direct Nicholas's letter back to him. But I had to know if the sixteen-year-old boy who had once meant so much to me was safe over there in France. And the bruised part of my heart ached to know whether he had changed into the sort of man who didn't care if a woman was married, or whether Vivian had betrayed him in his absence.

My eyes crept back to the letter.

I know you are not one for talk of war or politics, Vivian, so I will try to keep this short. Suffice to say that I am already weary, so much wearier than a 26-year-old should ever find himself.

I write to you from [redacted], France, where our 79th Regiment is currently training. But if this is merely a training ground, I can't imagine the fronts. This is horrific enough. The first thing you see when you disembark in [redacted] is "Cinder City," a tent city for convalescents built on the ruins and the ashes of abandoned ships and swampland. Women creep around in black mourning crepe, shops are boarded up, orphans run through the streets. There are no fewer than five hospitals here, and an ever-growing cemetery.

They tell us we are safe here, but I don't know. The Germans could push their way through at any moment.

God forgive me, I'll almost be glad to leave for the front lines. There, at least, I may prove to be useful.

I apologize for this dismal talk. I always imagined France as beautiful, but all I see is death. Just knowing you're there, that you're reading this, is what keeps me going. I even keep the picture you gave me on my person at all times to remind myself there's a world at home that remains whole and unscarred.

I'd nearly scoffed when I'd read that. A man *would* keep her picture on him, wouldn't he? Vivian was a ringleted beauty, a veritable Mary Pickford. I'd scowled then as I'd pushed my own straight, dark hair behind my ears; I did the same now in the narrow ship bunk as Ava snored lightly beneath me.

I'll make it back home to you so we can be together as far from this mess of war as we can get.

At that, I'd dropped the letter to the table, and my hand had fluttered to my throat. It didn't seem Nicholas had any idea that

Vivian was married, and she'd simply returned his letter unopened without the decency to tell him.

I'd grasped again for the letter.

> *They said it's luck whether you make it or not, but*
> *I don't believe it. There's no such thing as luck in war—*
> *not good luck, at least. But knowing there's still a world*
> *beyond all of this, and that it's waiting for me, keeps me*
> *going.*
>
> *In the meantime, I've had to rely on books. They have*
> *a few old copies donated from the States that we can*
> *borrow, though I hear they end up serving as shields*
> *against bullets as often as they do reading material once*
> *they're taken off to the trenches. But books here calm me.*
> *Things end happily in books—and when they don't,*
> *there's a reason. But who the hell knows how things end*
> *in real life?*
>
> *Write me something good. Please.*
>
> *Devotedly yours,*
>
> *Nicholas*

The letter made me hate myself for losing touch with Nicholas. But it had been hard to keep up with my mother's friends after she died. From D.C., the nearest Russian Orthodox church was in Baltimore, and so the celebrations and the get-togethers had shifted north after my mother's death. Only my mother, with her boundless energy and passion, had been able to bring together the Russian Orthodox Russians from Baltimore, the Shtundists from Virginia, and the Russian Hebrew community from Pikesville, Maryland. She'd mediated peace between the Shtundists, who carried the New Testament in their pockets, and the Jews, who had survived pogroms in the old country and were wary of anything overtly Christian. She'd taught the Russians who worked in garment factories and mines to read. She'd even raised money for their train fare to D.C. for our celebrations of Russian holidays, and we'd spend the week of Maslenitsa making the traditional pancake blinis that represented the sun, and on January 7 celebrating the Orthodox Christmas with a feast of pickled delicacies. For those, only our fellow Russian Orthodox came, but we had a full house for nonreligious holidays like Ivan Kupala Night.

Until Mama died. Then, each community had solidified into a distinct group—Shtundist, Orthodox, Jewish—and my father and I had no longer fit into the Orthodox group with my mother's yawning absence. I lost contact with the Russian-American community entirely when I disappeared to Garrison Forest School in Owings Mills, Maryland. After Father died, I didn't even return home for the Orthodox Christmas or Easter.

So maybe it was my guilt over losing touch that made me write back to Nicholas, or maybe it was the childish fantasy I'd once enjoyed of Nicholas and me together, of his hands on the small of my back and of us curled beside each other in bed with books in our hands.

Of course I told myself I wrote because it was the patriotic thing to do. The newspapers and war morale posters reminded women constantly that our role in the war was to write our men, and to write them good news only.

My pale hands had shaken as I'd slid the paper back into its envelope and into the pocket of my skirt. And then, in the safety of my parents' old townhouse, I had written Nicholas back as if I were Vivian herself.

Dearest Nicholas, I'd begun.

I'm thrilled to hear from you. Everything is lovely here.

You write that books are bringing you solace. I hope you'll be happy to hear that, after receiving your letter, I donated a pile of books to the Library War Service. Arthur Conan Doyle, Jane Austen, Dickens, the Brontës. I hope they bring you and your comrades as much joy as they've always brought me, and perhaps inspiration too. I've always wished I were as brave and self-assured as Jane Eyre.

I know you're brave, there in France, even if you don't feel like it.

My prayers are with you.

Your,

Vivian

I had cringed as I etched Vivian's name into the paper. The rest of the letter had felt so honest, but signing it as Vivian cemented the lie.

Now, looking at Nicholas's letter as I sat hunched over in the top bunk in my cabin on the USS *Aeolus*, I couldn't muster up any guilt or regret. I had lied, but I'd done it for Nicholas's sake. And that lie had changed my life.

The next morning, I ate a quick breakfast with the other girls and then returned to the library belowdecks. I'd let the captain know it was organized and ready for the men, and I had no doubt they would come. I had learned in my four weeks of training at Camp Meade how desperate for books these men were. The Books for Soldiers initiative had begun a year earlier, when the

Committee on Mobilization and War Service Plans partnered with Herbert Putnam of the Library of Congress to form the Library War Service. By the time Nicholas had written me—no, written *Vivian*—the ALA had raised nearly two million dollars, built thirty-six camp libraries, bought three hundred thousand books and collected over a million more, distributed five million magazines, and trained one hundred and seventeen librarians to sort books and work at camp libraries. The program had only grown as more and more men were drafted and sent overseas.

Midmorning, two men came into the ship library. Like me, they had to duck their heads to navigate the small space with its low ceilings, but they didn't complain.

The taller of the two looked at me. "Are you the librarian?"

"Yes, sir."

"Good deal," said the other one. "The librarian at Fort Leavenworth was a crotchety old man."

I cleared my throat, uncertain as to what to say. "Are you looking for anything in particular?"

"I'd like something on the funny side," said the first man. "Dave?"

The second one, Dave, shrugged. "Librarian's choice."

I knelt beside the bookshelf, conscious of the men's eyes on me, and rummaged through the selection. I'd gotten good at "prescribing" books at Camp Meade, where I ended up after dropping off my book donation and volunteering for the position. I'd been at the Dead Letter Office for five years not because I loved it but because it was easy and comfortable, and I'd figured after reading Nicholas's letter it was time to do something for the war effort. I didn't have the nerves to be an ammunition tester or the training to be a nurse, but it had seemed like a sign when the librarian taking my donation said more women were needed to serve as hospital librarians nearby in Camp Meade. It was perfect, a way to serve the soldiers without going any farther from home than I'd gone for school at Garrison Forest.

Or so I'd thought. I'd spent only a month at Camp Meade, a mere thirty miles from D.C., and had worked on administrative and organizational tasks the first two weeks. Just as I had here, I'd alphabetized books, tossed copies that were too worn to share with servicemen, and screened for things like used diaries or decades-old almanacs. I'd served my second two weeks in the wards with the men, most of whom were in bed with tuberculosis or awaiting minor surgeries for maladies like tonsillitis or appendicitis. They weren't war injuries, and for that I'd been grateful. I was surprised to discover that the men were grateful for me, too—not only because they'd been desperate for distraction, but because I was good at my job. I'd had a knack for knowing what types of books each man had needed, which the superior librarian called prescribing books just as doctors did medicine. The ones who'd been laid up for weeks on end needed adventure—westerns and mysteries and stories like *Robinson Crusoe*. The ones awaiting surgery needed books that were laugh-out-loud funny, books that would distract them from their fear.

Now I selected Charles Dickens's *The Pickwick Papers* for the first of the two sailors and *A Study in Scarlet* for Dave.

"These should do," I said. "The characters in *The Pickwick Papers* are as humorous as they are ridiculous. And you can't go wrong with Conan Doyle."

Both men thanked me, Dave with a mock salute, and then they were off. I sat beside the bookshelf with my knees pulled to my chin and wondered if the job would be so simple in France. I'd gone to bed each night at Camp Meade exhausted but satisfied, glad I was doing something for the war effort. But I also hadn't been able to keep from wondering, as I folded Nicholas's letter into my pocket each morning, why Camp Meade had gotten two librarians when the men overseas didn't have any at all.

When I finally mustered up the courage to ask the superior librarian, Mrs. Lipscomb, about the discrepancy, she'd turned to me with a finger on her chin, and for the first time I'd noticed how striking she was. With high cheekbones and crystal green eyes, she was far too pretty to be a librarian. I, with my awkward height and limp hair, fit the part perfectly.

Mrs. Lipscomb's eyes had shone especially bright that day. "In fact, Miss Balakin, the ALA has recently sent its first librarian overseas."

Just one? That hardly seemed sufficient, and Mrs. Lipscomb continued as if she'd read my mind. "But the ALA is partnering with the YMCA and the Red Cross to allow us to train several of their volunteers as librarians in France." She'd smiled. "I'll make a note that you're interested as well."

"Oh, no," I'd stammered, so surprised by her suggestion that I hadn't been able to gather my words. "I was only curious."

But three days later, Mrs. Lipscomb had approached me with the opportunity to go to France myself. She said that I'd distinguished myself as a top-notch librarian in my short time at Camp Meade, and that—despite my not being officially trained as a librarian nor registered as a YMCA volunteer—she had sent Frances Burton Stevenson, the ALA librarian in France, a telegraph personally recommending me for overseas service.

I hardly remembered my response. Most likely, my jaw had dropped and I'd stuttered something incomprehensible. It had seemed impossible; of all people to pick, why me? I had never left the D.C. area, never worked as a librarian before, never considered leaving the States.

"Think on it," Mrs. Lipscomb had told me, and I'd promised I would. But I didn't intend to do any such thing.

Until I lay in bed that night and thought of Nicholas's letter, of my parents, of all the books that had raised me. Jo March would have gone. And more importantly, the Emmaline Balakin my parents had raised would go, too. They'd raised me to do what was right even when it was terrifying. They'd raised me to believe that one person's choices and actions could make a difference. And most of all, they'd raised me to believe that books could change the world. My future had changed when my parents died; all my parents' money had gone to keeping my room and board at Garrison Forest, and I could no longer afford Mount Vernon College as had been the plan. But here was a new opportunity. I understood the men's need to escape into books to hide from reality, because I'd spent most of my life doing the same.

And it was time to stop. I'd been living a half-life for years, timid and stagnant and alone. Going to France would make me the heroine I'd always wanted to be, the heroine my mother believed I *could* be. In France, I would matter. I would live.

And perhaps a small part of me had wondered if perhaps this journey was fate. If I'd ended up with Nicholas's letter on purpose, and if I was headed to France now because a thread connected the two of us across time and distance. I knew it was unlikely I'd see Nicholas, but still I chose to take his deployment in France as a sign. He was there for a reason, and soon I would be too.

Maybe knowing that, I wouldn't feel quite so alone.

Chapter 4

—◈—

Kathleen Carre

July 1976

I was alone on day one. The other plebes were being dropped off by their families, but Nana never drove. Not since the Great War.

This morning, she'd wished me farewell at the door to our apartment unit, her face shining with pride despite her misgivings. I looked back at her thin frame in the doorway and considered for a moment whether it was a mistake to leave her. In saying goodbye to my family to pursue my dreams, was I doing what Jane had done?

No. I would only be thirty miles away, and Nana had raised me to fight for what I wanted. She was a fighter herself, a veteran of war and loss and widowed motherhood. She would be fine.

No worry could dampen my excitement. A single suitcase in one hand and my purse in the other, I marched straight to New

York Avenue NW. Nana claimed the Greyhound station had been something special in her day, but God knew it was far from its glory days now. Homeless men took up rows of plastic seats in the waiting room, and the sticky smell of spilled liquor blended with the buses' exhaust to make a fume so noxious I had to breathe through my mouth.

I was early, naturally, and so I stood along the side of the lobby and watched the V8 vegetable juice commercials playing on the cracked television screens. I considered snatching an extra forty minutes of sleep when I finally made it onto the bus, but I was too excited. Even after receiving my acceptance and spending months in preparation, this new life had hardly seemed possible. I'd given my notice at my bookkeeping job two weeks ago with the secret, unspeakable fear that I'd invented this new life. That I'd end up crawling back to the old one.

But there'd be no crawling back. I was here on the bus, the city fading behind me.

I was bound for Annapolis.

There were people everywhere when I arrived, but I looked past them to the glorious curve of the field house. A welcoming pale blue, Halsey was the first place I'd been instructed to report.

Shoulders held back, I pushed past the clusters of families and through the large doors. Though parents and siblings waited outside, there were enough plebes and officers inside to make check-in appear, for only a moment, hectic. Then my eyes adjusted to the patterns, and I realized that the hundreds of people crammed into the building were standing in lines and moving through stations in orderly military style. I could hardly hear myself think over the steady roar of background noise, but still I grinned. I appreciated little more than order.

I joined the line for incoming plebes with last names A–F and watched to learn the procedure. The men and women in front of me—mostly men—had to shout to be heard by the detailer, and then he'd give them their Alpha Codes and company information.

"Carre!" I yelled when it was my turn. "Kathleen Carre!"

"Carre . . ." The midshipman in front of me ran his fingers down a list of names. "Company Five." He handed me a card with my alpha number and company, platoon, and squad information.

And just like that I was in the thick of things. The detailer rose and taught me to salute: right arm out, right forefinger to right eyebrow. I recited back to him the rules: salute all officers, but only outdoors; begin salute six paces away, then hold until returned.

"Do you understand!" the man barked. It was an expectation, not a question.

"Sir, yes, sir!"

As if I hadn't just done it, the midshipman glared. "From now on, your first and last response will always be 'sir.' Understood?"

"Sir, yes, sir!" I kept the annoyance from creeping into my voice. Was he skeptical of my understanding because I was a woman? Or was he like this with everyone?

When I was dismissed, I scanned the crowd for a flag with a 5 on it. The flags were bright yellow and triangular, and fifteen of them rose above the crowd. So many companies and so many men, but so few women.

Five, when I found it, was no different. A dozen or so men stood around the flag, and I pushed my way toward it.

"So it's true." One of the plebes, a blond-haired guy who

looked fresh out of high school, stepped forward. "They really are letting girls in."

"Now, now." The upperclassman with the flag, a firstie based on his uniform, stepped forward. "Welcome to Company Five. I'm Officer Howe, the Plebe Summer detailer for the company."

"Kathleen Carre, sir." I turned back to the blond who'd spoken first. "And you are?"

"Robert."

I stuck out my hand, but he didn't take it. "Nice to meet you," I said anyway. The man was in my company; I had to be civil. "Nice to meet you all."

The other men introduced themselves with varying degrees of hostility. Mark seemed neutral, David smug, Pat friendly enough. Tom's eyes turned toward me appreciatively, taking in my red high-waisted pants and bright yellow buttoned shirt. I'd dressed in bold colors to show the men I wasn't scared of being here—but now it felt like I was just drawing attention to myself when what I needed was to fly under the radar. I made a note to remember that even as I couldn't help noticing that Tom wasn't bad-looking himself: clean-shaven with dark hair, no sideburns. But when he grinned at me, I merely nodded back. The rules about dating were hazy, but I wasn't going to risk my professional appearance here for anything. I wasn't here for an MRS degree.

Several more boys introduced themselves, and then a second girl joined our group. "Linda," she said. "Burr."

I watched as the boys reacted to a second woman in their midst. Some of them seemed less shocked this time around; several even angrier.

Linda came to stand next to me, already blushing. "What platoon and squad?"

We exchanged information and learned we were in opposite platoons and different squads.

"Figures." Linda pursed her lips. "There are only eighty-one of us, six percent. Some squads won't even have one girl. Let alone two."

"At least they won't be grouping us by sex," I said. "God forbid we be our own 'special' company."

By the time our company swelled to its full eighty plebes, one final girl had joined. She had short dark hair and introduced herself as Susan Silver before coming to stand beside Linda and me. All three of us, we found, were in separate squadrons.

Officer Howe instructed us to remain with our company as we lined up for processing. Uniformed upperclassmen checked our permission to report papers and then warned us: last chance to dispose of any contraband. I couldn't imagine anyone stupid enough to have brought drugs or alcohol into the field house. Once the upperclassmen had taken what we didn't need—civilian clothes, perfumes, and other non-essentials—they gave us our copies of *Reef Points*. Though the booklets were small, they were thick, and I knew they contained thousands of naval sayings, facts, expectations, and traditions. We were expected to know everything in the book by the end of the summer, and quizzing would start almost immediately.

I opened *Reef Points* while standing in line for the next processing station. I reviewed the five basic responses, the expectations for saluting, and how to "chop" rather than walk, then tucked the book into the waistband of my pants as I saw the men do when I got to the front of the line.

At the attendant's orders, I breathed into the red tube of a Breathalyzer and watched the foil bag expand. The upperclassman clipped the tube, inspected the numbers, and moved me along with a nod. Next was a doctor, who checked me for tattoos and piercings while conducting a general health screening. "All good," he said gruffly. "Now, just for the pregnancy test."

"The pregnancy test?" I nearly yelped.

The doctor raised his bushy eyebrows. "You have a problem with that? Something to hide?"

"Sir, no, sir."

What kind of fools did the academy take us for? I knew I wasn't pregnant, couldn't be pregnant, but still my cheeks burned as I peed into the vial. I walked out of the restroom with my fingers curled protectively around the glass, terrified that the men would judge me on my walk of shame.

At the doctor's station, the man shook the test tube, labeled it, and put it aside. "Results will be back within two hours," he told me. "You'll be alerted only if there is a problem."

"Sir, yes, sir." There wouldn't be.

The next station was a vaccine in my shoulder. I kept my face carefully impassive as I felt the sting of the needle; I couldn't afford to look any less brave than the men.

We continued to the vision screening, check-ins with the chaplain, and questions with the alumni association. Then, a thrill ran through me as I approached the final two stations. Linda had tears in her eyes at the thought of cutting off her hair, and Susan's was already short. But I couldn't wait to have my long, straight hair chopped off at the ear. I would fit in better with my hair shorn. There was something ritualistic about it, and even the girls who already had short hair went through the line.

The cut itself was unceremonious. My hair was trimmed straight around from my chin in the front to the base of my skull in the back. Short enough that it didn't graze my collar—the requirement—but long enough that I could still pull it tightly back.

"Thank you," I said as I left. I had no idea what my hair looked like; the stylist was the same for the men and the women, and the haircut had been done in a matter of minutes. But I was grateful even if I looked like a cabbage, because what mattered was that I was beginning to look like I belonged.

Men and women were separated at the final station. Linda, Susan, and I filed into a line to select standard-issue white underwear to accompany our uniforms. Any bras or panties we'd brought would be mailed home.

"Size?"

Linda bit her lip. "Maybe if I just pointed . . ."

"Size," the woman repeated.

"36D," Linda whispered.

I gave Linda a sympathetic look as I took my own 32Bs and my white cotton underpants and moved on. Here was the part I'd been craving: the real uniforms. The Navy might have made me pee in a cup and announce my bra size to the world, but I'd look the part now.

We put our uniforms into the large knapsacks we'd received at the beginning of processing and rejoined the men in our company. Officer Howe informed us it was time to split into squadrons, and I nodded to Linda and Susan as we parted.

Another upperclassman marched down my squad of ten. "I'm Midshipman Ensign Michael," he announced.

"You will call me and all other officers and upperclassmen 'officer' or 'sir.'"

I clenched my toes. There would be no women in the upper classes. Many a "sir," never a "ma'am."

Midshipman Ensign Michael led us through the parade rest and facing routines, which we practiced several times. I concentrated to make sure I turned on the correct toes and heels, at just the right degree—and thank God. One man put his weight on the wrong foot and received a lengthy verbal bashing. Only Tom got a compliment.

When Midshipman Ensign Michael was satisfied with our performance, he led us outside. The material of the sack slung behind my shoulder scratched my skin in the heat, but I worked to keep my face neutral. *Don't show any weakness*, I reminded myself. *You're in the Navy now.*

"Welcome to Bancroft Hall," Ensign Michael said. The building was impressive, with stone columns and dormer windows. "All midshipmen live in its eight wings."

The man next to me, Pat, leaned over and whispered, "I heard it has its own zip code."

"Barry!" Ensign Michael spun on his heel and faced Pat. "You do not speak out of turn in formation!"

Pat's face flushed deep red. "No excuse, sir."

"What did you say?"

"No excuse, sir!"

Ensign Michael nodded. "I do not expect you to make that mistake again."

"Sir, no, sir."

The officer surveyed us all. "I do not expect *any* of you to make that mistake again."

We chorused our response, and Ensign Michael led us up the marble steps and through Bancroft's grand entryway.

My shoes clicked across the pink and black floor as we ascended a marble staircase. "Memorial Hall," said Ensign Michael.

A sparkling, domed skylight cast rays of sun across the wood-paneled floor, and a collective sigh of appreciation came from our squadron.

JFK had spoken here in 1963; he'd said there was no more rewarding career than this one. I shivered to be in the spot where he'd been and fixed my eyes on the DON'T GIVE UP THE SHIP flag across the lobby. Below it was a large plaque dedicated to fallen midshipmen, and I made a promise right then to memorize it. *Dedicated to the honor of those alumni who have been killed in action defending the ideals of their country, with immortal valor and the price of their lives—*

"Carre!"

I jumped. "Sir?"

"You failed to salute the flag."

"I'm sorry, sir." But I couldn't let him think I was incompetent. "I was under the impression that we saluted outdoors only, sir."

"That rule applies to the saluting of officers," he snapped. "The American flag is saluted at all times." Arms clasped behind his back, he marched up to me. His heels clicked with rhythmic precision on the wood floor. *Deck*, I corrected myself. It wasn't called a floor here.

"And you do not respond to a question with an excuse, Miss Carre." His *miss* dripped with condescension. "You respond with 'No excuse, sir.' So I will ask you again. Why didn't you salute the American flag?"

I swallowed my pride. "No excuse, sir."

"Will you make this mistake again?"

"Sir, no, sir."

"What did you say?"

I consoled myself with the fact that Pat had received the same treatment for his mistake; this was not because I was a woman. I took a breath and shouted louder. "Sir, no, sir!"

"Good." The officer turned stiffly on his heel. "Because it's going to take a lot to convince me you belong here."

Not the same as with Pat, then. My knees trembled as we marched up to the fifth deck.

"Room 201," Ensign Michael called out. "Crawford, Skinner. Fall out." The handsome Tom and hostile Robert obeyed. "Room 202. Barry and Gleeson."

The other men peeled off one by one and two by two, those on their own to be joined by boys from other squadrons in Company Five. Each door was marked with their black name plates and graduation year, and I couldn't wait to see my own name beside the '80 like a promise.

When I did, it was on a white placard that differentiated our room from the men's. *Burr, '80, Carre, '80, Silver, '80.* Linda, Susan, and I would be three to the room.

I nodded thanks to Ensign Michael and stepped into the room. The space was small and bare, and I took it all in in a matter of seconds: three beds crammed into space for two, three shelves, three desks in the center of the room.

The door opened again before I'd moved from my spot between it and the sink. I stepped sideways to make room and found myself practically inside the shower.

Linda staggered into the room under the weight of her knapsack, her big blond curls trimmed short. "Kathleen, right?"

I nodded.

"How was your day?" She let her bag slump to the ground.

I laughed. "No 'was' about it, I'm afraid. We've still got plenty to do after lunch."

She groaned. "I'm starved. They should give us two lunches when our day goes so long."

"If only." I ran the calculations in my head. "Seven hours left, right?"

"Exactly. We're not even sixty percent of the way through!" Linda moaned. "Much less two-thirds."

I snorted. "I thought *I'd* studied the schedule."

Linda bent to pick up her bag, hiding her face. "It's the way I think," she said. I could see the red in her cheeks despite her crouching to hide it. "In numbers. It's not usually so obvious, but I get obsessed with it when I'm nervous. Keeps me calm."

I shrugged. "That's what running does for me. Will math be your major?"

Linda nodded, her face clearing of color. "What about yours?"

I sighed. "Naval architecture and ocean engineering, or operations research." I hated coming in undecided. "It's hard to decide when we don't know if we'll be allowed in combat."

Linda scrunched up her nose. "We *aren't* allowed."

"I know. But we weren't allowed at the academy a year ago, and that changed. I suspect combat won't be far behind."

It had been World War II's women who'd gotten the Women's Armed Services Integration Act passed decades ago, but it had been a false victory. Section 502 of the act forbade women from serving on Navy or Air Force aircraft, ships, submarines, or any other vessels that might engage in contact.

But as Bob Dylan said, times were a-changing.

We could enter the academies now; soon enough, they'd have to let us engage in combat. That was the entire point.

The door swung open again.

"Susan!" Linda turned.

Susan entered the room unchanged, though her short hair no longer stood out in a crowd. She gave a quick wave as she heaved her bag to the ground. "Girls."

I gave her a mock salute, and she laughed.

"How were y'all's mornings?"

I was surprised to hear her southern drawl. Somehow, I'd pictured her the New York type.

"Overwhelming," Linda confessed.

"And about to get a lot more overwhelming," I said, pulling out my uniform and getting the first good look at its pieces.

Linda and Susan turned and gasped. "Heels?"

"Looks like it." I dangled the black pumps from my fingers. "These are the only shoes in here."

Linda grabbed the left shoe and pressed her thumb up against its heel. "Three inches."

"There's no way!" Susan cried. "They expect us to march around the grass in *heels*? I won't do it."

I set my mouth in a firm line. "I don't think we have a choice."

We pulled on our uniforms piece by piece. The new white cotton underwear and bras, the tights. The white pants with wide waistbands and jackets with thick, crisp collars. And then, finally, the heels. When we were all dressed, we looked at each other's outfits in disbelief.

"This is ridiculous," Susan grumbled.

I agreed with her, but I wasn't going to let anything slow me down. "Could be worse."

"I don't know," Linda moaned. "I've never been good at walking in heels."

"At least they're not stilettos," I said. "You'll get the hang of it."

"You didn't see me at prom," Linda countered. "Total disaster."

The two of us laughed, but Susan didn't crack a smile. "*I* still think it's ridiculous."

A knock came at the door before we could respond. Time for lunch.

"Think they'll give us the same food the boys get?" Susan raised her eyebrows as we filed out. "Or will they give us the skinny versions?"

I snorted. "Bleu cheese for the boys, pink cheese for us?" This time, Susan did laugh, and we all three set out down the hallway, or, in Navy-speak, the passageway. I was painfully aware of our heels clicking, singling us out from the men.

"There are three hundred and two tables in the mess hall," Linda told us as we walked in. Then she winced. "Sorry. Not relevant."

"Hey." I turned to her. "Don't cut yourself down like that. Memorization is critical in the academy. Have you seen how thick *Reef Points* is?"

Linda didn't relax. Her shoulders threatened to swallow her neck, they were so high up toward her ears. "It's hard not to be nervous."

"Sure." I put a hand on her shoulder. "But we can do this."

"Thanks." Linda gave me a shy smile and then shook herself off. "Anyway, do you girls see your parents?"

I grimaced. "I came out here on my own, so no."

Susan nudged me. "My mom didn't come, either. She hates that I'm here. Come sit with my dad and me?"

I glanced at Linda, who was waving across the room to another blond-ringleted woman who had to be her mother.

"Are you sure?"

"It'll ease the awkwardness, honestly." Susan laughed. "He's tried to be supportive, but he doesn't much know how to talk to me. He alternates between pretending I'm a boy and asking me bizarre questions about clothes and makeup."

I chuckled and followed Susan through the crowd as she searched for him.

"There he is." A dark-haired, burly man waved at Susan through the mass of bodies. He was about three times Susan's size but looked as awkward and nervous as Linda.

"Told you," Susan hissed. "He's not quite sure how to act without my mother around to whip him into shape."

Susan rolled her eyes, but I imagined having a mother that whipped people into shape with envy. My mother didn't even have her own shape, I thought sometimes. She was amorphous. She never called from the same phone twice, and she was always talking about some new hobby or new purchase or new group of friends.

"Dad, this is Kathleen." Susan introduced me to her father, who shook my hand.

"Nice to meet you," he replied.

"And you. Susan said you wouldn't mind if I sat with you two for lunch?"

"Of course not!" The man looked back and forth between us for a moment. "Your folks couldn't make it?"

"No. It's just me and my grandmother."

"Hmm." The man twisted his cap in his hands, uncomfortable. "Well, glad to be of service." He issued a mock salute and then looked around. "I won't get in trouble for that, will I?"

"Of course not, Dad." Susan rolled her eyes as she led us to a table. The silence when we sat was uncomfortable, and so I jumped in.

"Give my regards to your wife," I said. "I hope she feels better soon."

This time, Susan didn't hide her eye roll from her father. "I'm sure she'll be magically cured in . . . hmm, four years or so?"

"Susan . . ." Her dad trailed off. "Be nice."

"I'll be nice when *she* starts being nice," Susan grumbled.

I stayed quiet but pursed my lips. If I'd waited for my own mother to grow up before doing it myself, I'd still be in primary school.

Though the conversation was stilted, the food was good. I gave Susan and her dad a few private minutes for their goodbye when we finished; we wouldn't be seeing our families again until December.

The day continued without sentiment until, finally, came the moment I'd been waiting for. All of us, men and women alike, funneled out into Tecumseh Court for the oath ceremony. I stepped gingerly so my heels didn't sink into the earth, but I didn't care that my toes were already sore or that blisters were forming. I was about to be sworn in as a midshipman, a plebe, a part of the United States military.

I swiveled my head. We stood with our hands clasped behind our backs in formation, long lines of white sparkling uniforms as far as the eye could see. With the identical white caps and short hair, I could hardly tell who was a man and who was a woman. We were just plebes.

A voice thundered from the front of the crowd. "Repeat 'I do.'"

Even in my heels, I couldn't see the man speaking. A thousand men and a few dozen women blocked my vision.

"Having been appointed midshipmen of the United States Navy, do you solemnly swear that you will support and defend the

Constitution of the United States against all enemies, foreign and domestic; that you will bear true faith and allegiance to the same; that you take this obligation freely, without any mental reservation or purposeful evasion, and that you will well and faithfully discharge the duty of the office which you are about to enter, so help you God?"

"I do!" Our voices wove together, echoed off the walls of Bancroft Hall, and lifted into the heavens. I imagined that Nana could hear us back in D.C.

The speaker proclaimed us the Naval Academy Class of 1980, and I felt tears prick at my eyes. But I wouldn't cry. Not with men on either side of me.

The first strains of "God Bless America" began, and I removed my hat in the same swift movement the rest of the class did, pressing it against my heart.

I sang, and I thought of my grandmother. *Look*, I thought, *how far we've come.*

Chapter 5

— ❖ —

Emmaline Balakin

September 1918

I held my breath as the USS *Aeolus* navigated into the port at Saint-Nazaire. The seasickness that had left me a week ago returned as I turned my head to see one razzle-dazzle-painted ship after another. It was like being at a circus, I imagined, except that the price of seeing through the illusion was death.

I snapped my eyes shut. What a morbid thought. Then I opened them again, eager to get my first glimpse of France. This was the world of Victor Hugo, Alexandre Dumas and *The Count of Monte Cristo*, even *Madame Bovary*. This was the land in which Sydney Carton had sacrificed himself for Lucie Manette. The world of the Enlightenment: of Voltaire, Rousseau, Montesquieu.

And now the background for war. The place for men to fight

and kill and, I reminded myself, heal. That was the part I was here to help with. Healing their minds and spirits.

I startled as a sailor came up behind me and joined me at the ship railing. "Ever been to France?"

I shook my head. "I've never been anywhere."

"Me neither." He fiddled with the cloth cap in his hands. "Never thought I'd leave Nebraska."

I glanced at him. He was shorter than me, and I wondered if his height made him as self-conscious as my height made me. Maybe he would still grow, though; I realized with a jolt he couldn't be older than eighteen. If that.

Other sailors swarmed the railings as we docked, most of them as young and fresh-faced as the one who'd just spoken to me. I felt for the knotted prayer rope on my left wrist, my mother's old chokti, and sent a prayer up to heaven for all these boys. Because they were just that: boys, not men.

We disembarked together, the boys with large sacks slung over their backs, the cable girls with their personal valises, and me with my own valise and the crate of books I'd been given at Camp Meade. On land, I stood surrounded by men wrestling with ropes, boxes, and pallets, awaiting instruction. I was unsteady on my feet after two weeks on the waves, and my fingers were already turning red where they gripped the case of thirty-five books. I finally dropped it just as a woman appeared before me. Her hair was silver, but her skin was as smooth and unmarred as an uncut plum. "Miss Isom." She stuck out a hand. "Portland, Oregon, librarian."

"Miss Balakin," I responded, shaking her hand and wincing as her fingers wrapped around my throbbing ones. "Washington, D.C. I trained at Camp Meade."

"Lovely to meet you. Grab your things. I'll be taking you to the train station."

I shook my head. I'd been wary of trains since the streetcar accident that had caused my mother's death. "I thought there was a driver coming for me? A man from the Red Cross?"

"A woman." Miss Isom shot me a distrustful look, her eyes narrowed. "She'll pick you up from Neufchâteau and take you to the hospital center at Bazoilles-sur-Meuse."

She marched off and I followed, squeezing my eyes shut to block out the overwhelming crowds and then opening them again when I stumbled.

Miss Isom waved me into a motorcar, and we bumped together over the cobblestone roads. I pressed my face to the window like a child and watched the city go by. I'd imagined France to be a beautiful, magical place, but Saint-Nazaire looked no different from Hoboken, New Jersey. Like a dreary filter had been placed over the ships, the warehouses, and the industrial plants we passed. A cluster of women hurried out of one building wearing gauze masks, and I turned toward Miss Isom. "What are the masks for?" They were thin and wispy, surely not good for protection against gas attacks.

"The Spanish influenza. Some of them wear camphor in sacks around their necks, too"—she sniffed—"as if the smell will ward off disease. Isn't it the same in D.C.?"

"It wasn't when I left," I admitted. But I'd been on the ship for two weeks and at Camp Meade for a month before that.

"Interesting. The entire city is quarantined now, I hear. Schools are out, libraries are closed, stores and movie theaters are shuttered. Even churches."

I gaped, my mouth opening and closing. How was it possible so much had changed so quickly?

That was how tragedy was, I supposed. One day everything was all right, and the next, it wasn't. One day my mother had been alive; the next, perished in a streetcar accident that killed a dozen. One day I'd composed a letter to my father about an exam I'd taken in school; the next, I received word he'd died of a heart attack.

Miss Isom and I continued in silence. It seemed as if there were locomotives everywhere, but none of them were ready for transport. They lay in pieces, having been shipped over from the United States in parts to be reassembled here in Saint-Nazaire. I didn't feel entirely comfortable getting on a train that had recently looked more like scrap metal than a vehicle, but I supposed I had no choice. There were nearly four thousand miles of ocean between me and home now. No turning back.

Our car stopped at a small wooden train station, and I followed Miss Isom to the tracks. Unable to lift my skirts with my valise and crate of books in my hands, I stumbled as I climbed into the train car. Miss Isom noticed, her sharp eyes darting toward me and away, but was polite enough to pretend she didn't.

I followed her along the length of the car, stepping over the long legs of soldiers who'd already found their seats. They had the same fresh-faced looks as the men on the ship had; they'd not yet been hardened by war. I hoped they never would be. I hoped *I* never would be.

Miss Isom led me through several cars and finally stopped in one that was nearly empty. We settled in the end opposite the smattering of troops, me taking the wooden seat near the window and Miss Isom the aisle. She pulled out a sheet of paper and a pencil, and so I turned to look out the window as we lurched to a start. The industry fell away as we moved east from Saint-Nazaire, and I gazed out at green farmland and tiny villages that I imagined depicted France as it was meant to be. France as it was in peacetime.

Miss Isom finished writing her letter after about half an hour and tucked it into her valise. "So." She settled back into her seat. "Where did you study?"

I hesitated. "The Garrison Forest School. It's in Owings Mills, Maryland. Near Baltimore."

"A college?"

"Oh." I remembered what Mrs. Lipscomb had said at Camp Meade about the other volunteers having been trained professionals, and I blushed. "No. Secondary school. I've worked at the Dead Letter Office since graduating."

Miss Isom cocked her head. "You weren't interested in going to college, then?"

"I was," I admitted. "My father was a professor at Mount Vernon College." When I was a girl, he'd take me to their commencement exercises to hear the winning senior essays on topics as wide-ranging and controversial as women's suffrage, child labor, and temperance. How I wanted to be one of them!

"But?"

"But he died when I was sixteen. He left enough money that I could finish at Garrison Forest as a boarder, but I couldn't afford college without a job. I moved back into the townhouse we owned and started working at the Dead Letter Office. I've been there since."

I tried not to show my disappointment at the way my life had turned out. I didn't want Miss Isom to hear it in my voice and pity me.

I directed the conversation her way. "Where did you grad-uate?"

"The Pratt Institute." Miss Isom grinned. "In 1901."

"Wow." I sighed. "I've never been to New York."

"I was only there two years." Miss Isom shrugged, as if spending two years in New York were akin to brushing your teeth in the morning. "I got a job as the head of the Portland Library Association and moved out west." She winked. "First woman in the position. *And* first free public library in the state."

"Are you from there?"

She shook her head. "My father was a Union surgeon in the Civil War, and he was stationed in Nashville, Tennessee, when I was born. We moved to Cleveland after the war."

I raised my eyebrows, impressed by this woman who seemed to have lived in every corner of the country. "How did you end up here?"

Miss Isom sighed. "My assistant librarian was a pacifist and refused to buy war bonds. I stood against the board when they tried to fire her, and my loyalty was questioned along with hers—even when she resigned at my urging. The entire affair soured me on the board's politics, and I wanted to come over to a place where I could be more directly useful to our men."

And, I imagined, a place where her loyalty would not be questioned.

As we continued to talk, I learned that Miss Isom too had lost both her parents, finding herself alone in the world at thirty-two. That was when she had gone to Pratt, she explained, upon realizing she was no longer tied to Cleveland or to her past. I supposed I was doing something similar now. My father's death had kept me from going to college as I'd planned, but this had come my way instead.

The train rolled to a stop three hours later in what Miss Isom told me was Tours, France. "This is where we part ways." She pulled another sheet of paper out of a coat pocket and handed it to me. "You will continue on through Chaumont and then to Neuf-château. The Motor Corps driver will pick you up there."

"But—"

"They don't need two librarians in the same hospital, Miss Balakin. We'll serve our country better this way."

"Right." I stood as she did, but she shook her head. "It was a pleasure to meet you."

"Likewise." She bit her lip, looking more uncertain than I'd yet seen her. "Good luck out there."

"You as well," I said. "Thank you."

And then I watched as she disappeared through the doors and I was left alone. Her head held high, she navigated easily through crowds of wounded: soldiers with bandages wrapped around their heads, using crutches with their legs amputated below the knee, sleeves flapping in the spots where arms had once belonged. Would my final destination look like this, or would it be even worse?

As the train set off again, I returned to staring out the grimy windows. But what I saw as we got farther east was no picturesque countryside. The muddy ground was pockmarked and torn open like a body, and I cringed at each outcropping of rock like I expected it to be a corpse. The few buildings we passed could no longer be called buildings, just jagged pillars of stone and piles of rubble. How many of these small towns, I couldn't help but wonder, had survived for centuries before this? The Romans had been here nearly two thousand years ago. These ruins could have been host to Charlemagne or Henry of Navarre, to Jeanne d'Arc or William the Conqueror. And now they were nothing.

Worse than the utter destruction, though, was the semblance of normalcy. Illusion that pulled me in, gave me hope, and then crushed it. The front of a grand cathedral rose in the distance before us, and I craned my neck to see, hungry for the sight of something beautiful. Smudging my nose on the window, I gasped when I saw reality. All that remained of the cathedral was the front facade, smooth stone like marble and a glorious archway. As we got level with the building, I could see the broken side of the wall that should have formed a corner. The arched doorway led nowhere.

I held my breath as the train flew past. The wall looked so fragile against the backdrop of gray sky that I was afraid it would collapse in the gust of wind our train created.

Eyes wet, I gazed out at the endless fields of destruction until we pulled into a train station late in the afternoon. The station was a simple building, but it was intact. That was all I could ask for.

I alighted from the train with my bag, stretching my stiff legs. My knees momentarily locked, and I squeezed my eyes shut. Could I really do this? I breathed deeply, coaxing myself to stay calm, and opened my eyes.

I surveyed the crowd for a woman, but men were everywhere. So different from at home in D.C., where only wives and daughters remained.

Finally I spotted a woman wearing a long, gray coat and a close-fitting hat that pressed down on short blond curls. The hat was stitched with a red cross, and an armband below her shoulder read *ARC*. Relieved, I pushed my way through the crowd until I reached her. She had bright eyes and round cheeks, and I towered over her.

Her gaze went to my case of books. "Miss Emmaline Balakin?"

"Yes, ma'am."

She laughed immediately. "Don't 'ma'am' me. My name is Nellie." She stuck out a hand, and I let my valise fall to the ground with a clunk so I could shake it. "I'm here to drive you to Base Hospital 42 in Bazoilles-sur-Meuse."

I nodded. Base Hospital 42 staff had been mobilized at Camp Meade just like Nicholas's 79th Infantry Division. Coming from Camp Meade myself, it made sense I would be placed there. But I knew little else about it. "Is it far?"

"Not at all. Four miles south. But"—she threw a smile over her shoulder as she stooped to pick up my valise and strode away—"we have to stop in Toul first."

I hurried to keep up. "Toul? What's in Toul?"

"Several base hospitals and an airfield," Nellie said. "I have to drop off an extra shipment of supplies. I'd keep them at our hospital complex if it were up to me—God knows we're overrun enough we'll need them eventually—but who am I to question the colonel?"

Her cheery tone hardly matched her words. How overrun was overrun? "How many beds are there at Base Hospital 42?"

"Counting just the barracks, one thousand. Of course, with all the casualties coming in from the Meuse-Argonne Offensive, we've had to break out the marquee tents. That adds another thousand cots. But," she continued as we reached the car and she swung my bags into the backseat, "42 is part of a hospital center with seven other base hospitals. We've got about ten thousand beds between them all."

Ten thousand wounded men. I could hardly imagine destruction on such a scale. Could Nicholas be one of them?

No. I couldn't think like that. However much I wanted to see him, I didn't wish injury upon him.

Remembering his gray eyes and his kind smile, I stumbled as I climbed into the car, but Nellie just flashed me a smile as she plugged her key into the ignition and gave it a twist.

The engine rumbled to life, and dust rose as we stuttered down the road. "How far is Toul?"

"About forty miles northeast." Nellie stole a sideways glance my way, this time without smiling. "It's only about ten from the front. The spot we're going is categorized as a base hospital—same as us—but has been functioning more like an evacuation hospital. Men coming straight from the field hospitals."

I shook my head. This was a whole new vocabulary for me. "What's the difference?"

"Field hospitals are just three or four miles from the troops at the front, and they only hold about two hundred men. The wounded are rushed there for emergency dressings and such, then taken by ambulance to evacuation hospitals. They're at those briefly, maybe two days, before taking hospital trains or ambulances to base hospitals for longer stays. Forty-two is a base hospital, but it's been acting more like an evacuation hospital, too, this last week. Too many men are coming in to keep them all."

"So where do you send them?"

"Farther back to base hospitals in the intermediate section."

I didn't respond out loud, but Nellie must have read the confusion in my face. "Don't worry. You're the librarian. You don't need to know about the sections or the evacuation system or the medical detachment. You just need to focus on the men at 42."

That didn't sound so simple, either, when I considered the sheer number of men.

"And you? How did you end up doing this?"

"Long story." Nellie laughed. "I was initially made a clerk, because I was a secretary back in the United States. But then one day when they were driving me back to the station, the brakes in the car failed and we hit a tree."

I gasped, and Nellie smiled. "I know. The driver was fine, but he was dazed enough from a bump on the head that he needed a moment to rest. I hopped out, fixed the brakes, and drove the rest of the way. By the time we got to our destination, he wanted me to work for the Motor Corps. I had to pass a mechanic's test and first-aid exam, but that was it."

That was *it*? It sounded impossible to me. "How did you know how to do it all? The brakes, the mechanic's test?" Even the driving seemed like a strange thing for a woman to know.

"Papa's a mechanic back home. He taught me and my sister both how to do just about everything there is to do with a motorcar. I've always loved it, but Mabel—my sister—can't stand the work." She laughed. "I suppose she's stuck helping Papa with all of it now."

Her face turned more serious. "I'll have to make it up to her when I get home."

"Mabel." It was a pretty name. "How old is she?"

"Four years younger than me. Twenty-one."

That made Nellie twenty-five, two years my senior.

I heard myself sigh. "I always wondered what it would be like having a sister."

"No siblings?"

I shook my head.

"Having a sister is infuriating," Nellie said. But then she softened. "And so special. Mabel's my best friend." She glanced at me. "You remind me of her, actually. Soft-spoken."

I grinned sheepishly back at her. I'd never had a sister nor a best friend, though I didn't say that out loud. My life in D.C. might not have seemed so empty if I had.

But I hadn't been as interested in the boarding school girls who returned home to happy households as I was in the orphans I read about: Oliver Twist, Huckleberry Finn, Jane Eyre. It was no wonder I'd hardly lived at all before going to Camp Meade.

Now I was here, maybe even risking my life in order to live. But my mother always told us that *dvúm smertjám ne byvàt', odnój ne minovát': one cannot have two deaths, but cannot run from one.* It mattered less how long you lived than how, and I had hardly lived a life worth protecting before.

Buildings fell away and forest began to encroach as Nellie and I continued on. I was relieved at first, glad to see the end of ruined towns and cemeteries.

But the forest was no better.

The trees rose like crooked spindles, like if I touched my finger against one, I'd fall into the cursed deep sleep of the Grimm brothers. Not a single trunk braved the sky; each one instead snapped at the halfway point or at the height of a soldier. What had happened, I wondered. Was this damage from a bomb? From artillery shells? It could have been either, or something else entirely. I could recite every street in D.C. and translate novels into French and Russian, but I knew nothing of war.

Whatever the cause, I shuddered. The trees stood like starched corpses, eerie and unsettling. It was September, barely fall, but not a single leaf remained. Not even on the ground. Instead, the ground was littered with branches. I realized with a start that that was what made the trees look so ghostly: not their lack of leaves, but the fact that they'd been wrenched of all their branches. They were straight lines, arrows up to heaven.

I tried to tear my gaze away but couldn't. A single tear rolled down my cheek, and I was grateful for Nellie's speed; she kept us moving too quickly for me to see more than snippets of barbed wire or flashes of stone fortifications that looked disconcertingly like portals to some sort of fairy-tale world.

If only. If only the stone huts were home to forest druids. If only the violent gash of each trench were a gently curving river of nymphs. Instead, the blackened, pockmarked land was a sign of anything but magic.

"I know," Nellie said, placing her small hand on my knee. I imagined Mabel, a smaller version of Nellie, being comforted in the same simple way.

"Do you get used to it?" I wasn't sure what I hoped her answer would be.

"Sometimes I think I have." Nellie sighed. "It's been a month, after all. But no. You simply find ways to cope."

I wanted to pat her knee the way she'd patted mine, but I hesitated. The opportunity passed, and I clenched my fist in my lap in shame.

And then the world shattered. A roar like the engine of the *Aeolus*, a hissing like an angry cat. An explosion of orange fire across the sky.

I screamed and couldn't hear myself. I could see my chest rising and falling, knew I must be breathing heavily, but I couldn't hear anything but the artillery exploding above us. My vision swirled, and I couldn't distinguish up from down or car from ground. All I saw was fire, and I squeezed my eyes shut and pulled my knees to my chest. Trying to quell my nausea, I rocked in the seat until the sound stopped.

Was I dead? I choked out a cry, but this time, I was able to hear it.

Then I heard Nellie. "Breathe. Emmaline, breathe. Inhale. Count to four. Exhale, two, three, four. Again. Inhale. Exhale." I heard her words from a distance, like she was talking to someone else, and only started to obey halfway through. I inhaled; I exhaled. "Can you see my hat?" The red cross on Nellie's cap wavered in front of me, and I tried to focus my eyes on it. "Just look at the red cross, Emmaline. Breathe. You're going to be okay."

When I could process my surroundings, I realized we'd pulled off the road and stopped. "What happened?" I managed. "Did the explosion—"

"No," Nellie rushed to answer. "I pulled off so I could help you. The explosion is miles away, on the front."

"How often—how often does that happen?"

"Enough that you *do* start to get used to it," Nellie said grimly. But still her lips went up in a slight smile, like we'd shared a joke or an understanding. This girl was so relaxed, so endlessly positive. I envied her.

In shame, I buried my head in my hands. "I'm so sorry." What I meant was *I'm so embarrassed.* To fall apart like this my very first day in France, at the sound of one explosion? Men like Nicholas lived through those explosions every day. What must Nellie think of me, I wondered.

Nellie shook her head. "Listen to me."

I kept my head bowed but let my eyes drift up to meet hers.

"This is war. We are *all* afraid."

"But—"

"No. Listen."

I could tell Nellie was the older sister. She was at once commanding and soothing.

"We're all afraid," she repeated. "But being scared like that just means you still have your humanity. And going on anyway makes you far braver than if you didn't have any fear at all."

I didn't trust myself to speak, so I just nodded. Nellie waited for a moment before starting the car again to be sure I wasn't going to crack, and then we continued in silence to Toul.

The city's white stone ramparts came into view first. They were at least twice my height and topped with grass, though the green was interspersed with brown. Behind the ramparts rose the turrets of a Gothic cathedral that took my breath away. *This* was the France I'd imagined.

But Nellie didn't stop. We continued another mile north of the town and its people and stopped in a desolate, barren field packed with wooden barracks. Each was identical, long and single-storied with small square windows at the end, and they made for a dreary picture against the brown of the land. An airplane buzzed above us. I cowered instinctively, but Nellie put a hand on mine. "Don't worry," she said. "The American Air Force is based here. That's our plane."

I didn't bother hiding my sigh of relief.

"You can wait in the car," Nellie said. "I'll be back in just a moment."

I waited with my fingers twisting in my lap as she darted off toward one of the wooden buildings. Would another explosion rip through the sky? Would the men waging their offensive a mere ten miles away come charging across the field with machine guns blazing?

I was so relieved when Nellie returned that I smiled at her broadly and without self-consciousness. She smiled back. "Ready to see your new home?"

"Does it look like this?"

Nellie pulled a face. "I'm afraid so."

Well. This was war. I couldn't expect luxury.

Something in my expression must have changed, because Nellie burst into laughter as she pulled us back onto the road. "What?"

"Your face," she gasped. "When I said 42 is set up the same way."

I scrunched my nose, somewhere between mortified and amused. "I didn't come from luxury," I said, "but a wooden shack in the mud does seem a bit . . . perilous. Not like it would do much against a bomb."

Nellie shook her head. "It wouldn't. Air raid sirens go off sometimes at night, and everyone goes outside to check for planes. But there's nowhere to hide if we see them."

Nowhere to hide. The words should have filled me with dread, but they gave me a much-needed jolt of adrenaline instead. "That's why the men need books."

Nellie shot me a quizzical look, her driving never faltering. "Books against bombs?"

"Books are the best place to hide," I said quietly. "When the world is just too much to take."

Nellie patted my knee once again, and then we drove on in silence. Back through the eerie forest and the ruins of small towns, back past Neufchâteau and south to Bazoilles-sur-Meuse. Night was falling, and I was in a foreign country in the midst of the war to end all wars. But somehow, with Nellie beside me and fog blanketing the landscape in silence, I felt almost at peace.

Chapter 6

—— ❦ ——

Kathleen Carre

July 1976

Susan, Linda, and I tumbled into our cots and pulled up our blankets after two more hours of "basic" instruction: how to hold and put on our hats ("plebe our covers"), chopping, the expectation that we shout responses loud enough to make us light-headed, and further lessons on saluting and responding to officers. It was hours past dinner by the time we returned to our rooms after sixteen and a half hours of training, and it had only been one day. It seemed like years ago that I'd been at the D.C. bus station.

Though I wanted to call Nana, I knew she'd be asleep by now. I should have been, too. Linda was breathing slowly next to me, a far cry from the nervous, shallow breathing I'd gotten used to during the day. Susan too was quiet, which could only mean she'd fallen asleep.

I stared at the ceiling and wondered how late it was. The ceiling was plain like the walls, but the lack of decor didn't bother me. Decor, in my opinion, was a waste of space and a waste of money. And decorating was a waste of time.

Speaking of time, I pulled a face. We weren't allowed to have watches or clocks; knowing the time was apparently a privilege too generous for us plebes. A cadre of officers would wake us at 5:30 a.m. every morning, but I hated that I couldn't set an alarm half an hour earlier to prepare.

I squeezed my eyes shut. Nothing I could do about it, was there? I kept my eyes closed, tried to push my anxiety away, and forced myself into sleep.

Before I knew it, whistles blew and knocks penetrated our door. I rubbed the sleep from my eyes, swung my legs off the side of my bed, and stood. Linda and Susan blinked at me as I immediately made my bed and changed into my uniform. We were allowed sneakers from home for the morning physical education, thank God. No heels.

I brushed out my short hair, pleasantly surprised by how quickly I could do so now that it was bobbed, and brushed my teeth. We weren't to wear jewelry or makeup, so that was it.

Susan, Linda, and I chopped outside for PEP, the plebe summer Physical Education Program. We began with calisthenics in our squadrons, and I found myself sandwiched between Robert and Tom.

"Still here?" Robert sneered.

I ignored him, keeping my eyes straight ahead, or "in the

boat." I certainly wasn't going to get myself in trouble by taking Robert's bait.

"Don't listen to him," Tom whispered on my other side. "He's just jealous because you look better in your uniform than he does."

I nodded a thank-you to Tom, and then the officer instructed us to begin. We did jumping jacks and toe touches to warm up, shoulder stands to stretch and wake up our abdomens, and then sit-ups in the still-wet, dewy grass. Next were push-ups.

"Women are permitted," the leaders thundered, "to do these push-ups on their knees." He paused. "Men must do complete push-ups, remaining on their toes. Understood?"

"Sir, yes, sir!" I joined the rest of the class in calling back, but my face burned. They were singling us out already.

I did the first two sets on my toes, which was easy after the twenty I'd done to get in. But halfway through the third set, my arms gave out and I dropped to my knees. I cursed under my breath, sweat stinging my eyes. Robert scoffed beside me and I gritted my teeth. I'd do push-ups every night if I had to. He wouldn't laugh at me again.

After calisthenics, we ran. They sent us on a two-mile route, going easy on us for the first day, and I smiled. My body was warm, and I reveled in doing something I'd done for years. I remained a few steps ahead of Robert the first mile, and I narrowed my eyes and practically sprinted to be sure I'd beat him the second. I couldn't do push-ups on my toes yet, but I could beat a snobby boy in a race.

When I was done, I stood on the other side of the finish line catching my breath. My lungs felt hollowed out and empty, but I had a smile on my face.

"Midshipman Carre!"

"Sir!" I turned to Ensign Michael. He'd told me yesterday I'd have to prove I deserved my spot here; I imagined I was on my way to doing just that.

"The Naval Academy expects cooperation and a sense of teamwork within squadrons, platoons, and companies."

"Sir, yes, sir." I didn't know what he was trying to say.

"Bilging your teammates, or making them look bad to make yourself look better, is not permitted."

I wiped my smile from my face, surprised I was being chastised.

"You left your team behind."

I blinked and looked back. Indeed, the other dozen men in my squadron were just crossing the finish line. I'd been so focused on beating Robert that I hadn't paid attention to the fact that I was beating Tom, Pat, and all the others.

Brow furrowed, I looked back at Ensign Michael. This was the Naval Academy. Didn't they expect our best?

Ensign Michael's face said otherwise, and I grimaced. "No excuse, sir."

Except that Robert was taunting me. That he doesn't want me to be here.

But neither, I supposed, did the squad leader.

"If you'd left your team behind in the field, they'd be dead."

I'm not allowed in the field, I wanted to say, but I kept my mouth shut.

"Do you understand the expectation?" he barked.

"Sir, yes, sir."

"Do you understand the expectation?" His voice was louder, his eyes darker.

"Sir, yes, sir!" I screamed. My throat rasped, dry after my run, and I was grateful when Ensign Michael left me. After a cool-down series, we were sent back to our rooms for showers before breakfast. I saw Linda and Susan walking together ahead of me, but I didn't run to catch up. After the way I'd been treated this morning, I didn't want to draw any more attention to the fact that I was a woman. I didn't need to glue myself to the other girls like we were something separate.

We each took two minutes to shower. I hardly had time to rinse my body and wet my hair before it was Linda's turn, and breakfast was no leisurely affair, either. We suffered through uniform checks in our heels before being permitted to eat, and then we had to keep our eyes in the boat and repeat our rates as we ate. The questions were easy: on the five basic responses, the uniforms to be worn at different events, the expectations for saluting officers and the flag. But our ensign warned us that the ease wouldn't last. I patted *Reef Points* in my waistband. There was a lot to learn.

The first few sessions after morning chow covered rank structure and the honor system, the NATO alphabet, and the expectations for memorizing *Reef Points*. When those were done, the men and women were separated for hygiene lectures.

"Thank God we don't have to sit through a hygiene talk with the men beside us," Linda whispered as we filed out. I shrugged. It might have been embarrassing, but I'd have preferred that to being singled out.

Eighty-one of us spread across the auditorium. We filled up so many fewer seats this way, just eighty of us rather than a thousand plus, and it was the first time I got a good look at the girls outside my company: blondes, brunettes, a redhead or two. They looked like any other girls off the street, except that none of them had the long, straight hair that was so fashionable right now. Otherwise, they could have been anyone. We ranged from thin and lean to stocky and muscular, and our expressions ranged from apprehensive to excited to guarded. The only unchanging variable was our hair length—and, but for one exception, our race. Out of eighty-one women, only one appeared to be Black.

It was still one more than I was used to. I'd been born the year *Brown v. Board* made integration a legal requirement, but de facto segregation remained the norm. The schools I'd attended had tracked students based on their alleged ability, with most of the white students in the college track and most of the Black students in the labor track. It didn't take a law degree to realize that rich white parents' preference for all-white classes factored into the tracking decisions far more than any real measure of potential did. Of the white families, only Nana had complained. She had written letter after unanswered letter to the school. I made a note to tell her about the integrated class here when we talked, not that one to eighty was any sort of equitable ratio.

The doctor appeared onstage. He repeated what we'd learned yesterday: no drugs or alcohol, no caffeine, no candy or chocolate. No medicine without visiting his office first.

One girl raised her hand. "Can we take Midol?"

The doctor shook his head. "Not without coming to me."

I suppressed a groan, not wanting to get called out for insubordination. The girl in front of me raised her hand, put it down, and then raised it again.

"Yes?"

She hesitated. "We don't have pockets in our uniforms, sir. How are we to carry—ah—hygiene products?"

A few nervous titters passed through the crowd, but I leaned forward in my seat. How, indeed?

The doctor looked to either side, as if someone might appear onstage to answer the question for him. "I will get back to you on that."

Susan muttered under her breath. "Doesn't he mean 'I'll find out, ma'am,' or 'No excuse, ma'am'?"

Linda giggled.

"Anyway." The doctor cleared his throat. "I'll leave you to the experts now."

We looked at each other. Who were the experts, if not a doctor? Would we finally see a woman in a position of authority?

The doctor scooted offstage, and the lights dimmed. A shaky image appeared on the screen up front.

UNITED STATES NAVY TRAINING FILM

Produced under the supervision of the
BUREAU OF AERONAUTICS for the
BUREAU OF MEDICINE AND SURGERY.

The naval anthem played in the background, and a shiver ran through me.

Until the next screen appeared.

PERSONAL HYGIENE FOR WOMEN: PART I.

Susan looked at us. "What does the Navy expect to know about feminine hygiene that we don't?"

I didn't respond, too busy squinting at the small copyright date in the corner. "It gets worse. I think that says 1943."

Linda's blue eyes bugged. "It's older than we are."

We turned our attention back to the screen. The women wore knee-length skirts and cardigans, their hair styled in victory rolls and curly bobs. They were the picture of '40s femininity, but the narrator's voice was a man's. This was "the expert"?

"Oh. My. God." Linda buried her face in her hands as he began describing the correct way to select a girdle for those "women who really need them."

He transitioned quickly into describing the correct fit of a shoe. I raised my eyebrows. The man depicted the natural curvature of the foot, cautioned against any shoe that disrupted it, and then explained that a shoe with a heel is suitable for any activity except for hiking. "For these purposes," he intoned, "you need a shoe which has a lower heel with a broader base."

"That shoe still has an inch-high heel," Linda whispered in horror.

"Yeah," Susan said. "I'm not hiking in that."

We listened to dry descriptions of how to fit stockings and avoid athlete's foot, how to keep a clean complexion and cuticles, how to treat lice, and how to shower and brush our teeth. What kind of women did they think we were, for God's sake? We knew how to use toothpaste.

A group of girls in the back laughed out loud when the narrator advised us to ask our friends if we suspected our vaginas smelled, and I was surprised when no officers reprimanded them. They must have been as uncomfortable as the rest of us.

Still, I wasn't expecting the next image: a labeled photograph of the anatomy of the vagina. "The hymen," the narrator told us, "is often broken during childbirth."

I couldn't help it this time; I snorted. Linda joined me when the doctor explained that menstruation should never be painful. "No wonder we aren't allowed chocolate," she whispered. "They don't understand how bad we need it." We breathed a collective sigh of relief when the film was over. I looked around the room and saw that most of our faces were red, and I'd wager half were colored in mortification; the other half, in the effort of holding in laughter. Maybe our mothers would have benefited from seeing this film back in their preteen years—but God, we were adults. And it was practically 1980. It was a new world: birth control was legal even for unmarried women now, and *Roe v. Wade* had passed three years ago.

The doctor appeared back onstage. "I have two additional announcements. The first is that this film makes no mention of birth control."

I stuck out my chin. The reason why wasn't exactly rocket science. Unmarried women couldn't legally access birth control until four years ago. Long after these films' time.

The doctor's voice brought me back to the present. "You'll remember that fraternizing is not allowed among midshipmen of different classes. There will be no dating at the Naval Academy." His next words suggested that this rule might have been one that no one expected us to follow.

"But as female midshipmen will be expelled for pregnancy, birth control can be prescribed in my office."

Chatter broke out among us girls. Five minutes ago, we'd been told the hymen breaks during childbirth. Now the United States Navy was offering us birth control?

"It's revolutionary!" Susan's eyes shone. "Who would have thought?"

Linda shook her head. "I'd be far too mortified to go in and ask for it." She shuddered.

"Dating isn't even allowed," I reminded them. "We won't need birth control."

The doctor called us back to attention. "The final announcement," he reminded us. We looked at him, half expecting him to pass out free condoms. "All female midshipmen will be required to wear purses."

"Purses?" some girl in the audience shouted. I couldn't help but feel the same way. We were naval midshipmen, not society wives.

"Purses for . . . feminine products," the doctor clarified.

I raised my hand. "Do we have to wear the purses at all times? Or simply when necessary?"

"At all times."

Grumbling spread again throughout the auditorium. How were we supposed to chop everywhere with purses flying around? And what would the men say?

At the conclusion of the doctor's awkward speech, we filed out of the auditorium. I blinked in the sunlight, and it took me a moment to realize that camera bulbs were going off around us. Reporters again. I'd avoided them on I-Day yesterday, but they'd been eager to talk to any girl who'd let them.

I kept my eyes straight ahead and marched on, refusing to even acknowledge the hawkers. But I could see Susan out of my periphery as she broke stride to answer a reporter's question.

"Don't," I hissed, but it was too late. I heard her voice as I marched away, her outrage over the outdated videos and the purses. Another woman chimed in with a comment about the heels, and I soldiered on. We'd quickly learned yesterday that any girl willing to talk to a reporter would get an immediate cold shoulder from the men in her company.

Our final drills of the day were in squadrons, and I was grateful we weren't in our larger companies. I didn't need to practice or draw more attention to myself alongside Susan, who'd surely be notorious from here on out after complaining to the reporter.

At evening chow, I set my tray next to Tom, who'd been kind to me so far.

I perched on the front three inches of the chair only; we'd be allowed to take up the whole space when we were no longer plebes. We were allowed one luxury today, however, as Ensign Michael granted us the freedom to speak freely throughout the meal. After the chaplain said the blessing and the gong rang for us to begin eating, we dove in.

"Kathleen." Tom turned to me with a practiced smile. "How are you?"

"Never better." I wasn't sure if it was the truth or a lie. "You?"

"Tired." He broke a roll in half and popped one entire piece in his mouth. "But I didn't expect anything else."

I nodded. "Good to know what you're getting into."

He finished chewing and then spoke again. "My father and grandfather were both Navy. I've spent my whole life preparing for this."

He did look the part.

"Was your dad a midshipman?"

"No," I said. "Actually—"

But Tom interrupted before I could tell him about Nana's stint in the Motor Corps during World War I or my late father's service in World War II and Korea. "Just take my word for it, then," he said. "It runs in the blood. When your family's been here, you spend your whole life preparing to come here too."

"My nana served in World War I," I finally had the opportunity to say. "Nellie Mayborn."

"My grandfather too. Forty-Fourth Regiment."

"Nana was in the Motor Corps with the Red Cross."

"Hm." Tom flashed me that charming smile with those straight white teeth. "Sounds like we have a lot in common."

I decided not to mention my absent mother or my grandmother's apparent aversion to my joining the military. "Guess so."

"Hey." Tom put down his fork. "We get Yard liberty Sunday afternoons. Any interest in meeting up for a game of golf at the golf club?" He winked. "Nothing better than good golf and good company."

My mouth opened and closed. "Statute 3.10 . . ."

The statute was a new rule, added only this year. *Unduly familiar personal relationships between midshipmen in the same Company are prohibited when prejudicial to good order and discipline or of a nature to bring discredit on the naval service.*

"Then don't call it unduly familiar." Tom shrugged. I envied his easy nonchalance. No one questioned whether he belonged here, but I would have to prove that I did. "I'll get some friends to come along. Just a group of midshipmen enjoying the Naval Support Activity."

Just a group of midshipmen. Not women, not girls, not ladies. Not "ploobs," or plebes with boobs; not "oinkers," as Linda had already been called by a man in her squadron. Just midshipmen.

That was what I wanted to be: just a midshipman like everyone else. So I pushed away my misgivings and smiled. "Okay," I said. "Let's do it."

We had thirty minutes of free time in the evening to write home or, if we were lucky, get a phone call in. After living with Nana for more than a decade, I felt like the few days since we'd spoken had been a lifetime.

The boy waiting for the telephone in front of me smirked. "Need to call home to Mama?"

"Nah." Another boy in line elbowed him. "I bet it's a boyfriend." He whispered something into the other boy's ear, and they both snickered as their eyes roamed my body.

I refused to look away. "Neither," I said with as much dignity as I could muster. "Not that it's any of your business."

The line moved slowly, and I had no way of knowing how much time was left before our nightly Blue and Gold company meeting. I bounced on my sore toes. Not having a watch was already driving me crazy.

By the time I was next in line, I'd bitten my nails short. I was near picking them to the point of drawing blood when it was finally my turn. I grabbed the receiver and dialed home, anxiously waiting for Nana to pick up. The phone rang and rang and rang. But no one answered.

"Give it up," said the plebe behind me. "Obviously they aren't picking up."

I shook my head. Nana knew that the only time I got to talk was in the afternoon, and she didn't go anywhere after dinner anyway. Her only social event these days was visiting with Mrs. Peregrine next door. So there was no reason for her not to answer.

But the phone kept ringing. I gave up only when tears threatened in the corners of my eyes, unwilling to let these men see me cry.

I replaced the receiver and turned. The boy behind me jumped up and grabbed it, his call answered on the first ring.

He didn't get to talk long. The horn sounded to signify our time was up, and the plebes still in line groaned. One of them, a tall Black man with long lashes, sighed as he turned away. He almost bumped into me and apologized profusely. "You didn't get to talk either, did you?"

I shook my head. "No answer."

"Sorry about that." He held out his hand. "Derrick, by the way. Nice to meet you."

I shook his hand. "I'm Kathleen. Sorry about your phone call."

He looked around and lowered his voice, a small smile playing on his lips. "I really wanted to talk to my mom." He grinned wider. "Not that I'd necessarily admit it." He turned serious again. "It's just that she knows what it's like to be somewhere people wish you weren't."

"Yeah." I swallowed. "That's why I wanted to talk to my grandma, too."

I couldn't sleep that night. God knew I was tired enough, but I couldn't shut my mind off. Nana should have picked up today.

I swung out of bed and positioned myself on the narrow strip of floor between it and the wall. I couldn't go on a run after lights out at 2145, but I *could* make sure Robert had nothing to make fun of tomorrow.

I stretched out for push-ups. I was okay in the plank position, since my core was strong from running, but the problem with the push-ups was in the arms. I'd inherited Nana's arms, long and thin with wrists so delicate that bracelets looked too large around them.

I breathed out all the prayers for my nana into the world as I bent my elbows toward my ribs. *Please let her be okay.* I fought the urge to fall to my knees just as I fought the urge to break the rules and run out into the hall to try home again.

Twenty-six push-ups. I'd get through two sets tomorrow without resorting to the modified version; by the end of the month, I swore, I'd get all four on my toes.

I'd do everything I could to make sure the next batch of girls was welcomed in a way I hadn't been.

Chapter 7

— ❧ —

Emmaline Balakin

September 1918

Welcome to Bazwillie Sure Moose." Nellie kept one hand on the wheel and waved the other about, gesturing to the small town nestled in the valley between two hills.

"What?" I was startled into laughter. "Bazwillie Sure Moose?"

Nellie shrugged. "That's what the soldiers call it. The French is too hard to pronounce."

"Bazoilles-sur-Meuse," I said. "Surely it isn't so difficult?"

Nellie raised her eyebrows. "We didn't all go to boarding school."

I felt my cheeks redden and hoped Nellie couldn't tell in the darkness of night. "I didn't mean—"

Nellie burst into that already-familiar laughter of hers, and I joined in after a moment of hesitation. "Okay," I said. "Bazwillie Sure Moose."

"They also call it Baz Eels on the Muss, if you'd prefer, or Bacillus on Mush."

"You're making these up."

"It's the soldiers," she swore. "They need something to entertain themselves when they're bedridden. Goedesversvelde is 'Gerty Wears Velvet.' Étaples, 'Eat Apples.' Of course, my favorite is 'Moo Cow Farm' for Mouquet Farm." She chuckled. "You can tell they're bored to tears." Then she cocked her head. "I suppose that's why you're here."

Books as an escape, I understood. But books as the sole form of entertainment for thousands of men? What a daunting task I had ahead of me. "Isn't there anything else for them to do?"

"The Red Cross sets up recreation huts at each hospital, but not all the men can get there. Many are confined to the wards."

She painted a rather dreary picture of hospital life, but her tone never faltered. "How do they keep up morale? How do *you*? You're so . . ." I wanted to say *blasé* but was afraid it would sound insulting. I didn't resent Nellie's attitude; I wanted to learn it for myself. "So cheerful."

She shrugged. "You have two options, I suppose. You can crack, or you can try to find pockets of joy."

"Joy . . ." We had just stepped from the motorcar, and I'd landed ankle-deep in mud. It plastered my skirt to the skin above my boots, making the cool air suddenly feel cold. Worse was the smell: a pungent mixture of filth, the iron scent of blood, and sharp antiseptic. "Where on earth do you find pockets of joy *here*?"

"People. Laughter." She spread her arms. "The occasional sunny day."

Nellie pulled me to the side of the building she'd parked in front of. Like the buildings on either side, it was long and thin and made of planks that looked soaked through with rain and snow. But in front of it was an ambulance, dozens of men on stretchers lying in the mud alongside it.

My breath caught. "Why are they out in the cold?"

"This is the receiving ward. They've just been brought from the field hospitals."

It was too dark to make out their faces or their injuries—except for the ones missing limbs, whose outlines were sickeningly incomplete against the fabric of their stretchers. "Are there always so many?"

"We've gotten dozens a day since the newest offensive started along the Meuse River and in the Argonne forest. It's the largest operation the AEF has undertaken. A million of our soldiers are involved—infantry, aircraft, everything. They're trying to cut off the entire German 2nd Army. They took Montfaucon today."

I swallowed. "Which means . . . ?"

"That they're beating back the Germans. But . . ." She looked at the men in the mud. "Not without casualties. Anyway." She shook herself off. "Let's get you inside."

Nellie marched me to the first building, a long wooden barracks-style structure like all the rest. "This is the administration building." She knocked on the door and wasted no time when it swung open. "Volunteer librarian reporting for commanding officer."

The man in uniform thanked Nellie and dismissed her, and I turned with wide eyes. "Where are you going?"

"I bunk at Hospital No. 18," she said. "It's centered in an old chateau, so there's a garage for me and my car."

"But it's part of this same hospital complex, right?" I asked less to understand how the base hospital organization worked and more to be sure Nellie wouldn't be far.

"Yes. I'll see you soon, Emmaline. I promise." She lowered her voice. "I'll find an excuse to stop by if nothing else. It can be so hard being away from home, away from my parents and my sister. I hope we see a lot more of each other."

She squeezed my hand, turned, and disappeared through the door.

The soldier who'd opened the door barked at me to follow him, and I obeyed. He deposited me in front of another, taller man with several pins on the breast of his uniform. His dark, limp mustache hung over his lip like a dead fish.

"Colonel Hodgson." The shorter soldier saluted. "The volunteer librarian, sir."

I bobbed a curtsy like a girl in a Regency novel and felt immediately foolish. "Emmaline Balakin, sir."

He raised a thin eyebrow, and I marveled at the oddity of his having so much hair on his upper lip and hardly any at all above his eyes. It put me in mind of an eel, thin and beady-eyed with a large, slimy mouth.

"I was under the impression," the colonel said, "that the librarian would be a man."

"Sir, no, sir."

"War is no place for women."

I thought of the wounded men lying outside in the mud. "I'd wager it's no place for men either, sir."

I nearly clapped my hand over my mouth as the words came out. Talking back to a superior was ill-advised in the best of cases, but in the army? I couldn't imagine it would be well-received.

The man's eyebrows came crashing down. "I am your commanding officer, Miss Balakin. You will speak only when you are asked a direct question."

I started to say *yes, sir*, then thought better of it. I nodded.

"I was going to have one of my men give you a tour of the place, but I think I'd like to do it after all. It doesn't hurt to keep an eye on your type."

I would have laughed if I hadn't been so cowed. My type? My type was shy and timid and quiet. My type was the type that lurked in the shadows.

Then again, I was here. I'd spoken my mind once already. Maybe I was more my mother's daughter than I'd thought.

Colonel Hodgson led me out of the headquarters building and into the dark night. We faced the receiving and evacuation buildings, and I watched as another man was unloaded from the ambulance.

"The receiving and evacuation ward," Colonel Hodgson said. "You've seen enough of that."

He steered me away. "The patients get cleaned up there and then get sent in for x-rays, to the wards, or the operation clinic."

I flinched. They'd done an operation on my mother after her accident, but it had been done in a shiny hospital building with all the newest technology. I still remembered the elevator that carried Mama up to the operating room, convinced that a place with such magic would be able to save her.

Here, they didn't even have solid walls.

Colonel Hodgson pointed to the left. "On this side of the camp are nine of the nineteen soldiers' wards. Each one has the capacity for fifty men. This one here"—he gestured to the nearest one—"is the officers' ward. Officer housing is also on this side—barracks, dining, and the bath. The other side is nearly identical, with ten wards and the nurses' housing."

"Will I be staying with the nurses?"

"You'll be in the recreation hut," Colonel Hodgson told me, "where the library will be."

He marched me past the officers' ward to the outskirts of the hospital, where dozens of white tents flapped in a muddy field. On many of them, the canvas sides ended a foot or so above the ground, and something about the unevenness made the whole expanse look like a gaping mouth of crooked, missing teeth. A guttural scream came from one of the tents, and I flinched.

"There are wounded soldiers in there?" I managed. "Exposed to the elements?"

"Our ward capacity is a mere one thousand, and the marquee tents allow us to double it to two thousand. I can assure you it has been an utter necessity since fighting began in the Argonne."

I nodded, barely absorbing the numbers. All I could focus on was the whimpering from within the tents.

But Colonel Hodgson was still talking. "We generally try to separate cases by type. Our specialty is maxillofacial injuries, so we have several of those wards, as well as a contagious disease ward, a head and abdominal ward, and so on. But with the rapid influx of casualties this month, the wards have become more mixed."

I nodded as if I weren't entirely overwhelmed, and the colonel steered me through the narrow corridor between wooden wards and marquee tents until we arrived at the end of the camp. We turned so we were walking alongside the barracks until we were at the back side of the camp opposite the administration building. There were positioned additional barracks, an ablution building, medical stores, and a cluster of latrines and an incinerator. I almost tripped over my own feet when I saw the incinerator for the waste coming out of the latrines. How were men expected to heal from life-threatening wounds when they were recuperating in a place that didn't even have indoor plumbing?

Colonel Hodgson was unfazed as he marched me past each building. We went back in the direction of the administration building, passing the patients' mess hall and kitchen, the dispensary, the clinic, the operating room, the x-ray, and finally—I held my breath as we passed it—the morgue. I only exhaled as Colonel Hodgson opened the door to the recreation hut, sandwiched unfortunately between evacuation/receiving and the morgue. The structure itself, like all the others, was utilitarian and bare, but it was crowded with all the things a soldier might need to remind him of home. A piano stood in the far right corner, and a phonograph sat right beside the door. On a large table against the left wall was a set of cards, a game of backgammon, and a chessboard. A bookshelf sat flush against the back wall of the room, but it was only about half filled with books.

"Is that my room?" I looked at the door beside the bookshelf.

"Yes."

I stepped forward and pushed open the door. My "bedroom" was obviously a storage closet. A small cot had been shoved in the corner, but it was surrounded by discarded objects: a deflated football with its stitches come undone, a precarious stack of papers and assorted pens and pencils, books of sheet music abandoned in a tipped-over wheelbarrow, and a roll of wrapping paper. I would hardly have room to get dressed each morning.

"Your gas mask and helmet are on the bed." Colonel Hodgson pointed. "Sleep with the helmet over your face."

I was horrified by the thought, but I forced myself to nod.

"A volunteer from Hospital 18 will come tomorrow to talk to you about your duties. Good night, Miss Balakin."

"Sir."

I stood shaking in the tiny space after the colonel closed the door, then waited until I heard the slam of the recreation hut door to fall onto the bed. I wished my mama or papa were here to wrap their arms around me and promise it would be all right in the end. Surely they'd felt the same way upon leaving Russia, overwhelmed by the new and unfamiliar. Like maybe they'd made a mistake.

I reached for my mama's chokti on my wrist and prayed. The familiar words of the prayer, the same from Moscow to D.C. to France, soothed me enough to stand and change into my night-gown. Then I returned to the bed and lifted the helmet from the table beside me. It was heavier than a book, but still I obeyed the colonel in putting it over my face. The metal dug into my skin like ice, and I winced. How could anyone bear to sleep under such a thing?

As if to answer my question, artillery rumbled in the distance, and I could see the flash of light through the slats in the wooden roof above me. I wrapped my arms around myself. The helmet wasn't comfortable, but it was better than being crushed by the building after an explosion.

I closed my eyes beneath it and tried to sleep. I was exhausted, having traveled hundreds of miles by train and by motorcar in a single day, but my mind wouldn't calm long enough for my body to follow. I couldn't help but imagine what it would be like if I really needed this helmet. If artillery like the explosion that had spun Nellie and me off the road landed here, or if a German plane flew overhead and dropped bombs on us like we were sitting ducks.

I could see the explosion, hear the men's screams, almost feel my skin crisping and burning and peeling off.

Despite my exhaustion, my mind whirred. My parents had called my imagination a gift when I was a child; now, it seemed more like a curse. Even when I drifted into sleep, I dreamed. And though I couldn't remember my nightmares in the morning, I woke up drenched in sweat.

Chapter 8

— ◈ —

Kathleen Carre

July 1976

By the time the end of our first week rolled around, Nana still hadn't picked up any of my calls. My nervousness had grown to fear and now to panic. This was not like Nana. At least, not like the Nana *I* had always known. Maybe she'd disappeared into herself during my mother's childhood, but for her to go AWOL now, during my first week of training?

I had an even worse feeling when I was called to the chaplain's office Friday morning. I chopped from Bancroft into the mess hall, then navigated deftly between the hundreds of tables set up for dining and into Mitscher Hall, keeping my emotions at a distance as if I could chop away from my fear. I tried to be rational as I went up the stairs toward the chaplain's office. A bad feeling meant nothing; there was no such thing as a premonition.

The chaplain swung the door open before I knocked, and I was surprised to note that he was in traditional Navy garb. With his brass buttons, Navy pin, and order of preference ribbons, he looked more like an officer—which he was, I supposed, as a captain—than a chaplain. I'd expected him in a robe or at least a tippet, but I found the naval attire comforting. This man looked like the men I saw every day, whereas a chaplain seemed someone to whom you'd turn in times of distress. Not that I'd ever done such; I preferred to put my faith in my own hard work. In the tangible, the things I could see and feel and—yes—control.

"Captain." I saluted.

"Midshipman Carre."

He gave me permission to sit, and I complied. But I sat the way we were required to as plebes in the mess hall, with my entire body poised on the edge of the chair. This wasn't a time to relax.

"Midshipman Carre," the chaplain began. "I am so sorry to inform you that we have received a call from a Mrs. Roberta Peregrine."

Mrs. Peregrine was our neighbor, an odd, magpie-like woman my nana spent time with often. I swallowed but did not speak.

"Mrs. Peregrine called with some bad news, Midshipman Carre. Your grandmother, Nellie Carre, has passed away."

The room seemed to spin suddenly. I gripped the arms of my chair tightly, though I wished I were anywhere but here, and closed my eyes.

But I'd been afraid of this, hadn't I? I'd had a feeling this news was coming. Part of me—some stupid, irrational, senseless part of me—had hoped Mrs. Peregrine had called because Nana's apartment had flooded and she'd moved in with her, or that Nana's phone had been disconnected. I'd even half hoped Nana had come down with a cold, that she'd been too ill to talk but would make a full recovery.

How could she be dead? She'd been fine just a week ago. I ticked through all the boxes in my head. She'd reported good health after her last doctor's appointment, she was taking her arthritis medication, and she'd been spry enough to go out with Mrs. Peregrine at least once a week until I left. What could have happened? How could her proud face as I left for the bus station be the last I would see of her?

I listened numbly as the chaplain explained how the American Red Cross had confirmed the death as well as my designation as executor of the estate.

"Me?" I supposed it made sense. My grandfather had died before I was born, and Jane was off God-knew-where.

"Yes, you. Do you think you can handle that?" The chaplain's voice was so gentle that I wanted to break.

"Of course I can." It wasn't as if I had a choice, was it? "Will I be permitted to leave for the funeral?" My mind was racing already. "I can schedule it for next Sunday's Yard liberty." Plebes didn't have permission to leave the Yard until the second summer session, but we had free time Sunday afternoons.

"I'm afraid it isn't up to me," the chaplain said. "But I have recommended to the chain of command that you be allowed leave, considering your role as executor. I also understand that your grandmother raised you?"

"Sir, yes, sir."

He nodded. "I have communicated that to the officers. Grandparents are not usually considered close family for special dispensation of leave, but I believe they will make an exception in your case."

I cringed at the word *exception* but forced a smile to my face. "Thank you."

"Now." He folded his hands on the desk. "Would you like to stay and chat a while?"

Absolutely not. If I stayed to chat, I would fall apart. I was barely holding it together as it was, however calm I hoped I appeared.

"No, thank you, sir," I said politely. "I need to get to morning chow and to class."

I joined my company for the last few minutes of morning chow. Ensign Michael didn't care that I'd hardly gotten situated and hadn't eaten a bite; he began grilling me on my rates right away.

"Midshipman Carre! What is the mission of the Naval Academy?"

I had to repeat it verbatim. "To develop midshipmen morally, mentally, and physically and to imbue them with the highest ideals of duty, honor, and loyalty in order to graduate leaders who are dedicated to a career of naval service and have potential for future development in mind and character to assume the highest responsibilities of command, citizenship, and government." I took a deep breath. "Sir."

"What is the order of responsibilities?"

"First to the Constitution of the United States, sir. Then to the mission, the service, the ship, the shipmate, and finally to self. Sir."

He still wasn't satisfied. "What three things does a midshipman not do?"

That was an easy one. "Lie, steal, or cheat, sir."

Ensign Michael pursed his lips. My fellow company members,

though not allowed to turn their heads to face me, were sneaking looks out of the corners of their eyes. I could see them darting back and forth. It wasn't typical to be grilled so relentlessly unless you'd gotten your first rates wrong. Ensign Michael was targeting me, and we all knew why.

"And how long have you been in the Navy, Midshipman Carre?"

I grimaced. I hated this one. "All me bloomin' life, sir!" I tried to say it with sincerity. "Me mother was a mermaid . . ." I couldn't continue. My mother was my nana, and she was gone.

"Midshipman?"

"Me mother was a mermaid," I tried again. "Me father was King Neptune. I was born on the crest of a wave and rocked in the cradle of the deep . . ."

I couldn't continue. Never again would I be cradled or rocked. The one person in the world who'd ever taken care of me was gone. I was completely and irrevocably alone.

"One thousand fries," Ensign Michael barked.

I glanced down, ashamed, trying to hide the tears swimming in my eyes. One thousand fries wasn't a lot—I'd get five times that for something like drinking. But I had a feeling Ensign Michael would take every opportunity to fry me, and I couldn't afford any demerits.

"Sir, permission to shove off, sir?"

Ensign Michael narrowed his eyes. "Why should I permit you to shove off when you don't know your rates?"

I took a deep breath. I could do this. "I was born on the crest of a wave and rocked in the cradle of the deep. Seaweed and barnacles are me clothes. Every tooth—"

"Midshipman Carre! I did not ask you to recite your rates again."

I shut my mouth, but I didn't escape the ensign's scrutiny. He squinted at me. "Stop crying."

I clenched my fists under the table. My nana was dead, and this man was tearing me apart in front of all the men in my squadron. I wanted nothing more than to jump up and run, but that wasn't me. That was what my mother would do. Jane loved to run from place to place. But I faced my problems head-on.

"They told us you girls would cry," Ensign Michael muttered. He didn't seem satisfied, though he'd driven me to tears himself.

"Permission to speak freely, sir?"

"Not granted."

I bit my tongue to keep from protesting. I wanted to tell him my grandmother was dead. But maybe—I remembered the chaplain saying he'd spoken to the chain of command—he already knew.

My despair was replaced by ice-hot anger. Ensign Michael was a bully and a brute. I wouldn't let him get the best of me.

"Sir, yes, sir." I sat up straighter and took a bite of my cereal. I chewed like I was tearing into the ensign himself. Anger, I was realizing, was an effective distraction from grief.

I made it through the rest of the day, too busy with drill sessions and lectures to wallow in my grief. But when we had free time from 2100 to 2130, I ran to my room and collapsed onto the bed.

Neither Susan nor Linda was there, to my relief, and I let myself bawl for the first time. I told myself it would be the last, too. As the executor of Nana's estate, I didn't have time to grieve for her. I had to take care of her apartment, her things, her funeral. I had to notify my mother somehow, and my nana's friends. I had to write an obituary and send it to the paper.

But now, I cried so hard that my throat felt blistered and my abs were as sore as if I'd just done several rounds of push-ups and crunches. My small, austere cot shook, and my pillowcase grew soaked with water and snot.

I was grateful there was no mirror in our room when I had to force myself up at 2130 for our nightly Blue and Gold meeting, where each company met separately for a review of the day's performance. I wanted nothing more than to stay in bed forever, but I had no choice. The Naval Academy was all I had to live for now. Not only for myself but also for my nana. It was my way to honor her legacy, her work in the war that had inspired me to get to this point.

So I pulled my body from bed despite the ache in my chest and the swelling around my eyes. I couldn't afford to be late to the meeting and receive yet another demerit.

I'd already lost Nana; I couldn't lose this, too.

Chapter 9

— ❖ —

Emmaline Balakin

September 1918

When the Red Cross volunteer appeared at my hut in the morning, I was ready. I wore the uniform dress made out of pongee that ended six inches above my ankles, a hat, a tie, stockings, and low-heeled boots. I couldn't imagine the dress would do much against the elements, but I did love the patch on my arm. The outline of an open book with *ALA* stitched into its pages, it reminded me what I was here to do.

When the recreation hut door clicked open, a redheaded girl in a Red Cross uniform not unlike Nellie's walked briskly in, her posture erect. "Miss Balakin?"

"Yes." I raised my hand like a schoolgirl, though no one else was in the room.

"Martha," she said by way of introduction. "I have to be back at 18 in half an hour, so we're going to make quick work of this training. That okay with you?"

"Yes." I got the sense she wasn't really asking.

"You've already done training in the States, correct?"

"Yes, ma'am. I served at Camp Meade." I chose not to mention how briefly I'd been there.

"Splendid. The basic tenets are the same. I'm just here to walk you through what might be different. First off, there are nineteen wooden wards and close to thirty smaller marquee tents here at 42, and you'll need to visit each one at least once a week."

I scrambled for a sheet of paper to write everything down.

"The men need entertainment, hence our huts." She gestured around her with confident ownership. "But many of them can't make it out of the wards. Books serve as portable entertainment. You wouldn't believe how relieved the men are to get them. But many of them also want books they can use to learn vocational skills for when they return home."

Many of the Camp Meade soldiers had preferred nonfiction, too.

"Most librarians use tea carts to carry books from ward to ward," Martha continued. "Occasionally a wagon or a wheelbarrow. There should be something in the storage closet for you to use."

I nodded. "A wheelbarrow."

"Excellent. And you know the policies for lending books? No fees, no fines. Cards for checkout are in the back of each book, and they're all labeled with a bookplate so soldiers know to bring them back to you."

The bookplate had a picture of a soldier with a bayonet and a towering stack of books, and it read *WAR SERVICE LIBRARY: This book is provided by the people of the United States through the American Library Association for the Use of the Soldiers and Sailors.*

"There's an inscription as well," Martha continued. "'These books come to us overseas from home; To read them is a privilege; To restore them promptly unabused a duty.' Doesn't mean they always come back, though."

There were greater crimes, I supposed. Especially to a man who might have seen his comrades shot and killed in front of him.

"The biggest thing you'll need to know here that you didn't at Camp Meade is how to order new books. The ALA and YMCA share a headquarters at the papal legate palace in Paris."

A Parisian palace sounded like the version of France I'd wished to see. I knew now how deeply the country had been brought to its knees, but part of me still imagined the palace as a place of beauty and refuge.

Martha continued matter-of-factly. "Requests are sent there, and we handle most of the distribution."

Was Nellie the one to drive to Paris for new books?

"Most of the books here at 42 were donated by the YMCA. You're the first ALA librarian onsite, so you can request a large order from Paris. Miss Carre, who you met yesterday, will pick them up."

That answered my question. I hoped I'd be able to see her in person to give her my list.

"Until then, you'll have to rely on whatever you brought as well as whatever you can find here." She pointed to the bookshelf against the back wall. "Just be warned—books will go fast. Men want them, desperately. And remember there's also a books-by-mail program. Men can write to the Paris headquarters on their own to request books, which will be shipped to them as soon as possible. The headquarters handles about a thousand requests a day."

Martha handed me a sheet of paper. "Here are the regulations and suggestions you're already familiar with, I'm sure, from your training. I'm at Base Hospital 18 across the complex if you have questions, but do remember I'm not a trained librarian."

Me neither, I wanted to say. But I kept my mouth shut.

"You're the expert here," Martha said, "and the men will look to you."

Never in my life had men looked to me for guidance, and I wasn't sure if the chill that ran through me was thrill or fear.

"Any questions?"

Too many to count.

"No," I said anyway. "Thank you."

Martha bade me farewell, gathered her skirts, and plunged back outside into the mud. I was left alone in the recreation hut with half an hour before it opened to the men, so I settled down in front of the bookshelf and surveyed the offerings. They were slim, as Camp Meade's Mrs. Lipscomb had warned me they would be; she'd said the YMCA and Red Cross libraries were full of repeat copies and little variety. My task for this week, then, would be determining what books to order from Paris.

I stood and brushed off my skirt, grabbed my notepad and pen, and sent one last glance at the bookshelf. However spotty its collection of books, it was the only familiar, comforting sight in this godforsaken place. Then I turned toward the door and stepped outside.

It was cool, and goose pimples rose on my skin when the wind blew. I couldn't conceive of any way to lug a cart full of books through this mud, but I tried to push that concern from my mind. Before worrying about transporting the books, I needed books to transport.

I walked up the row of hospital wards until I got to the first wooden building, then stopped at the door. I'd seen all sorts of horrors at the receiving ward yesterday, and I knew I had to prepare for worse in the light of day. I thought of what my dad would have told me: *Derzhi khvost pistolyetom*, or *Keep your tail up with a gun*. It meant not to give up, but the reference to guns didn't seem as innocent out here as it had in our townhouse in D.C. At least I had that place to return to if this didn't work out.

I tucked my notebook under my arm and rubbed my thumb across my prayer rope as I stepped through the door, but even the chokti couldn't protect me from what was inside. I was hit immediately with a chemical smell that turned my stomach. It had a tinge of blood to it, metallic and sharp, with something lingering and rotten underneath.

Keep your tail up, keep your tail up. I was here because I had a job to do. I was here to bring the men books rich with humor and fantasy and romance and everything else that seemed a world apart from war. Things the men had to be desperate to remember. Nicholas had said so in his letter, after all. He craved the escape of fiction, the logic of a world that followed the structure of plot and climax and resolution.

Other men surely yearned for the same. And if they could fight in these conditions, so could I.

I forced myself to focus only on the first man in the row of cots. I knew if I tried to take all the misery in at once, I'd break.

"Good morning," I whispered, afraid to breathe in too deeply. "I'm Emmaline Balakin, the new hospital librarian."

The man groaned in response, and I looked at his face. The left side was wrapped in a thick band of gauze, flat where his ear should have been. When he cupped his hand to his good ear, I repeated myself. But he squeezed his eyes shut and shook his head when I did. "Too dizzy to read."

"Right," I said, "of course." We'd been trained not to give the men the pity or sympathy that might come naturally, but it didn't prevent me from feeling them. "I'll just—move along then."

I turned to the second bed and nearly recoiled in shock. The bottom of this man's face was gone; he had no lips, no mouth, no chin. Half his jawbone had been torn off, and what remained jutted from his cheeks in a blinding white. The color was stark against the glittering red of his throat. When I approached him, all he did was shake his head. No books. No conversation.

How was I supposed to help these men when all I could do was suggest books they couldn't even read?

With these injuries abounding—I remembered the colonel saying maxillofacial wards were 42's specialty—we'd need funny books and happy endings. Lots of them.

I continued down the row of cots. Bed after bed of men with missing ears, empty eye sockets, flattened noses. I saw jawbones, cheekbones, nose bones.

When I finally stumbled out of the tent, I collapsed into the mud. It soaked through the fabric of my uniform, but I hardly noticed. I was taking great gulping breaths. My head spun, and I started doubting my ability to differentiate the gray-brown mud from the gray sky. Which way was up? And what was wrong with me, that I couldn't tell?

The cold of the wet ground eventually brought me back, and I rose and shook the mud from my dress the best I could. That was it, I tried to tell myself. I'd gotten the panic out of my system early, and I could carry on and do my job now that I had.

At least, I hoped that was the case. I stumbled into the next ward and the next, both maxillofacial wards like the first. The injuries were gruesome.

The fourth ward, finally, granted me a reprieve. The first man I talked to had a cast on his leg, which was suspended from strings attached to tall poles on his bed. It was nothing compared to the injuries I'd seen earlier, nor even was his neighbor's injury of two missing fingers. Somewhere in the back of my mind, I realized how wrong it was that missing fingers had so quickly become a minor injury in my mental rankings, but I didn't have time to think deeply on it now.

"Good morning," I told the man, continuing with my same script. "My name is Emmaline Balakin. I'm the new hospital librarian."

The man's face, almost as pale as his cast, lit up. "You have books?"

"I—no. Not this very moment. But I'm taking a survey. What sort of books do you want?"

"Anything." The man emitted a sound that might have been a cough or a laugh or a grunt from the pain. "I've had nothing to do for days but count the swirls of grain in the wood." He lifted an arm and pointed to the ceiling. "I'll take anything."

The man next to him, the one with three fingers, rolled to face us. "Our injuries aren't as bad as some of the others', though." He gestured around. "We don't all stay long enough to read a whole book."

I remembered what Nellie, Colonel Hodgson, and Martha had all said about the hospital acting like an evacuation hospital recently and having to send many of the casualties back into hospitals in the intermediate or base sections of France. If the majority of these men wouldn't stay, I had to have a way for them to enjoy my books regardless.

I thought for a moment. "I can leave a box in each ward. If you're moved to another hospital before you finish, you can drop the book there on the way out." It was an imperfect solution, and certainly not a groundbreaking one. But still I stood just a hair taller as I moved on to the third bed, because I'd come up with a plan. Soldiers had looked to me for answers, and I'd provided them.

I continued my rounds. Another ward made mainly of maxillofacial cases, another miscellaneous. And then a gas ward, which I entered with a sense of relief. I wouldn't have to see blood or shrapnel or bullet holes in here.

But still I found myself nauseated when I stepped into the ward. "It's the gas," a nurse told me as she whisked by. "Still on their clothes and skin and hair."

I clamped a hand over my mouth and nose. "Should I be wearing a gas mask?"

The nurse was already gone. I made my rounds in a haze, taking in the men's blisters as I wrote down their requests. Most of them were too nauseated and disoriented to read, and I was out of the building quickly.

I moved to the next ward, and the patient nearest the door sat bolt upright when I entered. A harsh cough burst from his throat, but he was smiling. "The librarian is here!"

His announcement was met with whoops and cheers. "Having

a book to read will be like attending the biggest party of the century," one man cried.

His joy was infectious, and I couldn't help but laugh at the comparison. "Do you have a book in mind?"

"Adventure," he answered immediately. "Do you have *Treasure Island*?"

I made a note. "I think I might. If not, I'll have it ordered immediately."

"Where do the books come from?"

"I'll be ordering them from the ALA headquarters in Paris."

The boy shook his head. "But where do *they* get them?"

"Different ways. In March, the ALA started sending every soldier coming to Europe with a book. They would read them on the way over and then turn them in upon arrival so they could circulate among other men. But the ALA gets them from all over the United States. Kids go door to door collecting books, people throw book drive parties, churches and libraries take up collections." I smiled, thinking of the books I'd donated after reading Nicholas's letter. "If you ever get one with *Emmaline Balakin* or *Maria Popova* scrawled across the inside cover, it came from me."

"Maria Popova?"

"My mother's maiden name." I didn't want to tell the cheerful boy that my mother had been dead for years, so I changed the subject back to the books. "Though I'm afraid both she and I owned primarily women's books. I'm not sure how much of a market there is here for the Brontës and Jane Austen."

The boy chuckled. "I'd read anything."

I moved throughout the ward, taking down the men's interests as I went. Like several of the men in other wards, they were eager for all manner of novels and poetry—Tennyson, Wells, Ruskin,

Shakespeare, Emerson—and I had to flip to a fifth page on my notepad to keep track.

Three days later, the tents had joined the wooden wards at full capacity. Casualties just kept coming: from Nantillois in the Argonne; from Ypres, Belgium; and from a battle over St. Quentin Canal. My task today was to tour the marquee tents the way I'd already toured the other buildings.

I steeled myself on the long, muddy walk over and entered the first tent. The smell was a shade less potent than it had been in the solid buildings, I supposed because the tents were exposed to the open air. This small blessing came with its own challenges; the occasional gust of wind would pick up any letters the soldiers were writing or reading and scatter them to the floor. A radiator stood in the front of the tent, but its heat was uneven. It warmed my legs more than anything else, and I imagined that the boys on the far side of the ward would barely feel anything from it. In the first week of October, the weather was tolerable. But I imagined it would get worse.

Aside from the intrusion of the elements and their smaller size, the marquee tents weren't significantly different from the wards I'd spent the last three days visiting. There were several maxillofacial tents and a few with assorted artillery injuries, then a row for men who had been victims of gas.

I took a break for meat and beans in the mess hall after visiting the gas wards, still woozy from the haze of gas that clung to the men. In the afternoon, I trudged back through the mud to the far end of the camp to resume going through the tents.

I stepped into the one where I'd left off and launched into

my prepared greeting. "Good afternoon," I said to the first patient. "I'm—"

I stopped short when I saw the man's face. His eyes were closed, but there was something familiar about him. I felt a magnetic pull toward him too strong to ignore. He had muscled arms and big, calloused hands, but there was something about his calm face that warmed me, made me feel at home. I couldn't quite place my finger on it.

As I inched closer, the man's eyes opened and settled on mine. *Nicholas.*

Chapter 10

—— ❖ ——

Kathleen Carre

July 1976

I lay awake late into the night, unable to escape my memories. There was the birthday where I'd eschewed a traditional birthday party and instead begged Nana to take me on a political tour of D.C.: the Washington Monument, the Capitol building, and the Lincoln and Jefferson memorials. Nana had added the Library of Congress to the itinerary too, and I'd stood awed by the grandeur of a building designed to house documents. Nana pointed out the painting of the Roman goddess Minerva, but she was of no interest to me in her two-dimensionality. Instead, I looked at the bronze statues that circled the room: Michelangelo, Robert Fulton, Solon, James Kent. Only now as I relived the memory did I realize none of the statues had been women.

There were smaller moments to remember too. The hugs, the way Nana's body and mine fit together like mirror images. The sliced sausage and thin pancake blinis she made me every Monday morning, the stories she told me of knights and wolves and falcons before bed every night of my childhood.

All of that was gone.

I had to think about moving forward. I'd do what I'd always done—use all the negative in my life to push me on. I could collapse and give up, or I could use my grief to fuel me. I'd prove that I was stronger than my sadness. I would be faster than the boys in my squadron, do more goddamn push-ups, memorize every last word of *Reef Points*.

I rose from my bed and checked on my roommates' sleeping forms. Our work each day was so exhausting mentally and physically that once we fell asleep, it was nearly impossible to wake us. My only problem was that it was impossible to fall asleep, too, what with thoughts of my nana swirling through my head.

Instead, I lowered myself to the ground and practiced my push-ups. When my arms gave out, I did sit-ups, then toe touches, and then, when my breath came out too ragged to continue, a series of stretches.

But I still couldn't sleep, and I didn't want to lie in bed and think of what I'd lost. So I pulled out *Reef Points* and my tiny flashlight, curled up under the sheets, and read until morning.

I was still awake when the pounding came on the door at 0530. I leapt from my bunk and into my PEP wear before Susan and Linda even touched their feet to the deck, and I chopped to the bathroom—the head, in Navy-speak—down the hall after brushing my teeth and pulling back my short hair.

When I walked into the head, the two girls inside stopped their conversation and turned to me with wide eyes. I glanced at them but kept walking, knowing we had no time to chat before PEP. And then I closed the stall door behind me and realized what it was they'd been discussing: the large, messy graffiti scrawled on the back of the door reading *Hang it up, bitch!*

Knowing the other girls were outside, I didn't react. I closed my eyes and told myself the same thing I'd told myself last night. I could lie down and hang it up, sure. Or I could funnel all my fury and indignation into proving the boys wrong. Into being the best plebe they'd ever seen.

The girls looked at me as if to judge my reaction when I came out of the stall, and I shrugged. "We'll prove them wrong," I said.

Both girls grinned back, one a little surer than the other. "I suppose you're right."

"I am," I promised as I washed my hands. "What other choice do we have?"

When Robert positioned himself in line beside me at PEP, I tried to ignore him the same way I'd ignored the graffiti. I only let myself look his way during push-ups, allowing the hatred I felt toward him to crackle into strength.

And when we ran, I let myself go even though I knew the consequences. I flew free, each footfall a word in the chorus: *hang, it, up, bitch, hang, it, up, bitch.*

Then I was falling. I must have hit a root, because my knees and palms hit the spongy grass. I heard footfalls around me, and my face burned to imagine how many men had watched me collapse. I rose quickly, knees wet and grass sticking to my palms, and saw Robert just two feet ahead of me. The ground was flat, but Robert was smirking.

The bastard had tripped me.

Tears and sweat in my eyes, I pushed harder than I'd pushed before. My lungs burned and my stomach felt like it was full of shifting rocks, but I didn't slow down. I ignored my thighs and my calves screaming for air, and I pumped my arms so they'd take some of the burden.

I didn't spare Robert a glance as I sprinted past him. Only once I'd left him far behind did I let my breath come out in the ragged gasps it needed, did I let a moan of exhaustion escape my lips. But still, I didn't slow down. By the time I crossed the finish line, even my shoulders ached. I stumbled to a stop, my legs moving with such momentum that it was harder to slow them than to keep them going. My breath was hard and fast and shallow; black spots danced in my vision.

"What was that?" Ensign Michael appeared in front of me. "We've talked about this. You run with your squadron."

"No excuse, sir." I wheezed out the words.

"You beat them on purpose."

I couldn't pretend otherwise. I was still doubled over in pain, and I could hardly speak. It was no secret that I'd put all my effort into that run.

"Do another lap."

"Sir?" My voice had a squeaky quality I'd never heard before.

"You heard me. One more lap."

A lap was nothing, I told myself. And usually, it wasn't. But now? I shivered, my sweat cooling on my skin.

"Now!"

I stumbled off, aware of Ensign Michael's gaze on my back. My legs were almost relieved to be moving again, and I breathed deep. Once I got into the rhythm of jogging, my heartbeat started to slow. I refused to look at Robert—at any of the men watching me on my lap of shame—though I felt them looking.

I wouldn't let anybody derail me again.

I tensed when they separated us by sex again in the afternoon, resenting the unequal treatment. But once we'd been funneled into different rooms, the eighty-one women going one way and the thousand-plus men going the other, my chest began to loosen. I hadn't realized how tight it had felt among my hostile squad mates, how hard it was to breathe. Especially now that my grief threatened always to spill out of me like a fountain.

I wiggled my shoulders, trying to relax, and my purse smacked against my side.

"God, these stupid things." Susan might as well have read my mind.

We perked up as an upperclassman appeared in the front of the room and told us he had an announcement on exactly that. "Women will no longer be required nor permitted to wear purses," he said.

A ripple of relief spread through the crowd.

"We've received several complaints from the men," the upperclassman continued.

Our relief suddenly became indignation. The *men* complained that we had to wear these clunky things around?

"They fear that women will get an edge being able to carry around their study materials."

I rolled my eyes as he continued.

"Instead, we're going to have pockets sewn into your clothes for feminine hygiene products." He cleared his throat and moved on quickly to his second announcement. "Additionally, the physician has reported several cases of shin splints among female patients. For this reason, we have made the decision to reduce the size of your heels. We expect you to take your heels to the cobblers by the end of next week to have them altered."

"God only knows why we can't just get new shoes," Susan grumbled. "Clomping around in heels all day is ridiculous."

I shrugged. She wasn't wrong, but at least this was an improvement. And in a world that wouldn't have allowed us to even be a part of it a year ago, what more could we ask?

Sunday afternoon brought our first taste of Yard liberty. We weren't allowed to dress in civilian clothes or leave the Yard, and we had to be back for evening meal formation. Most plebes spent the time studying, cleaning our rooms before the next week's room checks, or calling home.

While my fellow members of the brigade cleaned their rooms, I stood at the phone banks preparing for my grandmother's funeral. Mrs. Peregrine had found a way to fax Nana's will to the academy, and my commanding officer had brought it to my room with his condolences. My list of duties was extensive: paying debts and funeral expenses, dispensing of the property, closing bank accounts, and hiring lawyers and accountants. Half of Nana's funds had been left to me and half to my mother, with the stipulation that my mother come forth to accept them in the next five years. Otherwise, it would fall to me too.

But I would give my half and my mother's too to have Nana back.

My most pressing task as executor was scheduling the funeral. I'd gotten chit papers granting me leave for the following Sunday, so I called the funeral home and scheduled a service for eleven a.m. Nana had never been an avid churchgoer, to my eternal relief growing up, and so I accepted the officiant the home provided and arranged for a simple graveside service.

Transportation in the city was never convenient, and Nana's friends were old and frail. No point adding an extra stop.

I rubbed the bridge of my nose as I finished with the funeral arrangements. Dates and times and monetary amounts were easy; it was the final, emotional task that I knew would wreck me.

I dialed Mrs. Peregrine's number.

"Is this Kathleen?"

She knew before I spoke, and I shivered. As a child, I'd thought the woman was a witch—before I realized such things were impossible—and that sort of prescience was why. Now I knew that Mrs. Peregrine made me uncomfortable because she saw through me. She could tell when I faltered, even if the rest of the world thought I was keeping up. I attributed it to her work as a midwife and a nurse earlier in life; she'd seen humans at their most vulnerable.

But I didn't want to be vulnerable now. If I so much as let myself frown, I was afraid I'd begin to cry and never stop.

"Yes, Mrs. Peregrine. This is she."

"Oh, darling. I am so sorry about your grandmother. Knowing it was coming didn't make it any easier, did it?"

I froze, my hand on the receiver.

"Kathleen, dear? Can you hear me?" Mrs. Peregrine squawked in that overly loud way that older people did on the telephone.

"Yes, Mrs. Peregrine. I'm sorry—knowing it was coming?"

"The cancer, dear. Of course we hoped it wouldn't end like this, but . . . we knew."

I gritted my teeth. "The *cancer*?"

"The breast cancer." Only now did Mrs. Peregrine's voice falter. "Didn't you know?"

"No!" My voice came out shriller than I'd heard it before, and I swallowed. "No."

"Oh, Kathleen. She had so many appointments . . ."

It dawned on me. "You went with her, didn't you?"

"Of course. She didn't want to keep you from your work."

"No," I said. "She didn't want me to know at all. I thought she was going to some sort of meditation class with you every week."

"Oh, my."

I fisted the hand that wasn't holding the telephone. "The doctors. Couldn't they cure it?" I'd heard that doctors were beginning to perform radical mastectomies on women with breast cancer, and that they were working on development of a drug that had helped push back cancer in rats. "Treat it, at least?"

"She didn't want them to, darling. She wanted it like this."

"Like what? Like giving up?"

"No, Kathleen. Like peace."

"Why didn't she tell me?" I was ashamed that my voice broke.

"Nellie wasn't like you," Mrs. Peregrine said. "You want to do, and fix. But she could see a thing a hundred different ways. And sometimes that's all it takes to accept it."

You want to do, and fix. That was true, and I took strength in it. I couldn't let this revelation derail me when I had too much do-ing to do. I had things to do for Nana and for myself, too.

"And"—Mrs. Peregrine's voice came again—"she didn't want you to give up your life for her. Would you have gone to the acad-emy if you'd known?"

Of course not. I was like Nana, not my mother. She had taken me in and raised me; I would have taken care of her.

"Exactly." Mrs. Peregrine spoke as if I had responded aloud. "She knew that."

I took another deep breath, suddenly unnerved by Mrs. Pere-grine the way I'd been as a child. "Thank you," I said. "For every-thing. Now." I hoped my voice sounded brisk and businesslike, though I was on the verge of tears. It seemed like I was always on the verge of tears now. "Anyway, can you possibly read me the phone numbers in Nana's address book?"

I spent the next two hours calling Nana's friends and acquain-tances to tell them of her death and invite them to the funeral. It was a painful, thankless task, and I kept each call short to keep from breaking down. My only saving grace was the age of Nana's friends; they were accustomed to death, and they didn't weep or wail in ways that would overtly trigger my own grief. I tried to see them as checkboxes to tick off my to-do list, focus on moving for-ward, forward, forward.

My plan fell apart when Derrick joined me at the phone bank. He picked up the telephone beside me, flashed me a smile, and then froze. He set the receiver down again and turned to face me directly. "Kathleen."

I blinked furiously, trying to pretend I wasn't on the cusp of crying. "Derrick. Hi."

His eyes darted to either side, and then he seemed to make a decision. "Your grandmother . . . ?"

"Gone." I nodded. "Cancer."

Somehow, telling Derrick was so much worse than telling Nana's friends, and I sealed my lips to keep in the wail that threatened to emerge. It came out instead as a wavering, high-pitched whine, and Derrick leapt forward as if I were about to fall. He wrapped his arms around me and patted my back, a kind gesture I hadn't realized how desperately I was missing until now.

"I'm so sorry, Kathleen."

I sniffled, mortified. "Yes, well." I searched for something to say. "The funeral is a week from today." Easier to focus on the future than dwell on the emotion of the moment.

Derrick stepped back and searched my face. "And they're letting you leave for it?"

I nodded.

"Good," Derrick said. "I'm glad."

We both fidgeted for a moment, and then Derrick took a few awkward steps away from the phone bank. "Well," he said. "I'll give you a moment. But let me know if you need anything, Kathleen. I'm on the top deck." He grimaced. "Those of us who don't quite fit in here need to stick together, right?"

I bristled even below the crush of grief. "Don't fit in? This is exactly where I'm meant to be." My voice came out harder and more combative than I had intended, but Derrick seemed to understand.

"You're right." Derrick shook his head. "I didn't mean we don't fit in. I meant . . . those of us who perhaps the others see as different. Those of us who have the most to prove."

I nodded at this. That was the feeling exactly. It was why I was glad it was Derrick, rather than the men in my squadron, who'd come across me weeping in the passageway. I didn't need my fellow Company Five midshipmen to see me as anything but unbreakable.

I wished Derrick a good evening and returned to my telephone calls. I was so absorbed in the task that it wasn't until evening meal formation that I realized I'd missed my non-date with Tom and the other midshipmen at the golf course across the Severn River. It wasn't like me to forget an appointment—but then, my nana had never died before. Who knew what I was like without her?

I sat next to Tom in King Hall, hoping to explain my absence, but we weren't granted permission to "carry on" this meal. That meant no leaning back in our chairs, no exchanging so much as a look with our fellow midshipmen, and certainly no speaking.

No matter. Talking to Tom was around number one hundred on my list of priorities right now. I ate quickly with my eyes in the boat and waited to be dismissed, at which point I returned to my berth for the final task of the day: writing Nana's obituary. But how could I fit all that my hero was into a few black-and-white lines in the newspaper?

In the end, I stuck to the facts. Nana never did like to brag or talk about herself much.

Nellie Rose Mayborn Carre was born February 15, 1893, in Washington, D.C. She served as one of only 300 female American Red Cross Motor Corps drivers in France in World War I, then returned home to raise her daughter, Jane Carre, and later, her granddaughter, Kathleen Carre. She was preceded in death by her parents and her husband, William Carre, and survived by her daughter, Jane, and her granddaughter, Kathleen.

Burial will occur at Oak Hill Cemetery on Sunday, July 18, 1976, at eleven o'clock in the morning.

I resisted the urge to tear up the obituary when I finished it. Words felt meaningless right now. I'd spent all day talking to people and taking care of business, but none of that could bring Nana back. Nothing could.

From now on, I was on my own.

Chapter II

———— ❖ ————

Emmaline Balakin

October 1918

Nicholas's face had changed. His jawline was sharper, his hair darker, his nose slightly off-center. There was a birthmark below his left ear that I didn't remember from our childhood.

But those impenetrable gray eyes looked just the same as they always had, and sinking into them transported me back to the night that I'd last seen Nicholas.

It had been the last Christmas before my mother died, and I'd been an awkward, gangly fourteen-year-old. I'd grown half a foot in a matter of months, and I didn't know yet how to move my legs or my arms or my neck as I wobbled above the crowd. But Nicholas, at sixteen, had had all the assuredness of a man. His serious gray eyes had been so different from those of the boys at school, who at thirteen and fourteen still found it funny to tug on girls' braids and tag them on the playground. I'd expected Nicholas to treat me differently that year. I'd thought he would raise his eyebrows and look away when he saw my ill-fitting dress and my too-long arms. I'd thought he would laugh at grown-up things over my head and treat me like a child. But he'd talked to me the same way he always had. We'd laughed about the embarrassment of using Russian idioms translated into English at school—strange things like "when the crawfish whistles on a mountain" or "even a hedgehog would understand." We'd exchanged book recommendations. We'd defended his mother's blinis to the other children, because Mrs. Agrapov had overcooked them for the third year in a row.

When he'd disappeared after dinner, I'd picked up *Jane Eyre* to entertain myself, and then the time had come for each single woman and girl to step outside and ask the name of the first man who passed by, the legend being that it would be the name of the man the woman would marry. Because it had been my mother's party, I'd been selected to go first. Though I'd been much more interested in *Jane Eyre*'s Mr. Rochester than any stranger on the street, I'd reluctantly set aside my book and stepped outside.

But there'd been Nicholas, his eyelashes casting long shadows across his face under the soft light of a streetlamp. Mortified at the prospect of bringing his name inside, I hadn't stayed out long enough to ask him why he was there. I'd darted inside before he could see me and told the gathered crowd that no one had been outside. When they'd asked why I hadn't waited, I'd made up a lie about the cold.

One of the other children had laughed. "That means you'll never get married," she'd teased.

I'd looked down at my awkward body and my fingers twisted

in mortification and thought maybe she was right. But when Nicholas had walked in a few minutes later, he'd whispered into my ear, "I knew you'd be first. Why else do you think I was waiting there?"

My mama had died two months later, and I'd never seen Nicholas again. Hardly thought about him even, as consumed as I'd been by the dreary ins and outs of helping my father run the household.

Until his letter to Vivian had landed on my desk this summer.

And now I was standing before him again.

I stared at Nicholas, my heart racing. And then I said the most ridiculous thing. "You're hurt."

His lips, which blood loss had turned velvety purple against the pale of his face, quirked into a smile. "Most of us here are."

"I'm sorry." I swiped my clammy hands on the skirt of my dress. "I didn't mean . . . let me start over. I'm the new librarian. My name is Emma—"

"—line," he finished, his eyes widening in recognition. "By God, is it really you?"

I nodded, any doubts about whether the man really was Nicholas evaporating. "Yes. Nicholas, I can't believe it's really *you*."

It was like something out of a book. I'd found Nicholas's letter, and it had led me straight to him. Like Jane Eyre hearing Mr. Rochester's voice on the winds or Heathcliff returning to Catherine after years away.

"I know it's long overdue, but I was so sorry to hear about your mother," Nicholas said. "She was an incredible woman."

"She was," I said quietly. "Thank you."

Nicholas grinned. "Remember when we ruined her pelmeni?"

I covered my face with my hands. "Oh, it was awful. She was so sick, and we made such a mess of things."

Nicholas shook his head. "But she just laughed. She wasn't a bit angry." He laughed now. "Not many women would have put up with us."

"And not many boys would have cooked with me."

It was true. In the old country, only women cooked pelmeni. Women gathered in droves to make the meat dumplings before winter came in Russia, and Mama used to give the cook a day off to make them alongside her mother, her sister, and her sisters-in-law. In America, she would coordinate times for women in Baltimore and Virginia to meet at our townhouse and do the same. But she'd caught a bad flu when I was twelve and had to cancel, and I decided to make the comforting food myself. I made all of the phone calls for Mama telling her friends not to come to D.C., and when I called Nicholas's mother, she clucked. "Nicholas will be so disappointed," she said. "He was looking forward to seeing you."

I made an impulsive decision. "He can still come. Maybe he can help me make the pelmeni."

Nicholas's mother had laughed. "Nicholas has never cooked, Emmaline." But then her voice had gone fuzzy as she'd talked to Nicholas. "Emmaline?" She returned to the telephone. "He'll be there in half an hour."

Nicholas and I had worked hard at the pelmeni, but we'd made one huge mistake. I could tell now that Nicholas was thinking about it, because he smirked. "Can you believe we thought the dough needed . . . what, 225 ounces of water?"

I burst out laughing despite our dreary surroundings. Mama's recipe hadn't included units, and we American-born children had assumed that 225 referred not to milliliters but to ounces. We'd done all the math, dividing it by eight to get twenty-eight cups.

"Poor Mama was so hungry," I said, trying to stop laughing. We'd kept telling her to wait, we had a wonderful surprise coming, but the pelmeni never materialized. The dough was nothing but liquid.

"She must have thought me an utter fool," Nicholas said.

"No," I protested. "Never. She loved you. She loved your whole family."

The laughter seeped out of Nicholas's expression. "Mama tried to go by and drop off food for you and your father after the funeral, but . . . your father didn't want anything to do with us. With anyone."

"I'm sorry."

Nicholas waved his hand. "Grief can do strange things to a person." He hesitated. "How is he doing now?"

"He's gone. Heart attack."

Nicholas's hand fluttered like he wanted to reach out but couldn't. "I'm so sorry."

I forced a smile. "And your parents?"

"Also gone." He didn't elaborate. "But what about you? How are you?"

I didn't know how to answer. I was in the most terrifying place I'd ever been, with reminders of war and destruction all around me. But I remembered the joy I'd brought the young boys and the confidence I'd felt in the injured limbs ward and realized that despite the fear, I wouldn't go home if I had the option. Because I had the potential here to continue my parents' work. I had the opportunity here to live a life bigger than the one into which I'd retreated in D.C.

"How are *you*?" I asked instead of answering. And then,

realizing the question was foolish, I continued, "That is, what happened?" I gestured to the bandage around Nicholas's side.

He winced. "Artillery shell shrapnel."

I thought of the sixteen-year-old boy who'd made me feel comfortable in my awkward years and the fourteen-year-old who'd baked with me in my mother's kitchen. I thought of the nine-year-old boy who'd split the last piece of cake with me on Easter. I thought of the seven-year-old who'd stood up against the boys who'd said I couldn't play tag with them in a dress. How had he ended up here, in a hospital bed in France with shrapnel in his side?

And how had I ended up beside him?

"We had no idea," I said quietly. "No idea what the world had in store for us."

"Perhaps not. But we were as well prepared for it as we could have been, don't you think?"

I stared at Nicholas. I'd been anything but prepared, holed up in the Dead Letter Office like a recluse.

But Nicholas smiled. "Look at you. I should have known that the Emmaline I knew would end up here."

"What?" I nearly laughed. "Are you hanging noodles from my ears?"

Nicholas didn't hold it in like I had. He burst into laughter, low and rich and melodic. "I've missed those Russian idioms. *Pulling my leg* doesn't have the same imagery as our noodles do."

I let a smile escape. "Nothing does. But truly—are you?"

"No." Nicholas's eyebrows drew together. "Of course not. You were always so full of ideas. So insistent that everyone had something to say. It makes sense that you wouldn't be content to sit at home. That you'd end up here championing our American authors while we champion America at the front."

"I'm hardly championing anything," I said. "I'm just here to pass out books."

"You came all the way to France to do it, Emmaline. You wouldn't have done that if you thought it was so trivial a job."

I chewed on my lip, deliberating. My role was to be a light, comforting presence to these men. But Nicholas's honesty made me want to be honest, too.

"You're right," I admitted. "I like to think I'm doing something that matters. Helping you all escape, at least in your minds, because I can't help you escape in the flesh."

"The Emmaline I knew cared much more about the mind than the body, anyway."

Obviously he hadn't noticed the furtive glances I'd sent his way that last Maslenitsa season, then. I blushed at the thought.

"Me too, of course." His gray eyes clouded like I was seeing them through fog. "I always thought my only fighting would be done with the pen. It's mightier than the sword, and all that. But I'm starting to wonder if there's anything mightier than artillery." He made a sound somewhere between a snort and a sob.

"Don't be foolish," I surprised myself by saying. "Our parents didn't leave Russia because Czar Alexander was taking their weapons. They left because he was banning books. He saw books—ideas—as so much more dangerous than weapons of war."

"See?" Nicholas shook his head, but there was a hint of a smile on his lips. "I told you. You're the same girl I knew in D.C."

Surely I had changed. I always felt I'd lost the spark that I'd had before my mama died.

Or at least, I thought I'd lost it. Maybe I'd simply buried it. Maybe I'd hidden that spark, afraid the world would snuff it out the same way it snuffed out my mother.

And maybe here, I'd have the chance to light it back up.

I smiled at Nicholas. "And you're the same little Kolya that I knew. Always something kind to say."

"Kindness is more important here than anywhere," he said.

I wanted the whole world to be opened to Nicholas, to this kind and honest man who'd been through so much. "If you could read any book in the world right now, what would it be?"

Nicholas took the question seriously. He cocked his head and thought for a moment, silent. "Something with a happy ending," he mused. "Something to remind me we just might get out of this war alive."

"*Oliver Twist*," I said promptly. "Dickens himself said it was about good triumphing over adversity."

Nicholas looked at me as if I'd just read his mind. "Yes," he said. "I think *Oliver Twist* would be just right."

I made a note and then hesitated. I didn't want to move on, but I had to complete my rounds.

"I'll be back soon with your book," I promised Nicholas. "I'm staying in the recreation hut, if you need anything."

What on earth he might need from me, I had no idea. But I couldn't help letting him know I was close.

I continued tent by tent until I got to the last one on that side of the hospital, not knowing what type of injuries to expect, and stopped short. While several of the wards had been mixed—half burn victims and half surgical cases in one, or abdominal wounds and maxillofacial wounds in another—this one bore no semblance of organization. Several men were bundled up in casts with limbs suspended from their bed frames, while others bore the telltale peeling skin of major burns. Still more had bandages around their midsections, seeped through with blood. The man closest to the door was coughing in his sleep, and he turned so his arm was flung onto the cot belonging to the man beside him. I grimaced. Surely no one could be expected to heal in these conditions.

But the disorganization wasn't the only anomaly in this tent. While I'd seen the occasional colored man in the other tents, his injuries corresponding to his ward mates', this was the first one to be entirely segregated. It looked like the 92nd Division's ward at Camp Meade, where colored influenza, tuberculosis, cholera, and pneumonia patients were all housed together, only it wasn't entirely full. The few dozen colored patients were crowded in the back of the tent, and I picked my way toward them. I realized as I shivered that there was no radiator in this tent, and the cold of the muck on my legs and the nip in the air conspired to make even the first week of October feel overly cold without one.

One of the men swung his legs over the edge of his bed and limped over, his foot swaddled in a bandage. "I'm Burt Watson. We were hoping you'd make it down here."

"Sorry for the delay," I said. "It's a long walk." It occurred to me as I said it that the semi-isolation was likely intentional. "But yes. Of course I'm here. I'm Emmaline Balakin, the new hospital librarian."

"We can check out books as well, then?"

Colonel Hodgson hadn't said anything to the contrary, so I assumed yes. That was the point of my job here, wasn't it? To give everyone books. It was the whole reason my parents had loved the libraries so much in America—because *everyone* could have books, and every book could be in the library.

"Of course. Any requests?" I held my pen over paper.

"*Tarzan of the Apes.*"

"That's a popular one. I'm ordering several from Paris." I looked around. "Any others?"

I took down the other men's requests and then smiled at them. "Wonderful. They should be in the library in the next week, whenever you're ready to stop by."

Burt's smooth, dark brown forehead wrinkled under his bandaged ear. "Stop by?"

"Those of you who are able, that is." I winced at my misstep as I looked at some of the men's wounded legs and feet. "I know many of you are confined to bed."

A small man with velvety eyelashes piped up from the next bed. Perlie, he'd said his name was, and he'd requested a love story or something about family. "We aren't allowed in the recreation hut, ma'am. Whites only."

I turned in a circle and took in the sight of these men, who'd lost noses and limbs and eyes and ears in service to America. These were men who'd suffered shell shock and influenza and trench foot.

"Well," I said with a confidence I didn't know I'd possessed. "I will certainly bring you books. And . . ." I hesitated, my voice dropping to its usual quiet register. "I'll talk to the colonel about changing the rules for the library, too."

My legs quaked as I waited outside the headquarters building. What had possessed me to think I had the courage to do this?

I knew the answer, of course. Just that one conversation with Nicholas had reminded me how my parents had raised me to speak my ideals into existence, to stand up for what was right. I was the hospital librarian here, and it was my duty to give these men access to books.

Taking a breath and using one boot in a fruitless attempt to scrape the mud off the toe of the other, I knocked on the door.

Colonel Hodgson gazed down at me when it opened, and I gulped. I hadn't remembered him being so tall.

"Paying me a visit so soon?"

I kept my eyes trained toward the uneven wooden floor. "I have a question about the library."

"A question."

"Yes, sir. A question." Something about the way he repeated my words made me feel as if I'd said something faintly ridiculous.

Still, the colonel ushered me into the office, and I sat in front of his desk as he gestured toward the seat. I crossed my legs at the ankles to hide them and buried my shaking hands in the folds of my dress. "The colored soldiers have brought to my attention the fact that they are not permitted to use the recreation hut."

"Trying to stir trouble, are they?"

"No, sir. I mean to say that I have become aware that they are unable to use the hut. They by no means complained about it, sir."

"Hm."

I cleared my throat and told the colonel what I'd rehearsed on the way over. "The American Library Association takes great pride in providing books for free, because doing so allows for men from all walks of life to read without impediment. As their representative here at Base Hospital 42, I would like to request that all men, regardless of race, be allowed to access the hospital library, just as they are in our nation's own capital city." I exhaled. "Sir." Though libraries were segregated across most of the country, D.C.'s libraries remained one of its few integrated spaces.

Colonel Hodgson seemed to grow even taller as I spoke, if such a thing were possible. "Our men are segregated for their safety," he said. "To avoid friction between the races."

It seemed to me like there would be more friction between two groups treated like different species than between men treated like equals, but I kept my mouth shut. "What if we arranged separate hours for the white and the colored soldiers?"

The colonel raised his eyebrows. "And limit the amount of time the majority of our men can access the recreation hut? Absolutely not."

I swallowed. "I can't help but wonder, sir, why the men must be segregated in the recreation hut but not in the wards."

"I can't help but wonder, Miss Balakin, why you think it is your place to ask."

I blinked, fighting the urge to dip my head.

"I'll have you know, however, that the surgeon general of the United States himself has asked us to segregate hospital wards as far as possible. In fact, it is a requirement in convalescent camps. We are given more flexibility because we must first and foremost separate patients by casualty type. Do you understand?"

"Yes, sir."

At least I understood that he was afraid of things he didn't understand. I understood that he'd never read Ida B. Wells or W. E. B. DuBois.

I understood that I had to get out of his office before saying something I'd regret.

"Thank you," I said quickly. "Sir." And then I rose and fled.

My feet carried me back to the recreation hut. I needed a moment to process what I had heard, to maybe even lose myself in one of the books I'd set aside for myself. But I stopped when I entered the building and saw Nicholas playing a game of cards with another three soldiers at the table in the corner.

Nicholas. The boy who shared his cake and his games of tag. The man who didn't mind cooking, even if it was supposed to be a woman's job. The man whose parents, I dimly remembered, had read Karl Marx and Eugene Debs with the same open-minded curiosity as my own.

I shook my head. It wasn't just Nicholas in here. One man pounded away at the piano while another sang in a high, comical falsetto. A man on mud-encrusted crutches stood against the wall beside the bookshelf, another soldier stooping to find him books. Two men played an intense game of chess beside Nicholas and his card game.

I couldn't retreat into my room when I was supposed to be out here working, but I was certain that my pale face revealed every bit of frustration I was feeling.

I ducked back outside. Early autumn in France wasn't cold yet, but it was cool enough that I wrapped my arms around my torso as I leaned against the wooden planks of the recreation hut. Just as I tipped my head up, the door opened.

"Nicholas." I pulled away from the wall and tried to rearrange my expression into something more friendly. I was here to spread joy, not dismay. "How lovely to see you again so soon."

Nicholas raised one dark eyebrow. "What's the matter, Emmaline?"

I tried to smile. "That obvious?"

"Obvious to me." Nicholas lifted a shoulder and then winced, his hand going to his wounded abdomen. "I've known you for twenty years."

It was interesting that he thought of it that way when he hadn't seen me in nearly a decade, and the sentiment emboldened me. I stumbled through an explanation of what had happened, keeping my head low to hide the tears that threatened at the corners of my eyes. When I looked back up to Nicholas, his face was flushed and wide-eyed. I was so used to his steady calm and his easy laughter that I almost began to cry anew. The horror on his face was new to me. Did it mean that he, too, disagreed?

I didn't want to believe it. I couldn't reconcile his usual kindness with such blind prejudice, especially considering his parents' class politics. Like me, Nicholas had been brought up to question what society told him was the truth.

Then again, he'd courted Vivian. A woman from the upper echelon of society who never had even a pinky out of place.

"I'm sorry," I said, even though he was the one who'd disappointed me. "I shouldn't have assumed you'd feel the same way as me."

"No," Nicholas cut me off. "Of course I do. But Emmaline, talking to an officer like that is dangerous. What possessed you?"

You, I didn't say. *You're what possessed me.* He'd reminded me once again what I was capable of. That I had a voice and ideas.

"I don't want you to misunderstand," Nicholas said. "I'm impressed. And not entirely surprised."

He wasn't? Because I was shocked.

"But please, Emmaline. Remember to be careful. Because it's like you said before: men—especially those like Colonel Hodgson—are far more afraid of words than they are of war."

Chapter 12

——— ❧ ———

Kathleen Carre

July 1976

I ran into Tom and Robert in the passageway after the Blue and Gold that evening. I was afraid that Robert wasn't the ideal witness for my conversation with Tom—for any conversation of mine, really—but I wanted to clear the air. I couldn't have Tom, who had been one of the few kind men in my squadron, thinking I was irresponsible and feckless.

"Tom." I forced a smile, which felt unnatural under the stifling weight of my grief.

"Kathleen."

"I hope you had a good game of golf this afternoon?" He didn't answer, and so I forged ahead. "I'm so sorry I couldn't make it. My grandmother . . . I received word that she'd died."

I didn't let my voice falter or my emotion show. I could have been talking about the weather, I was so stiff, and that was exactly my intent. I couldn't let any of the men—Robert especially—sniff out any further weakness in me after my tears at mess.

Tom's face fell. "Oh, no."

I hoped that would be the end of it, but Robert interjected. "You couldn't have been too upset about it, seeing as you spent the afternoon with another guy."

"What?" I'd spent the afternoon making phone calls to Nana's friends. Unless the guy in question was Nana's eighty-nine-year-old bridge friend Stefan, I had no idea what Robert was talking about.

He didn't bother elaborating, just pulled Tom back and whispered something into his ear. I strained to hear his words, wondering why Tom's face had contorted and his lip had curled in something like disgust, but Robert was too quiet.

"Goodbye, Kathleen," Tom said. "I'm sorry about your grandmother . . ."

Robert grabbed Tom by the shoulders and marched him off, leaving me standing bewildered in the passageway.

Well. It didn't matter. Not really. I wasn't here to make friends, I was here to serve the United States. I was here to prove myself.

I was here for myself, and I was here for Nana.

I wasn't here for the boys, but I was jealous of them. They didn't have to spend their free time limping to the cobbler shop to get their heels altered. When Susan, Linda, and I went down on Monday afternoon, it seemed that every other woman was doing the same. The cobbler shop was downstairs in Bancroft Hall along with other necessities like the dentist and optometrist. The line stretched out of the cobbler's and past the barbershop and bookstore. But there was no such thing as wasting time at the Naval Academy, so Linda, Susan, and I took the line as an opportunity to quiz each other on our rates. Susan had us in stitches reciting hers in a horrific Alabama-inspired British accent that she swore helped her remember them.

The line moved quickly, and I was first of my roommates to reach the cobbler and hand him my shoes. He took a carving knife, hacked at the heel of one shoe, and then handed it back to me.

"Wait," I said. "Don't you need—"

He hacked off the other heel before I could finish my question, and I was left staring dumbfounded at two profoundly uneven shoes. "Sir," I said. "These are not the same—"

With a grumble of exasperation, he took them back, held them next to each other, and whittled off the half-inch difference between them. He passed them back again without a word and then called for the next in line, and I stumbled out of the way with bewilderment. My shoes were the same height as each other now, but I wasn't so sure they'd been cut flat.

I slid them onto my feet as I waited for Linda and Susan, and my shoulders tipped back. The heels were shorter now than the thick sole of the shoe, and I couldn't stand without rocking backward like a domino. Linda and Susan, when they appeared, had the same problem.

"What are we going to do?" Linda wailed. "I could have done a better job myself. At least I know how to use a ruler!"

Susan waved her arms to catch her balance as she skidded and almost fell in her own butchered pair of heels. "Should we complain?"

Linda sighed. "I don't know if there's any use."

"And we don't want to look like we expect the higher-ups to fix all our problems," I added. "They already think we're weaker than the men."

"True."

I glanced between the two girls. "Did you see the graffiti in the bathroom?"

"Yes." Linda looked mournful.

Susan laughed. "Don't tell me that's the first time you've been called a bitch."

Linda's eyes widened even more, her face pink. "Definitively the first time."

"We can think of it as a good thing in a way." I jumped in. "Now we have all the more incentive to prove them wrong."

Susan met my hand in a high five. "Yes, ma'am."

"If you say so." Linda sighed, but her shoulders straightened infinitesimally. All three of ours did. It didn't matter that we were destabilized by our uneven shoes or that the men didn't think we could do it—didn't even *want* us to do it. We wouldn't have been here at all if that sort of thing could stop us.

But we *were* here, and we wouldn't leave. We owed it to each other, and I owed it to Nana.

By Sunday morning, I was run ragged. I was working fourteen-hour days like the other plebes, dodging tricks from the boys every moment. Some mornings, we woke up to water spilled in front of our doorways so we'd slip; others, we'd find words like *fat* and *ugly* scribbled across our bathroom mirrors. At meals, we'd open a jar of peanut butter to find obscene images carved in by butter knives, and we knew better than to stand too close to the men during PEP or they'd smudge dirt on our uniforms and get us citations for uncleanliness.

To make matters worse, I hadn't slept well since hearing about Nana's death. I stayed up each night poring over *Reef Points*, preferring the exhaustion to the nightmares that plagued me when I closed my eyes. Any moment of leisure I had was spent agonizing over my nana's decision to hide her cancer from me, and the fact that she was able to. How had I not seen the pain she was in? Could I have done something to change her mind and save her?

I couldn't bear to think about it even as I sat on the bus headed toward D.C. for her funeral. I held *Reef Points* up before my face, mumbling the recitations aloud so I'd never trip up in front of Ensign Michael again.

Avoiding thoughts of Nana meant that I hadn't prepared myself for what to expect stepping into our apartment, where I stopped first to pick up Nana's crucifix—her one religious concession. The sterile smell in the apartment was sharp and cutting, and it ushered to mind images of gloves and toilets. It smelled like a hospital, I realized, but Nana hadn't wanted to die in a hospital. She'd chosen to keep the cancer quiet, not to treat it, and to die at home. She'd hate this smell.

The apartment was also too quiet. How many times had I sat here and talked, Nana simply listening? She'd heard all the stories, good and bad: of the essay-writing contest I won in third grade, the track coach in middle school who wouldn't let a girl on the team, the boy who took me to prom and got so drunk I had to drive him and myself home without a license. She'd heard all my dreams: to join the military, to do something that mattered, to be as disciplined as my mother was wild. And she'd heard all my fears, too.

I pushed the door to Nana's room open. It looked just like it always had. The bed was meticulously made. A book sat on the bedside table next to the crucifix I'd come to collect, a case of vitamins, and a glass of water. On Nana's dresser were photos of my mother and me, though I took up most of the space. There I was with Nana as a child, and in the picture next to it I was graduating from high school. In another I was sweaty and red-faced with the track team.

I paused over a picture of Jane and me on my first day of kindergarten. Nana had been the one to braid my hair and take the picture, but Jane's arm was thrown around me protectively. You'd never know from this picture that she'd leave me.

But I supposed she hadn't ever intended to leave me, just as my goal in entering the academy had never been to leave Nana. We'd both wanted nothing more than to pursue our own dreams. And maybe I could understand that a bit better now. I knew what it was to be a woman who didn't want to play the role she'd been cast.

Squeezing my eyes shut, I slid open the door to Nana's closet. Her dresses hung in neat rows from identical wire hangers. She hadn't owned a pair of pants in her life, I suspected. I sifted through, remembering times when I'd seen her wear each outfit. I pulled out a dark gray dress made of thick, starchy wool. My heart fluttered. It was Nana's Motor Corps uniform—and according to the clock, I had time to try it on.

I threw my clothes to the floor and pulled on the long, dark skirt. It hung low on my hips, but that wasn't a surprise. With PEP every morning this week, I'd probably lost enough weight to be thinner than Nana was at the same age. But the length of the skirt was all wrong, too. It hit just below the knee. I'd seen photographs of the Motor Corps; the skirts reached the women's ankles and ended where their lace-up boots began. This skirt was too short, and I swam in the jacket.

I stared at myself in Nana's mirror. I looked like I was playing dress-up. And I supposed I was. These were Nana's clothes, and I'd put them on for the same reason a child slips into a princess gown or stretches her arms out like a fairy. I'd wanted to feel powerful, in control. Purposeful.

I lifted Nana's watch box from her dresser and wrapped the watch around my wrist. Nana had had links removed so it would fit her frail wrists, and it fit mine like a glove. How I wished I were allowed to wear a watch at the academy, but no. I folded it carefully back into the box and glanced one last time at my reflection in the mirror. It was time to change and go.

I joined the officiant at the gravesite early. "Mr. Stewart. Nice to meet you." I shook his hand firmly. "Thank you for doing this."

"Miss Carre. My deepest condolences for your loss."

We went over the readings a final time before the guests arrived. Mrs. Peregrine showed up first, then came a cluster of elderly women that I recognized vaguely as acquaintances of Nana's from various volunteer and activist groups. No sign of Jane, of course. I hadn't known how to reach her.

The priest began the service with Psalm 62, which he had assured me was customary. But I didn't like it. I couldn't rely on God alone; he was not my rock. I'd always been my own rock.

Especially now, without even Nana to anchor me.

When it was my turn, I read a William Wordsworth poem that I knew Nana had loved.

"'What though the radiance which was once so bright/Be now

forever taken from my sight,/Though nothing can bring back the hour/Of splendor in the grass, of glory in the flower;/We will grieve not, rather find/Strength in what remains behind.'"

I hadn't picked it solely for Nana, but for myself too. I needed to find strength in what remained behind. At the academy, I couldn't be consumed by grief or despair. I'd never survive.

I took a deep breath as I finished the poem. That had been the easy part. Now I had to speak from the heart, which I tended to keep behind closed doors.

"My grandmother raised me," I began. "She was a mother to me. And she was the best mother I could have asked for. She was a listener first. She didn't talk about herself often or brag—not about her service in World War I, not about anything. I'm sure you all can think of a hundred times she looked at you with those unblinking eyes and just . . . listened.

"She was quiet, but she wasn't passive. Most of you here know her because you worked with her for some cause, maybe with the NAACP or the school board or for various women's causes. She's the one who inspired me to join the military; I wouldn't be at the United States Naval Academy without Nana." I took a deep breath. "What I'm trying to say is that we don't have my nana here with us anymore, but we won't forget her."

There was nothing in what I'd said that went beyond what anyone else could have said about my nana, but how could I describe her better? How could I describe her quiet strength, her occasional ability to surprise you?

No matter how insufficient my words, they left me in tears. And the sight of the gaping hole in the ground did nothing to comfort me. My nana didn't belong down there in the earth. She didn't belong underneath layers of grime and dirt; she deserved to be remembered. Honored. Celebrated. There should be an American flag folded over her now; there would be, if she'd been a man.

But the officiant concluded the service quietly and without fanfare, and the coffin was lowered into the ground. I watched it without emotion, forcing myself to disconnect from the moment. *That's not my grandmother*, I told myself. *Not anymore.*

Her remaining friends, used to death, were teary-eyed but calm. They came and kissed me on the cheeks, gave me their love and their sympathies. I thanked each one in turn: Ethel from Nana's occasional forays into church, Florence from the apartment building, Beth from the volunteer group. It went on and on.

I didn't recognize the final woman in line, but I wasn't going to admit that. "Hello." I accepted her hug, her ample bosom pressing against my collarbone and a hint of sugar and butter tickling my nose. "Thank you so much for coming."

"I had to," she said. "Because . . ." She paused. "You are Nellie's granddaughter?"

"Yes. But remind me—"

"I'm Nellie's sister," she interrupted, grasping my hand. "Which makes me your great-aunt."

Chapter 13

—— ❦ ——

Emmaline Balakin

October 1918

We needed hope more than ever as the tide began to turn against us along the Hindenburg Line in early October. On the 2nd, the Germans halted the Allied advance into Belgium, and nine companies from the 77th Division of our American Expeditionary Forces pressed forward into the Argonne without the promised support from their left and right flanks. From what we'd heard, there were over five hundred men completely surrounded by Germans—and though our patients didn't say it to my face, I could tell they didn't expect the soldiers to make it out alive.

With such bad news flooding into the camp along with the injured, providing solace to the men became more critical than ever. But without the books I'd travel to Paris to get with Nellie the next week, I couldn't even supply one full ward with reading material. Much less all two thousand wounded soldiers.

It was a memory from Camp Meade that gave me a solution. There'd been a man suffering from debilitating headaches and vision problems. The only way to comfort him had been through poetry, so I'd sat by his side and read aloud from John Milton and Rudyard Kipling. Surely I could do the same here.

I picked Jack London's *The Call of the Wild*, partially for the popularity it had enjoyed at Camp Meade and partially for its length. With just seven chapters, the book would be short enough to read in a week if I focused only on the wards where men stayed more than a day or two. Right now, that seemed to be the maxillofacial wards due to 42's doctors' specializations. And the men in the head and abdominal wards, I rationalized, because surely those wounds were too dangerous to risk transportation? A shiver ran through me at the thought of reading to Nicholas, and I quickly forced myself back to practical matters. I would also read to Burt and Perlie's tent, since they had no access to books beyond what I could physically bring them.

When I walked into the first maxillofacial ward and told the men of my plan, they let out a cheer that sounded as if I'd just announced Germany's surrender.

"This is the best news I've gotten in months," said a man with a bandage around his forehead.

"Let's get started, then. 'Chapter One: Into the Primitive.'"

And immediately, we were whisked away from the mud-drenched front to the sun-soaked San Francisco Bay.

By the time I finished the first chapter, my voice was dry. But the men's faces made it worth it.

"I never learned to read," one of them said with awe. "I had no idea it was so . . ." He paused as he searched for the right word. "It's like a magic carpet, is what it is. It carried me right out of this blasted place."

"Just wait till you read *The Arabian Nights*," another man joked. He had gauze over his nose, the shape of which seemed uneven and incomplete. His companions groaned good-naturedly.

"You'd better come back real soon," one of them told me. "Otherwise, all we've got to entertain us is Sid and his bad jokes."

I smiled, so overwhelmed by the attention that I couldn't summon up anything to say in response. And so it continued in each ward. One man told me the sound of my reading was more comforting than his mother's blackberry pie. Another told me he'd have hugged me had his arms not been encased in plaster. And one absolutely mortified me by getting down on his knee and jokingly proposing marriage.

When I told Nicholas about the proposal later that day, I expected him to laugh. But instead he nodded, not a hint of surprise evident on his face. "You don't know what they've seen out there, Emmaline."

My smile dropped as he continued. "We've held men who were like brothers to us as they died. We've been buried under collapsed trenches and wondered why we, rather than the better men among us, survived. We've watched men make miraculous recoveries from gunshots or shrapnel wounds only to fall prey to trench foot or influenza. We've tripped over dead bodies and waded through mud and guts."

"I'm sorry," I said. "I didn't mean to make light—"

"No," Nicholas interrupted. "I'm not saying you did. And even if you had, what other choice is there? Take the man who proposed to you. He did it out of desperation, because how could he not see this beautiful librarian as the perfect wife after everything he's lived through? I just mean to explain why it is we compare you to a magic carpet or a homemade pie. You're helping us escape this hellish reality."

My skin prickled with emotion. "Stories are the only thing stronger than artillery fire," I said, remembering our conversation from the other day.

"Yes," Nicholas said simply. "It may be the only thing that gets us through."

Only as I crawled into bed that night and placed my helmet over my face did I realize that Nicholas had called me beautiful.

The Lost Battalion still hadn't been rescued come Sunday, but Nellie promised that it was safe enough to drive to Paris. The capital city was west of the fighting, and it wasn't likely to be bombed now that Germany's new Chancellor von Baden had sued Wilson for peace. We had yet to hear what our president would say in response, but our soldiers doubted he would accept the suit. "We can't accept peace until Germany embraces democracy," one man had said yesterday in the library.

"Forget democracy," argued another. "As soon as they get their soldiers off Allied land, we should call it quits."

But Germany had neither become a democracy nor retreated from France, Belgium, or their colonies, and so the war waged on.

Only Nellie managed to look serene in the middle of the chaos, her blond hair glowing against the monochrome sky and muddy ground. "How has your first week been? Let me guess." She held up a finger before I could respond. "Utterly rotten?"

"Utterly rotten," I said. "But not *entirely* rotten. You wouldn't believe how desperate these men are for books."

Nellie flashed me a grin. "Good thing we're getting more."

"How many do you think they'll let me take?" I held up my clipboard and its many pages of requests.

"I would have said a lot," Nellie snorted. "But maybe not *that* many. We'll find out, though—are you ready?"

"I'm ready."

Nellie looked me up and down, a smile spreading across her soft features once again. "You've changed a lot in a week."

"Is that a good thing?" I tucked a strand of hair behind my ear, suddenly self-conscious. "Or bad?"

Nellie raised her eyebrows. "You tell me."

She turned and headed for the door, and I trotted to keep up. Change was a good thing, I decided. I wasn't any more confident in my ability to host parties like my mama had or find a man who'd propose as anything other than a joke. I wasn't any more confident in my ability to carry a conversation with a stranger without a book to link us.

But I knew, for the first time, that I was doing something that mattered. And it made me carry myself differently. Differently enough that even Nellie could tell.

Nellie flashed me a grin when we got to the car. "Does the new Emmaline want to drive?"

I shuddered. "Absolutely not." This was another thing I was no more confident doing than I had been a week ago. I imagined it was going to be hard enough for Nellie to get us to Paris safely, with artillery shells whizzing overhead and roadways decimated by war. I had no interest in taking over and making the journey more difficult than it had to be.

We settled into silence as Nellie navigated northwest out of Bazoilles-sur-Meuse. I watched the way her foot slid smoothly and confidently from one pedal to the next. She didn't even flinch when the back tires stuck in a patch of mud and the car roared in protest. She simply changed gears and bore down on the pedal to launch us back into motion.

I was relieved when we emerged from the bowels of the torn-up countryside and found ourselves on the straighter, more developed road toward Paris. I toyed with the idea of telling her about Nicholas. Like a schoolgirl with a crush, I just wanted an excuse to say his name. But what was there to say? Officially, I'd seen him only in the same capacity I'd seen the other men. It was comforting having someone to talk to who'd known my parents; in a way, it brought them back to life for me. But that, plus our common Orthodoxy and taste for Russian food and quirky idioms, was all we shared. Nicholas loved Vivian. And I knew that from reading a letter never meant for my eyes.

I was playing with my fingers in my lap, still debating telling Nellie, when she started talking. "I think I'll drop you off at the library while I pick up the supplies I need to get," she said. "Will you be all right on your own?"

I grinned. "At a library? Absolutely. What do you need to pick up?" I envisioned weapons: machine guns and bayonets, hand grenades and artillery shells.

"Mostly construction materials," Nellie said instead.

"For more hospitals?" I found the thought as chilling as the idea of weapons, and my skin went clammy to think there were thousands more injured men than were already being housed.

"No." Nellie slid her eyes toward me like she was sharing a private joke. "Paris Mark Deux."

"A second Paris?"

"They're building a fake city that will be identical to Paris from the sky. The idea is that the Germans will bomb the sham Paris rather than the real one."

"A tale of two cities," I whispered. It seemed too improbable to be true.

"Dickens, right?" Nellie flashed me a grin. "Even I know that one."

"Yes," I said. "But only one of the cities was Paris."

I settled back into my seat and thought about a second Paris. Dickens or not, it seemed more like something out of a storybook than real life.

Nellie laughed, and I realized I'd spoken my thoughts aloud. "It always comes back to books with you, doesn't it?"

My cheeks flushed. "Books are safe. Especially compared to this." I waved my hand to indicate our surroundings: the rubble, the craters in the earth, the remnants of shrapnel and strips of barbed wire.

"That's how I feel driving," Nellie said. "Surprising, maybe"— she chuckled as we flew over a pothole—"but true. It connects me to my father, for one. But it also gives me a sense of control."

"A sense of control," I repeated. That sounded both glorious and unattainable in this world.

"It's better with you, though," Nellie admitted. "Sometimes

when I drive hours and hours alone, I get mired in my thoughts. And however cheerful I seem—" She flashed me a smile. "It gets hard, being on my own all the time in the middle of all this."

I squeezed Nellie's shoulder. "I know what you mean. You're not on your own, though."

She flashed me a grateful look. "Thank you." Then she laughed, like she was uncomfortable with her own vulnerability. "Anyway, are you looking forward to seeing the library headquarters?" Nellie asked me.

"Yes," I admitted. "But it seems wrong to be excited about something when so many lives are lost each day."

Nellie shook her head. "It's not wrong. It's necessary. If you can't be excited about the good things, you'll lose yourself entirely."

We continued talking as we drove and as the sun rose weakly in the sky. It took half the day to get to Paris. I kept my eyes pasted to the window as we approached and took in every detail of Paris's suburban Vincennes. It had become a site to industrial buildings and munitions factories, and the women in rough-spun dresses and head shawls didn't look up as we passed.

"*Munitionettes*," Nellie said in her awful French accent. "They make one hundred thousand artillery shells a day."

My stomach turned. What had those women's hands been doing before the war? Delivering life, baking bread, sewing clothes? And now they were creating weapons that could outlive their fathers and husbands and sons.

I tried to shake my sense of discomfort as we approached Paris itself. I never expected to see the famous city outside of books and newspapers, and I doubted I'd get the chance to come again. I wanted to see the Sacré-Coeur and the Eiffel Tower. I wanted to pass under the Arc de Triomphe and imagine who had walked the same path before me. I wanted to read in the shade of a tree at Le Jardin du Luxembourg or Jardin des Tuileries, to wander the Louvre. I wanted to say a prayer for my parents' souls at the Cathedral of Notre-Dame and maybe even attend a service. The Roman Catholic mass was not so different from our own, except that we allowed no instruments in our churches.

I tried to temper my expectations as we drove through the eleventh arrondissement. We were in the Paris of the Great War, not the Paris of the Enlightenment.

Still I held my breath as we wound through cobblestone streets like something out of a fairy tale. We followed the curve of the Seine and passed the fronts of buildings straight out of history. I closed my eyes and sent a fervent prayer of gratitude up to heaven that Paris, at least, had not been ravaged.

The building took my breath away when we arrived at 10 rue de l'Elysée. The rain that seemed so brutal in Bazoilles-sur-Meuse just made the gray stone of this grand building shimmer, and the intricate designs on the wrought-iron balconies glistened with water. Rivulets ran down the windows, which were topped with elaborate stone crests, and the windows themselves framed a magnificent entryway in the form of an arch. In my eyes, it was the most splendid setting for a library I could ever imagine, though I was surprised France had felt the same way. The library at our hospital center, after all, was shoved in the back of a shaky recreation hut exposed to all the cruelty of the elements.

Nellie laughed at my reaction. "You're like a child on Christmas."

"My Christmas present was always a new book," I acknowledged. "So, it really is the same."

"I didn't think you'd want me to leave you on your own for too long," Nellie said, "but you're looking at this place like you could live in it."

I raised my eyebrows. "You've seen the place where I'm living now. Can you blame me?"

She laughed. "No. But I'm afraid it'll only take me an hour to pick up the supplies I've been sent for, if that."

She must have seen my face fall, because she held up a finger. "But," she said, "the delivery site is northwest, not on our way at all. I could drop the supplies off before coming back for you. Are you all right being alone that long?"

I almost laughed. I'd spent the last several years of my life alone. This was different. "Yes," I said. "Thank you."

I gripped my uniform skirt in my palm and stepped into the damp street. How different the mud was here in the city, caked in the gutter rather than spread across every conceivable surface. Nellie waved as she drove away, and I waved back.

Then, with the same shiver of apprehension I'd felt crossing the Atlantic and meeting Nicholas, I stepped through the doorway and into the library.

The interior was more glorious than the exterior. Everywhere, amid frescoes of Cupid and gleaming mirrors and stiff-backed chairs, were books. I was met by a fellow female librarian, whose job was to catalog books, and given a quick tour of the facility. There was almost too much to take in. Reference and reading rooms flanked the grand hallway, and both appeared to have been converted from former parlors or sitting rooms. Desks had been dragged in to accompany formal plush chairs, and bookshelves covered richly painted walls and whimsical wallpaper. In the kitchen, books covered stoves like skillets, and even the ovens were crammed with excess copies.

All my shyness fell away. "I could *live* here," I said. "I'd never have to leave."

"You'll love this part," my unofficial tour guide said. I couldn't remember her name, because I'd been too enthralled by my surroundings to pay attention to her introduction. "Watch."

She tapped on a wall, and it spun to reveal a staircase. "Once a secret wine closet," she said. "Now, a secret book storeroom."

This place really was a fairy tale. I just shook my head, having no idea how to express the awe I was feeling without sounding like a child. "It's amazing," I finally said, though the passion didn't come through in my awkwardness. "Truly."

"Amazing," the girl agreed. "But terribly time-consuming." She led to me to a room in which a dozen girls were seated sorting and cataloging books with reference numbers and labels, then another in which the girls were preparing books to mail out to various hospitals.

"I worked sorting mail in the States," I offered, taking in the size of the stacks of books in relation to the workers. "Can I help? That is"—I immediately felt presumptuous—"if you need it."

My guide's face split into a smile. "Please," she said. "We need every set of hands we can get. Why don't we get you your books first, and then we can sit you down to help?"

I nodded.

"Wonderful. How many soldiers do you have at your facility?"

"Approximately two thousand."

"Here's what we'll do, then. We'll get the books you have specific requests for off the shelves, then I'll give you two of the boxes that just shipped in from stateside. They haven't been sorted yet, but it's really the only way to give you enough books for that many men."

I nodded. There was such authority in the woman's voice that I couldn't help it.

Together, we went through the list of requests. Most of the men had been willing to take anything or had specified only a genre. I'd fulfill their needs with the assorted books in the shipping crates. But for those who'd been craving specific books, the library didn't disappoint. I found Henrik Ibsen's plays, *Tarzan of the Apes*, Arthur Conan Doyle, Jack London, Alexandre Dumas, Mark Twain, and poets from Kipling to Milton. For some of the men who'd confessed they'd never learned to read in English, I selected English primers, Italian-English dictionaries, and a handful of magazines. "Thank you," I kept saying, hardly believing that I could really take all of these for free. "Thank you so much."

"Thank *you*," the librarian said. "We would have to pay to ship these otherwise. We send out a thousand a day as it is."

"Still." I shook my head. "Thank you for all of this. It's incredible work."

"And you're part of it," the librarian reminded me. "Speaking of which—still willing to help catalog?"

"Of course." I set the books alongside the two crates I'd be taking back to Bazoilles-sur-Meuse and joined the other girls in what had once been a sitting room. They used a simpler cataloging system than the Dewey Decimal for the sake of time, and I'd already picked up most of its rules in browsing. They passed me a reference sheet just in case, then slid over another paper. "And here's the new list of forbidden books."

"What? What is this?" I looked at the list. It was four pages long, but some of the titles jumped out above others: *The Bolsheviki and World Peace* and *Germany's Point of View.*

"Those are the books the War Department has banned," the other librarian explained. "It's rare, but they sometimes end up here as donations. If so, we have orders to destroy them. We have an empty oven in the back we use."

"An empty oven . . ."

"To burn the books."

I gawked. The last thing I'd expected in this glorious library was a book-burning. It felt monarchical. It felt like what my parents had fled Russia to avoid. It felt like what we were fighting *against* in President Wilson's war to make the world safe for democracy.

"They can't just be set aside for the duration of the war?"

One girl shot me a look so poisonous I withered like a plant in winter. Another shrugged sympathetically. "It takes some getting used to."

Just like the rest of war did.

I bit my lip. "Of course. I'm sorry."

I'd been raised to question. When I'd come home from school at nine parroting my classmates' criticisms of the International Workers of the World, my parents gave me the organization's manifesto so I could draw my own conclusions. When *The Jungle* had been published the next year, I'd read it in full. When the bank run hit in 1907, my parents had sat me down and frankly discussed with me the crisis rather than letting me succumb to blind panic.

But my parents hadn't just encouraged knowledge. They often took action. When Indiana passed compulsory sterilization laws, my parents wrote both the governor and legislature to protest. When the Monongah Mining Disaster killed nearly four hundred workers in West Virginia, my parents raised money for the victims' families and sent letters to the mine's leadership.

But when my mother had died, my father's passion for knowledge had lost its springboard. Mama had been the one to spearhead the human aspects of their activism; my papa had handled the written and theoretical side. On his own, he hadn't known how to fight. And so we had both retreated.

Now I looked again at the list. Surely even my parents would have supported getting rid of books that were pro-German and un-American?

But as I looked at the list, my brow furrowed deeper. Some of the forbidden books were about war generally, like an 1892 book titled *In the Midst of Life: Tales of Soldiers and Civilians*, or Barbusse's *Under Fire: The Story of a Squad*. At the bottom of the list was an addendum: *Furthermore, it has recently been brought to our attention that pamphlets of a pacifist character are being sent to libraries. Please watch for them and destroy them.*

Was it disloyal for me to think, as more and more men died each day and were carted to the morgue across from my bedroom, that peace was exactly what we needed?

I shook my head. "How often do you have to destroy books?"

"Not too often," one of the women responded. "Some of them, like *Under Fire*, are sent in with innocent intentions. They're usually destroyed before being shipped overseas, but we end up with the occasional copy. Others, like *The Vampire of the Continent*, are intentionally sent as propaganda. But I doubt you'll stumble over anything too egregious. Most of what we end up having to weed out is pure rubbish. Half-finished diaries, books of paper dolls."

I prayed that she was right. I didn't want to mar my time in

this magical place by having to destroy a book. That was the an-
tithesis of everything I had come here to do.

I began my work silently, using the system they'd devised to
catalog books by genre and author surname. The rote nature of the
work soothed me after all the talk of burning books, and I found
myself steadier and calmer than I'd been in all my time in France
so far. This was like the work I'd done at the Dead Letter Office. It
was all numbers and letters; no death or destruction or broken men.

By the time Nellie returned to pick me up, my eyes were trembling with fatigue and my back ached from sitting at a desk for
longer than I had since leaving D.C. But still I didn't want to go.

"I'm a little bit afraid that that's the sort of librarian I'm supposed to be," I told Nellie as we motored out of the city. "The kind
who works with card catalogs and books, not with people."

"But anyone could do that," Nellie argued. "It takes someone
special to be a hospital librarian. Someone with stamina, courage,
leadership."

"Exactly," I said. "I don't think that someone is me."

Nellie didn't respond, which I took to mean she agreed. I settled back into my seat, wishing I could shrink into it, when she finally spoke. "What did you do in D.C.?"

"I worked at the Dead Letter Office." I explained what it had
been like: the giant sacks of mail, the addresses that had been written incorrectly or in other languages or that had been smudged
beyond recognition.

"Were you comfortable there?"

"Yes. I'd done it for years. The work was easy."

"But you left anyway. Why?"

I hesitated. "Because being comfortable was a bad reason to

stay. A cowardly reason, when the rest of the world was at war. When—maybe—men over here needed me."

"Don't say 'maybe,'" Nellie rebuked me. "You've seen the way these men react to you and your books. They *do* need you."

"They need someone," I said. "But me?"

"Yes." Nellie gestured to the crates in the back. "Look what you've done for them already."

"But anyone could have—"

Nellie interrupted. "Your old job was safe, and you were good at it."

Stupidly, I blushed.

"But you left because you knew there were more important things for you to do. To me, that shows—what did we say? Stamina and courage? And as for leadership, you're one of the first women here. Same as me. Surely that makes you a leader by default."

"I suppose." But I didn't really believe it. I was a rule-follower, not a leader.

At least, I had been a rule-follower until I'd opened Nicholas's letter. But maybe here I was something more. I'd confronted Colonel Hodgson about the whites-only recreation hut, and today I'd questioned an order straight from the War Department. I didn't just blindly follow the rules anymore; I questioned them, as my parents had tried to teach me. And maybe, eventually, I would change them.

Nellie watched me as my back straightened and I sat taller. Her lips curled into a smile, and then the car stopped with a thud.

I instinctively cowered again in my seat.

But Nellie's voice beside me was cheerful. "I know exactly what you need."

"I'm afraid to hear it."

She laughed. "I want to show you what you're capable of. Come on. Move over." She hopped out of the driver's seat and waited for me to move.

"You want me to—but—" I stopped. "I can't drive."

"I'll teach you."

"Nellie. I have *never* driven a car." I felt like I was talking to a child.

"Neither had I, my first time."

"And I'm sure you practiced somewhere safer," I cried, "not miles from the front!"

I immediately regretted shouting at my friend, but she rubbed her hands together like it had been part of her plan all along. "I knew you could fight back."

"But—"

"You can do it," she promised. "I'm right here."

"I really don't—"

"Look." Nellie put her hands on her hips. "The longer we sit here, the more of a target we become. You heard the airplanes over the hospital last night?"

Fear propelled me into the driver's seat, but it couldn't make me start it. "What do I do?"

"The car is already on, the throttle is open, and the emergency brake is off. You're ready to go."

"And I go . . . how?"

"The leftmost pedal is for switching gears." Nellie pointed. "The middle is for reverse. And the right is the one you mustn't forget: the brake."

If I remembered one thing from this lesson, it would be that. I would remember how to stop.

"Now, release this hand brake here"—she gestured—"and push down on the gear shift pedal to engage first gear."

I moved my foot so lightly that nothing happened, and Nellie laughed. "Harder than that."

I tried again and nearly screamed as the car lurched into motion. We trundled down the road, my leg shaking, until Nellie gave me another command. "Release that left pedal."

"Must I? I was just starting to get used to it." And even that was generous.

"If you want to get back to Bacillus on Mush before 1919, yes."

I bit my lip and complied. The car picked up speed, bumping over pebbles and potholes, and Nellie settled back into her seat. I couldn't. I sat ramrod straight, eyes glued to the road and my fingers clutching the wheel so tightly they turned white.

By the end of an hour, I was too drained to continue. Even if there was an underlying current of something intoxicating and new. My calf ached, and my eyes were beginning to blur. "Nellie?"

She turned to me.

"I think I'm done."

My friend walked me patiently through changing gears and putting the car in neutral. "I'm afraid you'll have to admit you did a splendid job," she said as we switched seats.

"I have to admit no such thing," I said, but I couldn't hide my smile. My neck hurt from hunching over the steering wheel, and feeling was only slowly returning to the tips of my fingers. But I had done it. I, Emmaline Balakin, who had never ridden in a motorcar until two months ago, had just driven one through the dirt roads of a France at war.

"Thank you," I said into the silence.

"For what?" Nellie smirked, making me say it.

"For forcing me to drive."

"You feel better now, don't you?"

And I did.

Chapter 14

Kathleen Carre

July 1976

I stared in shock at the woman who claimed to be Nana's sister, taking in her gray-blond hair and plump figure.

"Nana never . . ." I stopped. "I didn't realize she had a sister."

The woman's open face scrunched in quiet pain. "We hadn't seen each other in over sixty years. Not since she shipped off to France."

I shook my head. That couldn't be right. Nana had said she'd had no family left after the war. She'd told me her parents died of the Spanish flu, and she'd never had siblings.

Someone was lying, and I was inclined to believe it was this stranger rather than my beloved nana. "What's your name?" The question came out like a challenge.

"Mabel Johnson, née Mayborn." She said it with some hope, like I might recognize the name. *Oh, right, that sister!* But I didn't.

"I'm sorry," I said, "but I've never heard of you."

The woman's blue eyes shone with unshed tears. "Nellie was initially sent over as a secretary, but then she fixed a car that had hit a tree and they realized she could serve better as a driver."

I stared at Mabel. "She had to take a mechanic's test to do that. Which was easy for her, because . . ."

"Our dad was a mechanic," Mabel finished.

I gaped at her. That story wasn't in the obituary I'd written.

But it wasn't impossible that Nana had told her other friends.

"I need more," I said. "Where was she stationed?"

"Base Hospital 18. Bazoilles-sur-Meuse, France." Mabel's pronunciation was rougher than Nana's, but she named the same city. "Look. I have letters." She pulled a sheaf of envelopes from her purse and held them out to me. Postmarked from France in 1918, each one was addressed to the Mayborn family in Washington, D.C.

"My God," I whispered. "Can I read these?"

"Of course." Mabel's voice was soft. "She was your grandmother."

I looked up at her, suddenly ashamed of my interrogation. This woman was my family; aside from Jane, who didn't even know that her mother was dead or that her daughter was in Annapolis, she was all I had.

I took a deep breath. "Do you want to go somewhere we can talk?"

Mabel's round face broke into a sweet smile. "I'd like that, Kathleen. I'd like that very much."

I led Mabel up to the third floor of Nana's apartment building and ushered her inside. I invited her to sit as I went to get two glasses of water from the kitchen, then returned to see the woman in the same chair Nana had sat in every morning and afternoon. There were others to pick from, but still Mabel had chosen Nana's favorite. Like the sisters had a connection that had remained un-severed through the decades they'd been apart, and even past death. I wondered if they would pick the same seat at a restaurant, if Mabel preferred the window seat like my nana had.

I handed Mabel the glass of water and sat in the hard-backed chair across from her. Mabel thanked me, but she didn't take a sip. She craned her neck to look around the apartment, and I tried to see it through her eyes: the old desk, cluttered bookshelves, a col-lection of 1910s car prints on the wall. What had my grandmoth-er's childhood room looked like, I wondered. Had she and Mabel shared?

"Please," I said. "Tell me what you know."

Mabel twisted limp hands in her lap. "Nellie shipped off with the Red Cross in 1918. As you know, she started off as a secretary, but wrote us after a month or so that she'd become a Motor Corps driver instead. My mother was worried it would be more danger-ous, but my father was so proud."

"And you?"

Mabel's smile peeked through again. "Of course I was proud. She was my older sister, and I thought everything she did was right. I wanted to be just like her."

"Did you go too, then?"

"No. Nellie said I was too young, and my mother agreed."

"She was afraid for me to attend the academy, too," I said. "Said it was a man's world."

Mabel lifted her shoulders. "I don't know. She was always so cheerful in her letters, but maybe she was just trying to protect us." Mabel trailed off, lost in thought.

"And then?"

Mabel's smile faded. Her face looked wrong without it. "Her letters stopped coming around the time of the Armistice, and she just . . . never came home. It was so hard." Mabel's hands, spotted with old age, clenched in her lap. "Everyone else was celebrating the end of the war, but we were torn between hope and grief. We didn't know if Nellie would ever come back." Mabel brushed her eyes. "I was disconsolate. Nellie was my best friend. I knew she'd do everything she could to make it back to me, because she'd promised. But she never came."

"And you never looked?" There might have been a hint of accusation in my voice, but I couldn't help it. How had Nana's sister merely sat and waited, when she could have searched?

"Of course I looked. Nellie was like a second mother to me."

To me, too, I thought.

"But I never could find her. Records showed that she made it on to a ship heading back to the States, but after that, nothing. She's not listed anywhere. And surely, I thought, she'd reach out if she came home. The fact that I never heard from her . . . I assumed she was dead. That the records were wrong. It was war, after all. Far more than records had been lost."

I shook my head. "Then how did you end up here today?"

"I saw her obituary in the paper. Nellie Mayborn Carre, with the same birth date as my Nellie and reference to time spent in the

Motor Corps. I knew it wasn't a coincidence." She put up her hands. "I spent decades thinking Nellie was dead and only found out I was wrong once she actually *was*."

I winced. The truth of it—of Nana being dead—was still too much to utter aloud. Even after I'd watched her body being lowered into the ground.

"I just don't understand," Mabel whispered. "Why did she never reach out to me?"

I took a deep breath as I fingered the letters Mabel had given me. Nana wasn't proud of her past, but her sister deserved the truth.

"Things were hard for Nana when she came back from France," I said carefully. "She had what we used to call 'dark days.' Days she couldn't get out of bed for the guilt of it all. It meant my mother didn't always get to school on time, that friends would come knocking and no one would answer the door. She was ashamed, I think, and perhaps she didn't want you to know. Especially if she'd always been a role model in your eyes. Maybe she just didn't want to disappoint you."

Mabel shook her head. "If she needed help, I would have been there. I would have been there the very moment she called."

We sat silently for a moment—both of us thinking, I imagined, about how different my nana's life could have been. How different would Jane have been if she'd had an aunt to fill in the gaps? How different would my world be?

Mabel whispered her next question as if she were afraid to hear the answer. "Was she happy?"

I considered my Nana's life. I could see so much of it from where I sat: the postcards from my mother on Nana's refrigerator, the framed photographs of me sprouting up through the years. It wasn't the life I wanted for myself, but she had chosen it. I had enough faith in her to think she would have done things differently had she wanted to.

"I think so," I said finally. "I hope so."

Mabel nodded. "I hope so, too." Then a soft smile crept across her lips. "She had a wonderful granddaughter, after all."

Uncomfortable with the naked emotion in Mabel's voice, I asked the only logical question. "And you? Do you have children?"

"No." Mabel's soft shoulders curved forward. "I never did have kids."

I was surprised by that. Mabel smelled like chocolate chip cookies and was shaped like a hug. But maybe my grandmother's disappearance had affected her more than she let on. Or maybe she was like Jane, a woman with little desire for a family.

I twisted to look at the clock on the wall above Mabel. "I don't mean to be rude," I said, "but I have to be back at the Naval Academy tonight. And I've got the whole apartment to go through."

Mrs. Peregrine had offered to store some of Nana's personal things until I had a space for them. The rest of it, I would leave here for the estate sale I'd arranged. I wouldn't be present, but that was fine. I wasn't one to form emotional attachments to old relics like chairs or potato mashers.

Mabel bit her lip. It made her look young, and I imagined her as Nana must have known her. She'd have been so young when Nana left for France.

"I understand if you need privacy," Mabel said. "But I would so love to stay and to help you." Her eyes grew rheumy with tears. "This is the closest I've been to Nellie in decades."

I hated to admit it, but I wanted Mabel to stay, too. I hadn't known she existed three hours ago, but now she was the nearest link I had to the woman I loved and worshipped more than anyone else. I couldn't have Nana back, but Mabel could bring to life a part of her I'd never known.

"Of course you can stay."

Mabel offered to clean out the kitchen while I dealt with the more personal parts of the apartment like Nana's bedroom and my old room, but I hated the thought of leaving a stranger unsupervised in the apartment. Even if that stranger was Nana's sister.

Instead, I sat in the living room, where I could keep an eye on Mabel, and pored over Nana's letters. Her handwriting had grown better with age, and it was difficult to decipher her young ramblings, but I was determined. I learned about the garage attached to an old chateau where she stayed in Bazoilles-sur-Meuse and the strange hours she kept. I learned about the occasional snatches of beauty she glimpsed between the battlefields as she crisscrossed the country, the flowers she picked and kept in her car to remind her of home. I smiled at that. Nana had kept a vase of roses in the kitchen the whole time I'd lived with her; I could so easily imagine her with wildflowers strewn about the car.

By the time I'd finished the letters, my eyes were wet. How young Nana had been when she'd served in France, how vibrant.

I rose and busied myself with the books on Nana's shelves so Mabel wouldn't see my tears fall. There was so little in here worth keeping. I'd save Nana's car prints, though I wasn't allowed decor in Bancroft Hall and would have to leave them with Mrs. Peregrine for a time.

Once Mabel finished in the kitchen, we moved together into my bedroom. I'd put a few framed photographs into a box to keep.

Mabel pulled one of the photographs out. "You and your mother?"

I nodded. The picture had been taken in 1955, a year after I'd been born, and Jane's dark hair was long and loose. The camera had caught her in motion: hair flipping and face blurry, arms outstretched to hold my hands. I stood on the ground, my chubby fingers wrapped around hers, completely still. Mom claimed we'd been dancing when the photograph was taken, though of course I couldn't remember.

"She wasn't at the burial . . ."

I knew what Mabel was asking in her polite way. Was she dead? Estranged? Too sick to come?

"She doesn't live in D.C.," I said. "She's hard to reach."

Mabel cocked her head like a puppy, just as eager to comfort. "She doesn't know about Nellie yet?"

"She'll call eventually," I said. "I'll tell her then." It wasn't a task I relished.

Mabel had moved on to rubbing her elbows now, each with the opposite hand. "You don't know how to reach your own mother?"

"Nana raised me," I said shortly.

Mabel's eyes welled with sympathy. "Oh, honey. I wish I had been around. I could have helped you both. I'm so sorry about everything."

"No," I said firmly. "I didn't need anyone but Nana." And I certainly didn't need Mabel's pity. "She raised me to be everything my mother wouldn't have—to be strong and self-assured and responsible and brave. I wouldn't be at the academy if I'd been raised by anyone else." I shrugged, a practiced move. "My mother found her own way to be happy. So did Nana and I."

The papery-thin skin on Mabel's neck pulsed as she swallowed. I waited to see if she would protest, but she didn't.

"You're right," she said. "I'm sorry. In my life, the absence of someone has always been the loss of them."

Of course. I already regretted my harsh tone. "I'm sorry, too," I said. I pulled the photograph from Mabel's hand and placed it back in the box, then grabbed another to put beside it.

"You ran?" Mabel studied the picture, which showed me and the other girls on my track and field team after a district win.

"I still run," I said. "Only now, I do it with a whole bunch of men."

Mabel shook her head. "I hardly believed they were letting women in. What's it like?"

I could tell her about the aggression from the men and the condescension from the officers. The uniforms that didn't fit right and the heels and the purses. I could tell her about the scrutiny, the pressure to prove that women belonged at the academy as much as the men did.

"It's everything I've ever wanted," I said instead. Because if I said it enough and acted as if it were true, I was sure it would become reality.

I stacked the rest of the photographs quickly so as not to invite comment, then led Mabel to Nana's bedroom. It felt like a private place. This was where I used to come when I missed my mother late at night but hated to admit it, when I claimed nightmares about dragons or war to keep from having to tell Nana what was really wrong. She'd always known anyway, and she'd wrap me in her long, thin arms and hold me to her chest until I fell back asleep. The nights I spent in her bed were the nights I slept best.

I still needed her now, I supposed. I was hardly sleeping at the academy at all.

But there had been times I'd taken care of Nana in this room, too. I'd brought her breakfast in bed when she was too depressed to eat and crept in for the key to the apartment when I knew she wouldn't be able to let me in after school.

It was as hard to admit that my war hero wasn't infallible as it was to admit I missed my mom.

I didn't blame Nana for her vulnerability. But inwardly, I promised I'd never fall prey to it myself.

Now Mabel and I stepped over the threshold gingerly. I didn't believe in ghosts or spirits, but we both tiptoed as if we did. Nothing much of Nana remained in the room. The furniture and most of the clothing could be sold; all I wanted was Nana's watch, her Motor Corps uniform, and the box of her personal effects. I pulled it down from the shelf as Mabel riffled through the dresses hanging in the closet and glanced at what lay on top. Three photographs were visible: one of me posing before the Lincoln Memorial with two teeth missing from my smile, another of my graduation, and one of my thirty-four-year-old mother pregnant with me.

I sucked my teeth and pushed that one aside. I hated the pictures of Jane's pregnancy, acutely aware that she'd resented every minute of it.

I rested the box on my hip bone. "I think that's everything. And I have to start heading back to Annapolis. Do you need me to walk you down, call you a cab?" My voice was brisk, but I didn't know how else to say goodbye. Not when I hadn't been able to say goodbye to Nana.

"Can I have your address?" Mabel asked. "I just don't . . . I just found Nellie, and I don't want to lose her again."

She was so free with her emotions, so honest. It was dangerous. Like I might let my grief spill out to match hers.

I scrawled my address on a piece of paper and passed it over. "I can call you every once in a while too, if you don't mind giving me your number?" I surprised myself by asking. But she was Nana's sister. And though I had lost my nana, I didn't have to lose this link to her, too.

Mabel pressed her phone number into my hand. "Thank you," she said. There were tears in her eyes. "Thank you so much."

I waved goodbye as she let herself out, but I didn't follow her down the stairs and get on the bus back to Annapolis like I'd promised.

Instead, I stretched myself across my nana's bed and cried.

Nana was supposed to be the one who'd never leave me.

Chapter 15

———— ❖ ————

Emmaline Balakin

October 1918

Less than a week had passed since I'd gone to Paris with Nellie, but already I was stretched too thin to breathe. On a grand scale, things were looking up for the Allies: Cambrai had fallen to the British, and the Lost Battalion had escaped what had seemed like certain death. But the destruction left in victory's wake was devastating. We were receiving hundreds of new casualties daily, and from opening to closing every day, the recreation hut was full to bursting with men. They gathered to play cards and piano, to listen to songs on the phonograph and visit with friends from other wards—but most of all, they came for the books. As soon as I had a book sorted, cataloged, and displayed, it was gone. They came back just as quickly, most men finishing entire novels in a day or two for lack of other entertainment.

One day I overheard a cluster of men discussing *The Call of the Wild* in the recreation hut. Men from seemingly every ward joined to share their thoughts on everything from the quality of London's writing to the nature-versus-nurture debate. The book inspired the men to share stories of the dogs they'd had as children and pictures of their families and puppies in America. One raucous group of soldiers even had a howling contest.

I loved how important the book had been to the men in stretching their imaginations, challenging their assumptions, and creating new communities. But the hustle and bustle of the recreation hut was too much for me most days, and I preferred to push my wheelbarrow full of books from ward to ward for the men who were bedridden.

Later in the week, I made my way back to the unofficial colored ward. It was already colder than it had been just a week ago, and I shivered without the heat of the radiator to warm me. The mud on my ankles and calves was clammy against my skin.

"Burt, Perlie. Joshua." I greeted the three men I'd come to know best as I'd read *The Call of the Wild* to the ward. All three men went through books like they were bandages. Most of their ward mates had moved on, but these three had injuries too prone to infection. "How are you all?"

"Better now you're here."

Burt and Perlie returned the books they'd borrowed previously, though Joshua admitted with a sheepish smile that he hadn't finished his quite yet. "Take as long as you need," I told him. "That's one of the beautiful things about a book. You can make it last however long you need it."

"Do you have any new ones?" Burt sorted through the wheelbarrow.

"Not yet, I'm afraid. I hope to get the chance to unload the second crate of books from Paris on Sunday."

"You've been busy, then?"

"Yes. The hut has been swarmed with men gathering to discuss *The Call of the Wild.* They've been arguing, debating, rereading, simply chatting . . ." I bit my lip as I realized that it was perhaps insensitive to tell these men about a world they weren't welcome to join.

Burt raised an eyebrow. "I wish I could participate. Much of my work at Morehouse is on the myth of genetic superiority."

"I won't pretend to know as much as the professor, but something did rub me the wrong way when you read us that last scene with the American Indians," Perlie said. "My wife is part Cherokee. Which means my girls are, too. And they're no savages."

"His daughters are real cute," Joshua said to me. "Makes me miss the days when mine were young."

I couldn't help but smile. "Do you have a picture, Perlie?"

"My wife Josephine just sent me a new one." He rummaged under his mattress and then presented me with the photograph. "Tess is seven, and Annie is four."

The two girls in the photo beamed with their arms around each other, sitting squished together on wooden porch steps. They had the sweetest, widest smiles like their father's, though Annie's had a hint of mischief in it. Tess's hair was lovingly braided in two thick strands, and Annie's was pulled back in a barely controlled mass of curls. They both wore white like little angels, the color bright against their dark, glowing skin.

"Look at them," I murmured. "They are too sweet for words, Perlie."

"I know." He ducked his head with a wink. "That is, thank you kindly."

We both laughed, but then his face turned dark. "I hate being gone from them. I'm afraid Annie will hardly remember me when I get back." He sucked in a breath. "But I try to stay positive. I'm fighting this war for them, after all. Surely things will be different once we go home. My family will be treated like patriots, not like second-class citizens."

"Do you really think so?"

"I don't know," Perlie admitted. "But I hope so. Otherwise, why am I here?"

Burt grimaced. "Why, indeed? It's easy for the rest of the country to forget we're risking our lives for them when we're put in segregated units and wards."

I rubbed my temple, hating the thought that a book I'd read in so many wards might have negatively influenced other soldiers' opinions of people like Perlie's wife and girls. But the only way to change the narrative would be through introducing another one. And unlike Jack London or even Francis Galton, whom several soldiers were citing with alarming frequency, these men weren't allowed in the library to share *their* stories.

A few short months ago, I would have been disturbed by this but not sure what to do about it. Perhaps I would have read something by W. E. B. DuBois or Paul Laurence Dunbar, and compared their writings to those of the classics I'd grown up enjoying. But I wouldn't have acted.

Now I took a deep breath. "What if we brought the library to you?"

Joshua gestured toward the wheelbarrow. "Is that not what you're doing already?"

I surprised myself with my next words. "There's more to a library than books." I thought back to my training. Benjamin Franklin had been inspired to create the first lending library after a social club meeting, and he had considered it a success because it had improved conversation among Americans.

"I can bring the conversation into this ward," I said slowly, still thinking. "The debates, the chatter."

"How?" Perlie ran his thumb over the photograph of his daughters.

I bit my lip. This was the part my mother was good at. It had never been my forte. Just one year before I'd started work at the Dead Letter Office, President Wilson had tacitly allowed segregation of federal organizations and incited a wave of firings and demotions across the nation. The few colored postal workers who'd managed to retain employment in D.C. were sent to the Dead Letter Office, where the public was spared the apparent indignity of having to interact with them. I always felt guilty that all I had to offer Robert, the colored man who worked beside me for several years, was a smile and daily "How are you?" when my mother would likely have lobbied his case until it ended up in the courts. But my mother was gone, and I owed it to her and the world I inhabited to use my own position for good. "What if we start a discussion group?" I finally asked. "The men are gathering unofficially now, but we could make a club out of it. Meet here, where there's more space anyway."

Burt raised an eyebrow again. "You think the men will be willing to come here?"

"I know some of them will," I said, thinking of Nicholas. "But we can try to entice others. I'll bring the phonograph."

"I don't think a jaunty tune will overturn centuries of hatred," Burt said wryly, and I cringed.

"You're right. I'm sorry. I wasn't thinking."

Burt, Perlie, and Joshua shared a look. "Bring the phonograph," Perlie said when they broke eye contact. "We'll need all the help we can get."

The recreation hut and its library were closed Sunday morning so men would go to religious services at Base Hospital 18's chapel. Bleary-eyed and tired after hours of sirens at night, I resisted the urge to sleep late and resolved instead to sort the unopened crate of books from the ALA and prepare for the book club that would be running in Burt, Perlie, and Joshua's ward.

I started with the crate, lugging it from under the bed in my room and forcing it open. It was packed as tightly as the first one had been, and I remembered hearing that the ALA was sending fifty shipping tons of books—something like seventy-five thousand volumes—overseas a month.

Most of these books were similar to those that had been in the first crate. I set aside a late-nineteenth-century almanac and a book about neonatal nutrition, but the other books proved quite valuable—poetry, the great British classics, westerns, detective stories, nonfiction on everything from mechanics to farming, Shakespeare's plays, modern plays, and satire. All the men's favorites seemed to be here.

I labeled the books and put them on the recreation hut shelf or in the wheelbarrow depending on whether we had duplicate copies and where they were stored. By the time I had just a few books left in the box, I was confident that I'd have time to make flyers regarding the book club before the recreation hut reopened.

And then I pulled out Leon Trotsky's *The Bolsheviki and World Peace*.

I dropped it immediately back into the box. Trotsky had been arrested for the first time just a few years after my parents had left Russia. Last year, he'd been instrumental in overthrowing the provisional government that had replaced Czar Nicholas II. He was Vladimir Lenin's second in command, the leader of the Red Army, and one of the major advocates for this war becoming a socialist revolution.

To even hold his book in my hands was likely considered treason. Especially as it was on the War Department's list of banned books.

I couldn't help furtively opening the front cover. A pamphlet fell out. This one was called *The Disgrace of Democracy: Open Letter to Woodrow Wilson* by Kelly Miller.

I gasped and shoved the pamphlet back into the box, afraid that Colonel Hodgson would somehow know I had touched it. If Trotsky's book was forbidden, this pamphlet had to be.

I rummaged through my things for the list they'd given me at the library. And yes, there it was. *Miller, Kelly. The Disgrace of Democracy*. Sandwiched right in between *Ireland's Case* and *Open Letter to Profiteers*.

The expectation was clear, just as it had been when I'd been faced with Nicholas's letter in the Dead Letter Office two and a half months ago. That letter, I should have forwarded back to him unread. These books, I should turn in to the colonel, also unread, so they could be destroyed.

But I hadn't obeyed when it had come to Nicholas's letter. And that decision had opened up a whole new world to me.

I scooped up both forbidden books and darted into my cubbyhole of a room, slamming the door behind me. Books deserved to be read, after all. Wasn't it my job, as a librarian, to be the one reading them?

I started with Miller's letter to Wilson. It was short and to the point, condemning lynching and—even more powerfully—condemning the government's response to it. I couldn't help but think of Perlie as I read. He lived in Virginia, where I knew nearly one hundred colored men had been lynched since the Civil War. Perlie, with his gentle voice and his sweet little girls.

Lost in my thoughts, I nearly screamed when I heard the hut door thrown open and the boisterous cries of men who'd just been released from the silence of a church service. Frantic, I stuffed both books under my mattress and ran to the door to greet them.

"Miss us?" A handsome soldier named Edmund threw his arm around me. "You seem eager to see us this morning."

I flinched away from his touch, cheeks burning. "I'm just excited," I said quickly. I needed to explain my nervous energy and my flushed cheeks somehow. "I'm starting a book club."

"A book club!" Edmund's shout was much louder than my original statement had been, and several men turned to look at us.

"Yes," I said, cursing myself for making such an announcement unprepared. "A book club."

"Tell us more!" This came from someone in the crowd.

"Right. Well. We'll be meeting to listen to music and discuss books in marquee tent number fifty."

"Number fifty." One man scrunched up his nose. "Isn't that sort of far?"

I searched for an explanation. "It's not as full as the other tents. There's far more space to gather."

This was *a* truth, if not the whole truth.

"We'll meet for the first time tomorrow to discuss *The Call of the Wild*, get to know each other, and decide what to read next," I told the men. "Tell the others in your wards. The more the merrier!"

I cringed as I said it. *The more the merrier* was my mother's sentiment, though she would express it the Russian way: *in a crush, yet without resentment.* I didn't feel resentment in a crowd, but I certainly felt self-conscious and tongue-tied. And now was no exception. I made my excuses to the men and then rushed off under the guise of finalizing preparations in tent fifty. Really, I needed to confirm with the men that they were still accepting of the idea of a group of men joining them in their hut, and that it could be tomorrow. And then I needed to talk to the eternally calm, level Nicholas to slow down the beating of my heart.

I checked in with Burt, Perlie, and Joshua, who took my announcement with glee. They promised that they'd confirmed with their ward mates, many of whom were sleeping now, and that no one had an issue with the club.

Then I headed to Nicholas's ward. I realized too late that I should have come with an excuse. Professionally, I couldn't be perceived as showing favoritism to any one man over another. Personally, I was mortified at the thought that Nicholas might question my frequent visits. But I was already at the entrance to his tent, and I couldn't turn back now. I squared my shoulders and stepped inside.

"Emmaline."

Nicholas's voice was a low rumble. Lower than usual, even, and I wondered if he was in pain.

"Nicholas. Are you all right?"

"I've been better," he admitted. "But I'm not in too much pain to see my favorite librarian."

My stomach flipped like a schoolgirl's, and I quickly directed my attention to Nicholas's wound. The bandage around his torso was stained brown with blood. "When is the last time they changed that?"

He shrugged as if it didn't matter. "The nurses are overwhelmed. They'll do it when they can."

"I'll talk to them," I promised. "Make sure they get out here." It wasn't hard to imagine that they'd linger longer in the wooden wards now that winter was nearly upon us. These marquee tents did almost nothing to prevent the steady encroachment of mud and the frequent onslaughts of sleet and freezing rain.

"No need," Nicholas said. But he winced as he spoke.

"Shh," I said. "Don't hurt yourself. I'll do the talking."

I realized only after I said it that I was not particularly adept at talking. But for Nicholas, I would try. "I'm starting a book club," I told him quietly.

He raised his eyebrows not with skepticism but in what I interpreted as a nonverbal *oh?*

"Yes." I nodded. "All the men were gathering in the hut to talk about *The Call of the Wild*. And it was wonderful, truly. It made me feel like I'd done something that mattered here already, no matter how small."

"You have," Nicholas managed, but I put my finger to my lips again.

"But then I mentioned it to the men in the last tent on this side of the hospital. They've got all sorts of different injuries and diseases, but they're all grouped together 'cause they're colored."

Nicholas's brow wrinkled, and I followed his gaze to the cot catty-corner from his bed. On it lay a dark-skinned man with a bandage similar to Nicholas's around his midsection. Even from here, I could see it was as bloody as Nicholas's. If not more.

"I know," I said. "They're not all there. It's called 'imperfect segregation.' The colonel told me the convalescent hospitals are required to segregate entirely, but that here, he can only do so much because of separation by casualty type. I suppose marquee tent fifty has become the colored overflow ward.

"Anyway, they aren't allowed in the recreation hut. None of the colored men are, regardless of ward." I looked back to the man Nicholas had indicated before. His skin shone with sweat, and I worried he was feverish. I'd have to mention him to a nurse as well. "They were disappointed that they couldn't join the discussions with the other men. Raised some good points about the book, too. So I decided we would bring the discussions to them."

I waited for Nicholas's reaction with my toes curled in my shoes. Though I'd told what seemed like every man in the hospital about the book club, only Nicholas knew the real reason behind it.

I sagged with relief when he responded. "I think that's a brilliant idea. Count me in." He looked at me so intently I had to force myself not to duck away. "You're as idealistic as you used to be."

"Me? Idealistic? I don't think so." I closed my eyes as I inhaled and then opened them again. "I was complacent for so many years after my parents died. I stayed at the Dead Letter Office for five years just because it was safe and easy." I thought again of Robert, of how I'd done nothing for him.

Nicholas lifted his shoulders and grimaced at the movement. "But you're here now, and the work you're doing is changing lives." Then his brow wrinkled. "You worked at the Dead Letter Office?"

I resisted the urge to cover my face with my hands. I shouldn't have shared that, not when Vivian's letter had come to me there. "Yes."

"That was important work, too," Nicholas said. His voice was gaining strength. "Do you have any idea how comforting words from home can be?"

Yes, I do. What else had compelled me to fabricate them? To break all the rules, to lie? But I didn't answer out loud. Instead, I forced a smile and a subject change. "What did you do?"

Nicholas blinked, and the link between our gazes severed. "I worked at the Library of Congress," he told me.

I gaped at him. "The Library of Congress?" I brought my hands to my eyes. "You must think me such a novice in comparison."

Nicholas laughed. "Not at all. I worked in acquisitions, so I didn't interact with the patrons like you do."

I hardly heard him. All these years, Nicholas had worked just a mile away from me. But it had taken both our deployments to France to find each other again. "That must be incredible," I breathed. "What's it like?"

"Challenging," he admitted. "But that's not a bad thing. Every manuscript or photograph or packet of letters I'm able to secure for the Library helps tell the story of the United States." He pulled a face. "It's not always a pretty story, but I like to think we're documenting progress."

"What sort of records have you acquired?"

"My favorite acquisition was a collection of Quaker meeting notes from the original Virginia colony. There are several years' worth of records, and they provide insight into everything from the Quakers' early abolitionist beliefs and push for religious freedom to women's roles in colonial America and relationships with Indians." He shrugged. "None of my recent acquisitions have been quite as interesting. I was negotiating for some letters exchanged between John D. Rockefeller and Chester Winthrop before I was drafted, but . . ." He trailed off. "Now I'm here."

I didn't respond immediately, too stunned by the name Chester Winthrop.

Nicholas's eyes met mine, but it wasn't the same intense unbreakable stare as before. This time there was something in his eyes that looked almost like fear. "Emmaline . . ."

"Yes?"

He closed his eyes. "I want to let you know that I've been seeing Mr. Winthrop's daughter, Miss Vivian Callahan."

I knew this. I'd known this for months. But still I stepped back like Nicholas's words couldn't be true if they couldn't reach me. "Oh," I said quietly. "That's . . . so lovely to hear."

"We met through her father, and it's gone from there." He chuckled uncomfortably. "I can't believe her father approves of me, a second-generation Russian immigrant, but I know my parents would be thrilled. You know as well as I do such a thing would never have been possible in Russia."

I narrowed my eyes. "What are you saying, then? You're with her because of who her family is?" This wasn't the Nicholas I'd known.

"Of course not!" This time, Nicholas was the one to jolt back. "I thought you knew me better than that." He paused. "She's like a spot of fresh air. My whole life is consumed by this war, and it's like she barely even remembers it exists."

Or that you *exist,* I wanted to say, but stopped myself.

Nicholas sighed. "I know that's not really something to

admire. Being able to ignore tragedy that doesn't affect you is more selfish than optimistic. But I wish I could remain so aloof." He shook himself off. "It hardly matters. Her letters have stopped coming anyway, so it may be a moot point." He forced a weak smile.

I didn't know what to say. Was this the moment to tell him the truth, or should I let him continue living in ignorance? "The mail is so slow," I said halfheartedly.

Nicholas nodded, but it was obvious he didn't believe me. Other men were getting letters, weren't they? Nicholas put on a brave face. "If I'm telling the truth, this is the most at home I've felt since coming to France, letters or no letters."

"How so?" I tipped forward on my toes to catch his next words.

Nicholas looked straight at me with those stormy gray eyes I knew so well. "Isn't it obvious? I have you."

Chapter 16

———— ❖ ————

Kathleen Carre

July 1976

It was dusk when I returned to the Naval Academy grounds, still wearing the service dress blues I'd worn to Nana's funeral. I hated the way the tight-fitting skirt limited my stride as I headed to Bancroft.

"Oooh!" A group of men jeered as I moved past them. "Someone looks fancy. Where are you coming from?"

"Or where are you headed?" Another wiggled his eyebrows suggestively.

"And can I join in?" a third man threw out to raucous laughter.

I paused only a moment, then decided they weren't worth it. I wasn't going to risk being reported for antagonizing these men when it would be their collective word against mine. I kept walking.

"Lay off her," another voice came. "You know all these Navy girls are lesbos. They've got no interest in a guy like you."

The group exploded in guffaws again, and it took everything I had to keep moving forward. My fists clenched at my sides, but I didn't raise them. I was better than that, I told myself. They didn't deserve a rise out of me.

And I didn't want them seeing my puffy eyes, either.

I let out a sigh of relief when the doors of Bancroft shut behind me. The men were gone, and I was so close to my room. I could go upstairs, change into my Navy pajamas, and wake up tomorrow to put on my PEP clothes and rejoin the straightforward, emotionless world of the military.

But before I could run up the stairs, Derrick appeared before me. "Emmaline." His weight leaned on one leg like he was nervous, and I could see the movement of his tongue worrying his teeth behind his closed lips. "I'm glad I was finally able to catch you."

"You've been waiting for me? What's wrong?" I couldn't imagine what he needed.

"I'm so sorry." He wrung his hands. "I know this is a terrible time. How is—how was the funeral?"

"It was fine," I lied, wanting to know why he was here. "What's the matter?"

He hesitated, then said, "When I got back after evening chow, my room had been ransacked."

"I'm so sorry." But even as I said it, I couldn't help a twinge of irritation. I had more than enough on my plate, what with my nana's death and the harassment I had to deal with simply by walking the passageways. What did this have to do with me?

"There's more," he said, like he knew I was questioning him. "They left this note."

He held out a jagged square of paper, and I took it. In large, cartoonishly blocky letters, someone had written STAY AWAY FROM OUR WOMEN.

"'Our' women? What does that mean?"

"Same thing it's always meant: white women."

He flipped over the note in my palm to show me the rough sketch of a noose.

I'd stayed calm and collected throughout my grandmother's funeral, my conversation with Mabel, and in front of those boys on the green. But now my legs grew shaky and weak, and I sagged against the wall. "Oh my God."

"Listen," Derrick said. "Janie is the only girl in my squadron, and she's Black. Other than her, you're the only woman I've really spoken to."

"So you think . . ."

"I think they're referring to you."

My instinct was to drag Derrick up into my room and slam the door so no one would see us together. But that was an offense that could get us expelled. So I looked furtively around the foyer before I spoke. "Derrick, you need to report this."

"I did," he said. "On my way here. But I don't know how much good it will do."

"This is the Navy," I said. "It's all about order and respect. What do you mean, you don't know how much good it will do?"

Derrick looked down at the gleaming deck. "Do you know

when the first African American was admitted into the Naval Academy?"

"Wesley Brown," I said. "Class of '49."

Derrick shook his head.

"Yes," I insisted. "I read all about it."

Derrick held up a hand. "Wesley Brown was the first to graduate. But there were five enrolled before him. The first one, James H. Conyers, was nearly drowned by other midshipmen. He survived but dropped out. And the ones who'd tried to kill him weren't even given a slap on the wrist. The academy called it hazing."

I didn't have time to absorb this, to think about why I'd never heard of Conyers despite my endless studying. To think about what the Naval Academy would be like for me if I were the only woman like Conyers had been the only Black midshipman. I didn't have time, because now, we needed to think practically.

I took a deep breath. "What are you saying? That there's nothing we can do?"

"I think we'll make things worse if we try."

I closed my eyes. "I'm sorry, Derrick. This is awful, but I think we have to stay apart for now. It's too dangerous to be seen together." The noose swam before my eyelids. "Especially for you."

"But . . ."

I interrupted. "Maybe once the boys who did this are found and punished, we can associate again, but it's too risky now. I would never forgive myself if they hurt you."

Derrick sighed. "I suppose you're right."

"They *will* be punished, though," I said. "They have to be. So don't worry."

Derrick raised an eyebrow. "I'm a professional worrier."

I had no chance to respond before the door swung open and a crowd of midshipmen entered. "Go," I hissed. "Up the stairs."

Derrick threw one last look over his shoulder as he chopped upstairs, and I waited a moment before following. I flew around the corners on the way to my own bedroom, eager to get inside and collapse onto my bed, but I stopped short when I reached the door. According to regulation, it was opened ninety degrees . . . but what I saw inside wasn't my regulation cleanliness.

Derrick's room wasn't the only one that had been ransacked.

My white bedsheets were balled under the shower head with the faucet turned on. My desk chair lay with its legs out in the center of the room, and the few items I'd had on my desk—the American flag, a collection of books—were scattered around it.

I ran to the shower and shut off the water, but it was too late. The sheets were soaked, and so I righted my desk chair and draped them over its back. Water dripped onto the deck, and my nostrils flared. This was more than inconvenient. A failed room inspection would mean a demerit for not just me but Susan and Linda as well, and "No excuse, sir" left no room for me to explain that it had been someone else's fault.

I bent to pick up my things and place them on the desk, then caught sight of a note on the bed as I straightened. I thought of Derrick's noose and my stomach clenched. But there was no use avoiding it. I picked up the note and read:

*Better you can't sleep at all
than you sleep with a spook.*

My hand tightened around the note. I was no stranger to racism. There were still buildings on my street in D.C. with boarded-up windows and burned-out walls from the riots after Dr. King was shot, and I had enough memories of Jim Crow segregation in everything from water fountains to swimming pools.

But despite all the integration efforts, I'd gone to a school with classes full of people who looked like me, lived in an apartment building with people who looked like me. Racism had never been personal.

But now, rage boiled in me until I thought I might burst. The muscles in my legs tensed, and my teeth ground together. This was the type of overwhelming emotion I usually would run to avoid: three miles, four miles, six. But I only had a few hours left of liberty, and I needed to report this.

I chopped to the plebe supervisor's office. His secretary smiled at me when I entered, but I didn't smile back. "I need to file a complaint."

She passed over a clipboard and the form, and I filled out my own name and rank, then described what I'd found in my room. I wrote it all down, from the mess to the note. Then I turned over the clipboard, ignoring the twinge of nervousness low in my belly. This was what I had to do to hold my peers accountable. Wasn't that what the Navy was all about?

When I let myself back into my room in Bancroft, Susan and Linda were back.

"Kathleen!" They turned to me with anxious expressions. Linda's blue eyes were wide, and Susan's forehead creased in concern.

"Are you okay? How was the funeral?" Linda asked.

At the exact same time, Susan gestured to the sopping sheets. "What happened?"

I didn't have it in me to discuss the funeral, afraid the thought of my grandmother in the ground would send me tipping into tears again. I answered Susan's question instead. "Do you know Derrick, Company Nine?"

Both girls shook their heads.

"He's a good guy. I've talked to him some at the phone banks, though God knows we don't have much time to socialize beyond that. He's been sympathetic about everything that's been going on."

"And?"

"And his room was ransacked tonight, too." I told the girls about the note he'd found as well as the one I had.

"Wait." Susan's eyes snapped to mine. "He's Black?"

"Yes." I narrowed my eyes. Even with Susan's thick southern drawl, I tended to forget she came from Alabama. But if Virginia and D.C. were still segregationist, I couldn't imagine Alabama. I just hadn't thought Susan would fall into that camp. My hands went to my hips. "What of it?"

"Oh, God." To my shock, Susan began to laugh. "You didn't think I meant—oh, God, no. I'm just worried about you both. A ransacked room is one thing, but the wrath of a good ol' boy when it comes to 'race-mixing'?" She shook her head. "That could really be dangerous."

"We aren't 'mixing.'" I rolled my eyes. "We're just friends. And I reported it, anyway. I want to move on and get back to focusing on my work."

Linda shuddered. "But aren't you frightened?"

We were too busy to have the luxury of being frightened. "I reported it," I repeated. "The supervisor will take care of it."

Susan arched her eyebrows. "Coming from Birmingham, I can tell you that that is not always the case. Not when race is involved." She whistled. "White men get away with a lot."

"Still." I held on to my insistence that it was over. "No use worrying about it."

I pulled out *Reef Points*, ignoring Susan and Linda's shared look. I couldn't use my stripped bunk or sit in my chair, so I sat on the floor against the wall—the bulkhead—and began to read.

I didn't care where I had to sit. The men couldn't scare me away, and they couldn't stop me. It was the same as it had been with the messages in the bathroom.

I'd just work even harder. No matter the cost.

I swung my arms in wide circles on Monday morning to wake up my shoulders at PEP. I was tempted to let them swing wider, knock against Robert just to annoy him, but I wasn't a child.

And then I remembered the last conversation I'd had with him and Tom in the passageway. *You couldn't have been too upset about it, seeing as you spent the afternoon with another guy.* I'd thought Robert was bluffing, trying to make me look bad. But he'd meant Derrick. He'd seen me with Derrick by the phones, when I'd learned my grandmother had passed and he'd pressed me into a hug to comfort me.

Robert had been the one to ransack both our rooms.

It took everything in me not to lash out. And when we ran, I had to will myself to slow down, to resist the urge to fly past the boys and beat them. I wouldn't let Robert know he'd rattled me. And I wouldn't give Ensign Michael any reason to cite me for bilging my classmates when Robert was the one who deserved to be under fire.

I was called up to the supervisor's office that afternoon. Derrick was already there when I arrived, but we both kept our eyes in the boat and didn't make contact.

"Midshipman Kathleen Carre?"

"Sir, yes, sir." Even in this context, a thrill shot through me when I heard my name attached to the honorific.

"You and Midshipman Derrick Moore each filed a report regarding an act of hazing committed Sunday evening."

"Hazing, sir?"

"Midshipman Carre. You will not interrupt me. As our male plebes well know, hazing is a necessary part of plebe initiation. It strengthens our plebes and prepares them for the adversity they will face in duty. Particularly considering that you have been unable to provide us with any way to identify the perpetrators of the act, we are not moving forward with an investigation at this time."

I put up a hand. "Permission to speak?"

"Granted."

"Respectfully, sir, I believe that the note left in Midshipman Moore's room suggests that this act was something beyond hazing. The drawing of a noose in particular appeared to be a threat."

"That brings me to my next point," the supervisor said. "I was rather disturbed by the content of the notes you each turned in."

As he well should have been. Derrick's was a threat, and mine labeled him with an epithet that was completely inappropriate.

"The notes suggested fraternization between you two plebes."

My jaw dropped, though I stopped myself from objecting until allowed.

"You both know fraternization is forbidden, Midshipman Carre." He turned to me. "As one of the first women at the Naval Academy, you must not allow yourself to be distracted by men, however natural it may seem to do so."

The same rage that overtook me yesterday returned with

a vengeance, and I knew my face was turning red. But still I kept my mouth shut.

"And Midshipman Moore. You too should know better than to fraternize with a member of the opposite sex. Especially considering the difference in backgrounds between you."

Derrick seemed to be undergoing the same struggle as I. His dark skin didn't turn red, but his nostrils flared and his whole body tensed. He too stayed silent.

"That being said, we have no evidence that there has been any inappropriate fraternization between you two, particularly because we cannot assess the notes' credibility without knowing who wrote them. We therefore will also not be investigating or citing you for these allegations. Assuming"—he held up a finger—"that no further fraternization occurs."

Neither Derrick nor I responded, and the man shouted, "Do you understand me?"

"Sir, yes, sir!" Derrick and I chorused, though the words tasted sharp on my tongue.

The supervisor nodded. "You are dismissed."

Derrick and I stood shell-shocked in the passageway after the door slammed behind us. "I know who did it," I finally said. "Should we tell him?"

Derrick shook his head. "He's never going to be on our side." He didn't sound surprised, just resigned, and I thought about how many officials must have stood against him before because of his color. "If we give him a name, he'll use it as a credible witness for our 'fraternization.'"

I made a sound of frustration. "But there hasn't been any! I'd never risk my place here for a date." I thought of the way the supervisor had looked at me. *You must not allow yourself to be distracted by men, however natural it may seem.* "What kind of airheads does he think we all are?"

Derrick shook his head. "I gave up trying to understand why people think the ways they do long ago."

We gazed at each other sadly for a moment. "I guess this is goodbye again," I finally said. "Now that we've been threatened by our fellow plebes *and* by a superior."

"Good luck, Kathleen."

"Good luck to you too." I paused. "Use the fury to fuel you."

"I know," Derrick said. "That's what I've had to do all my life."

Chapter 17

— ❖ —

Emmaline Balakin

October 1918

Nellie met me early Monday morning before the book club was set to begin. "You're stuck with me. There are hardly any roads in the Argonne, so right now it's mostly just ambulances being allowed through. I'm off-duty."

I wasn't sure how much I believed her. She had dark circles under her eyes like she'd been driving back and forth, too. But she was here today, and for that I was grateful. I wasn't confident I could lead this book club on my own.

Together, we loaded the phonograph and a number of records into Nellie's motorcar, followed by some folding wooden chairs from the recreation hut and a selection of books the group might choose to read next.

"You look nervous," Nellie said as I climbed in beside her. "Do you need me to make you drive again?"

"Please, no," I laughed. "Not through the hospital. I'm afraid I'd plow right into one of the tents."

Nellie made a comically horrified face, her lips a perfect O.

"What about another day?" she asked more seriously. "I'll have to drive to Dijon on Sunday."

"Dijon?"

"It's not far," Nellie promised.

The thought of driving again sent tremors of fear down my spine—but then again, what didn't? Something about that journey to Paris had made me brave enough to create this book club. Maybe I needed to experience that again.

And if it meant spending more time with Nellie, all the better.

"Okay," I said. "Sunday."

She squealed and clapped her hands together. "You'll be as good as me in no time."

I rolled my eyes. "That seems a bit optimistic."

"Mabel was terrified too," Nellie countered, "when she started out. It doesn't scare her anymore." She laughed. "But she does still hate it."

Was that how Nellie saw me? I wondered. As another little sister? I found I didn't mind. Nellie made me laugh. She made this world seem manageable. And while I'd been an only child like Anne Shirley or Jane Eyre, I imagined that was what an elder sister was for.

Nellie and I picked Nicholas up on the way to book club. His infection had worsened and he'd lost clearance to walk, but still he insisted on coming. Nellie gave me a meaningful look—all wide eyes and tilted head—as I helped him into the car, but I shook my head. "We knew each other as kids," I hissed.

"He's not a kid now," Nellie whispered back.

It was true. Even listed slightly to one side due to his injury, Nicholas was tall and broad. It was hard to tell when he was leaning on me for support, but we were about the same height standing up. Perhaps he was an inch or two taller.

"Don't distract me," I told Nellie. "I'm nervous enough."

"Nervous?" This from Nicholas, who I prayed hadn't heard the whispered portion of our conversation.

"Very nervous. What if no one talks? What if they take one look at where we are and just . . . leave?"

"There are a lot of good men here," Nicholas promised. "They wouldn't just turn around like that. And Emmaline—you know us soldiers. We could talk to a rock."

I laughed. It was true. The hospital should have been a somber place, and often, it was. But it was also full of laughter and friendship and excitable chatter.

"And you prepared," Nellie reminded me. "Don't you have a list of questions?"

"Yes . . ."

"And don't you know how to read?"

"Yes." I let out a wisp of a laugh.

"So you'll be fine." She flashed me a smile just as we pulled up. "Now, last stop! Everybody off!"

Nellie opened the back to carry in the phonograph as I helped Nicholas out of the car. The bumpy ride must have exacerbated his pain, because he put more weight on me this time than he had before. His skin was warm even through the fabric of my dress, but still it made me shiver. He smelled like wood chips, and I could almost taste the sweat on his brow.

We staggered into the ward and were greeted by its men. Burt sprang up and helped Nicholas to an empty cot as Nellie ran to get a chair from the car.

"Sorry I can't help," Perlie called from his cot.

"Benefits to just losing a measly little ear," Burt said. He touched the gauze on the side of his head. "Least I can walk."

Thankfully, Perlie would be able to walk again too once he regained his strength and started his rehabilitation.

Burt, Nellie, and I arranged a circle of chairs near Joshua's and Perlie's cots, and Nicholas set the phonograph to play Billy Murray. Then we sat and waited. I couldn't fall back on my questions until the other men arrived, and though I'd spoken to these men plenty, I suddenly had no idea what to say. I sent Nellie a panicked look, and she sprang into action.

"Where are you all from?"

Perlie answered first. "My family and I are in Virginia."

Nellie brightened with interest. "I'm from outside Washington, D.C. Where in Virginia?"

"Caroline County. You probably haven't heard of it—very rural."

"Show her your kids," I spoke up. "They're precious."

Perlie passed the image of Tess and Annie around to many adoring oohs and aahs, and Nellie handed it back to him with a smile. "What about the rest of you?"

"I'm from New York City," Joshua said. "Not used to these quiet little towns."

Nellie laughed. "I wouldn't call Bazoilles quiet these days. Burt? What about you?"

"Atlanta, Georgia. But I was born and raised in Chicago."

Atlanta, New York City, Chicago. I'd never been to any of those places, and I said so.

"Where are you from?" Perlie asked.

"I'm from D.C. like Nellie. As is Nicholas." I gestured to him. "We knew each other growing up."

"War is strange in that way," Burt said. "A man I went to school with was in the cot beside me here for a week."

Edmund, the man I'd first told about the meeting yesterday in the recreation hut, burst into the room. He opened his mouth and then shut it again as he looked around, but he didn't turn to go. "Morning," he managed. His voice sounded strained, but I doubted anyone who wasn't used to his lighthearted nonchalance would notice.

Nellie shot to her feet. "I'm Nellie," she cried. "You can sit here!" She gestured to the seat next to her, and I stifled a laugh. She'd dared tease *me* for the way I'd helped Nicholas into the car?

As Edmund made his introductions, two more men inched into the room. They stood together by the door for a moment, arguing, before one started toward us. The other followed, and they sat together next to Nicholas.

"I'm Henry," said the first man. He had red hair and freckles that looked out of place with the circles under his eyes. "This here is Marvin."

The other man, his arms crossed, nodded shortly. But the awkward silence ended when a swell of men crowded through the entrance flap. I turned to see who I might recognize, and my heart sank as several of them—men I'd talked to and laughed with, even—took one look at Burt and the others and turned right back around.

Nicholas leaned in and whispered to me, "More of them are staying than leaving, Emmaline."

I couldn't look at him, too afraid tears would fall. While the men who stayed introduced themselves—a Jamaican immigrant by the name of Delroy, a man named Juan with a cast around his arm, a fellow from Nicholas's unit named Stephen, brothers named Michael and Matthew, and a slightly older man named Joe—I stayed silent. Only when Nicholas turned to me with an encouraging smile did I speak. "Welcome," I said. "Thank you all for being here today. Before we begin, are there any questions?"

Marvin and Joe sent sidelong glances at the colored men in the cots around us but didn't speak.

"No questions," Nellie said brightly. "Just lots of appreciation to you for setting this up, Emmaline!"

I smiled back, my shoulders releasing some of their tension. "Thank you, Nellie. I have a few discussion questions to get us started, but first—what did everyone think of *The Call of the Wild* as a whole?"

The men chorused their responses, mostly positive. I imagined that those who hadn't enjoyed *The Call of the Wild* hadn't shown up.

"Great. Now . . ." I glanced at Nicholas for support. "For a few more robust questions. I've heard several of you discussing this in the recreation hut, but here we have the space for a more measured discussion. Do you think that Buck's return to the wild represents Jack London's belief that we cannot override our nature? And what do *you* think about the nature-versus-nurture debate?"

Joe spoke first. "I have two sons, and even though I was traveling for most of their childhoods—I was a salesman—they're carbon copies of me. Everything from little mannerisms to attitude and belief. I didn't have to teach it to them—they just inherited it."

"I'm on the nature side, too," Stephen said. "Especially in war. It's all about Darwin's survival of the fittest."

Nicholas interjected. "I don't know about that. War is random. We've all seen better men than ourselves die. God knows I didn't deserve to live any more than the other men in my unit."

Several of the other men nodded, and Stephen inclined his head. "Perhaps not on an individual level, then. But think about Francis Galton and his eugenics. There are *groups* of people who will always be trouble. They have criminality in their blood, poverty in their blood, savagery. We saw it in *The Call of the Wild*. The Indians showed up in the last scene and tore everything apart."

My head swiveled toward Perlie. Was he going to say anything? If he didn't, should I? Sweat gathered under my arms, making me shiver in the cold of the unheated tent.

Perlie did finally speak, and when he did, he spoke in his usual gentle tones. "My wife is Cherokee," he said. "And she is neither— what did you say?—criminal nor savage."

Stephen sputtered. "I didn't mean any offense. There are exceptions, of course."

"I don't think there are." Burt frowned. "There can't be exceptions to something that was never a rule to begin with." He held up a hand when Stephen tried to speak again. "Forgive me, but I study genetics, heredity, and the myth of racial superiority at Morehouse. Galton was a wealthy man with high scores on intelligence tests who had every reason to claim that these qualities were innate. But he was a pseudoscientist who also believed that clean pets were miserable because they missed the stimulation of fleas, and that the least attractive women in the world came from Aberdeen specifically. And yet the United States has adopted his alleged scientific racism as a way to keep out immigrants and disenfranchise African Americans. It's not science or biology; it's politics."

"You sound like the political one here," Stephen snarled. "Almost to the point of criticizing the United States government. Need I remind you that's considered sedition in wartime?"

"Stephen." Nicholas held up a hand. "Calm down. This is meant to be a civil discussion."

Henry chuckled uncomfortably. "I don't even know who this Galton fellow is." He looked at Perlie. "Though I'm right sorry that this book made your wife look bad. It's a shame. I really liked the whole thing."

"There's another question." I jumped in before the men could tear each other to pieces. "Can we enjoy books that have problematic elements?" I couldn't help thinking of my own favorite, *Jane Eyre*, and the cruelty of Mr. Rochester's locking his first wife in the attic.

"I think we can," Burt said. "So long as we recognize and discuss them."

"What's the alternative?" Michael asked. "To ban the books?"

If I hadn't already been sweating, I would have started then. "The War Department actually has banned several writings," I said quietly. It wasn't a secret, but still the words felt clumsy on my tongue. Perhaps because I had two forbidden books stashed under my mattress at that very moment. "Pro-German books, socialist books, even pacifist books."

Matthew leaned forward. "*Under Fire* is one of them. I requested it with one of the forms they sent out, and they wrote back telling me that it was too savage a depiction of war."

"Isn't it about *this* war?" Michael asked.

"Yes!"

All the men guffawed, suddenly united. "What the hell do they think the book will tell us that we don't already know?"

I shook my head. "I have no idea. But at least those are things you *do* already know. They also ban books about things we're largely ignorant about. Pacifism, bolshevism . . ." I trailed off, realizing how my words might sound.

"And about things of which we are willfully ignorant," Burt added. "Racism. The classism inherent in war."

"Whoa." Stephen stood, his chair tipping back into the mud. "I don't have to listen to this. I'm going."

Panic bubbled inside me like failure. I had tried to bring the men together, and I was tearing them apart. I had tried to create a healthy discussion, and men were abandoning it. And—oh, God—Stephen could report me. Colonel Hodgson could search my room. He could find the books I had under the mattress.

Nicholas's hand reached across the space between us and grasped mine. Nellie's hand did the same on my other side.

"Does anyone else want to leave?" Nicholas's voice rang out across the ward, colder than I'd ever heard it.

Marvin glanced at Henry, who shrugged. Michael shook his head. Joe glanced between Nicholas and Burt but didn't move. And slowly I could breathe again, as the rest of the men stayed in their seats and looked toward me for guidance.

"Well." I forced a smile. "Perhaps it's time to pick our next book." I pulled out the sets I'd brought. "We're limited by the number of copies we have, so we only have a few choices. *Robinson Crusoe*, *Tarzan of the Apes*, several of Dickens's works, *Huckleberry Finn*, a book of Poe's stories, and *The Invisible Man*. Thoughts?"

The men quickly ruled out Edgar Allan Poe and H. G. Wells for being too dark. In the end, *Robinson Crusoe* won by a slim margin, and I passed out the copies.

"I don't need one," Henry said cheerfully. "Can't read a word. Marvin here will read it to me."

"Do you want me to bring you some reading primers?"

"That'd be real nice, Miss Balakin."

"Emmaline," I said. "Please."

Juan, who'd been quiet throughout the meeting, spoke up. "Do you have a Spanish-English dictionary? It might help me get through the book faster."

"Of course." I wrote down his ward number and Henry's and promised to get them what they needed. "When do you want to meet again?"

"One week from today?" Joshua suggested.

Nods all around.

"Great." I stood, my knees a bit shaky from the aftereffects of panic. "Thank you all for coming."

I collapsed back into my chair as the men filed out. Nicholas and Nellie both appeared at my side, but I shooed Nellie away. "Go chase Edmund," I said. "I'll still be here."

She squeezed me in a tight hug and ran off, leaving me with Nicholas, Burt, Perlie, and Joshua.

I turned first to Burt and Perlie. "I'm so sorry," I said. "I had no idea anyone would be so vicious."

Joshua let out a short laugh. "I did."

Shame flooded my face, and I stared down at my feet. My boots were muddy and already coming apart at the seams. I was a mess all around.

"Emmaline," Burt said. "You don't have to apologize. I'm the one who argued with that man." He smiled a bit. "I have to admit I even enjoyed it a bit. I miss the classroom."

I tried to laugh even though my eyes were blurring with tears. "Do you want to stop these meetings? Because if you want to end them, I'll do it. I'll tell everyone not to come back." It wouldn't be a pleasant conversation, but I owed it to my friends to stop what I'd started if they wanted me to.

"No." The three men spoke in unison. "It's like you were saying about banning the books. Censoring discussion isn't going to get us anywhere. We have to hear the ugly thoughts if we're going to combat them. And God knows they need to hear what we have to say."

"You did a good job, Emmaline." Nicholas's voice was low in my ear. "I'm proud of you. And your parents would be, too."

I took a deep breath and looked up. Nicholas's smooth ivory skin was so close, his lips a velvety red. Behind him was Burt, his body shifted forward like he too would come closer if I asked him to. Perlie and Joshua were both propped up on their elbows in bed.

Nellie ran in, face flushed, as I looked over them. "I'm here, too!"

I stood up and turned in a slow circle, my legs solidifying under me. This world was scarier than my world had been in D.C. But it was also a lot more important.

And here, I wasn't alone.

Chapter 18

—— ❖ ——

Kathleen Carre

July 1976

Once again, I couldn't sleep in this new world. Part of it was the still-damp sheet clinging to my legs; part of it, my still-simmering anger. Linda and Susan had tried to give me sympathy, but I'd pushed them away. Acknowledging my hurt and my fear would just make me weaker. And like Derrick and I had agreed, I needed to use this to make me strong.

The only person I wanted to talk to was my grandma, but she was gone.

But I still had something of her. I'd forgotten to look through Nana's box of mementos in the chaos of returning to Annapolis. Maybe her things could bring me some comfort right now, even if nothing else could.

I moved the framed photographs out of the way, knowing they were of me and my mother rather than Nana. Underneath them in the bottom corner of the box was a yellowing envelope, its corners flaking apart.

I checked the postmark, and the ink was smudged but still legible. It read AUG 1918, but was marked from France rather than D.C. Could it have been a letter my grandmother's family had never received? My heart beat faster. Might it explain why Nana had disappeared at the end of the war, as Mabel suggested?

No. My shoulders slumped as I checked the recipient address. The letter was for Vivian Winthrop in Washington, D.C. No one I had heard of.

Then again, I hadn't heard of Mabel Mayborn Johnson before this week.

I slid the letter from inside the envelope and jumped to the closing, expecting to see *Nellie* scrawled across the bottom in the handwriting I'd seen this morning. But it was another stranger's name at the bottom of the letter: *Private Nicholas Agrapov.*

Disappointed but still curious, I began to read. Nicholas described his training at a British naval base in France, and I shuddered. Plebe training was nothing compared to what Nicholas had seen.

Some of the lines had faded over the years, and I had to squint to read in the light of my flashlight. *I always imagined France as beautiful*, Nicholas had written, *but all I see is death.*

The sentiment stuck. I had no idea what Nicholas had gone through, but I still felt that I could understand his disappointment and confusion. I'd always seen the Naval Academy as a place of purpose and ambition, but that wasn't turning out how I'd planned, either.

But who was Nicholas? And why did Nana have his letter?

Before I could puzzle it out, a knock came at the door.

I was so immersed in Nicholas's war that I jumped. My room-mates were both still asleep; nothing ever woke them. I went to the door and pressed my ear to it. "Who is it?"

"Admiral," the voice came back. "Looking for Midshipman Kathleen Carre."

I glanced down at my regulation pajamas, a Navy T-shirt over Navy shorts, and hesitated. We weren't allowed to wear pajamas outside our rooms . . . but we also couldn't keep officers waiting.

I swung the door open. I wasn't fast enough to swing it back shut when I saw a cluster of masked midshipmen on the other side; they were ready for me. Two pairs of arms shot out and yanked me into the passageway, and a third wound a bandanna around my eyes.

I stifled a scream. I didn't want them thinking I was some helpless little thing. "What's going on?" I demanded.

"Just plebe initiation," one of the voices came back. It sounded like the same one who'd claimed to be the admiral; otherwise, it wasn't a voice I recognized.

My body relaxed a degree. If this was standard naval proce-dure, I could handle it. I wished I weren't in my pajamas, but that couldn't be helped. What could be was my reaction. I would laugh off whatever these upperclassmen put me through, be one of the boys. Robert's threatening notes had been more than hazing, but this? This, I could handle. Plebes had been hazed since the begin-ning of time.

"In here."

The boys grunted as they shoved open a door and pushed me

inside. The floor was tile on my bare feet, and I recognized the feel of it. We were in the bathroom.

My toes curled and my legs tensed. Could this be right?

"Close the door."

My head snapped up. I knew that voice. It was Robert's familiar snarl.

"Wait," I said. This couldn't be initiation. Robert was a plebe himself. "Robert?"

"She recognizes us," a voice hissed. There was an undercurrent of nerves beneath his voice, and I stiffened. It sounded like Tom.

"Doesn't matter." One of the boys wrenched off my bandanna, and there they were. Two strangers held me in place, and Robert stood with a smug smile and crossed arms. Worst of all was Tom next to him, his handsome face looking down in something like pity.

"Tom? I thought—I thought we were friends." The words sounded pathetic as soon as I said them.

Tom barked a laugh. "Maybe. Maybe we were friends, until you chose that ape over me." The nervousness in his voice was gone.

Robert joined in. "No one wants you here. And no one wants those monkeys around here, either."

"It's too late with them," one of the strangers said. "JFK and Johnson gave them everything they wanted a while ago. But you gals?"

Robert's lips stretched into an eerie smile. "We still have time to scare you away."

"Away from the academy," Tom said.

I flinched, and Tom laughed. He brushed my jawbone lightly

with a finger. "I could call him much worse, Kathleen. But I'm a gentleman. I won't use that language in front of a lady. You see, Kathleen . . . you're the prettiest girl in the class. And you're going to let a colored man appreciate you, rather than me?"

"I don't think so," one of the boys holding my arms snarled. He pulled me into him. "It's our turn."

I twisted my wrists to break free, then lurched forward so my shoulders slipped from their grasp. I leapt sideways toward the door.

All four boys were on me before I could blink. They fell on me with urgency and without care, and I collapsed to the ground. My knees bruised on the cold tile, and one of the boys thrust the back of my head down so my forehead hit, too. I tried to reach back and tug at my short pajama bottoms, but one of the men slapped my hand back.

Tom's voice appeared close to my ear. "You. Humiliated. Me," he said slowly. Like I was stupid, like I couldn't understand if he didn't separate each word with a pause as heavy as his cronies' hands on my skin. "I told the boys I had the prettiest girl in the class coming out with me, and then she didn't. Show. Up."

"You think she's the prettiest girl in the class?" One of the other boys snickered. "I think her face is far too serious."

"How 'bout this part of her?" Robert smacked my backside.

I screamed and wrenched sideways, but I couldn't break free. Their weight was on me. I didn't know if I'd ever forget that weight. "Anyway," Tom continued. Like nothing was the matter. "We thought you'd appreciate this courtesy."

"Courtesy?" My breath created a cloud of fog on the cold tile.

"A warning, so to speak."

Robert jumped in. "Girls don't belong here."

"I belong here," I managed. "More than any of you."

Tom yanked my hair, and my neck bent backward at a harrowing angle. I gritted my teeth and refused to scream. "I . . . belong . . . here."

Tom let my hair go, and my head fell forward and slammed against the tile again. The bump reverberated through my skull, and tears threatened behind my eyes.

"Take this as a warning," Tom said. "You humiliated me. And we'll keep humiliating you until you leave here for good."

Suddenly, the weight on my back lifted. Half of me feared it was a trick, but I couldn't help my body's reacting. I jumped up, swaying and disoriented. No one touched me.

Knees pulsing, I ran for the door. I nearly slammed into it, but still no one was stopping me.

"Just one more thing."

I turned around, my hand on the knob.

Robert stood with his arms crossed. Nonchalant. "You mention this to anyone. *Anyone.* And that monkey you were with gets worse."

I fled before I could hear another word. I ran down the passageway and into the women's head, slamming the door behind me and locking myself into a stall. I sank to the deck and put my head between my knees.

Breathe, Kathleen. I forced myself to consider my options. I could report the men, but look how badly that had turned out already. And Robert had threatened Derrick if I reported.

Plus, that was exactly what they would expect me to do. I could fight my own battles.

Option two, I could get my revenge. I could—no. I stopped myself from going down that route. However tempting it seemed,

I knew it would backfire. I didn't want to risk my spot here for anything. Not even for justice, or safety.

So my only solution seemed to be to continue on. Prove myself. I'd need to work so hard that I was too exhausted to feel Robert's hands on my skin or the taste of bile in my throat, study *Reef Points* until there was no room left in my brain to remember Tom's threats.

A touch on my shoulder woke me up the next morning, and I leapt out of bed with my arms raised.

"Hey!" Linda came into focus as she backed away. "Sorry! I just didn't want you to be late."

Susan chuckled from across the room. "The judo training stuck, huh?"

I lowered my hands, feeling foolish. While the boys learned boxing and wrestling, our course was on judo and karate.

"Sorry," I muttered. "Bad dream."

Mornings before PEP were rushed, and I was grateful that my roommates didn't have time to pry further.

I yanked on my exercise clothes and brushed my teeth, scrubbing them with ill-disguised fury. I was mad at Tom and Robert and their cronies. But I was even madder at myself, for letting it get to me. I hadn't overslept in years.

Still, I managed to race behind Linda and Susan to PEP, grateful for their presence. I wanted to be strong enough to stand next to Tom in my usual spot, but I couldn't do it. I was afraid my body would betray me if I neared him—afraid my legs would buckle and my breath would stop and my stomach would rebel.

Nana's words came back to me now in a flash of pain. *It's hard to be a woman in a world designed for men*, she'd said.

What would she counsel me to do now? I wondered. Yes, she had told me there were other ways to serve my country and other routes to take. But she hadn't quit when she was in the war, and actions spoke louder than words. Nana had persevered, and she would want me to as well. I knew it.

So I did my crunches and my push-ups and my jumping jacks. I did my sprints and my distance run and my stretches.

But when I returned upstairs to shower, I froze. The doors to a plebe's room could only be locked after taps; even getting to close the door was a privilege reserved for showering. But a closed door didn't seem enough now. Not after Robert had ransacked my room and he and his goons had assaulted me in the bathroom. They could burst in at any moment, and I'd never know it with the sound of the water.

I backed out of the marble shower. Bancroft had no air conditioning, and it was nearly as hot inside as it had been out. I needed a shower desperately.

But I couldn't take one. I couldn't face the idea of stripping off my clothes and showering, naked, with the door unlocked behind me.

I bent over the sink and splashed my face, then lathered my palms with soap and scrubbed under my armpits and between the crevices of my toes. It would have to do for today. But I couldn't make this a habit. By tomorrow, I swore to myself, I'd be able to shower again. At the very least to get the feel of the men's grimy fingers off my skin.

I couldn't eat at breakfast. My stomach growled, but I couldn't bear the thought of food sliding down my throat. I didn't want to put anything into my body that didn't have to be there. I didn't want to touch anything to my lips, my tongue.

I sipped instead at my water, then forced down some orange juice. I saw Linda throw a questioning glance my way from her spot at the next table, but she couldn't ask me if I was all right. No conversation allowed. For that small mercy, I was grateful. Telling the whole sordid tale sounded like the same painful exposure the assault itself had been. I couldn't let anyone else bear witness to my shame or my weakness. And they had threatened Derrick, after all. Said he would get worse if I told.

So I wouldn't tell my roommates, and I wouldn't report the boys this time. I would show them I was here to stay—no matter what—if it was the last thing I did.

Chapter 19

— ❖ —

Emmaline Balakin

October 1918

After the book club meeting, Nellie drove Nicholas and me back to the recreation hut. We both tried to convince him to return to his ward for some much-needed rest—though I was rather halfhearted in my protests—but he refused. He wanted to see the library, and I had to admit to myself that I wanted to show it to him too.

Nellie helped us move the chairs, the phonograph, and the unselected books inside. Then she bade me farewell with a hug, promising to tell me all about her conversation with Edmund at our driving lesson together over the weekend.

Once she was gone, I helped Nicholas through the crowds of people in the hut to the back wall where the shelves stood. "It's not much," I said. "But I sorted it all and cataloged everything, so everyone should be able to quickly find what they're looking for." I showed him each section, pulling out the reading primer for Henry and the Spanish-English dictionary for Juan as I did so.

"It might not look like much to you," Nicholas said, "but to us? This is more escape than we've had in months."

I'd only been here a few weeks, and already it felt like a lifetime. I couldn't imagine months. "When did you get to Bazoilles?"

"September twenty-seventh. I only lasted a day once the battle started in Avocourt." He said it as if it were a personal failing. "I can't imagine why they think a book or a pamphlet would turn us into pacifists, because I don't think anyone who has seen modern warfare could be anything else."

I didn't know what to say, but I knew how to listen. "Does it help to talk about it?"

Though he didn't answer yes or no, he did begin to talk. "My best friend in the trenches was a man named Roy. We went through training together, bunked together on the transport over, and went into battle for the first time side by side at Avocourt. We were there the second week of September before the fighting began in earnest, but still there were German patrols to contend with. He never slept well, and we'd often talk late into the night. It seemed as if no matter what time I opened my eyes, he was awake beside me."

Nicholas stopped, swallowed, and started back up. "The night before I was injured, I woke up. I don't know what time it was, just that it was dark. But it was always dark in the trenches. I asked Roy a question, expecting one of his usual sarcastic answers, and heard nothing."

I involuntarily raised a hand to my mouth. "Oh, no."

"I reached over to see if maybe he was asleep for once. And—" Nicholas's voice caught. "I reached right into his skull."

"No," I gasped. "Oh, Nicholas."

"German patrols had shot him while I lay there, asleep. And I hadn't even woken up."

"You know you couldn't have stopped it . . ."

"Maybe, maybe not. But I do know that it could have easily been me," Nicholas said. "It isn't as if things were all fine before that," he said. "War shows you right away what humanity is capable of. But I was coping best I could until that night. And now, stranded here without the ability to do anything more for men like Roy, I feel as if I'm losing all hope."

So many men had. There were soldiers in the wards who didn't speak at all, soldiers who wept or screamed at every sound. And we didn't get sent the worst of the neuropsychiatric cases; they went to Base Hospital 79 next door. I couldn't imagine the horrors they relived.

But Nicholas. He seemed so levelheaded and calm. Serious, certainly. Even sad sometimes. But he didn't seem tortured.

"I would never have guessed," I said. "You hide it so well."

"Yes. We're opposites in that way, aren't we?" He smiled a strange, bitter smile. "I seem calm on the surface, but I'm barely staying afloat underneath. Whereas you, Emmaline, second-guess your every move and walk around like a mouse waiting for a cat— yet you have an iron will beneath it all."

I felt my body heat. "I don't think I do," I admitted. "I've spent the majority of my life afraid to do anything remotely dangerous or even interesting. Even just *living* still seems terrifying at times."

It was a difficult admission to make, but Nicholas laughed. "Nothing dangerous? Look at you, Emmaline." He spread his arms.

"Yes," I said, "but this isn't like me."

"This *is* you," he said. "Don't you remember? Christmas dinner when you were six, and you took the very last piece of cake out to a beggar on the street even when your father told you it might be dangerous?"

"That couldn't have been me," I said. "I always listened to my parents."

"It *was* you. Your father gave you permission after you told him that beggars were beggars by circumstance, not by nature. That the man outside was no more likely to be dangerous than your schoolteacher or"—Nicholas laughed—"my mother."

I covered my mouth. "I did not say that."

"You did. Your father was proud of you. And I was awed. I'd thought it was nice of me to share that last slice with *you*. But I wasn't nearly so brave or generous as to take it outside to the streets."

I sat frozen. I'd thought I remembered that Christmas so clearly. I remembered eight-year-old Nicholas and his mop of curly brown hair, and I'd treasured his kindness in sharing his cake with me.

But I hadn't remembered what I myself had done with it.

"Nicholas," I said fervently. "You're brave, too. Do you know what Nellie told me my first day here? She said that this is *war*. That we're all terrified, because we're human. That's why Roy's death destroyed you, Nicholas—because you're human. You feel. But the fact that you've gone on anyway means you're braver than any monster who doesn't feel the pain or terror."

Nicholas reached forward and brushed my hand with his. "Thank you, Emmaline."

I stiffened in shock. Nicholas's touch wasn't the soft, comforting touch of a childhood friend; it sparked like the artillery shells bursting in the air over the Argonne. Hot and terrifying and somehow beautiful all at once.

"My apologies." Nicholas pulled back. "I didn't mean—"

I shook my head, at a loss for words. They'd always come so much easier in writing anyway. Conversation was not my strong suit, and this conversation had laid us both bare.

Nicholas's eyes strayed like he was casting around for another topic of conversation. "So what would our brave Emmaline do if she came across one of the War Department's forbidden books?" he asked teasingly, obviously trying to lighten the mood.

But this line of questioning wouldn't lighten anything. "Actually . . ." I hesitated. A man on the other side of the room was hammering out a ragtime tune on the piano, and the sound of the group's laughter and conversations was a steady roar. But still I whispered and leaned closer to Nicholas, close enough that I could feel his breath on my skin. "I've come across two."

Nicholas's eyebrows shot up. "And did you destroy them?"

I shook my head slowly.

"Where are they?" Nicholas's voice rivaled mine in quiet.

I cupped my hands around my lips and mouthed the words. *Under my mattress.*

Nicholas recoiled, and my breath came out in a disappointed gust. Nicholas was open-minded, and he loved books like I did. But what I was doing could be considered treason. Of course he was horrified. "You think it's wrong," I said.

"No, actually. I don't think it's wrong. I think it's dangerous."

I bit my lip.

"America's not perfect, but we've had opportunities here that we never would have had in Russia. Despite its flaws, I am loyal to this country. And directly disobeying an order from the War Department—that's not loyal, Emmaline. It's treasonous."

"No." I spoke louder than I intended to. "At least, not intentionally. Shouldn't loyalty to a country mean you want it to be the best it can be? Sometimes that means learning what's wrong. Learning what's wrong so it can change."

"Yes," Nicholas said. "Theoretically. But no one's learning anything when the books are hidden. It's an unnecessary risk."

I deflated. "It just seems wrong to burn them. Wouldn't it be better to just set them aside for the duration of the war? Take them out again when we're allowed?"

"Maybe. But we don't make the rules."

That was something my father had said a lot: "We don't make the rules." But Mama had always corrected him. I echoed her now.

"We don't make the rules," I said, "but with enough hope, we can challenge them."

Nicholas exhaled slowly. "I find it hard to hope for much of anything these days. But still." He looked at me. "I'd like to think you're right."

After spending days with Nicholas's words echoing in my head—*I find it hard to hope for much of anything*—I woke up Sunday eager to spend the morning with Nellie on the way to Dijon. We left when the skies were still dark, but Nellie was already bubbling over with energy. "Good morning, Emmaline! Ready to drive?"

I blinked. "Here?"

"No." She grinned. "I'll get us out of Bazoilles, then you can drive the stretch before it gets busy again."

"Thank you." Learning to drive was one thing, but doing it surrounded by wounded men who couldn't run for their lives if I forgot how to brake was an entirely different one.

Nellie told me about Dijon as we drove. It was the site of another American base hospital as well as the French Air Force base, though she didn't specify which of the two locations was her target. I was happier that way. I could pretend we were just two friends—sisters, even—out for a driving lesson. Far preferable to two army volunteers buffeted by the winds of war.

When we got out of Bazoilles, Nellie stopped the car so we could switch seats. I still remembered everything Nellie had taught me before, but I hesitated. "Tell me again?"

She walked me through the moves, and then I was driving. We were headed south today, in the direction opposite the fighting, and for that I was grateful. But still we weren't far enough from the action that the country didn't bear its scars.

As my time behind the wheel went up and I felt more and more comfortable—or at least, less and less *un*comfortable—I found myself able to talk to Nellie. There was something about being in the driver's seat that made honesty easier—a lack of eye contact, perhaps. We both talked about our childhoods and our families; I admitted that I'd often been teased for my shy, bookish ways and even that I felt like I'd failed to live up to what my mother would have wanted for me. Nellie countered with the obvious point that I was here now, and I couldn't argue with that.

She told me about her gentle, kindhearted father, her little sister Mabel, and her mother. She laughed as she told me that her mother had no interest in her husband's mechanic business and perhaps wished Nellie didn't, either.

We were almost to Dijon when I saw the feather. It was a shocking, vibrant orange against the damp gray earth, and I realized as we got closer that it had a circle of black at the tip. It looked exactly like I'd always imagined the feathers of the zhar-ptica, the firebird of Slavic legend.

I slammed my foot into the brake pedal, and the car sputtered to a stop.

"Emmaline? What are you doing?"

"I just need—" I pointed as I scrambled down from my seat and picked my way through the mud to the feather. "This."

"Why?" Nellie's head was cocked to one side in confusion, though I didn't read judgment in her eyes.

"It looks like the feather of a zhar-ptica."

"More like the feather of a hoopoe bird," Nellie said. "But continue."

"The zhar-ptica is a mystical creature in Russian folklore. Seeing one means that a difficult journey is coming—but the stories always turn out happy in the end. Like in *The Hunchbacked Horse*, where the peasant Ivan lives happily ever after with the Czar-Maid." Ironically, *The Hunchbacked Horse* had been banned for many years for its satirical portrayal of feudalism and for casting the czar as cruel and foolish.

"So you want us to have a difficult journey?" Nellie's eyes sparkled. She was teasing me.

"We've already had a difficult journey," I said. "I want to have a happy ending."

Most of all, I wanted to give Nicholas the feather. He would know the legend of the firebird, and the feather would signify hope to him as much as it did to me.

I cast Nellie a shy glance. "It's not for me," I admitted. "It's for one of the soldiers."

"Nicholas!" Nellie clapped her hands, and I blushed.

"Yes. Like I said, we—"

"Knew each other as kids," Nellie finished with a smirk. "I know. But the way you look at each other, that can't be the whole story."

I shrugged even as my heart beat faster in my chest. "I didn't want it to be," I confessed. "I definitely had hopes as a girl. And I think he might have felt the same way once upon a time." I told Nellie about the night Nicholas had waited for me under the lamp-post. "But it doesn't matter anymore. He's courting someone else." I tried to sound unbothered, but my voice quivered. "In D.C."

I braced myself for Nellie's sympathy, but she raised her eyebrows. "Yet you got him this symbolic feather?"

Her skepticism pulled a laugh out of me. "Yes. But just as a family friend would."

"Mm-hmm."

I wanted to nod, but Nellie's gaze was full of mirth. "Fine," I relented. "Yes. I wish we could be more than 'friends,' because there's something special about him. Better, even: something special about *us*. But he's seeing another woman, and that's that."

Feeling terribly exposed, I rushed to turn the attention to Nellie. "Now, why don't you tell me about Edmund? You looked pretty friendly after book club."

I tucked the feather carefully into my dress as she began to talk, then shifted the car back into gear. When nothing happened, I looked at Nellie with wide eyes. "Oh, no. What have I done?"

"Oh, don't get in a flap about it." She waved a hand. "The wheels are just mired in the mud. Happens all the time here in this weather." She hopped out of the car, procured a plank of wood from the back, and went to work using it as a lever underneath the back right wheel.

"Can I help?"

"Yes," she called back. "Shift gears for me."

I strained to listen to her directions over the ever-present buzzing of planes and distant artillery. But as she yelled instructions, the interference got louder. It sounded like bees or radio static, but I'd been here long enough to know what it meant: airplanes.

I looked up. There were two visible over the tree line, both headed in our direction. "Nellie?" I heard the panic in my own voice. "Are those French planes?" We were close to Dijon's airfield, weren't we?

"No." She dove into the passenger seat beside me, hunched forward, and put her arms over her head. "German."

The Germans were getting desperate. The fighting had begun again in earnest after President Wilson and the other Allied leaders had rejected Germany's halfhearted call for peace last week, and tensions were high.

I glanced up one more time, ready to copy Nellie's protective motions, and screamed. "Nellie, look!" Something was coming down from the planes, something white and black and swirling.

She cupped her hand around her eyes and looked up. "Those don't look like bombs. Look how they're falling. Slowly, and in a spiraling pattern. They aren't dropping straight down."

I was too terrified to respond. What could I say, anyway? I knew nothing about bombs. So we both watched as the mass began to spread out, tiny pinpricks of white floating in every possible direction.

"They're not bombs." Nellie's voice broke with relief.

"Not bombs," I echoed, too stunned to say anything else and hoping I would come to believe the words the more times I heard them. But what were the things falling, if not bombs? Were they hand grenades, or capsules full of poison gas?

"Nellie!" I reached out and grabbed her hand as I recognized the falling objects. "They're papers!"

"What?"

"They're papers! Pamphlets or flyers, maybe. Look at how they're bobbing with the wind."

Nellie squinted. "My God." She let out a short, surprised bark. "You're right."

The relief bubbled up from my belly and spilled out in a laugh. Nellie followed suit, and we sat together in the automobile and laughed so hard we cried.

"I thought we were going to die." My words came out on ragged exhalations that could have been giggles or sobs or something in between.

"I did, too."

Once our hysterics subsided, we sat and breathed for God knows how long. Then, finally, Nellie spoke. "We should go."

"Oh. Yes."

I moved to get out of the driver's seat, but Nellie reached out to stop me. "You were doing great," she said.

"Please, no." I was too rattled to trust my body or my mind.

"If you stop now, the fear will grow. You'll never drive again."

I wanted to say I didn't care if I ever drove again. That all I wanted was a safe bed as far from the front as I could get. D.C. Alaska. Antarctica.

But Nellie believed I could do this. I knew Nicholas would believe it, too. He'd called me brave, said I had an iron will. I wasn't going to just let it bend now, was I?

My two closest friends believed I was brave. The only person left to convince was myself. So with a sigh, I pressed the leftmost pedal to shift the car into gear. We continued on in silence, me as stiff and focused at the wheel as I'd been my first time. Every sound made me flinch, and the car jerked and rattled along with my abrupt movements.

Dijon, when we arrived, was like the opposite of Paris. On one side was a quaint square with an old abbey, a fountain, and a statue; on the other, a camouflage factory for the war. Nellie directed me through the streets, which were thankfully devoid of people to hit, and straight through to the airfield. "Wait here."

I was all too happy to comply. I needed to stretch my calves and my toes, so I stepped out of the car and directly onto a sheet of paper lying in the dirty street. When I leaned over to pick it up, I saw that I'd left a muddy footprint on the back of the sheet, and that the front was covered in blocky, typewritten text. It was clean and unwrinkled aside from the corner I'd marked, and I realized with a start that it must have been one of the papers dropped from the German planes. Propaganda.

I was in public, and so I told myself to drop the sheet of paper. I couldn't be seen reading German propaganda in a little French town that had mobilized all its citizens for the war effort.

But my fingers stayed clenched around the paper.

Abandoning my desire to stretch my aching legs, I clambered back into the car and bent my head over the paper.

TO THE COLORED SOLDIERS OF
THE UNITED STATES ARMY.

I thought immediately of Burt, Perlie, and Joshua and gritted my teeth. Surely the Germans wouldn't dare criticize our country for allowing its Black citizens to serve, or for treating them at our base hospitals alongside the other soldiers?

But the first paragraph went in an entirely different direction.

Can you get into a restaurant where white people dine? Can you get a seat in a theater where white people sit? Can you get a seat or a berth in a railroad car, or can you even ride in the South in the same streetcar with the white people? And how about the law? Is lynching and the most horrible crimes connected therewith a lawful proceeding in a democratic country? Now all this is entirely different in Germany, where they do like colored people; where they treat them as gentlemen and as white men, and quite a number of colored people have fine positions in business in Berlin and other German cities.

Treating them as white men seemed an odd turn of phrase. I was certain that Burt, who was so proud to teach at Morehouse, had no interest in being viewed as white.

Come over and see for yourself. Let those do the fighting who make the profit out of this war. Don't allow them to use you as cannon fodder. To carry a gun in this service is not an honor but a shame. Throw it away and come over to the German lines. You will find friends who will help you.

Nellie reappeared in my field of vision before I could process what I'd read, and I quickly crumpled the paper into a ball and tried to hide it in my lap. But Nellie, ever-watchful, scrunched her brow. "What is that?"

I handed it over silently and watched as she read it. Her face grew redder the longer she gazed upon the Germans' words, and I feared her head would burst.

"'To carry a gun in this service is not an honor but a shame,'" she finally cried. "What rubbish! The only shameful thing is this propaganda. Look." She stabbed at the paper with a finger. "'Come over to the German lines.' They're trying to steal our soldiers out from under us!"

I was as outraged as Nellie. I'd come to France to support my country—the same country that, as Nicholas had pointed out, had given me so much more than Russia would have. And I had nothing but disdain for those who refused to serve as patriots in whatever way they could—for women like Vivian, who had lavish weddings and sent their men off to play golf instead of off to war.

But still, the Germans had their facts right. In D.C., colored people and whites could not share recreational facilities or schools. They could ride on the same streetcars, but I knew that just miles away in Virginia, that too was forbidden. And it was true that several colored men had been lynched in neighboring Maryland and Virginia even in my lifetime.

"How awful." Nellie shuddered. "At least it wasn't a bomb."

But I remembered what I'd said to Nicholas when he'd

worried that artillery was mightier than the pen. Words could be more effective and more dangerous than any weapon.

And so, again, I tried to unfurl my fingers and let the paper fly away into the wind. But my curiosity wouldn't let me. I wanted to read the flyer again, untangle the truth and the lies it carried. And so I thrust the sheet into my pocket as Nellie and I switched seats and she fiddled with the emergency brake and the pedals. "You did a dilly of a job driving today," Nellie told me.

"Thank you." I snuck a look at her, hoping she knew I wasn't thanking her just for the compliment but also for encouraging me to drive past the fear. It hadn't been easy, but I was glad I'd done it.

I thumbed the feather I still had tucked into my blouse, and I smiled.

Hope.

Chapter 20

Kathleen Carre

July 1976

It wasn't easy, but I forced myself to remove my shorts and shirt and step into the shower the second morning after the ambush. The cold water felt refreshing on my skin, and I tipped my head back and imagined it could wash away the memory of what had happened.

But when our squadron sat down for morning chow, I found that I still couldn't stomach my eggs, bacon, or French toast. I picked at the strawberries and grapes and forced down my orange juice, but the eggs felt too slimy, the bacon too greasy, and the French toast too gooey.

When I stood at the end of morning chow, my legs trembled

and my vision momentarily faltered, but I kept my gaze forward and my expression neutral. I wouldn't show my weakness to my squad. Especially to Tom or Robert, whose bodies I was now hyperaware of in every room I entered.

I positioned myself as far away from both of them as I could at our morning round of rifle practice. I was becoming accustomed to the recoil of the gun, and I didn't startle like Pat, who stood beside me. He cursed once, and I glanced over to see him cradling his cheekbone. "Forgot to tuck it under my arm," he said sheepishly. "Recoiled up and smacked me in the face."

I tried to look sympathetic, but I was reluctant to engage. After Tom's reversal in attitude toward me, I wasn't sure I could trust any of the men in my company.

We practiced at our usual twenty-five feet from the targets, but after the first several minutes we were instructed to shoot from a kneeling position. I gritted my teeth as I lowered my knees to the ground, hating the feel of it digging into my skin. I made the mistake of glancing up and meeting Robert's eye; he smirked and shimmied his backside. A visceral reminder, as if I'd needed one, of what they'd done to me when I'd knelt on the floor of the bathroom.

I breathed in and out, forcing myself to stay calm. Not least because I had a rifle in my hand.

My fingers ached by the time we made it to noon chow, and I pushed the food around on my plate. We had gray space in the afternoon, which meant it was up to our cadre to decide how we'd spend our time. Last week, it had been uniform races, and before that, calling out answers to rates.

Today was the worst yet. The detailer ordered us to stand at attention in the passageway. Straight spine, shoulders back, toes pointed out, chin up, and eyes straight forward. Arms at our sides with thumb and index finger meeting.

And then he simply paced back and forth, silently watching, as the minutes ticked by and our bodies grew more and more desperate for movement. I wanted to pedal my feet and massage my heels, roll my shoulders in my sockets. After what I estimated as a half hour of standing, my calves had started to ache and the muscles in my back pulsed. But worse than the physical discomfort was the mental downtime. I'd relied on the constant rigor of the academy to keep my mind off my pain—my grief at losing Nana, the fear and fury from Tom and Robert's assault. I'd done just one more push-up, memorized one more rate. Anything to keep from being alone with my thoughts.

But now there was nothing else to do.

I tried to run through my rates in my head. A for Alpha, B for Bravo, C for Charlie. But the NATO alphabet was too easy to keep my mind occupied, and so I shifted into reciting the chain of command. President Gerald Ford, Vice President Nelson Rockefeller, Secretary of Defense Donald Rumsfeld, Secretary of the Navy J. William Middendorf. I went all the way down to the executive officer, listing the name of each man—of course they were all men—in my head.

Silently, I recited the six articles from the Code of Conduct, the eleven general orders of a sentry, the Honor Concept word for word.

But it wasn't enough. Robert stood across from me in the hallway, and I wasn't permitted to take my eyes off him. No matter what I tried to think about, his presence sent an undercurrent of fear throughout my body.

Ensign Michael stopped in front of me. "Midshipman Carre!"

"Sir, yes, sir!"

"Why are you moving?"

Moving? I realized that my legs, weak from hunger, were trembling. I locked out my knees in an effort to stop them, even though I knew it would make me light-headed in the long run. "No excuse, sir!"

Ensign Michael turned around and bellowed at the rest of the squadron. "Midshipman Carre can't stand still! Twenty push-ups, now!"

Everyone dropped to the floor and complied, including me. I funneled all my frustration into my trembling arms. Sure, any plebe who'd moved would have been treated the same way. But they could have laughed it off later. For me, it would serve as proof that girls didn't belong here.

Of course, it didn't matter that I never would have been shaking in the first place had the men not terrorized me.

That evening, I wanted to tumble into bed and never wake up. Instead, I forced myself to call Mabel. She'd agreed to stop by Nana's for the estate sale tomorrow to make sure everything went smoothly, and I wanted to make sure she was still planning on doing so. I'd attend myself if I were allowed to leave the Yard, but the funeral had been my only allowance. The sale was the last thing on my mind right now, anyway.

I slumped against the wall as the phone rang.

"Kathleen!" Mabel's warm voice flooded the line, and she sounded like she was standing right there with me. "You must have gotten my package!"

I blinked. "Package?"

"I sent you a care package. Nuts, raisins, those space food energy bars. You're allowed all that, right?"

"Yes," I said, surprised at myself for being so overcome. This was the sort of the thing Nana would have done, but I never expected someone to be around to do it after she was gone. "Thank you. I'll go down and get it after we hang up."

"Well. Why were you calling, then?"

For a moment, I forgot. I hadn't been calling to tell her about the boys' attack, had I, or their rummaging through my things and threatening me with that note?

No. Of course not. I was calling about the estate sale, and Mabel assured me she still planned to go when I said as much. I thanked her and then lingered on the line in stilted silence.

"Is there something else?"

"No."

"Are you certain?" Mabel's voice was frayed with nerves. "I imagine the Naval Academy isn't an easy place to be."

Her words were so similar to Nana's that I startled. Was that genetic, I wondered, or merely generational?

"I'm okay," I said quietly. But still I didn't hang up.

Mabel sighed. "Okay," she said. "But Kathleen, just know that by the time you're my age, you don't care what people think of you or what stories they tell. If you have something weighing you down, share it with someone. Maybe with me, maybe with some other girls there. But don't carry it alone."

I thought of Mabel losing Nellie so young, never having her own children. Who had she gone to her whole life?

"Kathleen? Are you listening? Are there girls at the academy you can talk to, girls who would understand whatever it is you're going through?"

"You don't understand," I said. "We can't show any weakness here."

"Sharing your story is never a weakness, Kathleen. When we realize we aren't alone, we grow so much stronger."

Nana had been solitary; she never shared her problems or even talked about them.

But she'd abandoned a loving sister. A sister who'd spent her whole life grieving someone who wasn't dead. Why? And was that the example I wanted to follow?

"Okay." I swallowed. "I suppose I could talk to my roommates."

"That's a good girl."

The boy behind me tapped my shoulder. "I was really hoping I could call home . . ."

"Right," I said. "Of course. I have to go, Mabel. But thank you so much." The words were ones I wasn't used to saying recently.

"Of course, dear. Take care of yourself."

"You, too."

I hung up the phone. If I ran, I'd have enough time to get to the mailroom downstairs and find Mabel's package.

I made it to the wall of lockers and twisted my key in my PO box, surprised to see not just one package crammed inside but also a large envelope.

The envelope was from Mrs. Peregrine and carried an assortment of letters forwarded from Nana's. Most of them were junk mail. One was a sympathy card from an old friend of Nana's, and another a personal invitation to a volunteer event. I was getting ready to throw the whole lot in the trash when the address on the last envelope stopped me short.

Surely I was losing my mind. It was the stress or the hunger or the fatigue or—something. I had to be wrong.

I closed my eyes and then checked the address again—and yes. It was addressed to Nicholas Agrapov, but his address was no longer an APO box in France. Now it was a townhouse in Lincoln Park, right on the eastern border of D.C.

But that was his name there, as clear as any officer's command. Nicholas Agrapov.

And he'd returned something my nana had sent him.

Chapter 21

— ❖ —

Emmaline Balakin

October 1918

Men were flooding into the recreation hut by the time Nellie and I returned to Bazoilles-sur-Meuse in the early afternoon. Nellie dropped me off to staff the library and returned to Base Hospital 18, where she was going to take a nap, then start off tonight on another journey.

The men in the recreation hut greeted me with their characteristic energy. They were full of news as they jostled past each other for the card table and bookshelf and piano. There was talk of Germany retreating from Belgium and out of the Argonne, of British occupation in Turkistan and Belgium, and of the bolsheviks' claim that the Red Terror had concluded. But no one believed Lenin, and no one knew if we could hope for another German bid for peace.

I fingered the feather in my pocket as I hurried through the mud to Nicholas's ward and tried to tell myself that, God willing, the war would end. And soon.

Nicholas brightened when he saw me. "Emmaline!"

I couldn't help but wonder if Nicholas would smile as broadly for another librarian, were there one, or whether that look was reserved for me. Then I remembered Vivian and shook my head. The relationship between us was based on a shared childhood. Nothing more. And the fact that I even found myself wanting it to be something different was too frightening to explore.

"I brought you something," I said abruptly, trying to turn off the spigot in my brain. "Something small."

Nicholas's smile grew even bigger, and I wondered if I was overreacting to the story he'd told. He didn't seem like a man with no hope.

But I remembered what he'd said about being one thing on the inside, and another on the outside. I hoped my simple gift wouldn't disappoint him.

I took the feather from my pocket and held it out to him. "This made me think of the zhar-ptica."

Nicholas's smile vanished, and I stepped back. Had I done something wrong?

Then I realized this new expression was one of awe, like there had been clouds in Nicholas's eyes that were suddenly lifted. His lips parted in surprise. "You brought that for me?"

I shrugged, a casual move I was unaccustomed to making, to cover my sudden self-consciousness. "I just wanted to remind you that a difficult journey can still end in joy."

Nicholas's look was impenetrable as I leaned in to hand him the feather, but it was me he was looking at. "Yes," he said. "I think it can."

Our fingers brushed as I passed the feather to him, and I shivered. "You deserve it."

Nicholas smiled softly. "We all do. Perlie deserves to go back to his family. Burt deserves to give speeches at every university in the country. You deserve to . . . well. What is it you want?"

I blinked, taken aback by the question. "I don't know," I said. "I suppose I don't want to lose my voice again. Maybe I'll write. Maybe I'll save up enough money to go back to school and get a degree in library science." I thought of my parents, who worked as teachers, and of men like Henry who were never taught to read. "Maybe I'll teach. But even daring to give myself so many options is more than I would have done a few months ago," I said. "I think that counts for something."

"Of course it does."

"What about you? What do you want?"

"I love my work at the Library of Congress," he said, "so I want to go back to that. And I want a family eventually. A wife and kids."

"That sounds nice," I said softly. I wondered whether he was picturing blond, curly-headed kids like Vivian would bear him. God knew I was imagining kids that looked like us. "We can raise our kids to do better than all this." I gestured around us to indicate the injured men and the detritus of war. Then I blushed. "That is, the general 'we.' Our generation."

I forced a laugh, but Nicholas's face remained focused. "Yes," he said. "That's what I want, too."

T hat night, I flipped through the copy of the *Stars and Stripes* newspaper the men had brought back from Base Hospital 18. The front page was full of what the men had already told me, and so I flipped to the next in search of good news.

There was a story about war orphans being adopted for Christmas, which was supposed to be uplifting but just made me sadder. A story about a boy who remained loyal and steadfast to the Allies until his death—again, more tragic than inspiring.

The third page brought news of the home front: reminders to write, a story about rations, even an article about baseball. Then I saw the word *librarian* and leaned in.

Librarian fired for presence of socialist, anarchist, pacifist books, it said. *Criminal charges under Sedition Act likely.*

I breathed in sharply. Criminal charges? For the same sort of texts that languished under my own mattress here?

I read on. The story was about a civilian librarian in North Dakota who had defied orders to remove "anti-American" and "pro-German" books from circulation. He'd retained books written in the German language, texts by conscientious objectors, writings of the International Workers of the World, and religious pamphlets opposed to war. And though he swore he was loyal to the United States and produced records of having bought war bonds to support it, he'd been brought in for questioning related to sedition.

By the time I got to the end of the article, my breath was coming out in short, quick bursts, and the words of the paper were beginning to blur before me. Then there were low voices around me and hands on my shoulders—someone pulling me up, another someone grabbing the newspaper—the room spinning as I stood—and quiet.

I came back to myself in bits and pieces. First, I became aware of the sweat-soaked strands of hair plastered across my forehead. Then the wobbles in my knees. And only then did the crushing mortification dawn. "I'm so sorry," I said. "I don't know what got into me." But my voice still sounded breathless and desperate.

"Happens to us all," one of the men said. I recognized him now as Michael, one of the men who had come to our first book club session. Dimly, I hoped this wouldn't affect his attendance at tomorrow's.

"What was it that frightened you?" The man who'd picked up the newspaper was flipping through it.

"I have a cousin in the Argonne," I lied. "The front page—it talked about the aircraft bombardments and the German fortifications and I suppose I got overwhelmed."

The men accepted my explanation with so much sympathy I almost felt guilty. But I couldn't tell them what had really startled me. Not unless I wanted them asking questions about why I cared—and I knew my eyes would go straight to the door that hid the books.

By the time Nellie and I picked Nicholas up for book club the next morning, he'd heard about my breakdown. "I didn't know you had cousins in the States," he said, worry creasing his brow.

"I don't," I confessed. "It was something else that frightened me."

We climbed into the car, Nicholas leaning on me for support, and I whispered that I would tell him later. We drove to tent fifty in a silence that quickly ruptured once we stepped inside. Our friends were eager to see us and even more eager to discuss *Robinson Crusoe*. Henry loved the adventure, Juan had been irritated by the fact that the goat changed from "he" to "she" and back again throughout the novel, and Nicholas appreciated the way the book was written as a series of diary entries that made it feel more personal. Of course, we also pointed out the fact that Crusoe headed a slave ship and that the authors seemed quite supportive of colonialism—a relevant topic not only for Delroy, whose native Jamaica was a colony of England, but for all of us, as we relied on French colonial troops in Africa to rebuff German forces even while criticizing Germany for invading lands beyond its own.

Despite the rich conversation, however, Perlie remained unusually quiet. A sheen of sweat on his face suggested a fever, and I lingered after book club had ended to check up on him. "I'll be all right," he promised. "Burt here will make sure of it."

Burt nodded. "Next time the nurses or doctors pop in, I'll be sure they see him."

Only after making them promise to send word if they needed our assistance did Nicholas and I leave, Nellie already outside flirting with her handsome Edmund.

"So?" Nicholas prompted once we were safely ensconced in the car waiting for her to finish. "What was it that *really* upset you in the newspaper?"

I told him all about the librarian who'd been fired and brought in for questioning. "He was a civilian, Nicholas, and all he was trying to do was his job."

Nicholas's face was white by the time I finished. "I was already worried for you, Emmaline, but now?" He shook his head. "Do you still have those books?"

I nodded. "And it doesn't seem fair. He and I both did the same thing, only he was brave enough to admit it. Brave enough for it to actually matter. And he's the only one being punished."

"Well," Nicholas began dryly. "Let's not level the playing field by getting you punished, too."

"Of course not. But what if we could help him?"

"How?"

"We're serving in the army, Nicholas. We have clout. No one can doubt our loyalty. If we make it known that *we* support freedom of ideas even in wartime . . . public opinion may begin to change."

"Or we'll be court-martialed and shot."

I shivered, but still I forged on. "We wouldn't use our names. I was thinking something quiet. Something like a letter. We could send it to a local newspaper in the librarian's hometown in North Dakota."

Nicholas closed his eyes and rubbed his temples. "Maybe . . ."

But I could tell he was still unconvinced.

"Look." I pulled the German propaganda to the colored soldiers out of my pocket. "If the government keeps banning books like the one I found about lynching, things aren't going to get better. And if things don't get better, Germany has this leverage against us. Because nothing they say here is untrue. And that's dangerous."

Nicholas's face drained of even more color as he read the pamphlet. "Emmaline, you can't have this. Where on earth did you— why do you—?" He couldn't even finish the question.

"German planes dropped it over Dijon. I only kept it because I was curious." I pulled back slightly. "I'm not distributing it. I'm not a traitor."

"Of course not." He leaned forward and placed his hand on mine, genuine concern written all over his face. "I know you aren't a traitor. But Emmaline, if you get caught writing a letter advocating for distributing so-called anti-American texts, you'll be viewed as one."

Something clicked into place in that moment, and it wasn't just the touch of Nicholas's hand that made me feel empowered. I'd flown under the radar my whole life. I was good at staying quiet, going unnoticed, being ignored. Maybe I could finally put those skills to good use.

"Well, then," I said. "I don't intend to get caught."

I wrote the letter that night. Would I be brave enough to send it? I wasn't sure. But still I worked hard crafting the words, putting thought into each one.

> *I write to you as a loyal United States citizen and Army volunteer concerning the firing of Mr. Thomas Plunkett from his position as librarian in your district. As I am certain you recall, Mr. Plunkett was fired for circulating socialist, pacifist, and anarchist books despite efforts of American libraries at large to remove such texts from public access for the duration of the war. As a patriot helping to make the world safe for democracy abroad, I am dismayed and horrified by the attack on free speech at home. Benjamin Franklin founded libraries with the stated purpose of opening the doors of wisdom for all. Thomas Jefferson, in founding the Library of Congress, said that "bigotry is the disease of ignorance [. . .]*

education and free discussion are the antidotes." And of course, freedom of speech and freedom of the press are embedded in the Constitution that we fight to protect.

Americans—in times of peace and in times of war, in civilian life and in the military—should never be denied the right to express their views. Even if their views align more closely with the enemy's; even if their views are not popular with the masses. Even if their views are socialism, anarchism, bolshevism. Because this is what it means to be an American: the freedom to dissent.

I cannot help but wonder what democracy is worth if it is democracy without dissent, if it is democracy for a privileged few but not for all.

It is for this reason that I call for the reinstatement of Mr. Thomas Plunkett as Bismarck librarian, as well as for the dropping of any charges that may be brought against him.

By the time I finished, my hand was cramped and my eyes were grainy with fatigue. But still I couldn't tell if the letter was right or not. Did it make too much of a statement? Did it make *enough* of a statement?

A knock on the recreation hut door startled me so badly that I knocked my glass of water to the floor. Frantically, I stuffed the letter under my mattress with the other books and then trotted out into the recreation hut. The knocking at the door continued, and I took a deep breath. Who could it be? Not Colonel Hodgson coming to punish me for my book clubs, I prayed. But I couldn't think of a better alternative.

I pulled the door open and sagged with relief. "Nicholas!"

"Do you mind if I—?" His breath was ragged, and he gestured to the table.

"Please," I said, worried that he'd walked all the way here on his own. "Come in."

Only after he'd sat did I realize that I was in my nightgown with my long, straight hair loose down my back. I clapped my arms over my chest to hide the shape of my breasts and the skin of my shoulders. "Excuse me," I said. "Let me just . . ." I backed into my bedroom and slammed the door. I threw on my uniform and twisted my hair into a low bun. Then I reemerged—still red-faced, but presentable.

"Sorry." Nicholas looked chastened. "I didn't mean to startle you."

I settled into the chair across from him. "Why *did* you come?"

"I decided that you were right."

I shook my head. "Right about what?"

He leaned forward on the table. "I want to help you write the letter."

Relief swept through me. To know I wasn't on my own was more of a gift than I could have imagined it would be. "Give me one minute," I said. I disappeared back into the bedroom and returned with the draft I'd written. "This is what I've done so far."

Nicholas took the paper and scrutinized it, his gaze moving slowly across the page. I swallowed deeply. What if he hated it?

What if, I realized too late, *he recognized my handwriting from the letter I'd written as Vivian?*

But when Nicholas looked up, there was no suspicion in his eyes. "You're incredible, Emmaline."

"No," I said instinctively. "No. I just wanted to . . ."

"Do something that mattered? Regardless of the consequences?"

"I suppose."

"As I said. Incredible."

I bit my lip. "I really don't think I could have done it without you. You've helped me remember who I used to be. Who I *can* be."

Nicholas shook his head. "You would have figured it out. But I am willing to keep helping, if you want. I can add my support to your letter. Change all the *I*s to *we*s, add *soldier* beside *Army volunteer*. Put an extra signature at the bottom."

"Are you certain?"

Nicholas leaned back in his chair, wincing slightly and reaching for his bandaged abdomen. "Yes."

"Then you can help me revise it, too. Something doesn't feel right yet."

I crossed out and added according to Nicholas's suggestions, and we ended up with a draft that felt more powerful and more solid. But something was still missing.

"I don't know," Nicholas said. "To me, you've said everything there is to say."

"That's exactly it." I hunched over and started scribbling furiously.

"What?"

"I've said everything there is to say. But I haven't backed it up with action."

I slid the paper across the table so Nicholas could read my revised final paragraph.

> It is for this reason that we call for the reinstatement of Mr. Thomas Plunkett as Bismarck librarian, as well as for the dropping of any charges that may be brought against him. As an act of solidarity with Mr. Plunkett and other

protectors of our constitutional right to free speech, we
will work here in France to make all texts available to
those who request them.

Nicholas raised his eyebrows. "You don't think it's too much?"

"I think I'd rather it be too much than not enough."

Nicholas didn't slide the paper back to me. Instead, he took the pencil and etched his initials at the bottom: *N.A., 79th Infantry Division.* I added my own: *E.B., U.S. Base Hospital 42.*

Nicholas stood. "I should get back," he said. "But I thank you for letting me be part of this."

I stood. "Let me walk you," I said. "You aren't well enough to brave the cold and the mud on your own."

Nicholas laughed. "I got here fine."

"It's darker now," I argued.

Nicholas leaned forward and touched his lips to mine so quickly that I hardly realized what was happening until it was over. "Thanks to you," he said, "I know there's always light in the darkness."

And then he turned and went, leaving me stunned and full of longing staring after him.

Chapter 22

— ❖ —

Kathleen Carre

July 1976

Staring at the letter to Nicholas, which had been postmarked fifty-eight years later than the letter he'd sent Vivian, I nearly forgot Mabel's package. After checking the senders, I dumped the rest of Nana's forwarded letters into the trash, grabbed Mabel's box of goodies, and then sprinted back upstairs. I deposited them into my room just in time to join the company for the Blue and Gold. We got a real tongue-lashing, as usual, and then retired to our rooms. Linda slammed the door. "I'm sick and tired of being yelled at all the time."

Susan shrugged. "It's part of being a plebe."

"Yeah," I added. "At least they don't go easy on us because we're women."

"The opposite," Susan grumbled. "They hate us."

I looked up. "Has something happened to you?"

"What do you mean?"

"Nothing." I forced a casual shrug. "Just wondered if something had prompted you to say that."

Linda narrowed her big eyes. "Doesn't seem like nothing. What happened?"

This would be the perfect moment to tell them, but I just couldn't bear the pity in her voice. "Nothing new," I lied. "Just thinking about how Robert ransacked our rooms."

Susan shuddered. "I can't imagine what poor Janie must experience, as the only Black woman in the brigade."

"I did the math when we were running the other day," Linda said. "Women overall make up six percent of the plebe class, two percent of the entire academy. Black women—of which there are only one—don't even make a single percent of our class. And it's something like one-tenth of a percent of the academy as a whole."

"You're crazy." Susan laughed. "Math while running? All I can think about is how not to die."

"Running is the only time I *don't* think," I admitted. "That's why I love it."

Linda shrugged her round shoulders. "I don't know. The math makes it go faster. I despise running."

We all laughed. Linda's hatred for running was obvious, and she turned red as a devil with all the huffing and puffing she did. But she was fast, faster than several of the men in her squadron. She claimed it was only because she wanted it to be over sooner.

Linda yawned, and Susan followed suit. "I'm exhausted," Linda said. "Can Sunday come any slower?"

"Oh!" Susan sat up in her bed. Her short hair stuck up like

bird feathers from leaning against the wall. "That reminds me. Two of the other women are hosting a meeting Sunday afternoon in Mitscher Hall."

"What for?"

"To share our experiences," Susan said. "Like consciousness-raising."

I pulled a face. "Like, feminism stuff? No way. They treat us differently enough as is." I raised my eyebrows. "Have you forgotten about the purses? The heels? The fact that we *can't serve in combat*?"

Susan held up her hands. "Whoa. I didn't write the rules. But you know that's exactly why we need this meeting. To talk about those things. To change them."

Linda piped in. "Are you going, Susan?"

"Yes. You should both come."

"Sure." Linda shrugged. "Strength in numbers and all that."

"Exactly," I said. "Strength in numbers. In all thirteen hundred of us. Not in fracturing ourselves into groups like this. Because twelve hundred and something men is a hell of a lot more than eighty-one women."

Susan shrugged. "Your call. You don't have to come."

We all three tumbled into bed, and I scrunched my eyes shut. I'd tried taking Mabel's advice. I'd tried talking. And for a second, it had helped.

But then I'd thought about where talking to Derrick had gotten me. Where continuing to talk to these girls would get me. And it had seemed overwhelming, all of a sudden, the way we were fractured and pitted against each other. One of the girls in Company Seven had burst into tears after being reprimanded the other day— loud, messy tears—and every man at the academy had ribbed us all about it for days afterward. They offered us handkerchiefs on the way to the bathroom, called us hysterical and overemotional and babyish.

Maybe the Naval Academy offered its promised community to the men, but the girls were deprived it at every turn. I'd come here wanting to be on a team, but all I felt was isolated. I couldn't see how a women's meeting would do anything but accentuate that.

I waited until Linda's and Susan's breathing steadied before I rolled over and got out Nicholas's package from under my bed. I tore it open and found a note at the top.

Nellie, it began.

> *After what happened with Emmaline, I'm surprised at you for trying to contact me. Where did you get this letter, off her dead body? I don't want anything to do with it. Not after everything.*
> *Nicholas*

How dare Nicholas write Nana this way? I didn't know who Emmaline was, but I was certain my grandmother would have done all she could to save her.

I reached into the envelope and pulled out the next note. This one was folded into a small square with an index card held on by a paper clip. The index card said, in my nana's adult handwriting: *I thought you should have this.*

I removed the card and unfolded the sheet of paper, which nearly tore at the creases as I laid it flat. The letter was addressed to the *Bismarck Tribune*, which didn't hold any special meaning for my nana as far as I knew. I began to read.

We write to you as loyal United States citizens and servicemen concerning the firing of Mr. Thomas Plunkett from his position as librarian in your district . . .

I continued on, my anxiety mounting as I neared the end of the letter. Once I finished, I dropped the letter as if it were a grenade. It didn't matter that it was nothing but a flimsy piece of paper; it bordered on seditious. If I'd found it a year ago, I'd have thought it was contemporary, written in protest of the Vietnam War.

But if the distressed paper wasn't enough to prove it, the signatures at the bottom of the letter would be.

E.B., U.S. Base Hospital 42
N.A., 79th Infantry Division

The 79th Infantry Division had become the 79th Sustainment Support Command after World War II, and the Vietnam War had certainly not called for base hospitals in the north of France. This letter was from the First World War, that much was obvious. But where had my grandmother gotten it? And if Nicholas was N.A., who was E.B.?

I sank back onto my pillow. I would call Nicholas tomorrow. I couldn't talk to the girls here or to my nana, but I could find someone who knew her, and maybe he could give me answers.

It was a relief the next day to have something to think about during our half hour break at the phone banks—something other than Nana's telephone ringing endlessly without answer or the constant threat of finding Tom and Robert in line alongside me. I consulted the white pages for Nicholas Agrapov while waiting in line. Agrapov, which sounded like a Russian name to me, wasn't a common surname in D.C., and no wonder. Our governments didn't exactly get along.

I had a list of questions I'd planned the night before, and I gripped them tightly as I approached the telephone. My hands trembled, but I attributed that more to hunger than nerves. It was still hard to force food down my throat, and I hadn't eaten a full meal since the incident.

When it was my turn to make a call, I dialed Nicholas's number and waited as the phone rang. *Please answer*, I willed Nicholas. *Please.* If he'd fought in the first war, he was probably my grandmother's age; if so, he likely didn't get out much. I was counting on his being home.

Finally, someone picked up the telephone with a click. "Nicholas Agrapov." The voice was low with a hint of gravel. "May I ask who is calling?"

"I'm Midshipman Kathleen Carre," I said, hoping the title would give me credence.

Nicholas's voice was suddenly on edge. "Carre?"

"Yes." I'd known he knew Nana, but still my heart leapt at his recognition. "I believe you knew my grandmother Nellie. Nellie Carre."

"I'm sorry," Nicholas said abruptly. "I have to go."

"Wait!" I shouted into the phone and then looked around guiltily. "She's dead."

"What?"

"My nana, Nellie. She passed away recently."

Nicholas's voice was still stiff, but it seemed to soften, like he really was sympathetic. "I'm sorry to hear that."

"Thank you. She sent you a letter before she died, and I wanted to ask you—"

"I'm sorry. It was all a long time ago, Midshipman."

I appreciated his easy use of the title for a woman, despite his lack of cooperation. "But—"

He interrupted. "I'm sorry for your loss."

And then he was gone.

My vision swam as I returned to my room, from frustration or exhaustion I wasn't sure. I went to my desk to look again at the letter to the *Bismarck Tribune*, and my hand stilled over the wood. The letter was gone.

I checked underneath the desk, hoping it had fallen, then cursed under my breath. Those bastards had been in my room again. And this time, they'd stolen something that was mine. Worse, my nana's.

The bell for reveille sounded, and I stepped out of my room and presented for the singing of the "Blue and Gold."

Singing the anthem, men's and women's voices intertwined and indistinguishable, was always one of my favorite parts of the day. It made me feel like I was part of something that mattered, even if just for a few minutes. Singing a song that had united the Navy for over fifty years reminded me of that.

But today, I didn't feel like a part of something. I felt like I was on the outside looking in.

Sunday afternoon came as a blessing. I needed to get out from under Robert's and Tom's noses, out from under the eye of Ensign Michael. I knew I was one of the best. I'd studied *Reef Points* the longest, tried the hardest. But the ensign paid so much additional attention to me, just waiting for me to slip up, that he did catch me occasionally. I'd pivot on the wrong heel or think we were having peas for lunch and beans for dinner when it was the other way around, and I'd get cited for it every time.

So, when everyone else on Sunday went out in groups to enjoy the luxury of time together, I laced up for a run to clear my head. I pulled on my PEP uniform and pulled my short hair into a stubby ponytail. It was noon, the sun high in the sky, and I had no doubt the temperature was in the high eighties. I immediately took off at a fast pace, afraid my thoughts would catch up with me otherwise.

By the first mile, I had forgotten about the way Nicholas had hung up on me. In the second, I stopped seeing Tom's and Robert's faces leering in my mind. By mile three, I could remember Nana without wanting to cry. At four, I stopped worrying about Robert's and Tom's dirty fingers snooping through my room, because I could outrun anyone.

By five, I couldn't remember when I'd last eaten.

At six, my knees hit the ground and my vision went black. At six, I stopped remembering the stolen letter and the boys and Nana and the funeral. At six, I stopped remembering anything.

Chapter 23

—— ❖ ——

Emmaline Balakin

October–November 1918

The next time Nellie came by, I pressed a copy of *The Adventures of Tom Sawyer* into her hands. Nicholas's and my letter was folded into its back cover, but I didn't tell Nellie. No reason to implicate her in something that could get us *all* imprisoned for treason. Instead, I handed her the address of the *Bismarck Tribune* and claimed it was the address of a cousin. Nellie didn't question me, instead promising to drop off the book at the Paris post office.

She would still be gone when our third book club was scheduled to meet Monday morning, so I woke early that day to set up on my own. I decided we could go without the phonograph for one meeting, but we would need chairs, so I stacked two and braced them against my body as I staggered through the mud toward tent fifty. I was panting by the time I got there, and I hoped Burt, Perlie, and Joshua were up for a chat so I could rest for a moment before returning for the other chairs.

But as I entered the ward, I could tell something was wrong. The men by the door didn't meet my eyes, and none of my friends called out in greeting. I looked to the back of the ward and froze. Burt and Joshua lay in their cots, but the one between them was empty. Had Perlie been transferred to the convalescent hospital in Neufchâteau or shipped to one of the more stable hospitals in the intermediate section?

As I got closer, I registered Burt's appearance. The veins in his eyes stood out, and his lips were chapped and bloody.

"Burt! Are you sick?"

"No," he said. "It's Perlie. He's gone."

"He was transferred already, then?"

"No," Burt croaked. "Perlie is dead."

"What?" I remembered Perlie's sweat last week, the way he'd appeared to have a fever. But so had Nicholas his first week here, and he'd been better within a day.

"How? What happened?" I heard myself asking the same question over and over, but I couldn't stop.

"Infection set in."

"Couldn't they treat it?" *This is a hospital*, I wanted to cry. *This is what it's here for.*

"Maybe they could have. But they wouldn't."

"What do you mean, they wouldn't?" My voice was approaching hysteria, but I couldn't be bothered to modulate it. "Who wouldn't?"

"The doctors were treating the white patients. They said Perlie had to wait until their scheduled rounds were complete."

"But—*all* of them? Surely not all of those cases were urgently life-threatening?"

"Most of them weren't."

I shook my head. "I don't understand, Burt."

Burt looked at me with a hard gaze. "Perlie was a colored man, Miss Balakin. It was more natural for them to let him die than it would have been for them to treat him before attending to a white man. And so that is what they did."

He turned back toward the wall, and I knew I'd been dismissed.

I ran from the ward, tears near freezing on my cheeks, and straight to the first place I thought to go: Nicholas. I hadn't seen him since our kiss, but any anticipation or apprehension I would have felt an hour ago was wiped away now. Now all that mattered was Perlie.

I collided with Nicholas as I ran toward his ward, and he caught me before I could fall. We both teetered on the edge of tipping over for a moment before regaining our balance.

"Emmaline? I was coming to help you set up, but—" He cut himself off when he saw my face. "Emmaline, what's happened?"

"Perlie—" I couldn't say it. "Perlie—"

"What, Emmaline?" Nicholas's voice was patient, but there was fear in his eyes.

"He had an infection. They didn't treat it. He—he—" It took a moment, but I was finally able to say it through my sobs. "He died."

"What?" Nicholas's hands tightened on my arms.

"Yes." I wept, telling him everything Burt had told me.

"Dear God."

Nicholas and I sank together into the mud, ignoring the way it soaked through the fabric of our clothing and caked along our legs. We cried together, and though no words were spoken, I couldn't help but feel as if we were sharing the deepest parts of ourselves. We weren't hiding anything—our sadness or grief, our fury at the unjustness of it. We laid our emotions bare, and we were lucky enough to have each other to share the pain.

All of us from the book group and several other soldiers from the colored ward packed into Nellie's motorcar Tuesday morning for Perlie's funeral. It had been two days since Perlie's death, and the grief in the car was palpable and raw. We drove through the small town of Bazoilles-sur-Meuse and over the River Meuse itself, then turned right at the hospital where Nellie spent her nights. In any other circumstance, I would have been awed by the facilities compared to our own. Now I only wondered whether Perlie could have avoided infection in these improved conditions. Base Hospital 18 was located on an estate centered on a chateau, which was replete with curtained windows and balconies and a great stone crest above the entryway.

We continued past the chateau, the wooden barracks, and the overflow tents to U.S. Military Cemetery #6. Each grave was marked with a white stone cross, a sobering reminder of the lives we couldn't save at the hospitals.

Several groups were already clustered about, for there were six other men being buried today. Nellie told me that four had died of the Spanish influenza or related pneumonia, one during surgery, and one due to tuberculosis. Only Perlie had died of sepsis related to a wound.

Perlie's mourners climbed from the car. I stood between Nellie and Nicholas, hoping I could absorb their strength and share my own. Not that it felt like I had any.

The chaplain listed all six men's names: Private John S. Graham, Private First Class Eugene C. Taylor, Private Francis J. Schuyler, Captain Richard J. Roos, Private First Class King L. Larkin. And Lieutenant Perlie R. Little.

I shook my head. That couldn't be right. Perlie hadn't been a lieutenant. Officers had their own ward with private rooms, and Perlie had been in a tent.

I glanced at Nicholas, whose eyebrows were drawn together. He was as confused as I was—no. His lips were hardened in a flat line. He wasn't confused. He was angry.

Then I realized my naïveté. Perlie had been an officer; he'd just been barred from the officers' ward—with its private rooms and around-the-clock care—because of his color.

I couldn't focus on the priest's Latin sermon. Perlie probably would have survived had he been in the officers' ward with better heating, better care, and less exposure to other illnesses.

Tears froze in my eyes. Monday, I had cried of grief; today, I cried at the unfairness of it all.

When the short ceremony ended, we took our leave. We didn't want to watch the gravediggers, all of them colored men who had been conscripted, bury the coffins. Each coffin had the forty-eight-star American flag folded over it, and I gazed at Perlie's with a complicated mixture of pride and shame. Perlie had fought for our country, died for it. But so many Americans wouldn't do the same for him.

The men piled into the back of the motorcar, and I took my spot in the front next to Nellie. She sat stock-still in the driver's seat.

"Nellie?"

For once, Nellie didn't say anything. She didn't shift the car into gear or even twist the key in the ignition.

I glanced back for help, but the men in the back of the car were oblivious as they talked among themselves.

"Nellie," I said again. "What is it?"

She turned to me with a blank expression. "He's really dead." And then her tears started to flow, her shoulders shaking so violently that her curls bounced up and down.

I turned and tapped Nicholas's shoulder. "Tell the others Nellie and I have to check the tires." When he nodded, I scrambled from the car and opened Nellie's door. She climbed out after me, and I wrapped her in my arms.

"I'm sorry," she said. "It's just that no one I was close to ever died before." She pulled back, aghast. "I'm so sorry," she said again. "I shouldn't have said that when you've lost both your parents. I'm lucky, I know that, that I've never had to—"

"Shh."

Nellie let out a deep, shuddering breath. "It sounds silly. I've been at the front forever, and it isn't as if I haven't seen death. But I'm a driver. I never *knew* any of the other soldiers. Perlie . . . Perlie was more than a name. He was a person. Even a friend. And it's so different." She let out a deep, shuddering sob. "Of course I *knew* he was dead. But I didn't really *understand* it. Not until they lowered the coffin into the ground, and then . . ." She dissolved into tears again.

I wanted to cry too at the sight of my indomitable friend in pieces. But she'd calmed me down before, and it was time for me to do the same for her.

"I know," I soothed. "And there will be times again when it

doesn't feel real, and then you'll remember it is. But it gets less and less frequent. You'll stop crying every time you think of him and start smiling—at the way he loved his kids, at the gentle way he talked, at the kindness he showed everyone even when it wasn't reciprocated."

I felt Nellie nod against my chest. "I guess." Her voice was still thick with tears. "But it's so *wrong*. So much death all around us, and now one that could have been prevented?" She looked up at me. "Did you hear? He was an officer. They could have avoided it all."

I nodded and glanced past Nellie at the car for fear I would break down if I met her eyes. Joshua was gazing out the window with his eyebrows up as if to ask what was going on, and I couldn't blame him. These men needed to get back to their nurses and their cots.

I swallowed. "Nellie. Why don't you go ahead and get in my seat?"

She looked up at me, eyes shining. "Really?"

I wanted to say no. I felt far from comfortable driving such a packed car, especially if Nellie wasn't in any condition to help me. But this woman had so quickly become my best friend, my surrogate big sister. And she needed me.

"Of course," I said.

I helped Nellie into the passenger seat and then slid stiffly into the driver's. I turned the car on and shifted it into gear.

I was too afraid to drive any faster than a crawl, but no one seemed to mind. Though I expected silence on the way back across the river—it was how I grieved, after all—these boys had seen death too many times to let it crush them. They kept their chins up, telling stories and sharing memories of Perlie the whole way back to our base.

No one mentioned Josephine or their daughters. But I couldn't imagine what grief Josephine would feel when she learned of her husband's death. And, if she found out the circumstances, what fury.

That night, I dreamed over and over again of Nicholas and Nellie dying.

Nellie was encircled by fire, unable to turn the motorcar before the flames that had swallowed the Argonne swallowed her, too. Nicholas was struck by artillery as I stood by, helpless, and watched the shrapnel shred his side like scissors through fabric.

Nellie was ambushed by the Germans. Nicholas was feverish, but the doctors didn't hear his cries.

Nellie's car slammed into a tree. Nicholas climbed over bodies in the trenches, a German gun waiting for him on the other side.

I heard the insistent buzzing of a German plane. The bomb siren. It didn't stop, and I slowly became aware of my body in its bed and the ceiling above me.

This wasn't a nightmare anymore; it was real.

I opened my eyes, nightgown soaked through with sweat, and watched as the lights switched on and off four times before plunging into darkness.

A real bomb threat, then. That was the sign.

I threw a coat over my nightgown and staggered outside with my helmet and my gas mask. I'd never put the latter on before, and I had to wrestle it onto my face. My neck lurched forward with my head. I felt like a great blinking owl with the wide eyepieces, but I didn't feel safe.

Suddenly panicked, I clawed at the mask and ripped it off. I threw my head back and gazed at the sky. There was the plane, louder than it had been just moments before. Figures began to dot the desolate landscape: officers from the administration building, a mortician, the men in the wards on either side of me. All of them tipped their faces up to the sky so their bodies were shrouded in darkness and their foreheads and cheeks shone with moonlight. They looked like ghosts, like specters. I wondered if that was what we would all be, soon.

The Russian Orthodox faith considered a person's final resting place their home in the afterlife. Would I live here in the mud for all eternity? Would Nicholas? No one would be here to throw juniper behind my coffin or bake the koliva that symbolized life, death, and renewal. My loved ones wouldn't circle my body with kisses. Would I even have a body, or would the bombs destroy every last trace of my earthly form? Maybe I'd be completely obliterated, nothing left of me to visit on the third day or the ninth or the fortieth.

I knew too well the prayer for the departing of the soul, having repeated it for my mother and my father both. I began to whisper it now. "O Lord and Master and Governor of all, Father of our Lord Jesus Christ, who desirest not the death of a sinner, but rather that he may turn from his wickedness and live . . ."

I kept my eyes closed as I went through the prayer, arriving at the end with a trembling voice. "Receive in peace the soul of Emmaline and give her rest in Thy eternal dwelling with all Thy saints, by the grace of Thine only Son our Lord God and Savior, Jesus Christ, with Whom Thou are blessed together with Thine all-holy, gracious, and life-giving Spirit now and forever and unto ages of ages."

I opened my eyes to cross myself and utter the final *Amen*, and only then did I become aware of the silence. The buzzing of planes had ceased, and as I spun in a slow circle, I saw that the others in the hospital had retreated back into their wards and their offices.

I was on the ground before I fully realized I was safe. How did the soldiers in the trenches face death every day and overcome it? I didn't feel as if I could move from this spot. I'd been calm as the plane flew overhead, the words of the prayer giving me something to focus on, but now the tears began to flow. I was surprised I had any left after all the crying I'd done for Perlie. But I did, and the tears kept coming now. I rocked back and forth in the mud until they stopped. This war, this damned war.

Chapter 24

Kathleen Carre

July 1976

I came to flat on my back, blinking at an array of white ceiling tiles. I pushed up on my elbows, immediately anxious. What time was it? Did the officers know where I was? Had I missed check-in?

The academy doctor appeared at my side. "Lie down, now."

I ignored him. "What time is it?"

"I'll tell you when you lie down."

I huffed but complied.

"It's 1345."

One forty-five p.m., and I'd started running just after noon.

"Do you remember what—"

I interrupted, offended that he'd suggest I didn't remember. "I went for a run. I hadn't eaten in a few hours or had any water. I went too far, too fast."

The doctor nodded, his face creased in concern. "An upper-class midshipman found you and brought you to my office."

Well, that was mortifying. But I smiled. "How kind of him. May I go now?" I'd passed out, for God's sake, not suffered a heart attack.

"I'm afraid not." The doctor gestured to my arm, and I startled to see a needle inserted into the soft flesh of my inner elbow. Even in my surprise, I noted the boniness of the joint. Did a few days really make such a marked difference?

"I hardly think I need an IV," I said.

"Just a precaution. You'll also need to eat." He handed me a container, and I peeked inside. Cashews and almonds.

"Okay," I said. "Thanks." But the doctor didn't go away. I looked into the container again, and the thick smell of cashews hit me hard.

"I'm sorry," I tried. "I'm really not hungry right now."

"Eat."

I closed my eyes and fished out an almond. The feeling of it on my lips turned my stomach, but I bit half of it off and chewed. I felt like I was moving wood splinters around in my mouth, and I tried to keep from making a face.

I ate the second half of the almond and swallowed. As soon as I did, my stomach cramped. "Oh!" I gasped. I was starving.

I tore into the cashews and almonds with vigor, feeling beginning to return to my arms and legs.

The doctor watched approvingly, gave me a stern lecture on

being sure to eat enough going forward, and discharged me. My room when I returned was empty, but a note in Susan's bold, slanted hand waited on my desk.

We're at the women's meeting in Mitscher Hall if
you change your mind and want to join.
—Susan and Linda

I stared at the note for a moment. I'd said no before, but now? Sitting in my room with gauze taped over the spot where I'd received my IV, I thought of Mabel's words. *Sharing your story is never a weakness, Kathleen. When we realize we aren't alone, we grow so much stronger.*

God knew I needed strength, and facing these demons alone wasn't working. So I grabbed a packet of trail mix from Mabel's package and chopped off: through Bancroft's dizzying maze of corridors, through King Hall, and into Mitscher. I checked the auditorium first, but the girls weren't there, so I ran through the passageways checking each conference room until I found them in one. A few dozen girls were spread around the space, and I recognized a few of them: Linda, Susan, the woman who'd raised her hand and asked about feminine hygiene that first week, the two girls I'd seen in the bathroom after *Hang it up, bitch* had been spray-painted on the stall door.

One of the women in the front of the room rose to shake my hand. "Janice Buxbaum. Midshipman Tyrell and I organized this meeting."

The other woman stood. "Marsha. Marsha Tyrell."

"I'm Kathleen Carre."

I joined Susan and Linda in the back, and the girls resumed their sharing. Linda and Susan filled me in on what I'd missed: women who'd found dead rats in their mailboxes like threats, and one woman who'd found *slut* carved into the door of her room. The rest of it, I was as familiar with as the rest of them: shaving cream bombs, obscene taunts in the passageways after hours, threats from officers that they could drive us out.

But as I listened, the stories grew more harrowing.

"Maria has a story to share," one girl said, raising her hand. "Go on, Maria." She turned to the girl beside her.

"I can't," Maria hissed back. "What if—?"

The first girl interrupted. "No one will think it was your fault. Go on. Tell them."

Maria took a deep breath. "I was asleep last week. I heard a sound, felt something, and I opened my eyes." She paused there, and her friend gave her an encouraging nod. "There was a man in my bed."

A collective gasp rose around the room.

"He was masked." Maria's voice grew stronger, like our horror had emboldened her. "So I don't know who it was. I screamed, of course, and my roommates woke up. We chased him out." She flashed a grateful smile at the woman who'd made her tell the story. "But . . ." Her voice broke. "I don't know who it was. So I'm terrified of every single man here. *Every single one.*"

"Thirteen hundred men," her roommate added. "It's a constant state of fear."

That, I could understand. And so could the other women, it seemed. One nodded as she opened her mouth. "That's the worst bit," she said. "The fear. I can deal with the pranks—the dead rats, the insults, the shaving cream. But this constant fear—it's like there's a bird living inside my stomach, tearing at me with its beak and its claws, trying to fly away. But it can't. It's always there. And it's killing me."

Several women murmured their assent, and Susan nudged me. "You should tell them what happened to you."

For a moment, I was frozen. How did she know? And then I realized—she meant the wet sheets and the note.

Again, Mabel's words echoed in my mind. *Sharing your story is never a weakness, Kathleen. When we realize we aren't alone, we grow so much stronger.*

It was true. Already, having heard these women talk about their fear had made me feel so much less alone. Now I could do the same for them.

I raised my hand. "I had my room ransacked. They stripped the sheets from my bed and soaked them in the shower, knocked over my chair, scattered everything from my desk across the deck." I glanced to Susan and Linda, who—like Maria's roommate moments ago—nodded. "And they left a note," I said. "They left a note that said it was better I didn't sleep at all than to sleep with a . . . a Black man, though their language was different. And it was only because they'd seen me talk to him, once."

Janice was about to respond to my story when the officer of the deck appeared in the doorway. "Midshipman Buxbaum! Midshipman Tyrell!" His voice thundered throughout the space.

"Sir, yes, sir!" Both women leapt to standing.

"You were warned that a meeting of this scale, without an officer and flag present, would be considered a mutiny."

The rest of us stared, aghast.

"Sir, yes, sir."

"And yet you decided to go through with it anyway?"

"No excuse, sir."

"Ladies."

I winced at his language. These "ladies" were plebes, mid-shipmen.

"You will come with me to the commandant's office. The rest of you"—the officer raised his voice—"disperse. I expect that this will not happen again."

"Sir, yes, sir!" our voices chorused back, and then we stood and fled. I for one was afraid even to look at the other women, and I didn't make eye contact with Maria as she hurried past me despite our similar experiences. Our one chance at coming together, as spread across squadrons as we were, and now it had been ruined. I doubted we'd get the chance again.

Susan and Linda and I hurried together back to the fifth deck of Bancroft and slammed our door behind us like we were being chased.

"Will they get expelled?" Linda fretted.

"They can't," Susan said. "It wouldn't be right."

But I remembered what Susan herself had said. The powers that be could not always be trusted to do what was right—at least, not what was right for us or our Black comrades. Only what was right for men like Tom and Robert. For the men whom our silence would protect.

I had another of Mabel's snacks to fire myself up for PEP the next morning. It was easier to eat in the privacy of my own room than in front of my squad, and I certainly wasn't going to let myself pass out in front of them. Not only would that give them fodder to use against me, but it would turn the other women against me, too. Weakness in one of us reflected badly on all of us, as we'd learned from the crybaby incident.

I paced myself carefully on the warm-up run, not wanting to overdo it. Then Tom fell into step beside me, and it took all my strength not to speed away. But I didn't want to look afraid.

"Midshipman Carre."

I glanced at him out of the corner of my eye, surprised to hear him use my honorific. "Midshipman Crawford."

"I wanted to give you a warning."

For God's sake. As if I hadn't been threatened—"warned"— enough.

"A real warning," Tom said, like he knew what I was thinking. "A heads-up."

I kept running, and he matched my stride. "Look. I know you don't like me, but—"

"Don't like you?" I almost laughed. "You've terrorized me."

"I know." Tom looked contrite. "And it's been more than enough. It should be over now."

The nerve of him, to think that what he'd done was something that could be moved past. To think it wasn't as bad as other things he could have done. "But?"

"Robert's filled out a Form-2 for you."

I stumbled. A Form-2 was a Misconduct Report Form. "What for?" I tried to keep my voice level.

"UCMJ Article 134."

"What?"

Tom's voice turned patronizing. "The UCMJ stands for—"

"The Uniform Code of Military Justice," I snapped. "I know. And Article 134 is for prejudice to the good order and discipline of the armed forces, particularly through disloyal statement, or for noncapital federal offenses. None of which I have committed." I worked to keep the hitch out of my voice as I ran. "I might be a woman, but I know my stuff."

Tom held up his hands like he had a cramp. "I'm just trying to help."

"I don't want or need your help," I spat. "I just need you to leave me alone." I finally did speed up and run ahead. I controlled the spin of my legs so as not to draw attention to myself, but I wanted to flee. As if everything Robert had already done to me wasn't bad enough? Now he was trying to get me separated at best, court-martialed at worst.

I breathed in through my nose and out through my mouth. None of that would happen, because I was innocent. What disloyal statements could Robert even pretend I'd made?

I nearly stopped running as the answer hit me. He'd stolen the letter my nana had sent Nicholas. I didn't remember the exact words, but it had railed against limits on free speech imposed on the military. In today's context, it would be a commitment to the Free Speech Movement that had proliferated in California in the last decade, or a testament to anti-war and anti-military protests. The letter, if attributed to me, would position me as a protester, someone to whom the government would respond with tear gas and trials and jail time.

Without action to accompany the words, it might not matter for a civilian. But for a midshipman to speak out against the government? That would be treason.

My mind somewhere else, I jumped when our officer chose today of all days to quiz me on the menu. Missing just one item would be an infraction the likes of which I couldn't afford now that I had a Form-2 on file.

"French toast, sir! Broiled bacon, broiled hash brown potatoes, and fresh fruit, sir!"

"And for beverages?"

"Orange juice, sir." Coffee, of course, was forbidden.

Though I'd remembered everything, the officer wasn't satisfied. "Lunch menu," he demanded. "Go."

I squeezed my eyes shut, and he snapped at me. "Eyes on your officer, plebe!"

I opened them and pulled in my chin. "No excuse, sir." I took a breath. "Today's lunch menu consists of a choice of buffalo chicken sandwich or peanut butter banana sandwiches." I hesitated, trying to remember the vegetable. Was it snap peas or cucumber? We would be having one for lunch and the other for dinner, but I couldn't remember now which was which. All that echoed in my mind was Article 134; it left little room for anything else. "Also"—I crossed my fingers at my side—"snap peas. Sir."

The officer nodded gruffly and continued down the line. I nearly collapsed against the bulkhead in relief, but doing so would be another strike.

A strike I couldn't afford.

Later that day, I was relieved to finally be summoned in front of the preliminary inquiry officer. I'd be able to explain what had happened and clear myself of this ridiculous accusation.

The officer, or PIO, sat behind his desk and folded his hands. I stood in front of him, lopsided in my chopped-off heels, and straightened my spine. "Sir."

"Miss Carre. You've been summoned about allegations

regarding Article 134 of the Uniform Code of Military Justice, specifically the subsection regarding disloyal statements."

"Sir, yes, sir. I understand, sir. However, the allegations—"

The man held up a hand. "First, I need to notify you of your rights. You will receive a copy of the allegation. The maximum penalty for an infraction of this type is expulsion, the equivalent of a dishonorable discharge, and confinement for up to three years."

Confinement! What sort of criminal did he think I was?

The man went through the rest of my rights and then slid a form across to me. "Sign here to acknowledge your rights." He pointed to the line marked *Defendant Signature*, and I twitched. I shouldn't be a defendant.

I signed and then looked up. "Can I see the allegation now?"

The PIO pursed his lips and slid it over. The handwriting was blocky and slanted, and Robert's full name was signed on the bottom.

It took all my control not to tear the paper to shreds.

Name of Service Member: *Kathleen Carre, plebe, Company 5*

Location of Wrongdoing: *Mitscher Hall*

My stomach dropped when I saw the location. Mitscher Hall had been the location of the girls' meeting—the so-called mutiny. Being associated with that was not going to help me any. Janice Buxbaum and Marsha Tyrell, the organizers, were under review for expulsion.

I returned to the report.

In walking through Mitscher Hall, I, Midshipman Robert Skinner of Company 5, noticed a large envelope (attached) discarded on a chair. Knowing personal possessions are not to be kept in communal spaces, I approached the envelope so I could return it to its owner. Lying on top of the envelope (not inside) was the attached letter, which advocates for communism and anarchism and the allowance of disloyal statements.

When I saw Kathleen Carre's address on the envelope, my heart sank.

His heart sank? What a load of bull. How could anyone believe this?

I hated the thought that a fellow company plebe might be harboring treasonous thoughts, but still felt that I needed to turn the materials into the Battalion XO. Due to the severity of the statements in the letter, he asked me to come to the inquiry office and file a complaint so an investigation could be opened regarding the "disloyal statements" subsection of the UCMJ, Article 134.

I had no idea what to think after reading Robert's accusation. But I certainly knew what I was feeling: fury. He was the one who should have been charged—for breaking and entering, for theft, for reading another midshipman's mail, for lying.

The PIO slid over a copy of the policy on disloyal statements. The elements of the crime—I shivered to see the word *crime* so starkly on the paper—were as follows: the accused actually made the alleged statement; the statement was made in public; the statement was disloyal to the United States; the statement promoted or encouraged troops or the civilian population to be disloyal or hostile toward the United States; the statement impaired and/or interfered with the morale, discipline, or loyalty to the United States or a member or multiple members of the United States military; and the nature of the statement was such that it brought discredit to the discipline and good order of the armed forces.

Maybe the provisions were supposed to scare me, but they comforted me instead. I knew that the first part at least didn't apply to me; I hadn't actually made the alleged statement.

The context of the letter would make that obvious enough. After all, it referenced a division that had long since been renamed, and didn't the letter say something about working in France?

"I need to see the letter," I said. I'd read all the rules; I knew that, as defendant, I was entitled to view the evidence against me. "Request to see material evidence, sir."

Another officer chopped into the room with a box. Even in my desperation, I couldn't help but admire the academy's efficiency.

And its organization. The materials were neatly labeled. I glanced at the envelope, my name clearly marked, and then pulled out the letter. I'd read it before, of course, but not under these circumstances. Not thinking I could be court-martialed for its content.

This time, the letter was different. It had been cut at the top and the bottom so that the context was gone; it no longer mentioned Mr. Thomas Plunkett, which would date the letter.

A few lines stood out to me.

We are dismayed and horrified by the attack on free speech at home in America.

Americans—in times of peace and in times of war, in civilian life and in the military—should never be denied the right to express their views. Even if their views align more closely with the enemy's; even if their views are not popular with the masses. Even if their views are socialism, anarchism, bolshevism.

We cannot help but wonder what democracy is worth if it is democracy without dissent, if it is democracy for a privileged few but not for all.

My vision started to fade like I was going to pass out again, but I willed myself to stay present. I fixed my eye on the American flag in the corner of the PIO's office and tethered myself to it. One star, two stars, three stars, four.

I blinked my eyes and returned to earth, feeling the blisters on my heels and the sore muscles in my midsection.

"I did not write this letter, sir."

He had to believe me, but even if the letter was written in the past, it applied today. The FBI was after the Black Panther Party. The Russians were sending signals through our radios. We still had Air Force fighting communism in Thailand, and we'd only just left Vietnam while I was in high school after years of protests and calls of pacifism.

If I'd been trying to disseminate this letter, I would have been trying to undermine the United States government, the military.

I looked back to the PIO. "Are you moving forward with the investigation, sir?"

A curt nod.

"Then I need to tell you that Robert has been targeting me. I've already filed one complaint, which—"

The PIO held up a hand. "That incident was investigated, and no defendants were identified."

"But."

"Miss Carre!" The man stood to tower over me, and I didn't miss his second use of "Miss" rather than "Midshipman." On a civilian, I might consider it an oversight. But the Navy did nothing by accident.

"You do not," he snarled, "under any circumstances, contradict a senior officer. Offense Code 4.05."

I pulled my chin in. "No excuse, sir." Unless being falsely accused counted as one.

The man sat back down and gestured for me to do the same. I complied, my foot tapping anxiously on the ground.

"I'm going to ask that you fill out a report describing your version of events. We will use it as evidence in our pending investigation."

He slid yet another paper toward me, along with a pen. I swallowed as I picked it up. Nana had loved the adage that the pen is mightier than the sword, but I'd never bought it. Now I might have to.

I went back to the beginning. I explained how I'd come into my room to find it in shambles, then wrote about the note Robert had left. Then, I moved on to explaining why I'd ended up with Nana's package to Nicholas and how it had disappeared from my room on Thursday. *The materials in question were mine, but they were not written by me nor taken to Mitscher Hall for distribution. Rather, the postmark on the envelope—as well as details in the text—indicate they were written in 1918. Robert has omitted the authors' initials as well the other contextualizing information from the sample he's provided.*

I read over my statement to make sure it made sense, that all my punctuation was correct and my handwriting was neat.

"Sir." I passed it over. I was feeling better already, the ability to write my own story returning some of my lost power. What I'd written was the truth, and I knew enough about the Navy's thorough standards to assume they'd get to the bottom of things.

At least, I hoped so. They hadn't necessarily done so in the past.

"This concludes today's interview." The PIO tucked my account into a file.

"Thank you, sir." The words burned. "When can I expect the results of the investigation, sir?"

"In no more than five days. Good day."

And with that, he sent me stumbling into the passageway, nauseated and unable to breathe. I wanted more than anything to call my grandmother. I wanted to hear her soothing voice and listen to her words of comfort. I wanted to ask her whether she'd mailed that letter, and why. I wanted to ask her what to do.

Chapter 25

Emmaline Balakin

November 1918

When I woke the day after the air raid siren, I couldn't open my eyes. They were puffy and heavy, and my heart felt the same. I had to drag myself from bed and into my uniform, then nearly forgot to affix the ALA pin to my arm. What was the point of anything, when we could all be dead in an instant? What could lines on a page do to protect us from the finality of death?

We had canceled this week's book club in light of Perlie's death, but I forced myself to grab my wheelbarrow in my trembling hands and wrestle it through the mud, visiting the wards in the same order I always did as if nothing were wrong. But I wasn't fooling anybody. I named the wrong authors, mangled titles, and

lapsed into unfocused silence when the men asked me for recommendations. Finally, an older soldier with an amputated arm drew
his bushy eyebrows together and told me I needed a taste of my
own medicine. "You prescribe us happy books when we're feeling
blue," he said reprovingly. "Go read one for yourself."

I told him I was just fine, but I thought more about his words
as I pushed my wheelbarrow back into the snow. I only had
one more ward to do today, and it could wait until tomorrow.
When perhaps Perlie's death didn't sting quite so acutely. When I
didn't want to seize every doctor by the collar of his coat and ask
him *why*.

I left the wheelbarrow in the main room of the recreation hut
for the men to peruse and then slipped inside my bedroom. I
wished for the umpteenth time it had a lock, because I never felt
entirely safe in here when there were men just outside the door.

I reached for the old, worn copy of *Jane Eyre* that I kept beside
my bed. But there was another book on top of it. *A Tale of Two Cities* by Charles Dickens.

My brain searched for an explanation. Several of the men,
Nicholas included, had recently checked *A Tale of Two Cities* out
from our library. But why would they return it here, rather than in
the drop boxes in the wards or recreation hut?

I picked up the book. With a gold-embossed image of Dickens
on the deep red cover, it was an old edition of the book. The same
one Nicholas had been so excited to find in the library.

I cracked it open, looking for that famous opening line. But a
note that had been folded into the front cover of the book fluttered
to the ground, and Nicholas's handwriting was immediately rec-
ognizable as I bent to pick it up.

Dear Emmaline,

Already, I was so overcome that I had to sit. Months ago, it had been a letter in this very script that had started me on this journey. But that one had been addressed to Vivian, not to me.

> *I know the last several days have been difficult. I remember what it was like my first week in the trenches, when I was confronted with my own mortality and that of my fellow men.*
> *Don't forget about the power of words to keep us alive. A Tale of Two Cities in particular serves as a reminder of two things:*
> *That anyone can be a hero,*
> *and that love remains a miracle in the midst of war.*
> *Yours,*
> *Nicholas*

Overwhelmed with emotion, I had to consciously keep from crumpling the note in my hand. Nicholas had read my mind, the way he so adeptly addressed all of my fears. How did he know that I'd awoken this morning fearing that my work meant nothing in the face of destruction? How had he known that the world seemed devoid of heroes and miracles and heart?

And love. He was referring to Sydney Carton, of course, who'd taken Lucie Manette Darnay's husband's place at the guillotine out of love for her. But for Nicholas to write of love in a message intended for me . . .

I lay back in bed. So much had changed since I'd read Nicholas's first letter in the Dead Letter Office. Between the two of us—but also in me. I had fought and created, loved and lost. I was a different version of the girl who'd come to France a month earlier.

A *Tale of Two Cities* and Sydney Carton spoke to that, too. To the capacity for change.

I settled onto my cot and opened the book again. No notes fell out this time, and I was able to read Dickens's words from the beginning.

It was the best of times, it was the worst of times . . .

I read all throughout the afternoon and skipped supper; eventually, the voices in the other room faded. With them faded my awareness of where I was and what had happened. I was fully in Dickens's world. So when a knock came on my door, I nearly screamed.

"One moment," I called.

"Emmaline? It's me."

I dropped my book. It was Nicholas's voice. I opened the door and stared at him like I was seeing him for the first time. With the eyes of the confidante I'd become to him these last several weeks. My gaze ran over his strong shoulders, his gray eyes, his genuine smile.

The proper thing to do would be to join Nicholas in the main room, but I wasn't ready to reenter the real world just yet. "Do you want to come in?"

Nicholas nodded, taking a tentative step forward and letting the door shut behind him. The room was too small for the two of us.

Nicholas's face creased in concern. "How are you?"

I gestured to the book on the bed. "I've been feeling a little bit better in here. But I don't know how I'll go out and face everyone tomorrow. Especially the doctors." I looked up at Nicholas. "I just want to shake them, explain to them who Perlie was and who he's left at home." My eyes welled with tears. "Did you see the picture of his daughters? Tess and Annie." The tears were falling now. "They no longer have a father."

Nicholas guided me to the bed and helped me sit. "Oh, Emmaline. They'll always have a father. If you love someone, they never fully leave you."

I thought of how I tried to live out my parents' legacies and realized Nicholas was right. And then there was the way that Nicholas and I, even when apart, had always been intertwined.

We shared a past: the cake Nicholas and I had split and the dumplings we'd attempted to cook. We'd imagined a future, Nicholas waiting for me underneath the streetlight that Christmas evening.

And even when that future didn't hold, when we'd ended up in different cities and different circles, we'd followed similar paths. We'd both lost our parents and relied on working with words to provide us purpose and pay our bills. We'd both come to France.

But nothing felt certain in wartime. Not after Perlie's death, not after I'd stood under the night sky and stared mortality in the face. So I admitted the truth to Nicholas. "It feels like everyone leaves me eventually."

Nicholas covered my hand with his own. "Not me, Emmaline. I'm not going anywhere."

"You promise?"

Nicholas reached up and stroked my face. "Not even tonight." He looked at me with a question in his eyes.

My heart sped up at what he proposed, even as the idea of

keeping him close felt like comfort. I met his eyes. "If we get caught—"

He put a finger on my mouth, sending a thrill through my body. "We've done more dangerous things before."

He was right. I let him lay me down and tuck me under the covers, then watched as he removed his cap and his jacket and lay beside me. He stayed on top of the sheets, a layer separating us.

"Nicholas," I whispered in the dark.

"Yes?"

I was afraid to ask, but I had to know that I meant as much to Nicholas as he did to me. "The other day, when you mentioned Vivian Winthrop . . ." I trailed off. I didn't know how to phrase the question when I was so afraid to hear its answer.

There was a moment of silence, and then the cot shifted as Nicholas sat up. "Anything Vivian and I had is over, Emmaline. If we had anything at all."

"What do you mean?"

"She was bright and smart and funny, but she hated to listen. And God knows we had nothing in common." He paused. "I think it would have ended long ago if I hadn't been drafted. But once I was, I needed something to hold on to. I needed some connection to home, and with my parents gone, Vivian provided that. Does that make any sense at all?"

Even in the darkness, I could see the earnest, beseeching look on his face.

"Yes," I said. "That makes sense." I knew what it was to cling to something comforting regardless of reality.

I didn't need more assurance, but Nicholas continued. "I could never have loved her. But I've known since we were children, Emmaline, that I could love you."

That he *could* love me. Did that mean he did?

I was too afraid to break the spell to ask, so I closed my eyes and drifted into the blessedness of sleep.

Nicholas was still beside me when I woke up in the middle of the night. I'd had a nightmare I couldn't quite remember, and it had left me with this need to take everything I could from life while I still had the chance. Right now, with Nicholas beside me, all I wanted was him.

I propped myself up on an elbow, gasping, and Nicholas's eyes flew open. "What happened?"

"Just a nightmare." My heartbeat began to slow.

"Do you need to talk about it?" Nicholas propped himself up like my mirror image, and even in the darkness, his eyes flashed when they met mine.

"No," I said. I spoke quietly, my face just inches from Nicholas's.

We weren't supposed to be here. We weren't supposed to be doing this. But this was what I wanted, and it could all be gone in an instant. "I don't need to talk about it," I said. "But there is something I need to do."

I leaned forward and pressed my lips to Nicholas's. I felt his surprise, and then his instant response. His fingers danced across my back, and I could feel his heat through my thin pongee uniform. After a month in the cold, damp forests of France, Nicholas's warmth felt like coming home. He shouldn't have felt safe, not when everything we'd done and were doing together was an act for which we could be punished. But he did.

I closed my eyes and let Nicholas kiss me back. I pressed my lips to his cheeks and down the side of his neck; when he moaned, I lingered at the base of his throat.

"Emmaline." I loved hearing him say my name. He'd written first to Vivian, but it was my name he whispered in the dark.

I ran my fingers through Nicholas's hair, then traced his jawbone. The stubble on his cheeks prickled my fingertips and I leaned into him. He tumbled backward so he was faceup on my bed. I lay atop him, startled at the heat that bloomed in my lower belly and spread through my legs.

I knew I should stop, but Nicholas's eyes invited me in. And for once in my life, I was feeling instead of thinking.

I kissed Nicholas again. His hands on my waist sent a thrill up my spine, and I wished they could touch the bare skin burning beneath my clothes. My own hands snaked under the collar of Nicholas's shirt and lay flush against his heated skin. He grabbed my wrists as if he were trying to pull me closer, then suddenly let go and grasped the base of his shirt. I rolled to his side and watched as he pulled it off and cast it aside. An array of bandages crisscrossed his torso, and I inhaled. "Your wound."

Nicholas swore under his breath and looked up with eyes dark with desire. "Don't worry about it," he said.

But I couldn't help myself. I traced the outline of the gauze and frowned. "Does it still hurt?"

"Not enough to stop."

The low rumble of his words made me flush. I gasped when he rolled on top of me, then quieted when he pressed his lips against mine. With his body shielding me from the rest of the world, I reached with fumbling fingers to the collar of my blouse. Slowly, I unhooked the buttons that marched in perfect formation down to my waist.

Nicholas's breathing grew labored. As I threw my blouse to the side, he fell upon my chemise. His large fingers tugged at the ribbons cinching the sleeves and then gave up; this gentle, bookish man yanked at my chemise so hard that the straps snapped.

I gasped, but not in fear or pain. I didn't have a word for the why of it; no book I'd ever read had gotten quite this far. Not even *Madame Bovary* and its carriage scene had told me what went on behind closed doors.

I didn't know what came next—only that I wasn't supposed to allow it.

Nicholas pressed the bare skin of his chest against mine, and our bodies fit like two puzzle pieces. I looked down and marveled at the way our skin could feel so similar and yet look so different: mine, pale white and smooth; his, near-brown and sun-crisped, spotted with dark hair.

Pressed up against each other, it still wasn't enough.

He pulled me closer as artillery exploded above us. I rested my head in the curve of his neck, and we held each other until the echoes faded.

We moved slower after that. By the time I tugged Nicholas's belt loose and he unclasped the side of my skirt, the rest of the world was silent. When we came together, I heard nothing but our breath.

Chapter 26

—— ❖ ——

Kathleen Carre

July 1976

I walked to the principal inquiry officer's office after PEP on Friday according to Ensign Michael's instructions. The officer nodded to the chair across from his desk when I arrived, and I sat perched on its edge as required for plebes. I kept my back straight, my hands folded in my lap.

"Miss Carre."

Again, the use of "Miss" did not bode well for the results of the investigation.

"Sir."

"The results of our preliminary questioning have been inconclusive. Material evidence demonstrates that you were in possession of seditious materials; however, only oral testimony suggests that you both wrote and intended to distribute said materials. Were this not directly in contrast with your testimony, it would be enough." He gave me a hard look. "Need I remind you that lying is intolerable at the Naval Academy, and that evidence in that vein will result in your separation as surely as sedition would?"

"Sir, no, sir. I stand by my statement, sir."

"Very well, then. This will have to go to an Article 32 preliminary hearing."

I was to be put on trial? It was like a nightmare, a darkroom negative of what my life should have been. I was supposed to be exemplary, honorable, responsible. I *was* all of those things.

"Sir, yes, sir," I managed.

"The hearing will be a week from today."

"Sir, yes, sir."

"You are not obligated to testify on your own behalf. Would you like to do so regardless?"

"Sir, yes, sir." I signed the form he slid across the desk.

"And would you like to call any witnesses to the stand?"

Yes. Nicholas Agrapov. But I couldn't rely on him. "No, sir."

"You also have a right to free legal counsel."

I hesitated. A month ago, I would have taken it. But now, I didn't want a man digging into my life. I didn't want him uncovering the shame of what Robert and Tom had done to me in the bathroom, didn't want to relive it in front of a court. And I didn't think I could trust a military man to defend me against his peers.

"I can represent myself, sir."

The PIO raised his eyebrows. "You understand that your right to legal counsel is free of charge?"

"Sir, yes, sir. I can represent myself, sir."

He pursed his lips and looked distastefully at my sweaty PEP gear. "Understood. You will wear your service dress uniform to the hearing."

"Sir, yes, sir." I'd known that, of course. I'd spent all my free time recently—not that I had much—reading about the Navy's honor councils and courts-martial. An Article 32 hearing meant that I was being considered for a general court-martial, the most severe level. I could be confined, dishonorably discharged, or even put to death. I didn't imagine, of course, that I'd be put to death for a letter—but dishonorable discharge and confinement hardly sounded better.

The man nodded again and checked his watch. I envied him the privilege. "You may go to morning meal formation," he said.

I didn't have time for my two-minute shower. I changed into my service whites and then sprinted to Tecumseh Court. I joined my company as we completed our daily parade.

"Center, face!"

There, uniform checks were conducted for the public to see. Usually, I bristled with pride in these moments. I loved showing off to Annapolis, to the tourists, to those who looked at us and saw us all as midshipmen rather than as woman or man. But today, I could think of nothing other than my trial. Each sweaty tendril of hair plastered to my forehead reminded me.

After parade check, we marched into the dining hall and to our chow calls. In unison, our company recited the day's menus and today's officer on duty, and then Robert was called to name three world events that occurred this week.

"The USSR performed an underground nuclear test," he shot off. "An earthquake struck Tangshan in the People's Republic of China." He hesitated just for a moment, and I reveled in his uncertainty before Ensign Michael shouted, "Twenty push-ups!"

We dropped to the deck like we were dodging bullets, accustomed to the punishment. I gritted my teeth as I pressed my heels against each other, working to stay up.

Then finally was breakfast. Although it was still difficult to eat, I'd learned my lesson and forced the food down. I wouldn't pass out again, give anyone reason to doubt my competence when I already had a Form-2 filed and a trial coming up.

I went through my classes the rest of the day with a restless energy. I checked my wrist for the time every few minutes, hating that I couldn't wear a watch that would count down the minutes till our free call time. Now that I would be put to trial, I needed to talk to Nicholas again. Desperately.

But the lines were long, and reveille began before I got a chance to call, which meant that I had to wait. I called but got no answer on Saturday, and it was Sunday by the time the man picked up.

"Mr. Agrapov," I said. "It's Kathleen Carre again. Please don't hang up. I have no interest in incriminating you in anything, nor in stirring up traumatic memories. I simply need your help." Though I hated to admit needing help, my plea seemed to work. There was silence on the other end of the line, but no click. No dial tone. So, I continued on. "The letter Nana sent you was stolen from my room. One of the other plebes is framing me for making disloyal statements, and he's cut off the contextual parts of the letter so it looks like I wrote it myself."

I paused to give Nicholas a chance to respond, but he didn't.

"I'm going to be court-martialed and separated from the academy if I can't prove that he's lying. I need to prove that I didn't write that letter. That someone else wrote it sixty years ago." I didn't ask Nicholas whether it was him. The question was obvious enough.

"I'm sorry, Kathleen." Nicholas's voice was weary; I could hear the weight of every decade he'd lived, from war to depression to war again—and again—and again. "But I can't help you. I don't want anything to do with it. Not anymore."

"Do you have a copy of the *Bismarck Tribune* with the letter published, perhaps? Something that doesn't have your name on it but that would prove that the accusations are false?"

"I'm sorry, Kathleen. I do wish you the best, but I can't be involved."

"I just need one thing. One thing, and I'll leave you alone. I don't have much time." The desperation in my voice was embarrassing, but maybe it would sway Nicholas. "My trial is on Friday."

Nicholas's voice was less apologetic and more irritated when he spoke next. "You know life won't be all chocolates even if you're found innocent, don't you?"

Even through my frustration, a spark of fondness took hold. That was something Nana used to say. She said her life was *all chocolate* now that she had me. But I'd never heard anyone else use the phrase. "Is that something they said in France? My nana said it, too."

"No." Nicholas sounded puzzled. "It's a Russian idiom. *V shekalade*. Everything is in chocolate."

"Nellie wasn't Russian," I said, just to keep Nicholas talking. "At least, she never mentioned it. Nor did Jane. Not," I snorted, "that *that's* worth much."

"Jane?" There was suddenly a sharpness in Nicholas's voice, an alertness that hadn't been there before in his resigned, apologetic tones. "Who is Jane?"

"My mother, technically. But Nana was the one who raised me."

"Jane . . . Do you know why she was given that name?"

What an odd question. But if it kept Nicholas from hanging up on me, I'd answer. "Knowing my grandmother, it was probably after Jane Austen or something—"

"Not Jane Austen," Nicholas interrupted. "Jane Eyre."

I gripped the telephone more tightly, slightly annoyed. "Okay, maybe." What right did he have to pretend he knew my grandmother better than I did when he wouldn't even help me? When he'd returned the letter she'd sent him?

"What does it matter?"

"I'm sorry. I'm getting ahead of myself. I need to go," Nicholas said. Just like he had the first time I'd talked to him.

"Wait," I cried. But the line was already dead.

I chopped down Stribling Walk and across Rickover Terrace and entered the concrete mammoth of Nimitz Library. I had to see if there was anything about Thomas Plunkett in our wartime records or, even better, whether we had old copies of the *Bismarck Tribune*.

But when I surveyed the drawers of microfiche in the newspaper archives section, there was nothing. We had the *Washington Post*, a few New York papers, and news published by the military. But nothing from Bismarck, North Dakota, which I couldn't pretend was any sort of surprise.

I trekked back downstairs to check the card catalog for Thomas Plunkett. A female midshipman with a brown bob and sharp green eyes was coming up at the same time, and I placed her after a moment as Marsha Tyrell. She'd organized the so-called mutiny last week with Janice Buxbaum, and both of them were under review. We didn't know any more than that, largely because we women were afraid to be seen together after what had happened. We had no way to communicate, and the only girls I'd talked to since the failed women's meeting were Linda and Susan.

My instinct now was to ignore Marsha and continue down the stairs. I didn't want to be associated with her, both of us on the verge of expulsion, but if I was feeling isolated and terrified, I knew Marsha must be feeling the same way. So, I scrounged up a smile for her and a nod. "Midshipman Tyrell."

We faced each other, her on the step below me heading up, me on the step above and heading down. It would have been impossible for her to miss my nod and my greeting, but her shoulders shrank in as she passed me, and her eyes didn't drift my way. She continued hurriedly up the steps without a backward glance.

Odd. But I wasn't here to make friends. I was here to clear my name.

Downstairs, I flicked through the entries for *P* in the card catalog. A station-bill for the USS *Philadelphia*, Seaman Edward M. Pickman's papers from a World War I prison camp, an 1860 journal of the USS *Plymouth* . . . but nothing about a Thomas Plunkett.

I met Susan and Linda back at Bancroft Hall, and the three of us got to work cleaning our room. We had a formal room inspection in the evening, and though we kept our room neat at all times for informal room checks, this required extra thoroughness.

Linda swept the deck as Susan scratched soap scum from the shower with a razor and I dusted the blinds. We organized the lockboxes on our desks and the desk drawers themselves, and made sure our clothes were folded according to regulation.

Susan snickered as she pulled out her bras. "I'll never forget that firstie's face when he taught us how to fold a bra."

Linda laughed. "It was like he'd never seen one before."

Susan demonstrated the way the man had held the bra he used to demonstrate, his fingers pinched and his nose wrinkled in disgust. They dissolved into laughter. And normally I would have too—Susan's impression was spot-on—but I was too worried.

Linda turned to me. "Kathleen? You're not laughing."

I forced a smile. "I was distracted." I waved my hand. "Making sure my bras were folded right, you know?" It was a weak attempt at humor. Linda dropped the shirt she was folding.

"Kathleen, what's wrong?"

Susan put her hands on her hips. "Don't lie to us." She put on a mock authoritative voice. "Midshipmen are persons of integrity: They stand for that which is right."

Linda took over the next part of the Midshipman Honor Concept. "They tell the truth and ensure that the truth is known."

Both girls looked at me expectantly, waiting for me to finish things off with a hearty *They do not lie.*

But instead, I fell into my desk chair. "*We* can't lie," I said. "But the boys seem to get away with it."

Linda came closer and put a hand on my shoulder. "Is this about the boys who ransacked your side of the room? The ones who left that disgusting note?"

"Because the officers aren't the only ones who can dole out punishments," Susan said. "They failed you, but we can drum something up." She raised her eyebrows. "God knows the boys here could use a taste of their own medicine."

I looked at the girls: Linda, her eyebrows drawn together in concern; Susan, her eyes narrowed. I thought of what Mabel had said about sharing my troubles, and suddenly, I remembered too Nana's one piece of advice: *Find another girl there, another woman. Someone to be your friend. Someone you can always rely on.* I'd forgotten it, discounted it after a lifetime of counting on myself.

But now, maybe it was time to accept that that wasn't enough. That we weren't meant to be alone. That was why the Navy organized us into companies, after all, and why we competed against each other for Color Company each semester. That was why we weren't allowed to bilge our classmates—why I'd gotten in trouble for running ahead of my squadron rather than celebrated for it.

I took a deep breath and then let the story of Nicholas's letter spill out. I told Linda and Susan about the letters to Vivian, the letter Nicholas had returned to my grandmother, and Robert's formal complaint against me.

I braced myself for pity when I was done, but Linda's eyes were wide with excitement. "You said Robert reported having found the letter in Mitscher Hall?"

"Yes." I grimaced. Being located at the scene of the mutiny wouldn't give the court a good opening impression of me.

"But that's perfect," Linda said. "We were there. We can testify that you didn't have the letter with you."

I gaped at her, not sure whether to laugh or cry. I felt like an idiot for not having thought of it sooner; when the PIO had asked me if I wanted to call any witnesses to the stand, I'd said no. Now I tamped down the flush of embarrassment and focused on the hope instead. "Are you certain you don't mind testifying?"

"Of course not," Susan said. "You know they have it coming."

I didn't ask whether "they" was the Naval Academy or Robert and his cronies.

Linda smiled. "You don't think we would just abandon you to the wolves, do you?"

I forced a smile in return, because part of me did think that. Not because Linda or Susan had ever done anything to give me that impression, but because—well, why would they risk their own standing to protect mine?

The answer came to me in a flash: because we were a team. Just as I'd sprinted to the school cafeteria for a bag of ice when my relay partner in high school had sprained her ankle despite having just run my own leg of the race, Linda and Susan were there when I needed them. This was in part what I'd come to the academy to find, what was missing in my bookkeeping job, and I'd managed to forget it in my constant fear of looking weak or being singled out.

"Thank you," I said to Linda and Susan. "If I can ever do anything for you in return—"

Susan interrupted me. "You can make my rack every morning."

I looked at her, startled, until she burst into laughter. "I'm teasing, Kathleen. You don't need to repay us."

I still would, somehow, but I kept that thought to myself. "Thank you," I said instead. "Thank you so much."

Chapter 27

—— ❈ ——

Emmaline Balakin

November 1918

Faint light shone between the cracks in the walls. I never slept through to morning here. But with Nicholas beside me, it seemed that I had.

"Good morning." I felt a smile spread across my face like syrup, languid and relaxed and entirely unlike me.

Nicholas's eyes opened, and he stretched out on my bed. "Good morning." His smile was as unfamiliar as mine felt, unreserved and almost goofy. "How did you sleep?"

I gestured to the light coming in through the slats in the wall. "Well, apparently. You?"

Nicholas's smile disappeared, and he looked at me with an intensity almost as intimate as what we'd done together last night.

"Would it scare you if I said I want to sleep like this for the rest of my life?"

I laughed. "We're in a war zone. There's not much you could say that would scare me."

"You're the one who told me words were more dangerous than weapons, Miss Balakin."

I loved my surname on his tongue, pronounced with the same Russian vowels my parents had used, and leaned forward to taste the word on his lips.

His mouth twisted under mine, and I pulled away. "What is it?"

He ducked his chin. "I can't say the nurses expected me to be quite so careless with my injury."

I looked down at his abdomen and winced. The bandage across his wound was soaked through with blood, and it sagged loosely like it was too heavy to remain in place for much longer.

"Let me see what I can find," I said. "There must be something in here we can use to patch you up."

We both sat up and surveyed the room: the deflated football, a pair of abandoned mittens, a smattering of excess chess pieces.

"There?" Nicholas pointed to an unlabeled box in the corner.

"Maybe," I said. "Let me see."

But Nicholas had already swung his feet to the ground. "Oops." He leaned over and picked up a sheet of paper. "I stepped on this, sorry. Didn't notice it last night." He flashed me a mischievous grin, and I blushed.

And then I realized what it was he must have found. "I can take that," I said, my voice high-pitched and unnatural. "It's nothing important."

But Nicholas was smiling. "This is my handwriting. Are you

keeping my note in your pocket?" A glint appeared in his eye. "It must have fallen out last night."

"Must have!" I lied as I reached out to grab the letter before Nicholas realized what it really was. But I was too late. His mouth contorted in confusion, and it was obvious. He knew.

"This isn't the letter I wrote *you*," he said. "It's a letter I wrote to Vivian."

"I—"

"How do you have this? Do you know her? Did she give it to you?"

"No, I—"

Realization dawned on his face. "You got this at the Dead Letter Office."

I could only nod.

"So if Vivian never received my letter . . ." A storm was brewing in his tone. "Were *you* the one to write back to me?"

I couldn't meet his eyes. "I did," I whispered. I didn't know how to explain that Vivian *had* received his letter and had merely chosen not to respond, and Nicholas spoke before I could.

"Damn it, Emmaline." He'd never sworn at me before. He fell onto my bed, head in his hands. "We've *talked* about Vivian. And you were lying to me all along?"

"I never meant to lie." I wanted to explain, to tell Nicholas that I'd written to help him, not to hurt him. That everything since that letter had been genuine. But I was so thrown by his discovery that I could barely think straight.

"But you *did*," Nicholas said. "You *did* lie. What else was a fantasy?" He cast his gaze around the room. "This, between us? Have you just been using me for the book club and the censorship letter?"

"Of course not!" I was screaming now. The sound of it was as unfamiliar as the curses on Nicholas's tongue. Tears flowed down my face. "I love you, Nicholas." This wasn't how the declaration was made in a novel, wasn't how I'd said it in my daydreams. But I wanted Nicholas to see that this was real. "I love you."

Nicholas stood. "I don't know if I can believe that anymore."

And then he was gone.

I had to talk to Nicholas. I had to explain. But I had always been so much better with written words than spoken ones. Before I went to beg his forgiveness, I sat down and wrote. I wrote down how much I loved Nicholas's kindness and honesty and support, how everything had been true. How I'd only written back to preserve the one thing I knew he needed: hope. And while I knew better than to read the letter to Nicholas when letters had gotten us into this mess, it helped me organize my thoughts enough for me to feel ready to talk to him.

I wanted to run, but I forced myself to walk. I'd already screamed and cried, and it had done no good. I had to be calm now. Logical.

The day nurses were just coming in to relieve the night nurses, and there was enough bustle that I slipped in unnoticed. I skidded to a stop beside Nicholas's bed and nearly crumpled. An hour ago, his stubble had brushed against my chin, my breasts, my— *Stop*, I told myself. Now we were here.

"Nicholas."

"Miss Balakin." His voice was cold.

"Emmaline." I whispered it like a question. "Please."

Nicholas remained silent.

"I wrote to you for your sake," I said. "Not mine. Vivian was married. She sent your letter back unopened. But I knew how much you needed something to hold on to at the front, and I couldn't bear for you to find out like that. So I wrote back. I'm sorry."

Nicholas's face was as pink as if I'd slapped him. Vivian's marriage, I realized, was yet another betrayal from a woman he'd thought he could love. But he recovered quickly. "This isn't one of your novels," he said. "This isn't *Emma*. It isn't *Twelfth Night*. You can't play with people like you're Austen or Shakespeare."

"I never meant to play with you. I meant what I said earlier. And everything that has happened here, Nicholas, has been the truth. I've been more honest with you than with anyone." My voice broke. "I'm so sorry."

Nicholas rubbed his temples, and I saw for a moment the man I knew. "I'm sorry, too," he said.

I was afraid to ask him what came next. "Will you—*can* you—forgive me?"

Nicholas took a long moment before responding. "I hope so, Emmaline. Because I loved you, too."

More than anything else, his use of the past tense tore me apart. I turned from the ward and ran, not caring if I looked unhinged or that I was splashing freezing mud all over my uniform.

But when I burst through the door of the recreation hut, I wasn't alone. Colonel Hodgson stood before me, a smirk on his lips and a sheet of paper dangling from his hand. "Miss Balakin," he said. "So lovely of you to stop by."

Chapter 28

Kathleen Carre

August 1976

I was as prepared as I could be the morning of my hearing. I'd practiced my testimony and listened to Susan and Linda practice theirs. I'd highlighted all the inconsistencies in the copy of the letter I'd been provided, ready to point out that they made no sense in a modern-day interpretation.

But all the preparation in the world couldn't calm me. How I wished I could sit beside my grandmother with a mug of tea and soak up her quiet wisdom. But I could never do that again.

Instead, I left the room early in my exercise clothes and began to run. I was out before PEP, having been excused from the morning routine for the day, and I had the Yard to myself.

I practiced my testimony for the first mile, which I kept slow and easy. After that, I sped up and let myself forget it all, lost in the feel of my feet slapping the wet ground. I passed the gymnasium, Nimitz Library, Herndon Monument. I rolled my shoulders back as I looked up at the obelisk. I'd be climbing it at the end of the summer just like all the other plebes, I swore to myself. They wouldn't force me out.

I ran along the edge of the bay and marveled at the wide expanse of it, the knowledge that even the oceans weren't unknowable to the Navy. To the Navy that I was a part of. The Navy that I was determined to *stay* a part of.

By the time I returned to Bancroft, I was sweaty and alive. My thighs were too sore and my breathing too fast for me to summon enough energy to feel anxious.

I showered and dressed alongside my roommates. I put on my uniform as instructed, the buttons marching up my blouse like toy soldiers. When we were ready, Linda, Susan, and I stood in front of the bathroom mirror to check that everything was in place. My spine tingled as I stared at our reflections. We stood in a neat row, our hair bobbed and our covers on. We wore the same boxy white jacket and A-line skirt; all three of us stood straight despite the uneven shoes we were forced to wear.

"This right here is the Navy," I whispered.

Susan turned to me. "What do you mean?"

I twisted my lip in thought, not sure how to put it into words, then gestured at our images. "We look the part."

"Hardly." Linda turned and surveyed herself in profile. Her top bunched up above her hips, which were too wide for the jacket's straight, masculine cut. It was a common problem among the girls, and some had taken to rolling the hem under and stapling it.

I shook my head. "It's not just the uniforms, though. It's what we're doing. Standing up for honesty and truth. In your cases, being loyal. Being a team."

"Everything a midshipman stands for," Linda murmured.

"And rightly so," Susan said. "We're just as much midshipmen as the rest of them are."

"Let's keep it that way." I pulled a face. "Because despite it all . . ." I looked at the ghostly traces of *ugly* and *bitch* and *fat* and *dyke* that still lingered on the mirror. "Despite it all, I want to stay."

Linda's eyes floated from one word to the next, lingering on *fat*. "Twenty percent never graduate, you know. And we've got it harder than the rest."

Then she squared her shoulders, and I saw Susan's ferocity in her for a moment, Nana's quiet resolution. "But we won't leave," Linda said. "Between the three of us, let's keep the percentage at zero."

We turned heads on the way to D.C. Female midshipmen were mythical, legendary; sitting across from three on public transit must have felt like running across a unicorn.

By unspoken agreement, all three of us sat as if we were in King Hall: on the front three inches of our seats, our backs not touching. We kept our covers on and our eyes trained forward. This was our chance to prove to the public that women could be as military in bearing as men could.

A portly man in a blue button-down smiled at us, turning around in his seat. "Where are you ladies off to?"

"Midshipmen," Susan corrected. The man nodded and waited expectantly, but Susan didn't answer his question.

He cleared his throat. "Where are you midshipmen off to?"

Susan smiled. "I'm afraid that's classified, sir."

I wondered if the "sir" was her southern or her Navy coming out.

"Classified!" The man whistled. "My daughter's going to love this. She wants to be Air Force. Pictures up all over her walls." He laughed. "My older one's room is filled with covers from *Tiger Beat*—Bobby Sherman, John Travolta. I must say I prefer the airplanes."

The man's companion twisted back for the first time. "Be careful. Lindy's such a pretty thing. You don't want her turning into some sort of man." He sent a particularly hard look in Susan's direction. Though we all had our hair shorn, Susan's muscled arms and thick eyebrows lent her a more traditionally masculine look than Linda or I had.

Linda's lips parted, and mine pursed. Even Susan stayed silent—likely not wanting the men to see us as overemotional. Both men turned back around, the one in blue looking cowed.

"Sorry about my friend," he whispered as we passed him to exit the train. "Lindy'll still be excited."

I gave him a smile, glad Susan hadn't told him the reason for our visit today. His daughter didn't need to know that I was on trial—that, as female plebes, *we* were on trial. That was what this summer was, after all. We had to prove to the world that we could do this just as the men could.

I wondered how old Lindy was, and how much would change before she graduated from high school. I hoped she was young—kindergarten, maybe—which would put her graduation in 1989. Would women make up half of the academy by then? Would they be allowed in combat and on submarines? I squared my shoulders as Susan, Linda, and I hopped onto the Metro that would take us to the Washington Navy Yard. They better be.

Sweating in the heat, we walked from the Metro stop to the entry gate at the Navy Yard. The armed men checked our naval credentials before ushering us in, and we made our way toward the building that housed the Naval Criminal Investigative Service and the court judge. We passed Civil War cannons and rifles on display as we walked, and I lifted my chin. So much had changed in the century since the Civil War; so much more could change. *Would* change.

The three of us marched into the building and gave our names to the receptionist, a woman about our own age. She could have been me a month ago, back when I was a bookkeeper, and I prayed to God that wasn't where I would end up again. My life had been easier, then, sure. But it wasn't the life I wanted.

The bailiff led us down a long hallway and stopped before a closed door. "Midshipmen Burr and Silver, you will remain here until called."

"Sir, yes, sir," they chorused. Linda's arms jerked forward and then fell back down like she wanted to hug me and had decided against it. Susan flashed me a surreptitious thumbs-up, and I made myself smile back at both of them as the bailiff led me into the room.

Just left of the door was the witness stand, directly opposite the desk where the preliminary inquiry officer sat. It was a different judge advocate than the PIO who had first looked into the case, a change I'd argued for and won with the insistence that the old official had preconceived notions regarding my guilt. This one looked stiff and unforgiving sitting in front of the large American flag, but I hoped he was at least fair. That was all I needed.

The bailiff led me to a desk on the left side of the room. There were two chairs, and I assumed the other was for my counsel. I wondered if refusing the military lawyer had been the right choice.

Across from me was another desk, this one with an unfamiliar officer behind it. He was the government counsel, I knew, and I studied my opposition. He was an unassuming man with pale hair and the characteristic posture of a military man.

I forced myself to look away when he met my eye. I didn't want to antagonize him before the trial even began. Instead, I looked around the wood-paneled room, which was as perfectly polished as I'd expect from the Navy. We weren't allowed dusty vents or rumpled pillowcases in our own berths, for God's sake, and I imagined the expectations for publicly used spaces were far more rigorous.

Beside the judge, a woman with curled gray hair sat before a stenotype. Just as I'd thought upon meeting the receptionist, I wondered if this woman was my future. If I'd be relegated to the sidelines to type other people's words for the rest of my life.

No. I wouldn't be found guilty, because I *wasn't* guilty. No use agonizing over worst-case scenarios.

Proceedings began at 0800 on the dot. The preliminary inquiry officer, who served as judge, cleared his throat and began to speak. "This Article 32 investigation will come to order. Let the record reflect that the original session of this Article 32 investigation commences at 0800 hours, 6 August 1976, at the Washington Navy Yard in Washington, District of Columbia. In attendance are myself, Colonel Grant; government counsel Colonel Loewe; and the accused, Midshipman Kathleen Carre. Witnesses called to the stand will be Midshipman Robert Skinner, Midshipman Marsha Tyrell, Midshipman Linda Burr, and Midshipman Susan Silver."

I startled. Why was Marsha testifying? Was she doing so in my favor, as a fellow woman who'd been unjustly accused?

I knew I should feel grateful if that was the case, but a prickling feeling of unease crept along my spine. It wouldn't help me any to have a woman accused of mutiny on my side.

The judge continued. "The record will further reflect that the subsequent proceedings will be transcribed verbatim until the conclusion of this hearing by Miss Barbara Lansing, who is present."

I took a deep breath, willing myself to stay calm as the judge turned to me. "This is a formal preliminary hearing into the charge against Midshipman Kathleen Carre ordered pursuant to Article 32, UCMJ, by Midshipman Robert Skinner." He turned back to the room at large. "I wish to inform counsel for both sides that in accordance with paragraph 34 of the *Manual for Courts-Martial* I wish to conduct this hearing in a manner that is both fair and impartial, to review all the relevant and necessary evidence that either side may wish to present, and based on the evidence as presented, to make a recommendation to the appointing authority as to whether or not the evidence warrants a trial or any other appropriate action. I will now read to you the charge."

I resisted the childish urge to cover my ears.

"Charge: Violation of the Uniform Code of Military Justice, Article 134, specifically for making disloyal statements with the intent to promote disloyalty or disaffection toward the United States and to impair the loyalty to the United States or discipline of other members of the armed forces. Today, we gather to determine whether the alleged statements were made by Midshipman Carre, whether they were made in a public arena, and whether the statements at hand discredit the United States and impair loyalty or morale within its military.

"As you all know," the inquiry officer intoned, "the answer to that question will be determined based off whether there is probable cause to suspect that a crime has been committed and if the accused was involved."

His *if* and *whether* gave me hope.

"Colonel Loewe?" The judge gestured for government counsel to begin.

"I wish to call Midshipman Robert Skinner to the stand."

The doors opened, and my stomach lurched as the bailiff led Robert in. He strutted to the stand with an easy nonchalance that I envied and hated in equal parts. I hadn't seen him walk like that before, accustomed to his chopping, but now he swaggered like he knew the whole world was on his side. And why not? The whole world *was* on his side, and it always had been.

The judge asked Robert to state his name, grade, organization, and armed force. "Do you swear that the evidence you shall give in the case now in hearing shall be the truth, the whole truth, and nothing but the truth, so help you God?"

"I swear by God that the evidence I shall give shall be the truth, the whole truth, and nothing but the truth." Robert's voice was even and confident as he lied, and I wanted to spit in his smug face. This entire trial was a lie.

Robert went on to describe what had, according to him, happened. He talked about finding the letter in Mitscher Hall and then read it aloud as Colonel Loewe passed it over the witness stand.

I cringed as he did, glad Linda and Susan were outside.

Neither of them had read the letter, and I feared it was worse than they'd imagined.

I turned down my chance to cross-examine Robert, choosing instead to rely on the strength of my own testimony. Putting us head to head would only provide an opportunity for comparison, and I was afraid that the judge would tend to believe the man with the low voice over the woman in a skirt and uneven heels.

Government counsel Colonel Loewe took the stand. "We can see from Midshipman Skinner's testimony that the third through sixth clauses of Article 134 are violated. The words contained here promote disloyalty and hostility to the United States, impair military morale and loyalty, and discredit the United States of America. Namely, the letter criticizes democracy, calls our military a breeding ground of hypocrisy, and advocates for socialism."

I wanted to tell him that none of that was true. The letter didn't advocate for socialism; it advocated for the freedom to learn about it. And it didn't criticize democracy; it criticized hypocrisy.

But I couldn't defend a letter I sought to prove wasn't mine.

"Now, our job is to determine whether Midshipman Carre planned to make the statements public," Colonel Grant continued. "We call Midshipman Marsha Tyrell, fourth class, to the stand."

Marsha shuffled in alongside the bailiff as if she were the one on trial: head down, feet dragging—and I supposed she was, in a way. She and Janice both were still at risk of being separated from their role in the so-called mutiny.

Though I hoped she was going to tell the truth—that I had no intention of "spreading" my message—I wasn't hopeful. It was government counsel that had called her up, after all.

I watched nervously as she took her spot at the stand. Even in her heels, she appeared tiny behind the wooden structure. I wondered if her shoes were cut as unevenly as mine. If she too had blisters on her heels and the sides of her toes. We'd dealt with so many of the same things: ill-fitting uniforms, those stupid purses for our pads and tampons, marches in high heels. Boys hooting and hollering as we passed, officers who told us we didn't belong.

Marsha opened her mouth to answer the judge's initial questions and make the witness's oath, then took a deep breath. "Midshipman Kathleen Carre, the accused, approached me prior to our meeting in Mitscher Hall. Though Midshipman Janice Buxbaum and I had planned to keep the meeting constructive, Midshipman Carre had a different idea."

I gripped the table in front of me to keep from jumping up in protest. I hadn't even decided on going to the meeting until it had been halfway over, much less had ideas about how it should be run before the fact.

Midshipman Tyrell continued. "She told me she'd written something. Something she wanted to share with the rest of the women."

My teeth ground together. These were lies, and I was helpless to defend myself until my turn came around.

Marsha's voice grew more confident. "Midshipman Carre said it was something very important to her, something she'd spent hours writing and refining so it would have maximum effect."

It took all my long-practiced self-control to keep from launching out of my seat and wrestling Marsha out from the witness stand. *None of this happened*, I wanted to scream. *Not a single word is true.*

But why? Why was Marsha, who knew as well as I did how quickly the academy could turn on women like us, speaking against me?

She went on. "I told Midshipman Carre no. I explained that our meeting was supposed to be positive. We didn't intend to speak ill of the Naval Academy, much less challenge the very structure of the military. After Midshipman Skinner found the box and the PIO questioned me about Midshipman Carre's attendance at the meeting, I realized that Midshipman Carre had planned on sharing the materials anyway."

Even when she mentioned my name, she didn't look at me. I hoped the judge noticed.

"Is there anything else, Midshipman Tyrell?"

"Sir, no, sir."

The judge looked to me and gave me the same option I'd had with Robert. "You may now cross-examine the witness concerning her testimony, her knowledge of the offense, or her worthiness of belief. Since you are not represented by counsel, I will do this for you, if you will inform me in a general way of the matters about which you want me to question this witness. Do you wish to cross-examine this witness?"

I hesitated. Marsha had rehearsed for this for days, it seemed, and I hadn't even known she was speaking.

"Sir, no, sir," I finally said. The words tasted ashy on my tongue; inaction was far from my default.

"The witness is therefore excused," said the judge. Marsha scurried out of the room like she could feel the anger radiating hot off my body.

I also wanted to run from the heat of the room and its stifling lies. While I didn't imagine the judge cared at all about my own wishes, his must have aligned with mine in that moment. "Let's take a ten-minute recess," he said.

I flew from the room without stopping to speak to my

roommates in the hallway. I needed to breathe. I needed to stretch my legs and round corners in my midshipman uniform at least this one more time.

Because the way this was going, I might not get the chance to wear the naval uniform much longer.

Chapter 29

— ❖ —

Emmaline Balakin

November 1918

I stood frozen before the commanding officer, my hair half un-furled from its bun and my chest heaving from exertion and emo-tion. "Colonel Hodgson." I tried to sound calm and professional, not like someone who'd campaigned against censorship, started an integrated book group, and slept with a soldier. "Sir."

"I received a tip," he said, "about some discussions you've been having about War Department censorship."

My mind flashed first to Nicholas, but I knew that he would never betray me. Even in his hurt and fury.

"I searched your room," the colonel continued. "And I've found several items of interest. Where to begin?"

He held up the two books first. "A book on socialism and a book against democracy. Both forbidden, of course. And then this, tucked inside them." He dangled the rough draft of Nicholas's and my letter to the *Bismarck Tribune* from his long, skinny fingers. "With quite the closing line, I must say. 'As an act of solidarity with Mr. Plunkett and other protectors of our constitutional right to free speech, we will work here in France to make all texts available to those who request them.'"

I flashed hot and cold and hot again. There was nothing I could say.

"And then there was this." Colonel Hodgson continued, lifting the German letter to America's colored soldiers. "Pro-German propaganda. Which leads me to ask, Miss Balakin. Are you a German agent?"

"*What?*" I was so shocked by the accusation that I forgot my rank and my manners. "Of course not!"

"Merely a traitor, then."

"I never meant to betray our country, sir. I beg you to read the letter again. It's a plea for the protection of democracy."

"Which part? The part where you say 'We cannot help but wonder what democracy is worth'? Or a different bit?"

I shook my head, unable to argue. He had the German propaganda. He had the forbidden books. No defense would save me now.

"The question is not whether you are a traitor, Miss Balakin. That much is clear. But my question is whether you acted alone."

"Yes," I said quickly. "All alone."

Colonel Hodgson raised his eyebrows. "But the letter says 'we' and is signed by N.A. Who is N.A.?"

I couldn't let Nicholas go down with me. "I thought signing two names would make my argument more compelling, sir. N.A. was my mother."

"Your mother?" Colonel Hodgson raised those thin eyebrows, and I cursed myself for such an inane lie. "*This* might compel you to tell the truth," the colonel said. "You will be court-martialed for sedition. For a soldier committing this crime, the sentence would be death. For you? Perhaps they'll take pity, and you'll be imprisoned for the next several decades of your life. Or perhaps, considering the serious nature of your crimes, they won't."

I could barely hear him over the rushing in my head.

"But I've been known to be generous to those who aid the cause by reporting others who weaken our Army. In fact, it was that promise that led me to you."

I still couldn't imagine who would have reported me. But it didn't matter. I wasn't giving Nicholas up.

I'd lied to Nicholas and turned him against me. The way he'd said "Miss Balakin" like he'd never known me . . .

But another lie could save him now.

"It was just me," I said again. "I acted alone."

Colonel Hodgson stepped closer and folded into a chair at the card table. It should have made him less intimidating, but seated he was somehow worse. He was so confident, so relaxed.

"We could make prison comfortable for you," he said. "You are a woman, after all."

"I'm telling the truth," I said. "I acted alone."

"Fine." Colonel Hodgson snapped up to standing. "If that's the way you want it."

Chapter 30

—— ❖ ——

Kathleen Carre

August 1976

I tore down the passageway—or the hallway, as a civilian would call it. A civilian like I was afraid I'd be again if this trial didn't start going in a different direction, stat.

I rounded a corner, and skidded to a stop to keep from slamming into the elderly man coming the other way. His back was stooped, though he was still tall, and his skin was spotted with age. But his gray eyes were sharp.

"I'm so sorry," I said, ready to take off again. I needed to burn off this energy before I went back into the courtroom and did something stupid—like demonstrate my new judo skills on Robert.

I sidestepped the man and prepared to keep running, but his arm shot out to grab mine. "Wait," he said.

I looked at him again.

"Yes?" I tried to tone down the impatience in my voice; I was the one who'd nearly knocked him over, after all. "Do you need something?"

"Kathleen," the man whispered. "It's you."

"How do you know my name? Are you part of the trial?"

He looked from my face to a newspaper tucked beneath his arm. It appeared decades old, the print faded to a sea of soft grays.

I drew my hand to my mouth, inadvertently snatching my arm from the man's gentle grip. "Nicholas?"

"Yes," the man said. "Am I too late?"

"No." Hope flooded me as I said the word. "Is that the article?"

"Yes," he said. He handed me the paper. "Page two."

I flipped past the first page, and there it was: *Americans overseas protest firing of librarian accused of sedition.* After a short introduction from the editor, the letter I'd been accused of writing was printed nearly word-for-word in a paper almost three times as old as I was.

"Nicholas," I cried, "you've saved me!" I hardly had time to wonder why, to wonder what had changed his mind.

He didn't respond to what I'd said, instead looking at me with a plea in his eyes. "Please," he said, "please find me after the trial is over. At the main gates."

"Wait," I cried, but Nicholas was already moving away. I didn't have time to follow him. I had to get back.

I raced back down the hallway, passing a startled Linda and Susan on the way. This wasn't chopping, this was sprinting.

I skidded into the courtroom, breathing heavily, and stood before the PIO's desk. I smelled his coffee before I heard him reenter the room, and I turned with a deep inhale. Caffeine was a luxury we weren't allowed at the Naval Academy. "Sir, permission to speak freely, sir?"

"Granted." The judge settled behind his desk.

"I have just acquired new evidence to present to the court, sir."

"Evidence should have been turned in during the initial investigation for documentation."

"I understand that, sir, and I apologize. But this is evidence that I was unable to acquire until today. I promise you that it is—" I grasped for the words he'd used earlier. "Both relevant and necessary, sir." I knew the judge wouldn't want this to go to trial. The entire charge against me was related to making the military look bad, and that wasn't something they wanted to air to the public. It wouldn't look good for them to dishonorably discharge one of the first women they'd accepted, either. "I believe that this evidence may substantially change your recommendation, sir."

The judge put out a silent hand, and I passed over the newspaper. I pointed to the relevant column and watched as he began to read. Once upon a time, I would have tapped my foot impatiently; now, I stood at parade rest. Nothing on my face or in my stance belied the flurry of emotions and impatience inside.

The judge held his reaction in the same way. There was no gasp or raised eyebrow, just a systematic refolding of the newspaper. "I will enter this into evidence, Midshipman Carre."

"Thank you, sir."

I returned to my seat with renewed confidence. I didn't flinch when the government counsel Colonel Loewe returned and sat across from me, nor when the transcriptionist cast me a sympathetic look.

The judge cleared his throat and recommended the proceedings, again announcing the time and the individuals present. "We next call the accused, Midshipman Kathleen Carre, fourth class, to the stand."

I stood on sore legs and walked to the front of the room, conscious of keeping my steps even and my chin held high.

"Please state your name, grade, organization, and armed force."

"Kathleen Carre, sir. Fourth class midshipman, USNA, Navy."

"Midshipman Carre, is it true that you have voluntarily chosen to forgo legal counsel?"

"Sir, yes, sir."

"I caution you that the charge against you is very serious, and it is important that you understand all of your rights and the procedures that control this preliminary hearing. I suggest you need the assistance of a lawyer to properly protect your rights and to otherwise help you."

I'd been through this already with the original PIO and rankled at the suggestion that I needed assistance. I knew my rights; I'd done my research.

"You have the absolute right to a qualified, free military lawyer," the judge continued. "You are free, however, to give up this right. Do you understand what you are giving up by waiving your right to counsel?"

"Sir, yes, sir."

"If you decide to proceed without a lawyer, you do so to your own peril and may jeopardize your case. Do you understand what I have just told you?"

Yes, I understand! I wanted to snap. Instead, I kept my voice level. "Sir, yes, sir."

"Do you wish to have a lawyer to represent you?"

"Sir, no, sir."

He went over my right to remain silent, and I waived that as well.

He nodded. "You may begin."

"Two and a half weeks ago," I said, "I received a packet of letters forwarded from my late grandmother's estate. Inside one of the envelopes was a letter addressed to my grandmother, Nellie Carre, from Nicholas Agrapov. This letter stated that Nicholas wanted nothing to do with the contents of her original letter, which was also enclosed. That original letter was addressed to the *Bismarck Tribune* and addressed the firing of a librarian who had allowed circulation of allegedly seditious materials during the First World War. The envelope was postmarked 1918." I took a breath.

"I left the letter in my quarters when I attended the meeting hosted by Midshipman Marsha Tyrell. As Midshipmen Linda Burr and Susan Silver will testify, I did not have the letter with me at the meeting. When I returned from the meeting, however, it was gone, and I learned the next day that Midshipman Skinner had filed a Form-2 against me under UCMJ Article 134. When I met with the PIO, he presented me with Midshipman Skinner's 'evidence'—the original letter, but with the beginning and end removed so that the context was erased. I knew then that Midshipman Skinner must have stolen the letter from my quarters, as he had been in my room previously to ransack it.

"To prove that Midshipman Tyrell lied when she said I had written the letter with intent to distribute, I enter into evidence a 1918 edition of the *Bismarck Tribune*."

The PIO passed me the article, and I read it aloud to the court as the typist's fingers flew across the keyboard.

And then it was time to be cross-examined. Colonel Loewe

rose and approached the stand. "You say Midshipman Skinner ransacked your room. Yet there are no complaints listed against him."

"The incident was dismissed as hazing, sir. No charges were made."

The man nodded. "Midshipman Carre. I'm afraid that, even if this newspaper is genuine and the letter was pulled from it, we must ask whether you intended to distribute the letter. Notwithstanding the authorship, the charge against you would stand if you'd planned on using it to damage the good standing of the academy."

"As I said, sir, I left the letter in my room when I attended the meeting. Midshipmen Burr and Silver, who attended, can confirm."

And then it struck me. "Additionally, sir, Midshipman Tyrell stated that I claimed to have worked hard on *writing* the letter, which we now know is false. I dare to suggest that this calls into question the truthfulness of her other statements."

The judge interrupted. "Miss Lansing. Can you read back Midshipman Tyrell's claims regarding Midshipman Carre's writing of the letter?"

The typist's voice was surprisingly strong. "Midshipman Tyrell stated the following. 'She told me she'd written something. Something she wanted to share with the rest of the women. Midshipman Carre said it was something very important to her, something she'd spent hours writing and refining so it would have maximum effect.'"

I couldn't help shooting a triumphant gaze at the government counsel. "As evidenced by the existence of this newspaper, sir, Midshipman Tyrell was lying about my writing the letter. I suggest you ask her whether she was also lying about my desire to distribute it."

Colonel Loewe clammed up. "No further questions."

I returned to my seat as Linda and Susan testified. Neither of them knew what had just transpired, and they stuck to their rehearsed testimonies. Linda was first, cheeks aflame, and she promised she'd sat beside me at the meeting and seen nothing in my possession aside from my copy of *Reef Points*. Susan followed, her southern drawl particularly prominent in her anger. Both statements were short and probably unnecessary thanks to the discovery of the newspaper. But still they bolstered me, for I'd thought when Nana died that I was entirely alone. It turned out that couldn't have been further from the truth.

After Linda's and Susan's testimonies, the judge called another recess. I huddled in the hallway with my friends and told them in hushed voices what had just transpired.

Linda couldn't hide her squeal. "The charges are dropped, then?"

I hushed her as Robert looked over at us. "No. Not yet. But I hope so." I gestured toward the courtroom. "The judge is speaking to government counsel right now."

When we reassembled, Colonel Loewe called Midshipman Tyrell back to the stand. As a lawyer, he was obligated to ask her to recant her perjury. She seemed to know that as well as I did, because she looked even smaller than before as she slunk to the witness stand.

"Midshipman Tyrell," Colonel Loewe began. I didn't envy her the sense of being cross-examined by your own counsel. "Midshipman Carre has demonstrated that the letter you claim she wrote was penned in 1918. Did you perhaps misremember Midshipman Carre's words? Perhaps she just said that—"

The judge frowned. "Leading question."

"Did you perhaps misremember Midshipman Carre's words?"

Marsha froze for a moment, and I leaned forward. Was she going to take the out, or was she going to tell the truth? I jolted back as she burst into tears.

"I'm so sorry," she sobbed. "Robert made me."

Colonel Loewe looked horrified, but he soldiered on. "Robert being Midshipman Skinner?"

"Yes. He threatened me. See," she gasped, "I'm under review with the disciplinary board for co-hosting the women's meeting. Robert—Midshipman Skinner—told me his father had influence. The type of influence that could get the meeting reclassified from a mutiny . . . or to make sure it stayed that way, and to ensure that I'd be separated from the Naval Academy on top of it."

Her voice broke on the last sentence, and I couldn't help but pity her. She'd done this to stay at the academy, and I almost couldn't blame her if she'd been as devoted to it as I was. But now, after committing perjury and admitting to it, she had no chance of staying.

"He said all I had to do was tell the court that Midshipman Carre had written the manifesto, and that she'd approached me about distributing it." Tears were streaming freely down her face now. "I was scared. So, I said yes."

"Thank you, Midshipman Tyrell."

Marsha winced at the word *midshipman*. I wondered whether it was the last time she'd be addressed as one.

The judge rubbed his hands together as Marsha took her seat. His eyes were closed in thought.

"We have confirmed today that Midshipman Carre had material that violated the first two subclauses of the disloyal statement amendment. However, it was Midshipman Tyrell's statement that convinced me the accused had also violated the following clauses with intent to distribute. As Midshipman Tyrell has amended her statement, I do not think we have enough evidence to go to trial."

I leaned forward in my seat.

"Remember that my recommendation is advisory rather than binding, and the commanding officer will make the final decision on the disposition of the charges in this case. My recommendation, however, will be to dismiss the charges against Midshipman Kathleen Carre, Company Five. I will be speaking to the preliminary inquiry officer to investigate Midshipmen Tyrell and Skinner on the count of perjury. Midshipman Carre, know you may be called to testify if these cases go to trial."

"Sir, yes, sir," I responded in a daze, only able to get the words out because they were so familiar.

"Court is dismissed."

I tumbled out into the passageway and pressed Linda and Susan into a hug. "Thank you, thank you, thank you." It was probably the most I'd ever said such a thing, and both girls laughed.

"Is it over?"

"Yes! I'm free. At least . . ." I pulled back. "Maybe. The judge's recommendation isn't binding, and—"

"Oh, hush." Linda swatted my arm. "It's over!"

"I get to stay." It seemed impossible. For two and a half weeks—had it really been that brief a time?—I'd spent every moment terrified that I was going to lose everything I'd worked so hard for. Losing my spot at the Naval Academy would have been losing my dream, my purpose, my confidence. And it also would have meant losing a link to Nana, because I understood more and more each day at the academy what she'd meant when she talked about how this was a man's world.

"Susan, Linda." I threw my arms around them, surprising my-self. "I can't thank you enough, truly. But there's someone I need to talk to."

"Of course." Susan rolled her eyes, but she was smiling. "There's Kathleen for you, always on the move."

Linda sighed dramatically. "Here I thought we could throw a party to celebrate."

All three of us laughed, because life at the academy left no time for partying.

"Later," I promised anyway. It was time for me to speak with Nicholas Agrapov.

Chapter 31

— ❖ —

Emmaline Balakin

November 1918

I was too terrified to speak as the colonel marched me in the early-morning light across the muddy grounds of the base hospital, his grip on my arm like a tourniquet. I wanted to be brave like a book character, like Sydney Carton going to his death for Lucie's sake, but tears streamed down my face.

Above the sound of my own ragged breath, I thought I heard my name carried indistinctly on the wind. "Emmaline!"

I glanced at the colonel, shocked, but he didn't react. I looked back down at the ground. I was imagining the call, so desperate for someone to save me that I could almost convince myself it was true. But who was left to call my name? Perlie was dead. Burt was confined to his bed with grief. And Nicholas wanted nothing to do with me ever again.

I heard my name again, louder this time, and closed my eyes. This wasn't *Jane Eyre*, I tried to tell myself; I couldn't hear my lover calling to me across the moors.

But I couldn't help glancing back. And there was Nicholas, hand on his bandaged abdomen and gait lopsided. He was coming this way.

If he did, the colonel would know immediately who my co-writer had been, and Nicholas would be court-martialed alongside me. As a member of the military rather than a volunteer, surely he'd be condemned to death.

I twisted back and shook my head. Nicholas froze, and even from here I could see the expression of hurt flash across his face. I whipped back around before my own emotions were as easily telegraphed. He couldn't come after me. Not now.

My tears fell faster as Colonel Hodgson dragged me into his office. He fiddled with a clunky electric object that looked like a cross between a telephone and a cabinet, and then he lifted an attached funnel and spoke into it. "Miss Mayborn, this is Colonel Hodgson. Over."

A wireless radio. I'd never seen one in action, and I nearly jumped when Nellie's voice fizzled through the machine. "Colonel Hodgson, this is Nellie Mayborn. Go ahead. Over."

"I need you and your car at 42, now. I have a prisoner for you to deliver to the military prison at Neufchâteau. Over."

"Which military prison? Say again. Over."

Any other time, I would have smiled at Nellie's inability to hear the differences between one French town and another. But now, all I could think was that I was being carted off to *prison*.

"Neufchâteau. Nan, east, unit, fox, cast, have, able, tare, easy, able, unit. Over."

Apparently this string of words made sense to Nellie, because she continued speaking in that professional tone that seemed so unfamiliar in her airy voice. "To confirm: I will deliver a prisoner to Neufchâteau. Leaving 18 now. Over."

"Affirmative. Over and out."

Her voice crackled away, and Colonel Hodgson and I were left in the sort of silence that begged for speculation. My head filled with horrors: I'd be housed with the same sort of men who Nellie told me had been hanged at Bazoilles in July for rape, or I'd be lumped in with German POWs. I knew, logically, that German soldiers on the individual level were no different than our own, but that didn't comfort me now. I pictured them the way they were depicted in the propaganda posters that had littered the streets of D.C.: as apes and beasts, with helpless women in their hairy clutches.

Nellie arrived the polar opposite of those helpless women. She wore her Motor Corps uniform and looked alert despite the early hour. "Sir."

Then her gaze went to me, and her mouth opened and closed. I couldn't make eye contact, so I stared at the floor.

"Miss Mayborn. Miss Balakin is to be imprisoned at Neufchâteau for treason." He handed over the draft of the letter Nicholas and I had written. "Entrust the officer there with this letter to explain her charges."

I was awed by the responsibility Colonel Hodgson gave Nellie. What other state secrets had she ferried about in the back of her car while I sat oblivious in the front seat?

"Miss Mayborn. Do you understand your assignment?"

Nellie's jaw had gone slack, but she snapped now to attention.

"Sir, yes, sir!" Nellie saluted Colonel Hodgson. "I will take the prisoner there now. You can expect me back midmorning."

An hour ago, I would never have believed that Nellie would follow this sort of order blindly. But now, after Nicholas had left me and someone had betrayed me, I almost expected it.

Not that such a thing made it any less painful.

The familiar light-headedness overtook me. If even Nellie was abandoning me, who did I have left? My pulse throbbed in my wrist as Colonel Hodgson released my arm, and then my vision went blurry. I stood still, too shocked to move, until Nellie dragged me to the motorcar and shoved me inside, then slammed the door and went around to the driver's side. When she spoke, I thought I'd misheard her over the furious beating of my own heart and the desperate waves of my own breath.

"Where should we go, Emmaline?" Her characteristic laugh was absent, her voice trembling with fear. "Where will you be safe?"

She didn't even ask what I'd been accused of or if I had done it. But she was going to save me, anyway.

I burst into tears. "Remember," I sobbed, "how I said I'd always wondered what it was like to have a sister?"

"Yes." Nellie's foot tapped impatiently. She probably thought I'd gone insane from the stress.

"Now I know."

Nellie threw her arms around me as she cried, too. "I'll take you to Reims," she said. "You can catch a train west from there and get home."

"No, Nellie. You can't do that. You'll be charged with treason."

"Not if I claim you overpowered me," she argued. "I have

weapons to deliver in the back of the motorcar. I'll say you grabbed one and shot at me with it."

"I can't ask you to—"

"You didn't ask," Nellie interrupted. "And you know you'd do the same thing for me. Sisters, right?"

"Sisters," I said quietly. She wasn't wrong. I was sacrificing myself for Nicholas; Nellie was willing to sacrifice for me. Any one of us would do the same for another.

Nellie pressed down on the pedal, and the car sped up. "Reims is northwest. I'll tell them you commandeered the car and took it south to Dijon."

I watched Nellie drive, mesmerized by her quick decision making and confidence.

"But what if we're seen? Won't the roads get more populated as we get closer?"

Nellie's grip on the wheel tightened. "I suppose we'll just have to hope no one pays us any mind."

"Wait," I said. "Nellie, you taught me to drive."

"Yes?"

"And if your story is that I overpowered you . . . that's what any witnesses should see."

"I don't understand."

"I need to be driving, Nellie."

She blinked rapidly, though her eyes never left the road. And then she smiled as she pulled over and climbed from the driver's seat. I was ready to take her place when she stopped me. "If you really had overpowered me and taken the car, you'd force me to give you my uniform, too. You wouldn't want passersby to notice the discrepancy," she said.

"But if I'm in the Motor Corps uniform, they'll think it was you driving."

Nellie raised her eyebrows. "You're about ten feet tall, fifty pounds soaking wet, and have hair twenty shades darker than mine. Trust me. It's the best plan."

"Okay," I said, because I did trust her. And what else could I do but obey, when she was risking everything for me? "If you're certain."

"I am." Nellie was already unbuttoning her jacket and pulling off the tie beneath it. She unbuttoned her blouse, leaving only her ribbed undergarments on. She balled them up and tossed them to me, then began to unbutton and step out of her skirt.

Turning away, I did the same, then silently passed my clothes back so Nellie could take them. I pulled her things on and turned around. The skirt hung too low on my hips, too large to stay on my waist, and it fell high on my legs. Nellie, meanwhile, had left a button undone on my top to fit her bosom into it, and the ends of the skirt dragged in the mud.

We climbed back into the car, and I shifted it into gear. "Thank you," I whispered to Nellie. "How will I ever repay you?"

"You don't have to." She looked over and smiled, though a glint of fear shone in her eyes. "You've been my friend. It's hard to come by those as one of the only women serving. You know that as well as I do."

The sun rose behind us as we drove on, and I felt overexposed in the light of day. And then the heavy buzz of artillery replaced one fear with another. Nellie and I shared a grim look, both of us used to the sound by now.

And then the world exploded. Flames erupted fifty yards away from us, their blazing light creating orange spots in my vision.

Dirt burst from the ground like a reverse waterfall, like a thousand different land mines were going off around the automobile at the same time.

"Nellie!" I tried to scream but heard nothing beyond the deafening boom of artillery. "Nellie!"

Dirt coated the windshield of the car, and the interior was too dark to see. I groped sideways until I found Nellie's arm, and then the car shot forward like it had been hit from behind. We spun, or at least I thought we did; I couldn't see or hear, just feel. I flew forward and slammed my head against the wheel. It came off sticky with blood, and I cradled it in my hands. The car had stopped, thank God, and there were longer and longer spaces between the sounds of each shell bursting into flames.

"Nellie!" I reached again toward my friend, waiting for her to respond. "Nellie?"

I found her arm and shook it, but she didn't respond. "Nellie!" My voice grew high-pitched and hysterical. It felt like the Germans could hear me eighty miles away—as far as the artillery had traveled. But I couldn't stop screaming. "Nellie!" I shook her again, and her whole body slumped forward.

I fumbled for the handle and pushed open the door. I fell out of the car and into knee-deep mud; we'd spun off the path and landed in a ditch. Just behind us was a gaping hole in the earth, scorched and black. The results of whatever explosion that had propelled us off the road.

I hurried to the passenger side of the car, practically swimming, and wrenched open Nellie's door. Her body tumbled out of the car when I succeeded. Nellie, my Nellie, dangled upside down from her seat, her blond hair hanging in the mud. Her face was a swollen, bloody mess—unrecognizable.

I screamed and fell to my knees beside her. I hugged Nellie's head to me, praying. "Please, Nellie," I begged. "Please, no."

I rocked back onto my heels and howled. Nellie, sweet Nellie, was dead. And it was all my fault.

I tore at my hair like Baba Yaga. This was my doing. In trying to save one person whom I loved more than anything, I'd killed another.

Because of me, my closest friend was dead.

I don't know how long I clung to Nellie's body. I came to my senses as though from a nightmare. But Nellie was still gone, and what once was my friend, my sister, was unrecognizable.

I couldn't stop myself from screaming. When I never arrived in Neufchâteau, my name would be distributed across France as that of a traitor and a fugitive. The army would hunt me down as long as I was here in France, and the government in the United States would search for me, too. I'd never be safe again.

At least, not as myself.

I forced myself to look at Nellie again. Her face was beyond recognition, her hair stiff and discolored, and she was in my uniform.

Anyone who found her body would think it was mine.

I pulled my own papers from my pocket and put them next to Nellie's body on the seat. Then, holding my breath, I reached into Nellie's pocket and extricated her Red Cross identification papers. I gagged. What sort of monster was I, stealing my dead friend's identity after I'd killed her? But if I didn't take her papers, her death would be in vain. I'd be caught trying to escape, and we'd both be dead.

I had to squint in the dark, but I could read it: *Nellie Rose Mayborn, American Red Cross, Motor Corps.* Her identification number was beneath the title. A cold, distant part of my brain registered the fact that I'd have to memorize that.

I hadn't known her middle name. She'd never gotten a chance to tell me.

I placed Nellie's identification in my pocket beside Nicholas's letters and the rough draft we'd written together. I shouldn't have kept it, I knew, but I couldn't help it. It was the only place where Nicholas and I would live on together, his ideas and mine intertwined.

I yanked open the back door of the car and rummaged through the box of medical supplies Nellie was delivering. I stayed far away from the guns. At the bottom of the medical box were stacks of large, triangular bandages used for slings.

I recalled the way I'd seen them folded at the hospital and replicated it on myself. I draped the cloth over my shoulder so my left forearm rested in its hammock, and then I slid Nicholas's letters and our plea between the folds before tying it. No one would search a Red Cross worker's bandaged arm, and the injury would explain why I was returning home before the war's end.

Finally, I pulled out a blank final efficiency report from the box of documents Nellie had brought from Paris. Tears falling, I filled it out as if Nellie had been disenrolled.

Name: MAYBORN, Nellie R.
Appointed:

I remembered Nellie saying she'd been in France a month when I arrived in late September, so I marked her appointment date as *August 1918*. For *disenrolled* date, I put today; for reason, I put *injury to arm—unable to drive.*

Then came the hardest part: forging the Red Cross Motor Corps Superintendent's signature, when I didn't even know what the superintendent's name was. I scrawled something illegible in script and prayed it would work.

But before I left, Nellie deserved real prayers. I knelt beside her body and grasped for my chokti, but it was gone. I scrabbled around the mud on my hands and knees to no avail. Who knew how far it could have flown?

I wiped the mud from my hands and folded them together to pray anyway. I prayed for Nellie and the sister she'd talked about so often, Mabel. I prayed for Nellie and the father who'd taught her to drive. I prayed for Nellie and the men who wouldn't receive the supplies Nellie had crammed into the back of the motorcar.

"I'm sorry, Nellie." Tears leaked from my eyes. An apology wasn't enough; she deserved more. But all I could give her was my own survival. It seemed cruel to live when she was gone, but worse to render her sacrifice worthless.

"I'll never forget you," I whispered.

With one final sigh, I rose. "Nellie Rose Mayborn." I repeated the name, committing it to memory. Trying to make it sound like mine.

And then I limped off into the darkness.

Chapter 32

— ❧ —

Kathleen Carre

August 1976

I ran outside, hardly noticing the heat, and dashed up Dahlgren Avenue. I passed Leutze Park and its weapons displays, then stopped at Latrobe Gate. "Gate" was misleading; it was a huge brick structure with two guard lodges, a Marine barracks, and a set of symmetrical towers. But I didn't see Nicholas.

I hurried through the gate, exiting the Navy Yard and finding myself on the street. Nicholas sat on a bench, his shoulders hunched but his head upright. His gaze was trained on a medieval-style castle across the street, which Nana had told me was once a cable car station. It had spent its recent years keeping government records; now, it was abandoned. The paint chipped and the wood bubbled with heat damage.

I tore my eyes away and sat beside Nicholas. We sat in silence for a moment as I watched the civilians pass: two girls in tube tops laughing as they walked, men in jeans with earrings, groups walking in disarray instead of in lockstep, couples holding hands and nuzzling each other's shoulders. Everything so different from the Naval Academy.

I finally looked at Nicholas, not sure how to begin. "The PIO is recommending to the commanding officer that the charges against me be dropped," I said. "You saved me."

"I didn't save you." Nicholas shook his head. "Your grandmother did."

"Pardon?"

Nicholas pulled a sheet of paper from his pocket and handed it to me. I recognized Nana's handwriting immediately. It wasn't the handwriting she'd had as a young girl in the Motor Corps, but the handwriting I recognized from permission slips and grocery lists.

> *Dearest Nicholas,*
>
> *The last letter you read of mine, fifty-eight years ago, tore us apart. I hope you've forgiven me for my lies—not least because you're going to have to forgive me for a lifetime more of them, if you read this letter.*
>
> *I understand why you returned the letter I sent you last week. I thought you should have the piece we'd written to the Bismarck Tribune, but I didn't plan on telling you anything else. Now that you've rejected my outreach as Nellie, I must tell you the truth.*
>
> *I am not and never was Nellie Mayborn, Nicholas. I am Emmaline. Your Emmaline. Emmaline Vera Balakin.*

I pulled the sheet of paper so tautly that it almost ripped in half. "I don't understand."

The ghost of a smile played around Nicholas's lips. "Neither did I. Keep reading."

The morning you left, Colonel Hodgson came to the recreation hut on a tip and found the rough draft of the letter you and I had written to the Bismarck Tribune. He offered me lenience if I gave up my co-conspirator, but I couldn't do that to you.

Do you remember when you called my name as I was led away? I'm sorry I looked at you the way I did. I did it to save you. I hope you understood that, once you'd learned what happened.

I wouldn't give you up, and so the colonel carted me off to Nellie and told her to take me to the prison at Neufchâteau.

"Nellie," I said. "My grandmother."

Nicholas shook his head. "Go on."

There, I'd be imprisoned and then court-martialed. Maybe even sentenced to death.

But Nellie saved me. Nellie promised to drive me to Reims, to claim I'd overpowered her and taken control of the car. We switched uniforms, and I drove.

And then the world exploded. It was an artillery shell. Nellie was killed instantly, her face and body destroyed beyond recognition.

I could think of only one thing to do, and it shames me to this day. I took her identity and I fled, letting the world think it was Emmaline Balakin, the traitor, who had died in German fire.

But I don't regret what I did, because it didn't only save me. Nicholas, it saved our daughter, too. I found out she was coming as soon as I returned home to D.C., and—forgive me—I married a wonderful man who never asked if the baby was his. I named her Jane Rose Carre, and the three of us lived together until my husband passed in '29. I wanted more than anything to find you, to share her with you, but I couldn't implicate you further in my crimes.

Jane is not the daughter I imagined, and I don't always agree with her decisions, but I like to think you'd be proud of her regardless. She lives her life her way, without apology or fear or—dare I say it?—censorship. She's lived in Arizona and Alaska, traveled to Mexico and Canada and Hawaii. She's an adventurer just like I always wanted to be. She's a travel writer—it affords her a way to see the world.

If only you and I had seen the world so freely, instead of mired in mud and trenches.

Jane also gave us a beautiful granddaughter. Her name is Kathleen Carre, and she's a plebe at the United States Naval Academy now. She looks so much like I did at that age that it's like looking into a mirror, but she's so different from me. Focused and grounded in reality, rather than off in the clouds like I always was.

You deserve to know about your daughter and your granddaughter, and I tell you of them now because I am dying. I have cancer, and the doctors told me I have a short time left to live. They said there was no way to know for sure—that it could be days or months or even a year— but somehow, I do. Somehow, I know that I will be gone before this letter reaches you, because some things— though my granddaughter would be loath to agree—come down to fate rather than to science.

I think it was all fate, Nicholas. Fate that I got your letter at the Dead Letter Office, fate that I ended up at Base Hospital 42 alongside you. Fate that I survived despite all odds so I could carry our daughter home.

I believe all of it was fate, and though I've never recovered from my time in France, I do not wish I had stayed home.

I only wish I had told you the truth sooner. But I had involved you in enough lies; I couldn't embroil you in one that would last a lifetime. And I could not let anyone learn my true identity for fear of the punishment I would receive. It was a punishment I deserved, but one my infant daughter did not.

I never stopped loving you, Nicholas. Is that foolish? I hope you can forgive me. But most of all, I hope that you forgive Jane and Kathleen the sins of their matriarch. That even if you stopped loving me long ago, you will love them.

    Yours,

    Emmaline

I looked at Nicholas, but I didn't speak. I didn't know where to begin. With the fact that my grandmother wasn't Nellie, wasn't a Motor Corps driver, and had written the letter that had put me in court? With the fact that Nicholas was my grandfather?

I realized I was shaking when Nicholas reached out to put a hand on my shoulder. "Do you want me to explain?"

"Please," I gasped.

Nicholas closed his eyes, breathed in, and started to talk. The story unraveled slowly. He explained that he had known Emmaline Balakin, my grandmother, as a child, and that they reunited in France at Bazoilles-sur-Meuse. He explained that she'd been a hospital librarian, not a Motor Corps driver, and that they had fallen in love. He told me about the book club they'd formed, the letter they'd written to the *Bismarck Tribune*, and the German leaflet Nana had found in Paris.

"Colonel Hodgson found it all," he said. "He searched her room on a tip from another man in our book club, Marvin." He said the name of the man not with bitterness, but with sadness. Like he was summoning a ghost. "I just hate that I wasn't with Emmaline when it happened. I tried—I tried to follow her. But she looked at me with such anger that I thought it was too late. I thought my fury had ruined things between us."

"Your fury?"

He explained my grandmother's job at the Dead Letter Office and the letter he'd found in her room. "I acted like her lying was the worst thing I'd seen in the army, like lying was more unforgivable than everything else in that world of death and violence and racism and colonialism and cruelty. When she looked back at me like that, I thought she hated me for it. But then I learned why she was taken away. She lied *for* me, even though I'd abandoned her, and she told the officer the letter was her own."

The pieces were coming together now. "So, Nellie really *was* a Motor Corps driver stationed at Bazoilles-sur-Meuse. She just wasn't my nana."

Nicholas nodded. "She was entrusted with taking Emmaline to the prison. When she never returned, a search party found what they said was Emmaline's body. The body was wearing the ALA librarian's uniform and had Emmaline's papers in her pockets. I spent nearly sixty years thinking it was Emmaline who had died. And frankly, I blamed Nellie. I had no idea she'd sought to help Emmaline. So when I got the first letter from your grandmother, I sent it back. Thinking she was Nellie, I wanted nothing to do with her."

"And then?"

"And then I got this one a week and a half later. I wanted to send it back, too, but I was afraid Nellie would just keep writing until I stopped rejecting her. So I kept the envelope unopened. And then you called for the second time."

"When I used the Russian expression."

Nicholas nodded. "And when you said your mother was named Jane. Emmaline's favorite book was *Jane Eyre*. She talked about wanting to be more like Jane all the time."

"And my grandmother never drove," I said slowly. "Not once did I see her behind the wheel of a car."

Nicholas nodded. "I wondered on the phone if I'd been wrong all along, if Emmaline had been the one to survive. And so, I opened her letter—and who knows? Maybe it was fate that had kept me from throwing it away. Just like she wrote."

"So you opened the letter," I said, "and you learned that Emmaline was alive. That Nellie was Emmaline."

"Yes," he said. "And that you, Kathleen, are my granddaughter." He spread his hands wide. "I had to help you. It took me two days to track down the newspaper in my storage, and I couldn't get through to you at the academy. So I came here."

"You came here," I repeated softly. This man had saved me. This man was *family*. This man was the great love of my nana's life.

"I just wish I had had time to come to Emmaline's aid, too. I never told her I loved her, that I'd forgiven her or that I owed her my life. I didn't even know to go to her funeral."

The funeral. "Oh, no. Mabel."

"Mabel?"

"Mabel was Nellie's sister. The real Nellie's sister. I met her at the funeral. How am I supposed to tell her that her sister died sixty years ago? And that I'm not her niece at all?" My voice rose to a pitch I didn't recognize; it wasn't often that I didn't know what to do.

Nicholas straightened his back a bit, though I saw a spasm of pain cross his face as he did. "I would like to talk to her," he said. "I need to tell her that her sister sacrificed herself to save a dear friend."

I wished Nicholas could be the one to tell Mabel everything, but she deserved to hear it from me. "I need to talk to her first. Tell her I'm not who she thought I was."

Nicholas scrutinized me for a moment. "Emmaline wrote me as Vivian, and when I found out, that's why I felt so betrayed. I told her she wasn't who I'd thought she was. But that wasn't true." He stopped and thought. "She was exactly who I knew her to be— book-loving, braver than she knew, thoughtful and compassionate and smart as a whip. It didn't matter what name she went by."

"But—"

"If Mabel has come to care for you, it doesn't matter whether you're blood or not."

I thought of Linda and Susan, who had become my family.

"I suppose you're right," I said. "Maybe we can call her together."

"Together." Nicholas smiled. "I like the sound of that."

Chapter 33

— ❖ —

Emmaline Balakin

November 1918

Two months ago, I'd stood on the deck of the USS *Aeolus* as Emmaline Vera Balakin, and I stood now on the deck of the SS *George Washington* as Nellie Rose Mayborn. So many things were different about this journey. We were going west toward home, rather than sailing east into adventure. We no longer traveled with a convoy of Navy ships, as the threat of German U-boats had been extinguished with yesterday's signing of the armistice. And the air on the seas now, in the weeks before Thanksgiving, was a biting wind rather than the sticky humidity that had accompanied my first voyage.

But there were other differences, too. And while they were less visible, they were no less important. I was a different girl now in more than name. I'd fallen in love with a man who'd loved me back. I'd gained a sister.

And then I'd lost them both.

But what I wouldn't lose again was the voice they had reminded me I had. The power they had brought out in me. All that, I would keep. And I could hold on to hope, too—hope that I would find love again one day. No man could replace Nicholas, with his thoughtful gray eyes and his honest warmth, but I wanted what Perlie had had. I wanted a family. A child like his Tess and Annie. One I could teach both to think and to act, who'd believe that hope was stronger than fear.

I'd spent a grueling two days in the forest, hungry and disoriented, before I reached Reims. By the time I'd gotten to the shelled-out city, spirits had been high. The war was almost at its end, and it seemed that every Frenchman and Frenchwoman was willing to pay the train fare for a heroine once she shared her story. The story was a fictional one, of course. In this story, I'd been the one driving when the car was struck by artillery, and I was a martyr and a war hero.

I spent a night and a day on one train and then another, passing through shelled-out towns and between lines of trenches, past ancient ruins and modern ones. I finally arrived in Saint Nazaire just days before the armistice—a stroke of luck that seemed like divine intervention, for I was funneled onto the SS *George Washington* before demobilization orders solidified the procedure for sending troops home.

Though Orthodoxy would tell me the timing was God's doing, I wondered instead if it was Nellie looking down on me. I hoped so. I hoped she wanted me to make it out alive, to make her sacrifice worth something.

It had been my second day on the ship when the Germans and the Allies signed the armistice. It was done in a train car in the French forest just after dawn; we heard the news at eleven. Of course I rejoiced; how could I not? Hundreds of thousands of men would now be spared the horrors of war. But still I retreated down into my bunk while the others celebrated. I'd denied Nellie the chance to see the armistice; it seemed wrong to participate in the parties it brought with it now. I was glad not to be in France, where we'd heard that the streets were filled with parades and even the hospitals were hosting celebratory banquets. But I hoped Nicholas was able to celebrate despite my betrayal. I hoped he would find another person to believe in after the wretchedness of this war. That Burt was able to feel joy despite Perlie's death.

I stood on deck now and looked toward France, though I could no longer make out the shoreline. I was leaving so much behind there, and my heart ached to think I could never see Nicholas again if I wanted to keep him safe. By now, he'd heard of Emmaline Balakin's death.

Only I knew the truth. I was still here, standing on the prow of the ship with salt on my lips and wind in my hair. By sheer determination or luck or divine providence, I'd been granted a second chance.

I owed it to Nellie and to Nicholas, to my parents and to Perlie, to use it.

But most of all, I owed it to myself.

Chapter 34

Kathleen Carre

June 1977

We'd walked past Herndon Monument hundreds of times over the last year, but this was the first time we were seeing it like this: slathered in thick, gooey lard with the sod at the bottom turned to mud. And most importantly, the monument was topped with the cover we'd wear next year as youngsters, or third-class midshipmen. Once we replaced the plebe-style dixie-cup cap on top of Herndon with an upperclassman's cover, our time as plebes would officially be over.

Linda, Susan, and I linked arms as the crowd of plebes formed. Not all thirteen hundred plebes who'd begun the summer last year remained, but there were still twelve hundred of us, including sixty-five women, crowding T-court now. Around the perimeter were spectators held back by lines of rope, and I searched the crowd for familiar faces.

But then came the loud, uncontrollable cry of "Let's do it!" from the mass of midshipmen, and we surged forward as one. I couldn't help laughing as the movement swept me up, even as other plebes' bodies jostled against mine and the sun beat down on my brow.

Susan and I dragged Linda forward. Being smaller than most of the men, we were able to worm our way through until our bare feet sank into the mud at the base of the monument. Around us, the men were already whipping off their shirts and plastering them to the side of the monument to wipe off the lard; others linked arms to provide a base for peers to climb.

"Let's go!" Susan cried, letting go of Linda and me and charging forward. With our help, she clambered up the bare back of the midshipman in front of us and then stood on his shoulders, her hands scrabbling for a grip on the slippery surface. "Someone throw me a shirt," she screamed down. But none of the men heard her, or maybe they just didn't want a woman making the first successful moves up the tower.

Susan rolled her eyes and whipped her own shirt off, revealing the jogbra beneath, then used it to scrub furiously at the stone. Lard came off in slimy chunks, and I strained forward to try to get my own foothold to help my friend. But a body falling from the monument obstructed my view, and when I clawed my way up again, Susan was gone.

Linda's voice came from behind me. "They pulled her off," she said, "I swear."

I growled in frustration. We'd known that not all the men wanted us on Herndon; some had even gotten fried for selling shirts that read *NGOH*, or *No Girls on Herndon*. But this was an exercise in teamwork, and anyone making progress up the monument was *all* of us making progress up the monument. A lesson I learned the hard way.

With renewed fury, I pushed forward again and yanked myself onto a bare-backed plebe's shoulders. From here, I could see Susan, spitting mud from between her teeth, fighting to regain her spot on the base.

I removed my shirt just as she had, using it to wipe away some of the slippery lard, and then I swayed back as a tug came on my ankle. I lurched forward so my whole body was pressed against the monument, smearing lard across my cheek, but I didn't care. I wouldn't let anybody pull me down.

Then the pressure disappeared, and a plebe appeared beside me. "Thanks," he shouted, gesturing to me. "I was afraid I'd brought you down for a moment!"

I grinned at him as we linked arms, and then bore down on the stone as several other plebes clambered up to stand on our shoulders. The men holding me up shifted, but those on either side of me kept me from falling. Then came a familiar face rising from the crowd. "Kathleen!"

"Derrick!" I reached a hand down and helped pull him up. "Go, go!" I squared my shoulders so he could climb onto them, wincing as his heels dug into my shoulder blades.

For two hours, we climbed and fell and climbed and fell again. My throat grew scratchy and raw, and my torso was cut up where I'd scratched it on Herndon. I could swear there was mud in my hair, and I had lost Susan and Linda and Derrick in the crowd.

I pulled myself up onto the monument for the fourth time, and a hand came down to lift me up. I grabbed it and braced myself as the mass of bodies roiled beneath me, then pushed off them to make the leap. When I came even with the man who'd pulled me up, I nearly fell off again. "Tom."

"Hey." He seemed equally surprised to see that the plebe he'd helped up was me.

I pulled my hand from his, all of a sudden back in that bathroom with his hands on my skin. I'd realized over the last year that my shame at what had happened to me was unfounded, though natural, and telling Linda and Susan about the abuse had helped lighten the load. But still I'd never be able to touch Tom without feeling sick.

I turned to the plebe on my other side, a man I didn't recognize or know. "Help me up," I said.

He raised his eyebrows. "You think you can make it all the way?"

We were close, only the top quarter of the obelisk remaining. But it was still caked in lard. It looked nearly impossible to surmount.

"Yeah," I said anyway. "I can make it."

Without hesitation, the man pushed me up, and I wobbled precariously on his shoulders. Then Derrick appeared from around the other side of the monument, his skin dripping with sweat. "Look," he said, pointing down.

Just below us was a plebe who had to be something like six and a half feet tall. "I can reach," he cried. "Let me up!"

Derrick and I braced ourselves, our fingers clasped, as the man pulled himself up and placed one foot on each of our shoulders.

"Throw me the cap!" he called down.

From the crowd came the white-and-black cover, sailing

through the air until the man caught it. He wavered as he reached out, but a hand from below steadied him, and I gritted my teeth as I worked to keep my own footing.

"Go, go, go!" The chants grew louder, and I swore I could hear Linda's and Susan's familiar voices in the mass.

With a grunt of effort, the plebe on our shoulders strained up and wrestled the dixie-cup cap off the monument. He tossed the upperclassman cover just as a foot grasped my ankle and pulled down. I tumbled off, blinded by a blur of skin and mud and lard and even a *NGOH* shirt that had somehow made it past the officers. But I just laughed when I saw it. "Too late!" I pointed in the direction I thought was up. "We've already done it."

Linda and Susan caught me as I careened to the ground, keeping mud from splattering into my mouth and eyes like it had on some of the plebes.

"They pulled you down," Susan shouted, but I barely heard her. The whole crowd was celebrating, screaming and laughing in joy. It had taken two hours, but we'd done it.

And I had been part of it.

"Who cares?" I called back to Susan. "They've tried getting rid of us before, haven't they?"

Linda grinned back at me. "A zero percent dropout rate," she cried, reminding us of the promise the three of us had made that long-ago morning before my hearing.

Susan's glare softened as she looked between us. "Zero percent," she repeated quietly.

We hugged as the crowd pulsed around us in celebration, and then came the officers' voices over the speakers. Together—men and women in unison—we sang the "Blue and Gold," our voices rising. "'But still when two or three shall meet / and old tales be retold / From low to highest in the fleet / We'll pledge the Blue and Gold!'"

And then came chaos, the crowd dispersing to shower and talk to the news anchors and run to family in the crowd. Linda, Susan, and I split up to join our families, and I searched the crowd fruitlessly until I saw a head of snow-white hair floating near the back of the crowd. "Mabel." I pushed forward and stopped before Mabel and Nicholas, my chest heaving with exhaustion.

Mabel reached forward to hug me, and I laughed. "No," I said, "I'm covered in mud."

But she ignored me, and I felt Nicholas's arms wrap around me from behind.

I closed my eyes and breathed it in. The earthy scent of the mud, the ever-present smell of chocolate chip cookies I'd come to expect from Mabel, the faint tobacco smell that emanated from Nicholas's clothing. My own sour sweat, a sign of challenges weathered and challenges won.

When Mabel and Nicholas released me from their hug, Mabel had tears in her eyes.

"Here." Nicholas passed me a small box. "It's from your mother."

I took the gift and opened it, shocked to see that Jane had sent me a necklace. I squinted at the letters engraved on the silver. *MKC.* "MKC?"

"Midshipman," Nicholas explained. "Midshipman Kathleen Carre."

The perfect mother would have known that midshipmen were forbidden to wear jewelry. But I didn't need a perfect mother, just one who tried.

And for the first time, I had that. Jane had returned to D.C. after hearing about Nana's passing, and we'd held a second, private funeral. With Nicholas's guidance, we arranged the Russian Orthodox service Nana would have wanted had she not had to hide her faith and identity. In place of the body, we circled around a worn, knotted bracelet Nicholas said had been Emmaline's and her mother's before that. He called it her chokti and told us he'd found it at the hospital after she'd been taken away. It was Jane's now; one day, it would be mine.

The time together in the church had healed something between Jane and me. It wasn't God; I still didn't know if I'd ever believe in a world beyond the one in which I lived. But it was something, and I'd begun to forgive my mother for what she'd done. She'd known that Nana could raise me in a way she couldn't have, after all. And I'd learned that the separation had hurt her as much as it had me.

Mabel fastened the necklace around my neck as I fought tears, and Nicholas cupped my chin in his hands. "Emmaline would have been so proud," he said.

Mabel shook her head. "She *is* proud," she said. "Who says she's not watching, right now?"

I gazed up at the sky and thanked my nana for everything she'd given me. She'd inspired this dream in me, and she'd brought me this family—the grandfather I'd never known existed, and the woman who was not-quite-my-great-aunt. She'd brought me here to the academy, where I'd found Susan and Linda and Derrick and the others in my company.

She'd warned me about it being a man's world, and she hadn't been wrong. War was a man's world, the academy was a man's world, and the whole damn universe was a man's world.

But one painstaking climb at a time, my friends and I were changing it.

Author's Note

Reading has always felt as necessary to me as breathing. If you're reading this, it's quite possible you feel the same way. But governments do not traditionally view fiction through the same lens they do food or water; even as recently as 2020, bookstores were shut down as "non-essential" during the early stages of the COVID-19 pandemic. So I was shocked to discover that, during America's vast World War I mobilization of troops, volunteers, nurses, food, automobiles, munitions, and other standard military resources, the War Department and American Library Association generated $5 million (approximately $112 million in today's dollars) and seven to ten million books for soldiers' libraries. As a lifelong reader and writer, I was captivated by the very idea. But I was also conflicted upon reading about the censorship the War Department imposed on the ALA alongside its support. Librarians were forbidden from providing soldiers books that sympathized with the Central Powers or bolshevism as well as largely banned from providing books on pacifism, American racism, or even the experience of war itself.

On the one hand, it struck me as incredibly ironic that these champions for libraries were limiting the books allowed in them. But on the other hand, it made sense: both the dedication to providing books and the fear of subversive ones are rooted in the same belief that words have power.

Emmaline is living through a war, and Kathleen is preparing for one. But to me, this book is not about war or the military. It's about the magic and the power of words to give comfort and to effect change.

Emmaline's journey begins with words, not only in books but in Nicholas's letter. But I didn't want Emmaline on the sidelines of war, watching from D.C.; I wanted her in the thick of it. I wanted her where fiction's escape was absolutely necessary. In moving her there, I took a few historical liberties. Very few female librarians were sent to France before the end of the war, at which point several went to serve convalescents, and those who did travel overseas were highly trained. Red Cross and YMCA volunteers, however, did staff overseas libraries without training, and it is their experiences I imagine were similar to Emmaline's. I also lifted information about the conditions from letters written by the real-life war librarian Mary Frances Isom. Isom was a Portland, Oregon, librarian who arrived in France at the time of the armistice and traveled from hospital to hospital setting up libraries. In the book, I moved her arrival in France up to September so that she could make a cameo. I wanted to honor her and her contributions, and I hope I did so by having her escort Emmaline on the train through France.

The librarian Thomas Plunkett, who in my book is fired for providing socialist, anarchist, and pacifist books, is not a real person. However, his story is based on several real events. In February 1918, Los Angeles banned all German books from libraries; Cleveland, Ohio, followed suit in August and Queens, New York, in

October. Various cities, counties, and states across the country did the same, removing texts written in the German language, books written by German philosophers, or any materials that supported anarchy or socialism. In the spring of 1918, librarians were required not only to remove books on explosives from their shelves but also to report to the Army the names of any patrons requesting them. While some librarians were able to stand up against censorship without losing their jobs, the majority were not. Library historian Wayne Wiegand reports that several librarians across the country "lost jobs for sticking to principles." In fact, a librarian who worked under Mary Frances Isom in Portland was forced to step down after refusing to buy war bonds—despite supporting American soldiers in numerous other ways.

The other characters in Emmaline's storyline are invented. In Kathleen's timeline, Tom, Robert, Marsha, Derrick, Susan, and Linda are my creations. Janice Buxbaum is a real woman who graduated from the Naval Academy in 1980 and who organized the women's meeting that was labeled a "mutiny" by the administration. In subsequent talks with leadership, she became a powerful, much-needed representative for the female plebes—nothing at all like Marsha, who is a figment of my imagination alone.

If you are interested in reading more about the first class of women at the Naval Academy, I recommend *First Class* by Sharon Hanley Disher. Disher is a graduate of the class of 1980 and writes based on firsthand experience and interviews with classmates. Much of what Kathleen goes through is inspired by the experiences Disher shares in *First Class*, and I truly couldn't have written *The War Librarian* without reading it. My eternal thanks to Disher for being courageous enough to write honestly about her and other midshipmen's experiences. Emmaline would be proud.

Acknowledgments

Second Novel Syndrome is real, y'all. *The War Librarian* wouldn't exist without the tireless work of my agent, my editors, and—of course—my mother. The book is unrecognizable compared to the first draft thanks to them: to Melissa Danaczko and her early work on the book, to Tara Singh Carlson and Ashley Di Dio and their endless revisions, and to my poor mom and her willingness to read a dozen atrocious drafts. I also owe a million thanks to my husband, Jorge Nunez, and to everyone else who supported me throughout the writing process—plus those who so eagerly embraced *The Light of Luna Park*. I've been absolutely awed by the love from old teachers, friends and family friends, co-workers, and readers, and I hope you all enjoy *The War Librarian* as much as you did my first novel.

Thanks of course to everyone on Putnam's team beyond Tara and Ashley: cover designers, copy editors, layout designers, and all the others who have worked so hard. I owe another huge thank-you to Kaia Alderson, who not only provided me with a blurb but also with perspective on how to improve the historical context surrounding Emmaline's timeline.

Again, I couldn't have written this book without reading *First Class* by Sharon Hanley Disher. Eternal thanks to her for writing about her experience as part of the first class of women at the Naval Academy and for being courageous enough to go in the first place. I'm so grateful to all the other women throughout history who have forged the way for the rest of us.

The War Librarian

---❖---

Addison Armstrong

A Conversation with Addison Armstrong

Discussion Questions

PUTNAM
—EST. 1838—

A Conversation
with Addison Armstrong

The War Librarian is your second historical novel. What inspired you to write this story? What felt different, writing this book?

We hear so much about women serving as nurses, Red Cross volunteers, and even yeomen in World War I, so I was shocked that I'd never heard about the women who worked as war librarians. I wanted their stories to be told, but there was more to it. Something about how massive the Library War Service's undertaking was inspired me, because it demonstrated just how powerful the United States believed books could be, even—or especially—in times of war. I was also fascinated by the fact that the United States saw the vital importance of books and then, at the same time, went about banning many of the books that soldiers wanted to access. The irony of it seemed too powerful not to explore. As for Kathleen's timeline, it seemed a natural fit when I realized how recently women were accepted into the service academies despite centuries of war work.

That being said, this novel was a lot harder to write than *The Light of Luna Park*. I think part of it was the classic second novel syndrome; suddenly, writing was a job rather than a hobby, which meant all the insecurities and stressors and deadlines of any career interfered where they hadn't before.

This novel is rooted in the real history of both the first volunteer librarians during World War I and the first class of women to attend the United States Naval Academy. What research did you perform in order to craft this novel?

I did a lot of reading, that's for sure! I read newspaper articles, ALA minutes and bulletins, Naval Academy yearbooks, interviews, American and German war propaganda, ALA book lists, librarians' journals, and articles galore. Most of all, I have to thank Sharon Hanley Disher, because her book *First Class* gave me almost everything I needed to write about Kathleen's experiences at the Naval Academy. My eternal thanks to Lieutenant Disher for her bravery both in attending the Naval Academy and in sharing her and others' authentic experiences.

Now, my most *fun* research came at the very end of the writing process. The Naval Academy had been closed because of COVID until just before my final edits were due, but it had just reopened, and so my mom and I (both vaccinated) flew to Annapolis and toured the Yard. I was able to sharpen a lot of my descriptions and details afterward. If only I could have flown out to France, too . . .

Kathleen is such a strong, determined woman in a male-dominated field. How did you come to her character? Is she inspired by someone in particular?

Kathleen wasn't consciously inspired by anyone, but she's a lot like my incredible little sister Ryan. Ryan is studying to be a pilot, and the aviation field is still shockingly male-dominated; much of what the first class of women at the Naval Academy experienced is not as much a thing of the past as we like to believe. Ryan and Kathleen are both brave and determined and self-assured, as well as strong and assertive, but Ryan is not a lone wolf like Kathleen is for most of the novel. Ryan is bright and fun and the most loyal friend you'll ever have.

What about Emmaline? Is she based on a historical figure? Why did you want Emmaline to be a Russian immigrant? How do you think these details add to the story as a whole?

Emmaline is not directly based on a historical figure, but I did take elements of a librarian named Mary Frances Isom to create her. The name may sound familiar, as I gave Miss Isom a cameo in the book, though I had to move up her arrival in France so she could interact with Emmaline. Really, Miss Isom arrived in France just as the armistice was being signed, and afterward traveled around the country setting up libraries and training volunteers. Some of the details of the conditions in which Emmaline would have lived are pulled from Miss Isom's letters home, and the information Miss Isom gives Emmaline in the story (about a librarian in her charge refusing to buy war bonds) is all factual.

There were several reasons I made Emmaline a Russian immigrant, which was actually my agent Melissa Danaczko's idea originally. It gave Emmaline a childhood connection to Nicholas as well as an additional reason to feel like an outsider during her youth; more importantly, the issues of censorship and Marxism paralleled nicely in her parents' emigration story and in France. I also liked the idea of showing an immigrant as a core part of the American war effort. Most of the students I teach are immigrants, and nearly all their families are; America would not be America without them.

Kathleen's role model and guiding light is her grandmother, Nellie. What about Nellie and Kathleen's relationship do you think is special, and why did you choose to focus on this familial bond in Kathleen's story?

In some ways, I think the relationship echoes that in *The Light of Luna Park*. Nellie is Kathleen's mother for all intents and purposes. Their relationship is strong and supportive just like my relationship with my mom and with my grandmothers Mimi and Nan.

Emmaline and Nicholas's relationship has a complex history and is put to the test against the backdrop of war. Can you share your thought process while writing this romance, and if there were any surprising aspects you came to along the way?

War is a series of unimaginable horrors, but it's also a setting in which unbreakable relationships are forged. Emmaline makes the best friends of her life during her time in France, and she falls in love with a man she will never stop loving. I wanted something bright to shine throughout the chaos and destruction of World War I, and Nicholas and Emmaline's relationship became that beacon of hope.

Novels about women's voices finally being heard are gaining in popularity among readers. What do you feel *The War Librarian*

adds to this category of fiction? What are some of your favorite books in this vein?

I hope that *The War Librarian* shows that it isn't just women from a century ago whose voices deserve to be heard. It's not just Emmaline's story that needs to be uncovered but Kathleen's, too—and Kathleen, born in 1954, could be you or your mother or your grandmother. Women are also trendy to write about, whereas other marginalized groups do not receive the same privileges. I tried to include some windows into the historical experiences of people of color rather than just of white women. However, I encourage readers to seek out historical fiction by authors of color (I recommend *The Vanishing Half* by Brit Bennett, *Of Women and Salt* by Gabriela Garcia, *Yellow Wife* by Sadeqa Johnson, *The Water Dancer* by Ta-Nehisi Coates, *Conjure Women* by Afia Atakora, and *Hotel on the Corner of Bitter and Sweet* by Jamie Ford). Some of my other favorite historical fiction books centering women's voices are Kate Quinn's novels, everything by Kate Morton, Ariel Lawhon's *Code Name Hélène*, *The Book of Lost Names* by Kristin Harmel, and Sue Monk Kidd's *The Book of Longings*.

What do you want readers to take away from *The War Librarian*?

I hope they come away with a renewed belief in the transformative power of words and books. I also want readers to feel empowered by Emmaline's and Kathleen's stories and by the continuous progress we've made as a society.

Without giving anything away, did you always know how the story would end?

It's one of the few things I did know! I usually have a pretty clear idea of how my story will start and end, but I don't really know what happens in the middle until I write it.

What's next for you?

I'm currently teaching elementary school English language learners, which has always been my dream. I definitely want to keep writing historical fiction and am hoping to publish a middle-grade historical fiction book in addition to more adult novels.

Discussion Questions

1. What was the most surprising or interesting fact you learned about the United States Naval Academy or World War I while reading *The War Librarian*?

2. *The War Librarian* is not only a story about resilience in the face of hardship but also of the power women have within themselves to effect change. Share a time in your life when you were faced with an obstacle and overcame it or advocated for something you were passionate about. What did you learn about yourself and the world around you?

3. What do you think both Kathleen's and Emmaline's greatest strengths are? What are their weaknesses? How do these shape who they are throughout the novel?

4. Emmaline facilitates a book club in order to create an inclusive environment for all the soldiers. What other opportunities do you feel book clubs create for readers? What are some of the positives you've taken away from being in a book club?

5. Discuss how grief and loss shaped both Emmaline's and Kathleen's lives and the similar and different ways in which they dealt with their emotions. How do you think you would have handled their circumstances if you were Emmaline or Kathleen?

6. What was your favorite scene in the novel, and why?

7. If you were in Emmaline's shoes, how would you have handled her life-changing decision toward the end of the book? Do you feel Emmaline ultimately made the right or wrong choice, and why?

8. What do you think is special about Emmaline and Nicholas's relationship? How did each of them help the other grow and change throughout the novel? Do you have a favorite scene of theirs, and if so, what is it?

9. Discuss how Emmaline's identity as a Russian immigrant shaped her story and the choices she made throughout the novel. If her background had been different, do you feel her story would have changed? If so, how?

10. What about Kathleen? Do you think her life would have taken a different turn if her upbringing had been more "traditional" for the time period? If so, how?

11. What are your thoughts about the ending?

Ryan Armstrong

Addison Armstrong graduated from Vanderbilt University in 2020 with degrees in elementary education and language and literacy studies and received her master's degree in reading education from Vanderbilt in 2021. *The Light of Luna Park* was her first novel. She lives with her husband in New York, New York, where she teaches elementary school.

AddisonArmstrong.com

🐦 @AddisonArmstro7